This Blood Runs

J.M. Cannon

This Blood Runs

Table of Contents

Seen

Iris sat at the bar of the Willard Hotel's restaurant in downtown Memphis. It was 2019, a few days before Christmas. She was twenty-four and getting giddy drunk to celebrate the end of what should be her last semester of community college.

Her ribs were starting to ache from laughing, and her cheeks were crimson from alcohol. A redhead in her early twenties talked to Iris. She had a few rings pierced in her left eyebrow. Her lipstick was so dark that in some lighting it looked black. Iris watched her mouth as she spoke.

"All I'm saying is if that Ashley girl wore any more perfume, I was going to reach into the other row, pull out my lighter, and set her on fire."

Iris laughed harder.

"I'm serious. You could've put her in my car's gas tank and gotten thirty miles to the gallon. That bitch was straight combustible."

Iris looked her in the eye. "It wasn't *that* bad, Claire." Claire kept her expression serious, but as Iris began to laugh, her straight face fell, and they both giggled.

"Maybe I'm being a bit dramatic," said Claire, taking a sip of her wine.

"No, she stank. I agree."

"The worst part is she thinks she smells good!"

"Do you know the brand name of it? I want to get you some for Christmas."

The redhead punched Iris's shoulder with a limp fist.

"So, when do you want to blow this joint?" Iris asked.

Claire suddenly looked away. "I got called into work. They just texted me like twenty minutes ago."

"Oh." Iris tried to keep the disappointment from her face. She'd thought she had Claire to herself all evening. All night.

"You really have to work right before Christmas?"

"Shit doesn't wipe itself."

"It does in Europe. They've got those toilets."

"That shoot water up your butt? Yeah, well, this is America. And speaking of work..." Claire pulled out her phone to check the time. "I really got to go. I'm already late."

"One more drink?" The anxiety of being alone has already tunneled into Iris's gut. She knew her pleading was hopeless, but her lips kept begging.

Claire thumbed through the bills in her wallet and set a handful on the bar. "I'm late, Iris. I'll see you the day after Christmas, okay?"

"Okay."

"This was a great idea. I've always wanted to have a fancy drink here."

"Be safe tonight."

"I'm always safe. It's you, Iris"—she wagged her finger—"I worry about." Claire stood and leaned towards Iris. Iris knew she wanted a kiss. But she was hesitant. *Here? In public?*

"Come on, Iris. It's Christmastime. You gotta kiss me."

Iris's eyes found some of the diners who had been glancing at them now and again through most of the evening. They had likely assumed the nature of their relationship but not really known. Iris was buzzed enough to not be self-conscious. She leaned forward and gave Claire a quick kiss.

"Merry Christmas, Iris."

Iris didn't respond. She watched Claire's back as she walked out of the restaurant. Her mood had immediately changed. The loneliness that had been lying in wait now coiled itself around her. She distracted herself with people watching as she ordered another drink.

Five-star restaurants were filled with families this time of year. While she was by herself at the bar, the tables behind her were occupied by laughing children, uninterested teenagers, and buzzed parents ready to have the holiday season in the rearview.

There was the dull clatter of polite conversation and the ghost of Bing Crosby singing about snow in the background. There was a thud on the bar top as her next drink was put in front of her. She didn't touch it right away. She looked at herself in the bar mirror behind the bottles.

Her hair was short—shoulder-length. She wore a cheap black dress, and her face looked silky and without a pore in the shoddy light. The bar was dark, lonely, while the dining room behind her was lit up with chandeliers. She'd left her tattered gray wool coat lying over the stool next to her. She was just glad holey clothing was considered a style these days, because she couldn't afford anything else. She thought she should probably not have another drink. Celebration or not, she should call it.

But before tonight, she had never had a proper cocktail in her entire life. She'd had plenty of drinks hastily thrown together with tonic or cola, but nothing ever shaken or stirred or finished with one of those little red cherries she was too nervous to try to pronounce.

Her drinks here didn't taste all that much better, she decided. Maybe her palate was too immature. Either way, she was happy to drink something out of a chilled martini glass for once in her life instead of a clear plastic cup.

She wasn't sure what to do now that she was alone. She didn't pull out her phone or pick apart a bar napkin. At first, she stared into space to turn her brain off. Relax. Decompress. But she was too interested in people to do that for long. For much of the next half hour, she was half looking over her shoulder.

There was a table with two women that caught her attention. One of them kept looking at Iris and was doing a poor job of hiding it. She had long, flowing hair that blazed blonde under the restaurant lights and wore a dark-red dress.

Did she know her? There was a hint of confusion on the woman's face, as if she was attempting to remember Iris.

The woman simply couldn't keep her gaze off Iris. She would glance in her direction even as she spoke to her dining partner—a younger Hispanic woman just as finely dressed.

The woman wasn't the only person Iris noticed looking at her. There was a man dining alone in the center of the room.

He was in a cream cable-knit sweater that emphasized broad shoulders and a large chest, but it wasn't his muscles, his looks, or his lonesomeness that caught her eye. His posture was strange, at least outside of an English boarding school. It looked like he'd spent his youth getting whipped if he slouched an inch. His hands were under the table placed flat on his thighs.

Neck straight. Back straight. Shoulders pulled back and level. There was something unsettling about him beyond his posture. He didn't move his head as his gaze darted about the dining room. His stare would find Iris, now and again, and she'd glance back quickly to the bar.

He was just nervous. Waiting for a date, she assumed. He might be afraid he's getting stood up. She gave him another glance when he wasn't looking. He was still perfectly erect.

Penis man, Iris decided to name him, and she grinned without a wrinkle the way a girl her age could and took another sip of her Cosmo.

Not too long afterwards, the Hispanic woman and the blonde with wandering eyes stood to leave.

Iris could only see the Hispanic woman from where she sat, and they locked eyes. She had long, thin lips and a pencil-thin neck to go with them. She was pretty, but in the alien way some runway models are. Her looks were arresting, not breathtaking.

She only looked back at Iris for a fraction of a second before a faraway look occupied her eyes, and then she walked to where she was out of sight.

Iris realized she'd never been around rich people like this. She'd passed them in traffic and on the street and seen them courtside from the cheap seats at Grizzlies' games, but never has she been in the same space as them like she was now.

But then again, she's alone at the bar while they're with their families celebrating the holidays.

She still looked like the odd one out.

She pictured the house that woman was going home to. A sweeping staircase. A walk-in closet so big it had one of those dressing tables in the middle of it.

Iris thought about wealth often. She had no money, and her life felt like a mess because of it. The choices she must make... The work she must do... But there was something in that woman's eyes—a lifelessness. A reassurance that you can have everything yet still nothing.

Iris sighed and turned back to her drink. She was done trying to be pensive. Tonight should be a celebration. She could still have a good time, even if she wasn't getting laid. She stayed in the restaurant drinking until the chatter had died and been replaced with the clink of dishware as waiters cleared tables.

She was past tipsy and was a little drunk as she wormed her arms into her coat and paid the bill. The bar was open later than the kitchen, but Iris could tell she was the only thing keeping the bartender from wrapping up early.

But just as she was about to stand, a younger woman came to the bar. Iris watched her as she approached. She wore black eyeshadow and thick mascara and was maybe a few years older than Iris, in her late twenties. She had light-brown hair and plump rosy cheeks, and when she smiled, her dimples widened enough for Iris to fall into them.

"Hey. This spot taken?" She pointed at Iris's stool.

Iris wasn't done looking at her. She wasn't ready for a question yet. "Ah..." she stuttered. "I was debating staying for another drink. So yeah."

"If you do, I'll buy. I hate being the only one at a bar. Makes me feel like a sad drunk. Veronica," the girl added hastily and extended her hand.

"Iris." Iris shook it. Veronica's hand was soft but ice-cold, like she'd been outside all evening.

"I was just at Deacon's Bar," said Veronica. "The place is a madhouse."

"I bet."

"There was this redhead with the most ridiculous combat boots making out with a woman who had to be twenty years older than her, *right* next to me. I've never actually said 'get a room' before tonight."

Iris suddenly froze. Claire was a redhead with ridiculous combat boots. *Did she lie about getting called into work?*

"Did she have an oak tree tattoo on the back of her bicep?"

Veronica frowned. "Yeah. Yeah, what the hell? Do you know her?"

"This is a small town sometimes. Especially if you like girls."

Veronica looked shocked, and then her dimples collapsed her cheeks again. "Then how come I've never met you before?" Veronica stared into Iris's eyes for an extra second before flagging down the bartender. It was just long enough to let her know she was into her.

Iris grinned and turned to face the other direction to hide it. Maybe tonight wasn't a bust after all.

They got to talking. After as many drinks as Iris had, conversation came easy. Veronica turned out to be smart as a whip. Smart to the point she made Iris feel a little insecure.

She kept Iris laughing and drinking, and suddenly she forgot that Claire lied to her about having to work in order to get into someone else's pants.

After ninety minutes, the bartender let them know they were closing soon. "This is going to sound ridiculous..." Veronica said. "But I haven't decorated my Christmas tree yet."

"Really?"

"Do you want to come over and maybe... give me a hand with it?" Veronica bit her lip as she waited for Iris's answer.

Iris froze. Did she? Yes.

Veronica was out of her league. And a cutesy evening decorating a tree that led to sex? She didn't usually do this kind of thing. She'd never been to a bar alone before. Maybe she should start doing it more often. Besides, tonight just felt different. Felt like fate.

Ten minutes later, they were in the back of an Uber having trouble keeping their hands off each other.

However, Iris's mood changed when they reached their destination. They'd driven to North Memphis, and Iris could see the white smokestack of the old Firestone plant sticking up above the skeletal trees of December. They were on a dead-end block of buildings with a brick apartment complex at the end of it.

"I know it's not the Taj Mahal," Veronica said. "Girl's gotta make due. I spruced up the inside though. You'll be surprised. Well... maybe less now that I said you would be."

Iris got out of the Uber and took a deep, sobering, breath of the cold air. *What was she doing here?* She was no stranger to poor places, but the houses on the block looked abandoned. They were single-story shacks. There were no lights on inside them. No streetlights lining the boulevard. A lone window of the apartment complex they walked towards was lit up. A single orange square in the cold night.

Their Uber pulled into a U-turn, and Iris felt her stomach begin to twist in a similar direction. She didn't like this. She had found herself in plenty of sketchy places, but the isolation of this block was something different.

She found herself standing still while Veronica bounded ahead.

"You coming?"

"Yeah," Iris said but didn't walk quick enough to catch up. She stayed several feet behind, surveying the dark street.

"So it's not the most wonderful Christmas tree, but it's not a sad little Charlie Brown thing either," Veronica said as she unlocked the dinged and graffitied metal door to the apartment complex.

The stairwell was lit by a single weak bulb. Inside smelled like incense and marijuana, and Iris was fumbling excuses to leave in her head.

"Do you have like... um... neighbors here?"

"Yeah. There's six units. But only three are occupied and livable. Some yuppie from Nashville bought the building and is working on renovating the rest."

They reached the top of the stairs, and Veronica unlocked another door. Iris's heart stopped hammering when she saw the inside.

Veronica wasn't lying. She'd made her place cozy. It had a woman's touch. There were plush blankets and houseplants in every corner. An essential oils diffuser blew a stream of calming steam, and thankfully, an undecorated Christmas tree was actually sitting in the corner.

A brown Siamese cat with its black face silently appeared to greet Iris. It rubbed its back against her legs.

"That's Dylan. He was the neighborhood cat before I took him in for the winter. He's semi-domesticated, but he will eat your shoelaces, so put your boots on top of the shelf."

Veronica pointed up, and Iris undid her boots and set them next to another half dozen pairs of women's shoes on the top of a black bookshelf.

"Not bad, right?" Veronica gestured her arms out at the apartment. "Realtors say location, location, location, but I say six-hundred dollars a month rent, bitches."

"Yeah that's a steal. Except you might get kidnapped walking home."

"Eh. But I bite," Veronica said and barred her teeth at Iris.

Iris grinned and walked around. There were two bathrooms and a full-sized kitchen. Her wandering led her into a bedroom. There was a queen mattress in a white metal frame. Tapestries with psychedelic patterns were hung on the walls. Iris heard the wood floors creak as Veronica came up behind her.

"Come on. We got a tree to decorate," Veronica said, and Iris turned.

Iris was giddy again now that she felt like her organs weren't going to be harvested. She gave Veronica her widest, slyest grin. "That tree looks pretty well watered. I mean... it *could* wait."

Veronica didn't stutter. She walked into the bedroom and shut the door behind her. She gave Iris a playful push onto the mattress, and Iris obliged by falling back onto the blankets limply.

She felt Veronica's mouth on her body and closed her eyes.

"I'm a little kinky," Veronica said. "Do you mind?"

Iris wasn't sure what she was talking about, but at about the same time Veronica finished her question, she felt cold metal on her wrist as she was handcuffed to the bedframe. Then she felt the same thing on her other wrist.

Her own helplessness turned Iris on more, but Veronica didn't keep kissing her. She stood up from the bed and patted her clothes flat. "I'll be right back."

She turned and left the room. *What the hell?* Iris isn't a fan of being kept in suspense. Especially with strangers. After two minutes, she began to feel as stupid as she should for ending up here.

It was easy to trust another girl, especially one who was as pretty and smart as Veronica. Especially one who shared the same vulnerability of being a lesbian. But Iris sobered up enough to realize she was tied to a stranger's bed. Her pulse quickened, and as her blood moved faster through her veins, it turned her lust into fear.

"Veronica?" Iris yelled.

She came back in not long afterward. A spoon and lighter in one hand, she sat on the end of the bed.

"What are you doing?" Iris squirmed her feet.

"Do you ever party like this?" Veronica waved the spoon at her.

"Like what?"

Veronica said a single syllable. "H?"

"I don't fuck with hard drugs."

Veronica smiled. "It's the softest drug in the world, sweetheart. That's why everybody loves it."

Iris wasn't about to debate the dangers of heroin.

"Look, you can get high. That's cool. But I don't want any."

Veronica stopped responding. She opened the nightstand drawer and pulled out an orange capped syringe.

"Hey." Iris pulled at her cuffed hands, but they didn't budge. "Hey. Seriously."

She watched the shining point of the needle with wide eyes as Veronica heated the spoon and then sucked up the liquid with the syringe.

"Look, I'm not close with you like that. I don't want that shit. Please."

Veronica scooted up the bed so she was closer to Iris. "Quit moving your arm, or the needle will break off in you." She leaned forward with the syringe.

"I said no! You psycho bitch!" Iris bucked at her restraints and tried to move her feet so she could kick.

"Hey. Hey," Veronica said, her normal, empathetic personality returning. But it was just an act. "Trust me, okay?"

Iris's anger didn't last. She was scared. "I want to go home."

"This..." Veronica smiled and moved the needle to find a vein. "Is better than home."

Iris was too afraid of needles to fight anymore. The thought of it breaking off in her skin was enough to make her see stars. "Please, please, please. Why?" she whined through tears. "Don't do this to me."

"Shh," Veronica said as she depressed the plunger.

It was immediate. Iris felt the world slip out from under her. Her eyes rolled back. Her fear evaporated into a warm golden light.

"Shh," Veronica whispered again, but Iris didn't need any more coaxing. She was silent as the drugs waltzed in her brain.

She wasn't there anymore—tied to a bed in the wrong part of town. She was gone. But to just what extent she was about to vanish from the face of the earth, Iris had no idea.

Run

Two hours. That's all it's been since Annabelle tilted her head back and drank her glass of acid. Aurelia told Iris to spend the night. Jamie certainly won't be home for a while.

Iris stumbles up the staircase towards her old bedroom, drunk with shock. Perhaps Aurelia could see that in her eyes. She was smart to keep Iris away from the wheel. Iris closes the door to her bedroom.

She's read Augusta's letter several times now. Her mind changes every time she looks it over. One second, she thinks it's a trap, and the next, she believes it's a genuine invitation.

Paulo had the resources to kill Iris where she stood. There was no point in luring her to Mexico to do it. If anything, it would bring the unwanted eyes of the FBI onto him.

Iris looks around her old bedroom. Annabelle has made more than one change to Sweet Blood. A flat screen now hangs on the wall in front of the bed. It gives the room less of a historic feel and more like she's in a hotel.

Iris picks up the remote and clicks through the channels to the local news. Sure enough, there is a woman reporter standing in front of the event center for the Gala. Standing where Iris was waiting for the valet to bring her car around just a couple hours ago. There's a picture of Annabelle, younger and happier, occupying a corner of the screen.

"The police are saying this was no accident, but an intentional act of violence. Although they arrived at St. Luke's Hospital more than an hour ago, we still have no word on Annabelle Adler's condition or that of her baby."

The shot flashes to another anchor in the studio. "Do we have any idea what she consumed?"

The reporter appears again, nodding. "It could have been some kind of household cleaning product. Something like Drano. The police have not identified the substance used, but according to eyewitnesses, it was described as corrosive. An acid, essentially."

"Wow, horrible. Just horrible."

"Yes, the police *do* say they have a person of interest. However, they are not sharing names with the public. Witnesses described a scene of pandemonium—"

Iris turns off the TV and sits on the end of the bed. She didn't think she'd have sympathy for Annabelle, but it was the look in her eyes that she finds so haunting. It wasn't just pain or a fear of death. There was sadness in her expression. Like she was begging for the life of her baby.

Iris says a little prayer that the child makes it. She doesn't care that Annabelle's blood flows through its veins. The kid has a chance to be someone better.

She takes off her shoes and puts her earrings on the nightstand and finds a toothbrush in the bathroom. She brushes her teeth, and when she's done, she lies on top of the covers while still in her emerald dress.

She's sure Aurelia will wake her up in the morning, but she sets an alarm for 5:30 anyway. She doesn't want to be here when Jamie comes back.

As tired as she is, her eyes stay open. The person of interest must be Dominic. She doesn't think he's going to try to run from this. Annabelle's murder was too public. It wasn't something he was meant to get away with.

Iris suddenly becomes flush. If there were cameras at the event center, she would've been seen talking to Dominic just before Annabelle toasted to her own death. Iris ran to help her, sure, but the police might just see that as an act.

With all she's wrapped up in, the FBI would love to stick her with accessory to murder charges.

Then her mind finds a third meaning the card she got from Mexico could have. It wasn't a trap or an invitation. It was a warning—the FBI are closing in. *Get out.*

She stands from bed in a brief panic and begins to pace. Even with her own place, her own money, Iris has never stopped feeling trapped. To be back at Sweet Blood now feels like symbolism.

She's still a prisoner.

She begins to take deep breaths, and by the time she's done, she's distracted enough to be calm. But the room is softly vibrating.

Iris squints. First, she feels it in her feet—a gentle tickle. She thinks it's from the heavy breathing, but then the windowpane begins to rattle softly. She's still calm until her earrings start to *tick tick tick* as they bounce on the nightstand.

She steps towards the window just as she hears footsteps pound towards her room from the hall.

She pulls the shutters open and gazes out. A pounding sound now accompanies the vibrations. A red light blinks low in the sky. It sweeps over the sugarcane.

A helicopter.

For a second, she thinks it has to do with the harvest and the controlled burn of the crop, but then she sees its shape. The helicopter is a monstrous thing. Black and sleek. It soars over the fields and then slows to hover above the front lawn of Sweet Blood.

The room brightens as her bedroom door is opened to the hall. "Iris!" Aurelia shouts, but Iris doesn't turn. Her attention is at the gate. A shadow moves there, too. A vehicle bursts through the wrought iron, sending the metal halves flying into the ditch. A line of police vehicles races towards the house.

"Iris, honey. You've got to move." Aurelia is pulling on her arm, but Iris is stuck in place. *Am I the person of interest?*

Suddenly she finds her feet moving as she and Aurelia race down the hall and the stairs. "Where are we going?"

"Not to jail. Come on." Aurelia takes her through the kitchen and to the door to the basement.

Iris hears car doors slam and footsteps thumping up the porch, but the front door is locked.

Aurelia flips through a set of keys, plunges one into the lock of the basement door, and turns it. Just as it clicks open, there's a crack of wood as the police batter their way inside.

A series of shouts follow as if all the agents want to be the one to say it—"FBI!"

Aurelia guides Iris down the stairs and shuts the door silently behind them. Then she locks it again.

"They'll find us here," Iris says. She's doing her best not to cry, but she can't keep the quiver from her voice. This is it. Prison.

"They're finding nothing but canned tomatoes. Come on."

Iris is quiet as they descend. At the bottom, the floor is concrete with a drain, but the walls are original red brick.

There is a line of wooden shelves on the far wall filled with wine bottles, canned goods, and cleaning products.

"This house has many secrets," Aurelia says as her fingers begin to creep on the underside of a shelf. Something clicks, and the bottom half of the wood shelf swings open gently.

Iris has all but forgotten her fear. Her eyes are wide, her mouth a little agape in childlike amazement. She'd pictured this plantation having tunnels. Hidden rooms. But seeing it is another thing. Dank cool air wafts into the little cellar. It's rich and smells of black dirt.

Aurelia grabs her shoulder. "This will take you a ways away but not off the property. You'll come out into a culvert that runs under the farm road. Before you leave, there's a couple backpacks kept near the end of the tunnel."

Aurelia and Iris both look up as footsteps stomp above them. Dust cascades from the ceiling.

"They both have clothes and money in them, but most importantly, there's a phone. I'll respond to the letter you got and make sure whoever's after you in Mexico knows you have it. That phone is your lifeline. Don't lose it."

"Okay."

Augusta reaches into the tunnel and pulls a flashlight off a coat hook. She clicks the button until it's on its brightest setting and hands it to Iris.

"Don't waste any time now. I'll sneak upstairs and throw them off your tail."

Iris ducks and takes a step into the tunnel.

"And, Iris, sugar."

Iris turns and Aurelia holds out her hand. "Your phone."

"Right." Iris empties her pockets. She thinks about handing it to Aurelia but thinks better and smashes it against the wall. When the screen won't light up, she drops it on the tunnel floor.

"Be safe, Iris. Don't wait around here. Head south. There's a place in the bayou just outside the town of Dustin. It's run by an old friend of mine. A woman named Tilda. Tell her Aurelia sent you. They don't ask many questions. Pay cash. Wait for that phone to ring."

Iris nods. "Thank you, Aurelia."

"Don't thank me till you're outta here." She winks and closes the shelf. Iris listens to it latch, and then everything is suddenly very quiet. There's the sound of dripping water somewhere in the dark, but other than that, the tunnel is silent.

Searchlight

Maybe it's the darkness or the uncomfortable crouch in which she must walk, but the tunnel feels like it stretches for miles. Iris has been walking for ten minutes when she has to stop to take a break.

Her back is sore from the way she's bent over. She drops so she's on her knees and straightens out her spine with her hands on her lower back.

The tunnel is older than she had thought. At least from what she can tell from the timbers that line either side of it every six or so feet. They're nearly black with age. Some are buckled entirely. The purpose of this escape route isn't of the drug trafficking era of the Adlers. It goes back to fear of civil war and slave rebellion.

It's been upkept for sure. Some of the timbers have been replaced. It must've been repurposed by the Adlers in case their empire ever crumbled. Now it's Iris, the source of their very downfall, who is using it.

Iris gets back to her feet and brushes off her knees. It was foolish to stop, she realizes in a couple minutes when her flashlight illuminates the end of the tunnel and a circular door. The door is only a couple feet across. It'll be a tight squeeze even for Iris.

There are two backpacks, both covered with dirt and dust. Iris starts rifling through them both.

The first one she opens has men's clothes. Jeans. Flannel shirt. Raincoat. At the bottom there's $3000 in fifties and hundreds. She sets the money aside and starts going through the other pockets.

There's a compass. A folding knife. Toothbrush and travel toothpaste. A roll of nylon string. A lighter. A roadmap of Louisiana and a pint of Jim Beam.

No phone.

She keeps the map, compass, and lighter and starts going through the other pack. These go bags must've been for Augusta and Joseph Senior before his illness. Or Augusta and whichever one of her sons may have been home when the police came knocking.

The women's jeans are several sizes too big, but she is able to cut a strip of the nylon rope into a belt. She discards her dress and puts on the jeans and a heather gray sweater she found with them. In the bottom of this bag is another $3000 in cash. The other pockets in this bag have more practical items than whisky.

There's a little loaded revolver with no extra ammo and a brick of a flip phone. An old Nokia. It's heavy enough to be a weapon in its own right.

What Iris doesn't find is a charger for it. When she presses the power button, the phone's screen stays dark. "Come on," she whispers. "Come on."

She empties out the bags, but there's no charger. There are no tennis shoes left around on the tunnel floor either. She'll have to leave barefoot. Obviously, the Adlers had become quite confident they wouldn't ever need these bags.

They weren't wrong, Iris thinks.

She puts on three pairs of socks and thinks her feet are cushioned enough to run on gravel if she needs to. She shoulders on one of the backpacks to keep the cash, phone, and gun and then inspects the door in front of her.

The circular door is made up of scrap lumber. There's no obvious handle, which she thinks is strange, but when she pushes on it, the entire door moves. It's not latched. It's simply sitting in place from its weight.

She puts her shoulder into it and drives with her feet. The weight feels enormous until it's suddenly light as a feather. The door drops on the other side with a crack.

There's another tunnel in front of her now. A drainage tunnel that runs under a road, and she's peering into it sideways. This one smells like rot and murky water, not black dirt.

Suddenly she hears voices. For a moment she's frozen, thinking the police are waiting here for her at the exit, but then she realizes the sound is coming from behind her.

She turns to see two little blue points of light bobbing in the dark a couple hundred yards back.

They already found the tunnel.

Iris scrambles through the opening and lands with a wet plop. Her socks are already soaked, as are her jeans and sweater. A line of muddy water runs along the entire bottom of the concrete culvert she's in. It's even lower than the tunnel, and she has to crawl in order to exit.

The sound of the helicopter isn't far off, and when she's out, she stands and quickly tries to find her bearings.

She wishes she had the compass in hand. She knows she's on one of the farm roads but isn't sure which. The helicopter sounds about a half mile off, but it might've moved. There's no telling if it's still over the house.

There's sugarcane on either side of her, and Sweet Blood is not in sight. There's no point running if she doesn't know which way she's going.

She curses and yanks off the backpack. She unzips the side pocket and pulls out the compass. It takes a moment for her to read it. South is to her right. She hears the crunch of tires on the road. Shouts come from the tunnel. They're closing in.

She steps into the sugarcane, and then she's running.

The backpack bounces wildly, and she clenches the compass in her fist. Her lungs burn after what feels like only a minute, and then she hears a dog bark.

She stops and spins. It's coming from near the culvert, and Iris realizes she left her dress. She should've put it in the goddamn backpack, but now they've got her scent. They can make a beeline to her now.

She looks at the compass and holds it up so she can see by starlight. She changes her direction to the southeast and starts to sprint.

Iris is heading towards the highway, but what she realizes after a few minutes is that she's also heading towards the crop fires.

The smoke fills her nostrils. It smells nothing like the sweet product of these stalks. The scent is acrid, eye watering, the same as a pile of burning leaves.

She doesn't know if smoke can throw a dog off her scent trail, but she thinks it's possible. It could at least confuse it.

Iris hears the fire before she sees it. It crackles and roars in the distance. The stalks in front of her are as thick as a head of hair, and it's only in the sky above them that she can see the red glow of flames.

She walks slower as she comes upon a clearing. It's about as wide as a road. It looks like a swath that has been plowed for burn control.

Just across the clearing the sugarcane burns. Iris can feel the heat on every inch of her body. It makes the sweat on her hands shine orange. The fire is at least fifty yards long, and the flames reach towards the stars sending a flurry of sparks and debris up with its draft.

Suddenly the sparks are blown back towards the earth violently. The sugarcane on either side of Iris flails.

She hits the ground just before she sees the black shadow of the helicopter pass overhead. Its searchlight isn't far from where Iris lies.

The circle of searching light doesn't glide gently on the ground. It ticks and twitches. Searching feverishly. The orb covers twenty yards of field in a second and then pauses before speeding off again.

The helicopter has infrared cameras no doubt, but the fire must create one giant blind spot. She can picture the flames on the infrared screen—a mass of hot orange light hiding Iris's heat signature.

When the helicopter banks back towards the way Iris had come, she bounds to her feet and veers right around the fire. She passes as close to the flames as she can without burning herself. The fire was only fifty yards long, but the flames run deep into the field.

She runs alongside flames for a couple minutes before the night air has a chill to it again.

She can hardly hear the helicopter anymore. It must be staying clear of the fires to better see the fields. Iris looks at the compass again and breathes. She's not hidden by the heat anymore. She needs to get to the highway before the helicopter comes back.

She sprints with one arm out in front of her to keep the stalks from thwacking her in the face. She's exhausted, but she grits her teeth and keeps her legs pumping.

She doesn't know what's in her future, but she does know that behind her is life in prison.

The FBI must have enough to get her for Joseph's death. Annabelle's murder must've stirred Agent Long into taking action. Her superiors in the FBI have likely been demanding charges. With Annabelle's death, the case around the Adler family has reached a breaking point.

Handcuffs. Courtrooms. A life of utter boredom. It's what Iris is running from, but more than anything, she feels like she sprints from injustice.

Her husband deserved to die. Some people do. He was a monster, and the government couldn't do anything about it except punish Iris when she took things into her own hands.

After another minute of running, Iris can't think anymore. With every stride, she repeats a mantra in her head—*Don't throw up. Don't fall over. Don't throw up. Don't fall over.*

It's all she can do to keep from doing either. The burning in her lungs has morphed into nausea in her stomach. Her legs wobble beneath her.

Suddenly, above the sound of her beating heart, the pounding of the helicopter blades is back. She thinks about lying down, but that would only widen her heat signature.

They already saw her, she's sure. That's why it's gaining on her.

She slows her pace and searches the sky behind her. It isn't more than a couple seconds before she pays for her lack of attention and trips. She falls out of the sugarcane and flat on her face. But she's surprised to feel cool grass on her face. She looks up and sees that she's on the shoulder of a road. She's in the ditch. About fifty yards ahead up a slight hill is the whoosh of traffic.

It's the highway. Iris scrambles towards it. Not the highway. She realizes from the sound alone. She has run all the way to the interstate.

It's a weekend night, and there's a fair amount of traffic for how late it is. From where she stands, Iris can see the helicopter clearly. It's a half mile away. It's coming her way but not facing her directly.

She doesn't have time to look for a culvert to hide in. She has to look for a ride. This might get her killed rather than imprisoned, but she doesn't care. She throws off the backpack and digs inside for one of the rubber banded rolls of cash. She strips off the rubber band, fans the cash in her hand and walks on the shoulder facing traffic. She startles the first two cars, and they swerve and honk.

The next vehicle has seen her coming. It rolls gently onto the shoulder and honks twice. Iris runs to the driver's side. The window is down. A man in a dirty baseball cap and short beard is looking at her with one eye cocked. Man's a stretch—he's maybe twenty-three.

"Need a ride?"

"Yes."

"How much we talkin'?" He nods down towards the money she holds in her fist.

She's in no position to negotiate. He knows she's in some kind of trouble, and she has to pay a premium. What he can't tell in the dark is how much money she has. "Five hundred to take me past New Orleans."

"Well shit." He gestures towards the passenger seat with an open palm. "Get in."

Iris runs around the back of the truck and practically throws herself inside. She takes off her backpack and moves it to her feet. The man doesn't drive immediately. He hesitates a moment, looking at her.

There's nothing malicious about him. He wears an expression of curiosity. His New Orleans Saints ballcap is stained, and he frowns out from under its fleur-de-lis.

"Drive!"

"Alright, alright." He puts on his blinker and merges back onto the highway.

Iris realizes he might even be younger than she first thought. The beard is throwing her off. He's college-aged at most.

He doesn't give her bad vibes. She takes her eye off him to look out the back windshield. The helicopter comes into view just as they get up to speed. She doesn't think they saw her because its searchlight lingers in the area where she burst through the sugarcane. *Can they see the trampled stalks?*

"Boy trouble or law?"

Iris jumps at the sound of his voice.

"Didn't mean to scare ya."

She doesn't respond right away. She hoped he would take her gasping, ragged breaths as a clue that conversation could wait.

He keeps talking. "'Cause I don't want to get caught up and shot by some crazy boyfriend. The law's fine. Nothing illegal with picking up a hitchhiker.

"The law."

"You drunk? Crash your car back there?"

"Something like that."

"You don't smell drunk. Or talk drunk."

Iris ignores him and turns around to face the front windshield. One way or another, the police are going to figure out she hitched a ride on the interstate. The dogs will lose her scent there. The agents will see the crushed stalks. The question is, when will they figure it out? If they know this second, which they might, they can set up roadblocks long before she reaches New Orleans.

"Hey, you mind taking the back roads?" Iris asks.

"Can I see that money again?"

Iris pulls her backpack onto her lap. She counts out five hundred with her hands hidden and then wedges the bills between the dashboard and windshield.

He puts on his blinker and takes the next exit. "You want me to take Highway 9?"

Iris sighs. No. Nine was too obvious. They probably have a state trooper getting ready to check licenses. She bites her lip. "Drive west. Take the county roads."

He rocks his head back and forth gently, considering. "Where would we be going then?"

"South. Eventually."

"Eventually? Lady, where do you want to go?"

"Baton Rouge."

"Well shit, we're closer to there than New Orleans."

"Five hundred too much, then?"

"No, no." He grins. "Five hundred's perfect. But where in Baton Rouge we headin'?"

Iris sighs. She knows exactly where she wants to go. There's something that needs doing before she leaves this country. They've slowed to a stop at the end of the exit ramp, and Iris looks him in the eye.

"Lafitte Hill."

"Ah. You a rich girl?"

"Not anymore." They start driving, and Iris watches the patches of red sky that glow from the sugarcane fires. "I've got to see someone."

Hot Tea

They make it to town without encountering a checkpoint. In fact, they don't see a single cop the entire drive. Iris is confident by this point that the FBI have no idea where she is.

Iris's driver sniffs, and he takes one hand off the wheel and rubs the sweat off on his pants leg before extending his hand. "I'm Michael, by the way."

"Augusta," Iris responds. She curses herself. It was just the first name that wasn't her own that came to mind.

"Well, Augusta, have you got an address, or you just want to be dropped off around here?"

Iris looks out of the window. She hasn't ever been to her destination in Lafitte Hill without the help of GPS, but she thinks she's close. "What're you doing tonight, Michael?"

He shrugs. "This I suppose."

"You want to keep doing whatever *this* is?"

"If it pays more, hell yeah."

"Alright. Another five hundred. Or wait. Shit..." Iris acts concerned and looks into her bag. She doesn't want him thinking she has a pile of money. "I can do three fifty. Three hundred and fifty to take me south of New Orleans, Dustin, specifically."

"You got it!"

Iris realizes how lucky she got with this kid. He actually seems to be enjoying this.

"Alright. Wait in front of this park. And lie down on the seat. Don't be visible. The last thing we want is someone in one of these big houses seeing you waiting here and calling the cops."

"Right. When will you be back?"

"An hour, tops."

"Should I get your number? You know, in case I have to move or anything."

"I don't have a phone on me."

"Oh," he says, surprised. He looks her over from head to toe. She can tell he's trying to get a read on her. No phone. A bag full of cash and a baggy gray sweatshirt. She must look like a bank robber. But lucky for Iris, plenty of boys his age, criminals or not, think they're Clyde and are looking for a Bonnie.

Michael takes off his dirty hat and parts his hair. "You can trust me." He didn't have to say it, Iris thinks. Everything about his body language thus far has been genuine. "Is there anything else I can do for you? You don't have to pay me any more money."

Iris looks down at his feet. "What size shoe are you?"

"Twelve."

Iris sighs and pulls on the door handle. "No. There's nothing else. Just hang tight."

"Hangin' tight."

She almost considers giving him a wink, but her acting as a cool criminal can only go so far. She's still sick from adrenaline when she gets out of the pickup. She closes the door as quietly as she can and starts to walk.

She's still damp from the culvert, and it's cold when a light wind blows. The residential streets she walks down don't have sidewalks. The lawns run right to the road. Luckily, despite the suburban vibe, the houses have plenty of variance.

She'll recognize the one she's looking for even in the dark.

She tries to act as casual as possible, but if anyone in these houses were to see her socked feet, they'd know this wasn't some restless midnight walk.

Then there's the possibility that there is a private security detail patrolling around here. She'll have to get off the road at the first sign of headlights, but so far, the streets have been empty.

In another two blocks, her surroundings are even more familiar, and then she sees it. A fountain sits in the circular drive of a white colonnaded mansion. The shutters look black in the night, but she knows they're dark green.

There's no gate, and she doesn't want to be seen creeping in the shadows. She walks straight past the fountain and to the front door. Then she presses the doorbell. She waits ten seconds and taps it again. This time a dog barks.

It's another five seconds before she sees a light come on inside. She stands back so she's visible through the peephole and smiles. The door opens, revealing an older face with horn-rimmed glasses. It's her lawyer, Marshall.

"Iris?"

"Sorry for the night call."

He opens the door wider, revealing a cocker spaniel panting and wagging its tail. It seems happy to have visitors, despite the hour.

His eyes find her shoeless feet quickly, and he frowns. "Well, come in."

Iris steps inside, and he shuts the door behind her. The house is very *southern lawyer*. It's all wood walls and floors and heavy leather furniture. There are bookshelves housing hundreds of shiny law textbooks along the living room wall. The place even smells like a paperback book.

Marshall walks into the living room, and an older woman in hair rollers and a nightgown appears on the landing. She crosses her arms and stares at Iris without a word.

Marshall notices her and makes introductions. "Cherry, this is Iris—the brave young woman you know so much about."

Cherry doesn't say anything. With her arms crossed and her chin tilted slightly up, the message she gives Iris is clear; *My husband may have let you in, but this is my house. Watch yourself.*

"You can go back to bed. I'm sure we won't be long," Marshall says.

Cherry waits for Iris to sit in a leather armchair before she turns and heads back upstairs.

Marshall turns on a gas fireplace and sits in the chair opposite Iris. "I'm sorry you caught me in my jim-jams." His expression suddenly goes blank. "Shit." He waves his hand embarrassed. "My grandson. We've been watching him. That's what he calls pajamas."

"It's okay."

"I take it there's an emergency?"

Iris looks over her shoulder towards the stairs.

"Don't worry about Cherry. While it's not in the law books, there's such a thing as attorney-wife privileges."

"Meaning she knows everything?"

Marshall shrugs. "More or less."

Iris leans back in her chair. "The FBI moved on me. You heard about Annabelle?"

"We were watching the news until midnight. I wasn't a fan of her, but Christ."

"It wasn't me."

"Oh. I didn't think it was." He shakes his head quickly, suggesting he very much did think it was Iris.

"The FBI must think I'm involved. I was talking to the man who did it. He's the brother of the prostitute in Memphis that my ex-husband beat into a coma."

"Dominic?"

"You know about him?"

They're suddenly interrupted as there are footsteps on the stairs. Cherry has come back down. She has changed out of her nightgown and into a lavender lounge dress. Iris and Marshall are both quiet as she goes to the corner of the living room and turns on an electric kettle. She makes a racket as she prepares a teacup and saucer.

"Yes," Marshall says. "I know about Dominic. Again, Augusta was very transparent about her plans with me. There were no secrets between us." He gulps nervously as he says this.

"Then do you know Augusta's still alive?"

Marshall recoils a little, and Cherry spins from making her tea.

"Why on earth do you think that?"

"Dominic pulled her from the river. At least, I think he did. He was following the riverboat in a skiff."

"Did he tell you Augusta is alive?"

"No. He told me about a letter. It's from Mexico. From Augusta."

"Did you see this letter?"

"Yes, tonight. It was waiting at Sweet Blood."

"You're sure it was from her?"

"Pretty much. I compared the handwriting. She's at Paulo's estate."

He smacks his lips quietly. "She still owes me an invoice, then," he says jokingly, but Iris doesn't smile. He clears his throat. "So, how'd you get here?" He glances towards the front windows. "The police follow you?"

"Not a chance. I got away early."

"So what are you here for? You want to face the music?"

"The opposite, actually. Can you help get me to Mexico?"

Marshall sucks air through his teeth and sighs. "My connections were largely through Augusta. Without her... I'm not really the *guy* anymore."

Iris unzips her backpack and pulls out the Nokia. She wiggles it at Marshall. "Do you know about this?"

"No."

"It was in one of the backpacks kept in the tunnel."

Marshall isn't the best actor. His confusion looks genuine at the mention of the words backpack and tunnel. "I suppose there are some secrets I don't know."

"Forget it." Iris tosses the phone back in the bag.

"I'm sorry, but fleeing the country isn't really my expertise."

"That's fine."

Cherry has poured her tea, and Iris and Marshall are both quiet as she walks over and sits down in a third armchair. The cocker spaniel trots over and lies at her feet, and Cherry begins to watch them as one would TV.

A satisfied look spreads on her face, as if she's the luckiest woman in Louisiana for this first-class coverage of the Adler disaster.

35

Marshall seems to think her silent presence is perfectly normal. He doesn't even look at her. He crosses one leg over the other. "There was a guy I knew in the 90s who took people across the border, but he was old then. I could make some calls. He might know somebody. But you're *hot*, Iris. They're not saying your name in the news *yet*. But now that you're missing... Are you sure you don't want to wait around here for the smoke to clear?"

Iris fidgets uncomfortably.

Marshall stands to make a pile of money defending Iris if she gets arrested. Maybe he doesn't have her best interests in mind.

"Forget it, then," says Iris. "Can you at least get in touch with Paulo or his people?"

Marshall nods slowly. Like he can but may not want to.

Iris leans forward and tries to ignore Cherry sipping her tea. "Promise me. Tell them I need help getting out of the country. Tell them that I have the phone from the backpack. Aurelia said she would, too, but I want to be sure. I can't get out of here by myself.

"Alright. Alright, I can do that." He points at her. "But if you get caught you were never here."

"I'm not stupid. There's something else you could help me with."

Marshall makes it clear his help is conditional. He keeps his mouth shut and waits to hear the request.

"It's about the PI firm we hired to dig into my past in Memphis. I'm sure the FBI froze my accounts, but I want to make sure they keep getting paid."

"That can be arranged."

"And I want to know what they have so far."

"Funny you should mention that. They sent me the first half of the report just the other day." Marshall stands and goes over to a desk cluttered with papers and mail. Based on how deep he has to dig, Iris can tell this report didn't come *just the other day.*

He searches for long enough that the silence between Iris and Cherry grows awkward. Iris looks at her with a tight smile. Cherry doesn't change her expression any. She just slurps her tea.

"Ah-ha!" Marshall pulls out a large white envelope that's about a quarter inch thick. The top is ripped open already. "They emailed me a PDF as well, but I suppose you'd like the physical copy."

Iris stands and holds out her hand, but Marshall doesn't give it to her right away.

"You know what, there were some notes of my own I think I left in here." He reaches his hand in and pulls a handful of the papers out, but Iris walks closer. His voice gets clearly higher when he lies. She also noticed he speaks a lot less southern when he's around his wife.

Iris holds her hand out again for the envelope, and Marshall concedes. "Well, it's not the time for searching for a needle in a haystack, I suppose." He puts the papers back and gives her the envelope. His hand suddenly flies to rub the back of his neck. He's uncomfortable. There's something in these papers that he doesn't trust her with.

"And I've been remembering more. There was a woman in Memphis. A girl no much older than me. Her name was Veronica. Search the PDF for her name, and if it's not there, tell the PIs about her," says Iris, stuffing the envelope into her backpack and putting the straps over her shoulders.

"Are you sure you don't want to stick around awhile?"

"I should move while it's still dark."

"Move where?"

"I've got a place to wait for the call."

"You don't need a ride?"

"I've got one of those, too."

Marshall suddenly looks concerned.

"Don't worry. They're parked far from here."

"Right. Okay. You're certain you don't at least want something to eat?"

Iris is growing uncomfortable. "Thank you, Marshall. I'm fine." She makes for the front door.

Cherry and Marshall follow her, and the dog trots between them.

"Stay safe," Marshall calls after her. "I'll make sure your PIs keep getting paid. And contact me if you get to Mexico. Just call my office. I have my phones checked for wires weekly. It's a safe line."

"Okay."

Iris turns to Cherry, who has yet to say a word. She's looking Iris over from head to toe, and then she speaks. "What size shoe are you, sugar?"

Friends

The running shoes Iris wears are bright pink and a size too small, but she feels twice as capable of having to run if she needs to again. She walks back to Michael's truck much faster than she left.

She doesn't completely trust Marshall. He could've called the police on her to cover his own ass in case a neighbor saw her coming and going. Or because he'd prefer to have her locked up as a paying client.

She knocks on the truck window, and Michael gets up from lying in his seat and unlocks the doors.

"Let's not waste any time," Iris says, getting in.

Michael suddenly looks twice as nervous as he did before. He doesn't say anything as he starts the truck. *Did he have time to realize how crazy it was that he was helping an obvious fugitive?* That, Iris thinks, or he looked at his phone when she was away. Maybe she is in the news.

"Everything okay?" Iris asks and Michael immediately lights up.

"Totally! Yeah! I'm just tired. I was heading home from work when we crossed paths."

"And what do you do, Michael?"

"I work at a machine shop. Second shift."

"You like what you do?"

"Oh sure. Pays well enough. It's not exactly what I planned to do the year after graduating college, but hey... I'll save up some money."

"What did you study?"

Michael smiles, like he's embarrassed by the answer. "Philosophy."

Iris smirks. "And what the hell did you plan to do with that anyway?"

"I figured it would really help me think my way through the days when I ended up working at a machine shop. I wouldn't even need to listen to podcasts."

"Ah." Iris is relaxed again. She's glad to have gotten Michael talking. Perhaps he *is* just tired and a little stressed from abetting a fugitive.

"So did you do any philosophizing about what it means that you're helping me?"

"I was thinking this was the most excitement I've felt since my basketball team went to State my junior year of high school. And I spent the whole game on the bench."

"So you like the rush?"

"You don't seem like a bad person. It's funny to say that since I don't know you at all. You might've murdered your husband for all I know."

Iris's eyes widen, but she doesn't think he's fishing. His example is just coincidence.

Michael continues, "But you can tell a normal, moral person from how they talk for the most part. The way they look at you. I know you see the world similar to how I see it."

"Yeah?"

"Yeah. And I think you could've hijacked my truck with that pistol you got in your bag, but you don't think that's a good thing to do to someone."

Iris is quiet for a moment. She must've been sloppy when she first went through her bag for the cash and let the revolver show. "Are you just saying all this because you want me to open up about what I did?"

"Maybe."

"You're dying to know, aren't you?"

"I'll consider the truth part of my payment."

"Okay, Michael. Just get me to Dustin, and I'll spill the beans."

"Aye. Aye."

"I did murder my husband, for the record."

He laughs. "Understood.

"But the son of a bitch deserved it."

"I hear ya."

Iris moves her attention back to getting to her destination without getting caught. "Let's avoid I-10. I don't want to cross over any roads we've already driven on. Let's take 12 and come through New Orleans from the north."

"And cross Lake Pontchartrain?"

"Exactly."

"Alright. It's gonna be a longer drive."

Iris looks at him. "Do you want more money?"

"No. It's just that I usually eat when I get off work."

"We can eat."

"Yeah?"

"I'm not so wanted that we can't hit up a drive-through."

"Alright." Michael grins. "Let's do it."

In ten minutes, Iris has her new sneakers kicked up on the dashboard and is wolfing down a double cheeseburger and handfuls of fries. Her fear has mostly left her, and when she first smelled the fryers in the drive-through, she realized she was famished.

She takes a sip of her chocolate shake, and Michael talks with his mouth still mostly full. One of his hands is perched on the wheel. His other holds a burger in its yellow paper wrapper. "I think we would've been good friends if we grew up together."

"What makes you think so?"

"We're both not trusting of authority. We both like adventure. We like cheeseburgers." He raises his burger up in emphasis. "You don't need all that much in common to be friends."

"I'm not nearly as wild and adventurous as I seem."

"No?"

"There were circumstances that kind of... *pushed* me into this."

"Fair enough."

"I actually never had that many friends."

"Really?"

"Really."

"You seem like an interesting person."

"You caught me at one of my more interesting moments, Michael."

"Don't try to tell me you were a bore before you were running from the police. Because I doubt that."

"Being an outlaw isn't exactly my identity. I'm not John Dillinger is all I'm saying."

"So who are you?"

"You seem to stick to the script of being a philosophy major, huh?"

Michael smiles but doesn't respond. He wants her to answer the question.

Iris looks out the windshield. "I'm... I'm just someone who met a lot of really bad people. And I guess

I've been trying to give them what they deserve ever since."

"Oh." Michael raises his voice in surprise. "A vigilante."

"I'm most definitely *not* a vigilante."

"You just kinda defined one."

Iris thinks for a moment. "Vigilantes have some higher belief in justice. I don't care about any of that. These people I met. The shit they did... They just make me sick."

"So you're a punisher?"

Iris laughs. "Sure. Whatever you say. I'm a punisher."

"It sounds more badass anyway. Vigilante is a little lame."

"Agreed."

"I'd like to have something like that to fight for. To be honest, life is a little empty. Gym. Work. Watch YouTube."

"If it makes you feel any better, I'd kill to have a boring routine."

"Thanks, but I'd rather have the purpose that comes with having a shitlist."

"Don't be so sure," Iris says quietly. The conversation dies. She sips her shake, and when it's empty, she begins to struggle to stay awake.

The truck's cab is warm, and her stomach is full. She lets her eyes close for a moment, but it's harder than she thinks to open them again. And before she can even try, Iris is asleep.

Pursuit

Iris wakes in a panic, and her sudden movement causes Michael to whip his head from the road to look at her.

She blinks rapidly and bends over to see that her backpack looks untouched. Then she looks out the window to get her bearings. Trees. The glow of water and reeds under the moonlight. They've entered the bayou.

Michael is smart enough to understand what she wants to know. "We're not far from Dustin. Last sign said fourteen miles, and that was a couple minutes ago."

"How long was I asleep?"

"About an hour."

"Seriously?" She's upset with herself. Iris was beginning to feel a kind of satisfaction from her criminal skills. Falling asleep in a stranger's truck wasn't very pro. She's woken up with a tickle in the back of her throat, too. It could be stress related or just from the stale air of the cab. She's probably fine, she reasons. Iris can't deal with the thought of being sick on top of all this.

"Seems like you needed the sleep," Michael says.

"I guess," Iris says and stretches.

"Um. There is one thing that needs mentioning... That car behind us..."

Iris looks at the side mirror. "What about it?"

"It looks like a Charger. Maybe I'm being paranoid, but I think I can see a light rack, too."

"You're saying it's a cop?"

"I think so, yeah."

Iris can't tell what kind of car it is herself, but she does think it has a police-look to its outline.

"How long has it been behind us?"

"Only the last few miles. I don't think they've been tailing us. Unlucky coincidence, though."

"Just stay calm, then."

"Would they recognize you?" Michael asks.

"Maybe. We're pretty far from where they were looking for me." Even as Iris says this, she knows without a doubt that an all-points bulletin has been issued across the state by now. It would include a picture of her, along with the fact that she likely hitchhiked a ride on I-10. All this info would be sent right to the little computer that cops have in their cruisers.

Michael is so busy staring at the car in the rearview that he doesn't watch the road. They suddenly veer towards the shoulder, and he has to swerve back after hitting the rubble strip. "Fuck," he says, and then all doubt is removed whether it's a cop... The night begins to flash red and blue as the car behind them turns on their emergency lights.

"Oh shit. *Shit.*"

"It's okay," Iris says, but she's not confident he didn't do it on purpose. *Did he want her to get caught now?*

But Michael doesn't start to slow down.

"Alright. Okay," Michael says through a sigh. "I'm not going to be able to lose him totally, but it's dark enough..."

Iris feels the truck start to pick up speed. The engine begins to roar lightly. "Michael, what are you doing?"

"I bet I can lose them by a little bit. Just enough for you to slip out into the dark."

"I'm not letting you catch a felony for me. Just pull over."

"And what? Let you go to prison because I fucked up? I'll fix it."

"You didn't fuck up."

"Let me fix it!" Michael yells.

The truck's engine is hard to hear over now.

Iris tries to find the words to talk Michael down, but she has a feeling she can't. As he presses the gas pedal to the floor, she realizes who Michael is. He's not that much less desperate than she is.

He's depressed. A philosophy major working in a machine shop, who picked up a pretty girl who had a bag of cash on his drive home. For the first time in weeks, he has someone to talk to other than his online friends in video games.

It must've felt like the perfect night. Wild, spontaneous. And now he feels like he fucked it up.

"Michael!" Iris yells.

He's not listening. He's looking at the rearview and back to the road. "I'll find a place to turn around. When I'm halfway into my turn and the passenger door is facing away from him, get out. I'll finish the turn and blind him with my high beams. He won't even know you were here."

"He probably already saw the back of my head. He knows you have a passenger."

"No way. I've got heavy tints. Just trust me, Augusta."

Iris feels guilty. He doesn't even know her real name. But she stops trying to talk him out of playing savior. She knows his type. The bored young man looking for purpose. The burning building to run into.

"Okay," Iris says. They pass a sign indicating a junction with another highway, and she points. "There. The intersection should be wide enough to turn."

"Already on it."

Michael accelerates even more. He must plan on surprising the cop by slamming on his brakes. Iris closes her eyes. Her already watery guts shake from the vibrating engine. She braces her arm against the door.

"You don't have to be going so fast!"

Michael waits another couple seconds before braking. The tires squeal, and Iris already knows he really fucked up this time.

The wheels lock. She grits her teeth and gets ready for impact with the ditch, but just as they're about to pass through the intersection, Iris realizes they have a bigger problem.

The asphalt of the junction glows yellow, but it's not from their lights. She looks left just in time to see it—a set of headlights shines six feet off the ground.

It's a semi-truck.

Time freezes for a fraction of a second, and the cab erupts with a crash that comes with impact.

The semi hits where the truck bed meets the cab and splits them in two. Iris and Michael's half of the truck is sent spinning. The world blurs, but not so much that Iris can't see the trailer of the truck jack-knife and clip the front of the cop car.

Then the airbags deploy.

Hers hits her like a boxer's glove and brings the taste of blood to her mouth. By the time she can see again, the cab has stopped moving. They've fallen into the ditch.

Iris is on her back, and the truck is facing straight up at the sky, like the bed would be buried beneath them.

She never lost consciousness, and the entire crash must've only taken a second or two. She pats herself for injuries and realizes she's suddenly wet. Their half must be in water. They're in the bayou.

"Shit, shit, shit." She's afraid she'll be trapped in her seat belt, put when she clicks the button, it flies right off.

"Michael. Michael." Iris turns to him and freezes. Where his neck should be is a piece of gnarled metal. Blood dribbles down off it with the consistency of a fountain stream.

"Michael..." She sees his eyes are open. Lifelessly wide. The metal must've severed his spinal cord. She can see from the expression of surprise petrified on his face that his death was instant.

She hears yelling nearby. She looks right, expecting her door to be broken and trapping her, but there is no passenger door at all. She gets out and snatches her backpack up and throws it on.

Then she's on her feet, stumbling as she gains her balance. It's so dark out here in the bayou that she doesn't feel the need to run. No one can see her. Even as she hears the truck driver and cop approach the front of the truck, she only walks.

Michael's warm blood that soaks her skin is already cooling, and soon she has a chill.

Dustin

The first responders must be coming to the scene from the opposite direction, because Iris hasn't had to walk off the road once to hide from a passing car.

She's walking slowly, expecting to feel the burn of some injury that her adrenaline has masked, but after twenty minutes she still feels fine. She doesn't have a scratch. Not a broken nail. Just a headache from the airbag. Michael was on the side of impact, and she wasn't.

Tonight is the most she's ever felt like a murderer.

The more distance she gets, the more she wants to turn around. She can't stop thinking what Michael's family is going to think. They'll figure he lost his mind. Snapped.

Committed suicide probably. She can't leave them thinking that.

She got him killed when she got into his truck with a backpack full of cash and a handgun. Iris feels like a criminal.

Actions have consequences, and now a young man is dead because of her. He'd be alive right now if she hadn't run through those sugarcane fields. If she hadn't flashed cash on the side of the highway. If she hadn't been a murderer already.

A part of her brain fires back saying she didn't make him flee from the cop. She didn't tell him to speed up. She said the opposite.

He was old enough to think for himself. He made a mistake picking her up, and he made a mistake when he tried to play hero. There was no gun to his head. The only consolation was that as a philosophy major, she figures that he'd probably agree with her take.

He was responsible for his own actions.

It doesn't lessen the guilt. It feels like a brick in her gut. Her mind keeps racing on and on. Michael's wide dead eyes are all she can think about until she enters the town of Dustin and the horizon has the purple hue of dawn.

She didn't even realize she had been walking the right direction. She pauses and begins to focus on the situation at hand.

She's covered in too much blood to just waltz into the first gas station and ask for directions. She doesn't think there's any way for her to get to a bathroom and a mirror without being seen by someone.

She's been walking next to water this whole time, but she hasn't thought of cleaning herself off in it as an option. The black water is serene and still as glass but full of alligators.

She's seen a few sets of eyes already shining in the moonlight, watching her. She's been putting it off but knows she has no choice. Before sunrise, she has to get the blood off her.

She walks a little farther from the road so she won't be surprised by a car, and then she takes off her backpack and pools her clothes at her feet. It's October, but the shallow water is still warm. It stinks a little of rot, but she has to get this blood off her. She can feel it sticking her strands of hair together. She kneels on shore and dunks her head. She rakes her fingers through her hair and cringes as they bring out clumps of something slimy.

Congealed blood. Brains. Chunks of flesh. She flicks them away into the water before she can tell.

She takes off her sweatshirt and laves the water over her arms and face. She scrubs furiously, but she can feel some of the flakes of dried blood refuse to unstick from her skin.

Something splashes into the water nearby, and Iris decides she's cleaned off enough. She'd been chumming the water anyway. She puts her sweatshirt and backpack back on and keeps walking into town.

The tickle in her throat has come back, only this time stronger. Maybe it never went away and she'd just been in too much shock to notice it. Regardless, she's not able to pretend it's the air quality anymore. Her nostrils are stuffy as well. She's getting sick.

Soon, she starts to pass houses. It's still early enough that the town is asleep, but she decides she's not going to act suspicious and try to dodge approaching traffic. There's no reason for the police to think Iris Adler was in that truck. She needs to act normal.

She passes a quaint white church, and the first person she sees is its pastor. He's an old man with hair only on the sides of his head. He wears a short-sleeved black shirt with a clerical collar. Iris smiles at him as he steps off the sidewalk to open the door to the church.

She decides it's still dark enough for her not to worry about being remembered. She stops when she's still fifteen feet from him. "Good morning."

"Morning." He pauses, apparently a little confused why she stopped so far away. He looks over his shoulder guardedly.

"Do you know where I can find Tilda's place?" Iris asks.

"Four blocks down to Spring Street. Take a right there, and her place is at the very end of the road." His tone suggests the question doesn't surprise him. Like Tilda's is the home of all wet-haired vagabonds wandering the streets before sunrise on a Sunday morning.

"Thank you."

"Service starts at nine," he adds, but the comment is a chide more than an invitation—you need Jesus. He doesn't look at Iris again as he unlocks the door to the church and steps in.

Fine by her. The less time people see her the better.

She gets to Spring Street and takes a right. Here there's old wooden houses with peeling paint. Most are no bigger than shacks. There's trash in the yards—toilet seats and couches with rusted springs sprouting from their cushions.

A brindle mutt on a chain barks furiously as she passes. Slobber flies and the muscles in its gigantic head pulse.

There are no American flags. No political signage on the lawns. She can tell this is not a community that's eager to cooperate with the police. Here, meth is made in backyards, and if you're paying taxes, you're doing it wrong. This is good, Iris thinks.

She needs the company of thieves.

She walks faster, and by the end of it, the asphalt road she walks on is cracked and coming apart like a puzzle.

She sees the sign for Tilda's. It's wooden with white paint. There's a gravel parking lot with old American pickups and chopper motorcycles parked in it. The motel itself is half on land and half over the water.

She stops, panicked for a minute. Near the parking lot, next to a picnic table, a man in leather chaps and a leather jacket lies belly up on the grass.

It takes her a minute to realize he's passed-out drunk. When she looks back at Tilda's, she sees from the beer signs that half of the structure is a bar. She keeps walking and opens a squeaky door to reception. There's a clock over the counter that reads 6:47.

The room smells of cigarette smoke.

Iris rings the little bell. She can hear the laugh track of a sitcom from the back room, and a woman with a hoarse voice shouts, "Comin'."

Iris places her hands on the counter, but when she sees the dried blood under her nails and between her fingers, she puts them at her sides.

An older woman in a tank top comes out from the back. The word "Harley" is spelled across the top with sequins. Her face is carved in deep lines from a lifetime of tanning, cigarettes, and no sunscreen.

The woman doesn't look at Iris as she talks. She organizes some papers on the desk in front of her. "Lookin' for a room? We ain't got nothin' till 'leven."

"Um. Yeah. Are you Tilda?"

"Uh-huh."

"Aurelia sent me here."

Now the woman looks Iris in the eye. "Aurelia who?"

"I don't know her last name, to be honest. But do you know many Aurelias?"

"No."

"Do you know one? Black woman, 5'2". She's in her fifties."

"Sure I do. That's the Adlers' girl. Oh." The woman widens her eyes. Apparently, she must watch the news. She recognizes Iris. "You got to be shittin' me." She sighs. "Cops after ya?"

Iris nods nervously.

"Okay. It's hundred a night, then. Call it one fifty."

"Fine. But can I get a room now?"

"How'd you get here? Anyone see you?"

"No one. I got dropped off."

The woman walks out from around the desk and opens the screen door. She stands with her hands on her hips until she's content she doesn't see cops posted outside. "You *can't* get a room. I don't want you in gen pop. You're getting a villa. No extra cost."

"Oh." Iris's chest rocks with relief as she exhales. "Perfect."

There are three doors in this reception room. The one she came in from, one to the bar, and another that's propped open with a cinder block that shows a row of room doors that extend out on a dock, stilted above the water. The rooms over the water must be "gen pop." Iris assumes a villa must mean more privacy.

Tilda goes back behind the counter. "You pay now."

Iris digs into her backpack and takes out the cash. She keeps the bills out of sight as she counts out the money to pay for three nights.

"Give me another fifty, and I'll buy hair dye and give ya a trim."

Iris adds a fifty-dollar bill and hands it all over.

"Redhead or blonde? Or do ya want one of them anarchist colors?"

"Blonde."

Tilda says nothing and pockets the cash.

"Is three nights okay?" Iris asks. "I might stay shorter... or longer. I don't know."

"If you got the money, you could stay till ya get caught for alls I care."

"Great."

Tilda takes a room key off a hook. "Come on, sugar."

They go back out the screen door and cross the yard. About fifty yards from reception and a similar distance from where the residential houses on the street start is a dirt trail that snakes off to the right.

There's a porta potty near the trail entrance that stinks like the chemically blue liquid they pump into its tank.

Tilda takes the path, and Iris has to walk faster to keep up.

She can see water through the trees on either side of her. They're on a peninsula about the width of a tennis court. The first "villa" appears. It's what Iris would best describe as a moonshiner's shack.

It's a disheveled wooden structure. It's stilted to withstand flood waters but only about four feet high. Its sole window is green and black from mold. The building itself is maybe twelve by twelve feet.

They pass another shack identical in design, but its siding is newer than the last one. The wood is closer to brown than black, and the one window looks like it's seen Windex this century. Unfortunately, Tilda doesn't stop.

The peninsula ends with a third shack that looks more like the first. Lopsided. Rotting. The waterline of the bayou starts only twenty feet behind it.

Tilda goes up the stairs and unlocks the door, and Iris steps in after her. It smells wet. Mossy. There's a queen bed with surprisingly fresh-looking sheets, a stained tan couch Iris plans to never sit on, and a wooden kitchen counter with a sink. What Iris doesn't see is a toilet.

"Um..."

Tilda seems to read her thoughts. "Bathroom is the port-a-jon we passed. Where the path starts."

"Gotcha." Iris looks around the single room again. There's a distinct lack of anything breakable. There's a small table with chairs that the single light of the room dangles over, and a flashlight is set on it. But there is nothing on the walls or unnecessary furniture. No bookshelves or cupboards or board games.

This room is used for partying and sex. No one complains about a toilet because the men that stay here just piss out the front door.

Iris is willing to bet that the rooms in "gen pop" at least have their own bathrooms. This wouldn't have been so bad if Tilda didn't get Iris's hopes up with the word "villa," but she's still happy to have a bed and a door that locks. As badly as she needs a bath.

"I'll be back later to cut your hair. My dad was a prison barber. I know my shit." Tilda holds the key to the room out in a pinch, and Iris opens her palm. The key falls with a ping, and Iris closes it in her fist.

"Perfect," Iris says with as much genuine enthusiasm as she can muster. This woman is the only thing between her and a prison cell. She tries to be grateful so Tilda might think twice if the police end up offering a reward for her capture.

"I'll drop by at least once a day to bring you food and take any requests. You 'lergic to anything?"

Iris shakes her head.

"See you around three, then."

Tilda leaves, and, when she gets down the steps, Iris flips the deadbolt. She kicks off her pants and lifts her T-shirt over her head, but before she crawls under the covers, she opens her backpack and sets the revolver on the floor next to the bed.

Then she finds the thick envelope the PI firm sent to Marshall. Based on the sheer heft of the report, it seems obvious they didn't meet a dead end while digging into Iris's past.

There are things Iris has begun to remember— Veronica. A needle and a spoon. She knows enough to not be excited to read the thing.

She lifts the mattress and stuffs the envelope beneath it. If there are more secrets in there, they will have to wait. For now, she needs to forget.

She needs to sleep.

Fever Dreams

Iris wakes in wet sheets. She can't remember where she is. Her head pounds, and her insides feel like hot coals. "Oh shit," she says aloud and sits up in bed. She's sick. Sicker than she's been since she was a kid. She shivers violently. That's why she woke up. She feels like she's freezing.

Fever.

The memory of the bayou bleeds into her brain. Tilda. Her thoughts have a hallucinogenic feel. Colors splotch her vision in the dark. Violets and oranges explode and bounce around her field of vision. For a blissful moment, she isn't sure whether any of the last twenty-hour hours even happened. But it doesn't last.

The room is pitch black. She slept the entire day. She reaches up and touches her hair to feel that it hasn't been cut. Tilda never came by. Or maybe she did but Iris slept so deeply that she didn't hear her knocking.

The thoughts need to wait because she's hit by a singular want: water. Iris crawls out of bed and pulls the sheet and blanket out with her so she's cloaked.

She walks to the faucet, but when she turns the lever, there's no sound. No drip of water in the sink. She stumbles towards the front door and opens it. The night is still and quieter than it would be in midsummer. She closes her eyes as the breeze hits her like a balm.

Iris doesn't think she has the strength to make it to reception, but if she doesn't get water, she could be in trouble. She's adjusted to the dark to see more, but it's a long walk to the motel, and no telling if reception is open.

But she needs to take the chance. She's about to close the door and start getting dressed when she realizes something white shining near her feet on the porch—plastic shopping bags.

Iris pulls them inside and turns on the light. In one of the bags is a box of Oreos, a packet of Slim Jims, two bags of chips, and a two-liter bottle of Sprite. Iris is just thankful it isn't Coke and twists off the cap.

She sits cross-legged on the floor and swallows greedily. It's her fourth gulp when her stomach revolts. She pauses and then retches forward.

When she vomits the Sprite back up all over the floor, she knows she's in trouble. She groans and lets the residual snot and bile fall from her nose and mouth. She can feel the lemon zing burn in her sinuses. She doesn't attempt to have another drink. She feels twice as sick now. With the door still slightly open, Iris cocoons herself in the blankets and moves towards the table. She crawls into a ball beneath it, and very quickly she fades into a shallow sleep filled with fever dreams.

Iris wakes to something freezing.

"Oh hon," she hears. The cold sensation is the back of Tilda's fingers pressed against her forehead. The room is filled with morning light. It has the stale reek of sugary vomit.

Iris is helped up and into one of the chairs. She rests her head on the tabletop and listens as Tilda opens the single cabinet under the sink and starts cleaning. At some point she leaves and comes back with fresh bedding. She unwraps Iris from her blanket cloak and wraps her in a fresh one.

"I'll pick you up some Tamiflu. Water and Tylenol, too. You need anything else?"

"No," Iris manages to say. "No, thank you."

"I'm sure you're not eatin' yet, but I'll get ya some chicken soup for when you are."

"Thank you."

Tilda helps Iris outside, where she pees beneath the stairs, not bothering to make the extra trip to the outhouse. Iris is helped back to bed, and then Tilda leaves. It's hard to tell time, but Iris thinks maybe she sleeps for a fitful hour before she's awakened again.

"Alright," Tilda says as she takes things out of a plastic bag and sets them on the counter. "Dayquil. Nyquil. Tamiflu. Tylenol. I got some behind-the-counter tricks, too. You want a Brompton cocktail, hon?"

Iris has no idea what that is, but it sounds strong. She wants to sleep this sickness away. "Sure."

"Okie-doke." Tilda is at the table for a minute mixing things together.

Iris can smell the drink before it's even brought over to her in a clear plastic cup. It's a viscous concoction of cold medicine.

"You think you can stomach this?"

Iris isn't sure, but she nods, willing to take the risk. When she has the cup in her hand, she takes a few deep breaths.

Tilda goes to the table again and comes back with a little cup of Sprite, presumably to chase it down. Tilda then reaches out and pinches Iris's nose so it's plugged. "Down it. Don't even let it touch your tongue."

Iris throws her head back. She gags once, but the violet-colored liquid doesn't come back up.

She takes the Sprite and swishes it around in her mouth before swallowing. Maybe it's because her stomach is so empty or the sickness has left her so weak, but she already feels the drugs seeping into her bloodstream. Her eyelids grow heavy. She forgets the burn of her fever.

Tilda begins to tidy up. She's arranging things on the table. Another minute passes, and Iris is suddenly afraid. There's a familiar feeling overtaking her—a blanket of euphoria. She can't even fear it for more than a second before she begins to grin. She can't help it. "Tilda, what was in that exactly?"

"NyQuil, cognac, and a little bit of Percocet. On the house."

"Opioids?" Iris asks sleepily.

"Just enough to take the edge off, darling."

"Oh." Iris has already forgotten her fugitive status. She's forgotten Michael. Everything in this moment feels perfect, and that is the danger. But then a thought creeps in. One she's been putting off since she began to run.

She begins to remember another bed. Handcuffs and heroin. She knows how she ended up in prostitution, but will the report the PIs put together confirm her memories? Was it not Iris's fault?

She was imprisoned. Trafficked. Tricked.

She looks at her backpack. She should send it to the bottom of the bayou. She doesn't need to read about what she already knows. She lifts a limp finger, planning to tell Tilda to dispose of the envelope, but before she can even straighten her index, her eyelids shut like cement, and this time, she doesn't even dream.

Lizards

It's dark when she wakes again. Night again already. The drugs have worn off, and Iris is left with the panic of the comedown. Not only that, but her fever has fought back. She's burning up.

The room is moonlit, and she can see from the slant of blue light that hits the table that there's another Brompton cocktail already made for her.

Upon just seeing it, she feels as if she's drunk it. Her heart rate slows, and she leans back relaxed in bed. It's there. The next hit is right there.

She has to pee again, but there's the more pressing feeling of a bowel movement that gets her up from bed. She shucks off the blanket so she's in nothing but her shirt and underwear and flips the light on. She sits to put on her sneakers, and then she grabs the flashlight. She doesn't bother with the effort of putting on pants.

She debates leaving the Brompton cocktail for when she gets back, but the thought doesn't last long. She snatches the cup up before she can change her mind and downs the syrupy liquid.

She looks for the Sprite, picks it up off the floor, and takes a few deep glugs. This time it all stays down. The nausea stage of this sickness seems over.

She opens the door and stays still as the night breeze hits her. She can smell the sour stink of her armpits without bending to them. Her whole body must emit a similar odor of sickness.

She steps down the first stair to go to the outhouse, when she stops. There's a log at the bottom of the stairs that wasn't there before. She focuses the flashlight on it and jumps.

An alligator takes a stubborn step forward but otherwise doesn't seem bothered by the beam of light. It's medium-sized, fat in the middle, and its armor of scales glistens. It must've just left the water.

Iris looks around. The shack's porch doesn't wrap around. There's no way to get down without being within a few feet of the gator.

"Seriously. Dude, I gotta go. Go. Get." Iris clicks her teeth and waves the flashlight, but the gator stays put.

"Don't make me." She points at it firmly and then turns around and gets a bottle of water Tilda left. She thinks she's safe from where she stands. Alligators can't climb stairs. She splashes some water on the gator, but it just opens its mouth and hisses.

She could probably run past it, but she's already beginning to feel a little high and doesn't trust her balance. "Guy, get out of here. I gotta poop. Come on," she whines.

She's been in the bayou for two days and only a few conscious hours, and she's already standing on a porch scolding an alligator in her underwear.

She sighs and goes back inside. The gun is not an option. Even if a warning shot would scare it off, she most certainly doesn't want the attention that would come with the sound.

She opens the cupboard under the sink and finds an aerosol cleaning spray. She takes a practice spray in the cabinet. It shoots out a steady, smelly mist.

She goes back out the door, confident from the drugs and desperate from the pressure in her bowels. "You asked for it, bud. Come on." She sprays the cleaner at the gator.

It hisses again but starts to waddle forward slowly.

"Come on. You can shit anywhere. Get going."

When it's gone, she sweeps the flashlight over the little patch of swamp looking for more, but no eyes shine. When she gets to the porta-potty she can hear the music from the bar. She opens its door, and it doesn't smell nearly as clean as when she passed it the first time. She shoots a long spray of cleaning product inside before sitting down.

She's there for ten minutes. When she's done, she starts back down the trail. She wonders if these other shacks are occupied, and the thought makes her turn off her flashlight. But she's not afraid, her mood somber, she thinks about Michael. She thinks about his parents and the course his life would've taken if he'd left work twenty seconds earlier.

He was handsome. Clever. He would've met a nice girl at some point. Then Iris pictures this girl, asleep in bed, unaware of the soulmate she never met because Iris killed him.

Iris has broken something that can't be put back together. It doesn't matter her intentions. Actions have consequences.

The sickness has prevented her from thinking too hard about him, but now his death crashes over her like a wave. Guilt. Panic. Iris sits on the step of her shack and taps her foot, waiting for the drugs to kick in. She doesn't care that her bare butt presses against the dirty, splintered wood.

The cocktail isn't working as quickly as the first one did. She wonders if her tolerance is already that much stronger or if Tilda didn't share the Percocet this time.

She listens to the wind blow, rattling the leaves above her.

A minute passes. Two. Then it becomes hard to track time.

She's high.

She rationalizes this relapse with the fact that the best thing she can do for herself is to get as much sleep as possible. She needs to get better so she can get to Mexico. But to get to Mexico for what? Iris begins to cry. Her life feels meaningless. She doesn't have the drive to discover her past pushing her onward anymore.

The mystery was solved.

She thinks of the thick folder the investigators mailed and Marshall's reluctance to hand it over. She needs to read it, but it's becoming hard for Iris to hold on to a thought.

They begin to float around her brain, bumping into each other. No single idea lasts for more than a moment. She opens her mouth and takes a deep breath. Her skin tingles as the blood pulses beneath it. She stands to go inside, when suddenly her heart begins to pound in her chest. She sees something.

Someone is in the trees. They're lingering just off the trail near the second shack, but there's one problem: the figure she sees is simply too big to be a person.

It looks like a man, but from the height of this dark figure, they'd have to be more than six and a half feet tall.

Just as she thinks it's the drugs, the figure takes a step off the trail and disappears into the dark.

Iris bolts up. Her heart pounds. The breeze blows and the leaves whisper together. Her eyes scan the dark in front of her, but the figure doesn't reappear. She decides it was the drugs. Her imagination. She goes inside and locks the door behind her, and this time she brings the revolver into bed with her and tucks it into the sheets next to her like a little steel lover.

Blondie

Iris feels somewhat better the next day. Her fever hasn't broken completely, but it's noticeably lower. The downside to not feeling as sick is that Iris can't sleep the day away like she has been doing.

Tilda comes over early to cut and dye her hair. She brings a bucket and a gallon of water. She smokes two cigarettes in the time it takes her to slice Iris's hair into a bob. When she's brushed the hair off Iris's shoulders, she starts with the dye.

Iris can see from the box that the shade of blonde Tilda picked out is nearly white. With her bob and bright hair, Iris is going to look like the protagonist of a sci-fi movie. She's just thankful the room doesn't have a mirror.

When Tilda comes back in the afternoon, she has a Subway sandwich and a few old romance paperbacks.

"Thank you," Iris says, setting the items on the table. "Do you think you could get me a newspaper the next time you go out?"

"Sure." Tilda snorts.

"Have you been watching the news?"

"No. I don't know what they're saying about you. You been here nearly three nights."

"Yeah," Iris says.

"You gotta pay more if you plan to keep stayin'."

"Oh, of course. Can you just..." Iris holds up a finger and looks at her backpack.

Tilda doesn't look away to give her privacy, but Iris realizes if Tilda wanted to rob her, she's had plenty of chances when Iris was passed out sick.

Iris flips through the dollar bills. "How much?"

"Call it five hundred for another three nights."

Iris doesn't plan to barter. Tilda's been a blessing. She hands her the money. Just as Tilda's about to leave, Iris speaks again. "And by the way…" She digs the Nokia out of her backpack. "Could you take a picture of this?"

Tilda takes her phone out and snaps a pic. "You want another just like it?"

"No, the next time you're in town, can you try to find a charger for it?"

"Sure."

"Thank you."

"I'll bill ya."

"Of course."

"Alrighty, then." Tilda turns to leave.

"And Tilda?"

"Yep?"

Iris licks her lips. She's not sold that it was just her sickness that made her see the tall man last night. "Is there anyone else staying in the other shacks right now?"

"It's just you out here. The other *villas*," Tilda corrects her, "are empty."

"Okay. Thank you, Tilda."

"Mmhmm."

Tilda leaves, and Iris eats the sandwich. She's still not hungry, even though she hasn't had more than a snack in days, but she knows her body needs the food.

She tries to read the private investigator's report, but her mind is still too sick and foggy to focus. She doesn't mind having the excuse to not read it. She's afraid of what she might find. She hates herself enough as it is. Reading about the prostitute drug addict she once was is not something she looks forward to.

She picks up one of the romance novels and reads about one hundred pages before she stands up and stretches. She can't imagine how people put up with these un-airconditioned shacks in the summer. It's a seventy-five-degree day in October, and the room feels like it's swelling with heat.

Tilda left the cognac she made the Brompton cocktail with next to the other supplies she brought, and Iris picks it up and inspects the brown liquid. She reads the back, flips it over, and takes off the cap. She takes a pull and coughs but keeps it down. She sits at the table and drinks warm liquor like the generations of drunks that have occupied this shanty before her.

She wants to stop thinking about Michael. She wants to stop questioning why she's hiding.

She pictures a concrete jail cell. Sixty years of sitting in one. Just as much as she's afraid of losing her freedom, she fears the purgatory of prison. Then she thinks of Augusta. She's in Mexico, staring at the hazy mountains with a cigarette between her fingers, waiting for Iris to answer that damn phone she keeps trying to call.

Soon the room has cooled and the sun is setting. Iris feels sicker with the liquor in her stomach, but her bad thoughts have ceased.

She makes sure the door is locked and crawls into bed. If it weren't for the liquor, she thinks she'd probably be panicking at the sight of nightfall. Last night was no hallucination. There's a giant lurking outside her shack.

She picks up the revolver and works the cylinder until it opens. She counts the bullets and then snaps it shut and assures herself that no matter how big he is, he's not bulletproof.

Room

Another day passes, and Tilda has not brought a newspaper, nor could she find a charger for the Nokia. On the bright side, Iris finally feels normal. She only had the two Brompton Cocktails. Tilda didn't offer any more Percocet, and Iris didn't ask.

She's not going to relapse.

Now that she's not ill, Iris intends to get her shit together, and that starts with taking a shower. For that she needs a regular room. On the morning of her fourth day in Dustin, Iris puts on a purple T-shirt and a pair of light-wash jeans that Tilda picked up for her from Walmart. She stuffs her things into her backpack and starts off to the motel.

She doesn't pass anyone on her way to reception. There is no giant waiting to jump out at her or any bikers passed out in the parking lot. When Iris enters, Tilda is leaning on the counter, writing. She stares at Iris but doesn't say anything.

"I'd like a regular room."

Tilda looks her up and down as if considering how recognizable she is. She still doesn't speak.

"Are they still showing me on the news?"

Tilda gestures backwards with her head to the TV in her office. "They're talking about you right now."

Iris leans forward. "What're they saying?"

"That you're still missin'."

"That's it?"

Tilda crosses her arms. "That and you're wanted for questioning in connection to multiple murders."

Iris smiles awkwardly.

Tilda sighs and raises a single brow. Her expression says enough. *Girl, aren't you somethin'.*

"I'll pay double."

"You ain't gotta do that. Come on. You got your things?"

"Yep."

"Key?"

"Yeah. It's locked." Iris hands over her old key, and Tilda takes a new one from a peg.

Tilda goes out the reception room's back door, and Iris follows. They walk down a dock to a connected, floating structure. They pass a row of doors that aren't numbered. Instead, they're different colors—red, blue, yellow, green, black.

Tilda stops in front of an orange door. It's the last in the row. She unlocks it and hands the key to Iris. Iris doesn't care for the coloring system. All she can think about is some colorblind biker trying to barge into her room in the middle of the night.

"Try not to go anywhere. You don't look much like the picture they're showin' on the news. But if someone stares at those bruises long enough to see past em', they'll figure it out."

Bruises. Iris hasn't looked in a mirror for days. The airbag must've done a number on her. "Okay. I'll be smart. I promise."

Tilda doesn't respond. She walks back down the dock, and Iris steps into her room and locks the door behind her.

The inside is like any other cheap motel room. Stained carpet. Starchy-looking sheets. Light smell of cigarettes.

There's no TV. Perhaps to deter theft, or maybe drunk bikers kept breaking them. The room shows the abuse of decades of drunk men. There are fist-size depressions in the wall and chips taken out of end tables.

Still, after that secluded shack, she might as well be in paradise.

Iris strips immediately and heads into the bathroom. She turns on the shower, and as soon as the water is warm, she steps into the stream. She cleans herself in a few minutes but stays in until the hot water runs out fifteen minutes later.

When the mirror is no longer foggy, she inspects the bruises that the airbag left. They were probably black and blue when she was sick, but now they've faded to greens and yellows. Iris is shocked Tilda didn't mention them before. They take over the entire right side of her face and stretch down to her breast. She thinks she's only a neck tattoo and a cigarette away from fitting in perfectly with these rough-skin bikers.

Her blonde bob is also as jarring as she thought. She moves her head as if her reflection is so different from her that it might not move back.

She parts her hair to look at her scar from where she shot herself. It's as unnoticeable as ever with her bruising competing for attention. She told Michael that she didn't identify with John Dillinger, but the woman who stares back at her is a criminal.

Iris Adler: famous fugitive murderess.

When she leaves the bathroom, Iris is already nervous. She knows she can't put it off any longer. She stares at her backpack while she's still dripping wet.

It is time to read the report.

Pasts

Iris sets herself up in bed and begins to read the private investigator's report.

The first few pages detail her early life and paint a picture Iris can more or less remember. She lived with her mom and sister in a rough neighborhood in Memphis. Her dad is a deadbeat who has never even met Iris, having moved to southern California a few weeks after her mother said she was pregnant.

Her half-sister Laney's dad was around more but didn't care for Iris. He was never any kind of stepfather to her.

The first thing that surprises Iris is that the report has interviews with her schoolteachers going back to fifth grade. It misses only a few high school instructors who either didn't remember Iris or had passed away.

Iris was remembered by her earlier teachers as a quiet girl, possibly on the spectrum but certainly facing trouble at home. She often had visible bruises on her arms. There were no reports of CPS visits, however.

She didn't participate in any extracurriculars until she was in theater in high school. This she also doesn't remember at all. Theater? The acting training certainly came handy for putting up with Joseph, she thinks.

Her high school teachers remember her as a different girl entirely. Smart, but at times disruptive in class. Again, there was mention of trouble at home. But apparently Iris was open about having an abusive mother and absent father. Still, she earned good enough grades to get accepted into Memphis City College, a technical school, where she attended for two semesters, achieving a 4.0 grade point average. She withdrew at the end of her second year's second trimester, having failed to register for classes that January.

A counselor at Memphis City College says he remembers a determined girl who looked like Iris talking about transferring to either the University of Tennessee or even Vanderbilt, depending on the scholarships offered, but he couldn't be certain it was her when shown a picture of Iris.

However, when investigators contacted UT's and Vanderbilt's admission departments, there was no record of any applications ever sent by Iris.

December 2019. That's when she fell off the map, and the interviews with her mom and sister confirm the same. Iris stopped pretending to be friendly with her family. *"No contact at all starting December 2019."*

Iris remembers the apartment. That dull block of crumbling buildings. The Firestone stack.

Iris pops back up a few months later.

The interviews turn from being with former teachers to people she doesn't remember. One's with a man named James who was her landlord for a couple months at an address on Lauderdale Street.

Iris was thought to be involved in prostitution, if not the drug trade as well. There's another interview with the owner of a corner store who says Iris was a regular. His suspicions as to her line of work were the same.

Iris cringes. She's picturing herself in stilettos. A cheetah print skirt. Was that the kind of person she was?

Why can't there be a description? Even just a picture of her during that time.

Iris has a Hollywood idea of a prostitute stuck in her head, but she probably didn't solicit on street corners. Her lack of a criminal record suggests she may have been discreet. Maybe she kept her dignity and wore baggy sweatshirts when she wasn't working. Maybe she was embarrassed but desperate, scratching her needle marks and itching for the money to afford that next hit.

Iris has to close the folder for a minute.

She pinches her brow, and the image of Michael's torn neck plays over in her head. This all started with the plunge of that needle. First, it's pulled back so the blood mixes with the heroin. Then it's depressed, and it sinks you into what feels like a jar of warm honey.

When Iris was given the lethal dose of fentanyl on the riverboat, it had reminded her what opioids were like. The disassociation. The enveloping hug of the drug. She hasn't craved any since then, but it did open a window to her past self. That was when she started to remember, as much as she didn't want to.

The irony is that if she hadn't met Joseph, she would probably be dead. The report is filled with dead ends— girls who worked in Iris's trade that had fatally overdosed in the last couple years.

Fentanyl isn't a dirty word anymore. Apparently, addicts seek the stuff out specifically because the high is so much stronger. They don't care that they walk a tightrope with death beneath them. The high is somehow worth it.

As fat as the envelope is, most of it is the explanation of their investigation methods. Not information itself. It's wordy and sparse on actual important details. Maybe they have been stonewalled.

Iris skips to the last interview. It's the one with the corner store owner. The investigator's initials are only listed as PI. The shop owner is KR—Kevin Renner. Iris reads the interview. She focuses on the middle paragraphs.

PI: *"And when was the last time Iris came into your shop?"*

KR: *"It's hard to say exactly. I didn't notice she'd stopped coming in for weeks."*

PI: *"If you had to guess."*

KR: *"Towards the end of 2020. Maybe early 2021. There were rumors a couple years ago."*

PI: *"Rumors about Iris?"*

KR: *"Yeah."*

PI: *"So you knew her well enough to know her name?"*

KR: *"I knew most of the girls' names. Some guys in the neighborhood gave them trouble. Called them names. I liked being friendly."*

PI: *"And what were the rumors about Iris?"*

KR: *"That she got a big score. Met some hotshot that was keeping her as a mistress."*

PI: *"Do you know any girls in the neighborhood who might've worked with Iris?"*

KR: *"Sure. There are two that still live on Preeker Street a couple blocks down. Katie and Jasmine. They're in the business."*

PI: *"How long have they been active? Would they have known Iris?"*

KR: *"They knew each other. The three used to come in here together in the past. I think they were all* roommates. But come to think of it, I haven't seen either of those girls in a couple weeks now."

PI: "And you usually see them often?"

KR: "A couple times a week at least."

PI: "Do you know their address?"

Iris sees that the shop owner gave him directions to their house. The interview ends. The final page of the report details the investigator's trip to the house on Preeker Street, but there is no interview with the girls attached.

The description is long, and Iris frowns. There's nothing else in the report like this. She already has a bad feeling.

Arrived at 5408 Preeker Street at 2 pm, September 30th. The property is listed under the name of a real estate company—Mississippi Rentals and Management. I contacted them regarding the current lease at 5408 but never received a response. The company uses a PO box and has no physical office. We plan to investigate Mississippi Rentals and Management further.

5408 Preeker is a single-family residence and did not look habitable from outside. (Broken window on the second floor. Sections of the roof have collapsed.) The property is isolated. Its neighbor to the east is a church, and the house to the west is foreclosed and boarded up.

Iris looks at a picture that's been printed out and paperclipped into the binder. There's a brick house with faded, peach-colored paint. The whole structure leans heavily to its left. The lawn is just dirt and clumps of dead grass. She keeps reading.

There was no answer to a knock, but I was able to successfully gain entry as the door was unlocked.

Upon entering the residence, it was clear from produce in the kitchen that the house had been occupied recently. Fruit was in various stages of decomposition, but nothing appeared older than perhaps a week. Most items in the fridge were not past their expiration dates. In the living room were two mattresses on the floor. A television and a couch.

Again there's a picture. Two twin-sized mattresses are laid with about two feet of space between them. They both have sheets, but the blankets are tossed about on the floor. Iris can see one comforter all the way across the room that had been dropped on a steep staircase. It's a weird place for a blanket. It looks like someone was woken up in a panic.

The living room in the picture is dark. The plaster walls are painted maroon, and dark cracks web across them and the white ceiling. However, the house doesn't have the look of a drug den.

Other than the bedding, the floor is clean. There are no empty bottles or food wrappers. No strewn clothes or cigarette butts.

Still, there's something unsettling about the two mattresses in this dingy room. Iris's stomach sinks further as she reads on.

Upstairs were two bedrooms—both had empty bed frames that fit twin mattresses. From how the frames were crooked and disturbed, it looks as if the mattresses had recently been removed and taken downstairs to the living room. The bedrooms were otherwise empty, apart from women's clothing.

The upstairs bathroom (not pictured) was greatly disturbed. The doorjamb was broken, suggesting forced entry. This is where the upstairs window seen from outside was broken. The mirror, vanity top, and cover to the toilet tank were also broken.

A significant amount of what appeared to be dried blood covered the floor, walls, and bathtub.

The police were then called to the residence and are currently investigating.

Iris flips furiously to the next page, but that's all there is on Jasmine, Katie, and the house on Preeker Street. "Come on," she says out loud. "Come on."

The fact that there's no picture of the bathroom leaves her livid. She's paying this PI firm close to fifty grand for this report, and they think she's too delicate to receive a photo of a gory bathroom?

Then she reasons they were probably already breaking the law by documenting the house and sharing it with Iris. It was an active crime scene.

Iris tosses the report next to her on the bed. It's left more questions than answers. She lifts a few pages up and looks back at the picture of the twin mattresses on the floor.

The photo makes her think of fear. Like two siblings who decided to share a bed when they heard a creak in the closet. The girls moved the beds downstairs so they could sleep next to each other. But what were they afraid of?

Whoever chased them to the bathroom.

The answer had to be Annabelle. Or people sent by her. She had been tying up loose ends the last few months. She was willing to kill girls who knew about Joseph's abuse in Louisiana. She must've gone after the prostitutes who knew about Iris and the Adlers' human trafficking operation in Memphis.

The last page of the report is a bulleted list of what steps investigators are taking next. It's plain to see that their biggest frustration is finding someone who worked with Iris when she was a prostitute. The girls are all gone—overdosed or vanished.

It's like Iris is the last one left.

But she knows of one. Veronica. She's glad she got the name to them. Hopefully Marshall shared it, but she can't help but think maybe he isn't on her side.

She hears rain on the metal roof of her room and crosses her arms over her chest.

She pictures the girls sleeping on the floor. Being woken to a break-in in the middle of the night. They ran upstairs, blankets falling off their shoulders, and locked themselves in the bathroom. The old window was stuck, so they broke it, but before they had a chance to climb out, they were murdered. Their bodies dumped in the Mississippi.

Iris stands from bed and walks to the back of her room where the only window is. The pane of glass is four feet long and perhaps three high. She pulls the blind back and looks out at the bayou.

Raindrops ripple the water, and the trees that rise out of this swampland are gray and ghostly. The Spanish moss on their branches doesn't look like an adornment. It doesn't hang like a southern garland the way it does on the live oaks of Sweet Blood. The strands of moss crawl like raggedy, moonshiner beards.

She looks to her left where she can see dry land by the bar. There are picnic tables with umbrellas, but at this hour there are no bikers drinking beneath them.

There's a man leaning on a picnic table. A giant, Iris realizes with a start.

He looks obscenely tall, and she wonders if it's some kind of trick of perspective, but she doesn't think so. The top of the picnic table comes up to the middle of his thigh. He looks 6'8".

Taller. And he's looking directly at her window.

He must see her, because the man immediately sticks his hands in his pockets and begins to kick at the ground like a bored kid. He wanders back towards the bar, and soon he's out of sight.

Iris feels sick to her stomach because his casual wandering was a poor performance. It was obvious he was out there to watch her. But the fear doesn't eat at her for long. Her heart is hammering for another reason.

She can't stop thinking of the house on Preeker Street and the girls on the floor because the scene reminds her of another mattress. One in a white metal frame with Iris bound in the middle of it.

Prisoner

The first two days she was cuffed to the bed hadn't differed for Iris. Once in the morning and again in the evening, Veronica came into the bedroom and administered a syringe full of heroin into her arm.

When Iris woke up after the first dose and found her hands locked to the frame, she knew this wasn't simply a fetish for Veronica. There wasn't anything sexual about it.

Iris got her answer as to why she was here the second night. From about six p.m. to midnight, the apartment building filled with the sounds of sex. Beds banged and women screamed and men grunted from the floors below.

She was in a brothel, and she was smart enough to know what was coming for her next.

It had been thirty-six hours since she was first cuffed to the bed, and Iris had been high for most of it. This was as sober as she had been. Veronica was taking her time bringing her the evening shot of heroin, and Iris found herself in an anxious sweat.

Her body was already screaming for the drugs.

She didn't have any hope of escape. The only time she was somewhat free was when she had to go to the bathroom. And even then, Veronica undid just one handcuff, and Iris hung off the bed over a five-gallon bucket that acted as a bedpan.

Finally, the bedroom door opened, and Veronica came in with her spoon and lighter. Eagerly, Iris sat up as much as she could in the bed.

She had already come to look forward to the drugs. They took her away from here. Away from the smell of cigarettes and the sounds of sex downstairs.

Veronica sat on the bed and began preparing the spoon.

Iris was calm now that the drugs were in sight. She asked the same question she had every time Veronica had come in. "Can you tell me why? Please... You know I won't tell anybody about this. I won't go to the police. I swear."

Veronica glanced up from heating the spoon. She did her job with the care and efficiency of a nurse. "Why?" She chuckled at Iris's question. "You're pretty, but more importantly, babe, you're poor."

"I can still pay you. I have two thousand dollars saved for school. Just—"

"Honey... you have no idea what you're worth." Veronica tore off the corner of a cotton ball and set it in the melted heroin. "My advice to you—don't fight this. They'll break you either way."

"I don't even like men. Okay? You know that. Why make me a prostitute?"

"That doesn't really matter. A lot of men like a girl who doesn't enjoy it."

Iris's eyes bulged. She hadn't really contemplated her fate. She'd been too busy being high or jonesing for the next hit. "You don't seem like some soulless monster. Please, just let me go home."

"You'll go home. I've told you that. We're not going to kill you."

Iris was about to ask another question when there was suddenly a knock from what sounded like the front door of Veronica's apartment.

Veronica put the syringe down immediately.

"Wait," Iris pleaded. "Wait, where are you going?" Iris's eyes went back and forth from the heroin syringe to Veronica.

"Veronica?"

"Shut your mouth," she said and left the room.

Iris heard Veronica open her front door, and a woman came inside speaking Spanish. Iris heard Veronica respond in Spanish, too. The women talked for a few minutes before the bedroom door opened again.

Veronica strolled in alone, pulled a bandana from the nightstand, and wrapped it around Iris's eyes. "Don't make me gag you. No begging, you hear?"

"Okay," Iris said and accepted the blindfold. Then she heard heeled footsteps making their way over to the bed. The other woman had entered, and Veronica didn't want Iris to see her face.

"She's pretty," the other woman said. Her voice was younger—twenties or early thirties—and heavily accented.

Iris felt Veronica move her chin from side to side, and then to her shock, Veronica yanked up Iris's T-shirt to expose her breasts. Iris was being inspected.

The two women exchange a few sentences in Spanish. Their voices got quieter as they went back out to the living room. A single pair of footsteps came back to the bed, and the world brightened as her blindfold was ripped off.

"What was that?" Iris asked, but she was afraid she already knew. "A buyer?"

"You're smart," Veronica said and started to prepare the drugs again.

"You probably prefer dumb girls."

"That's the beauty of this stuff." She sucked up the liquid in the spoon with the syringe. "It makes everybody who uses it an idiot."

Veronica leaned forward to find a vein, and Iris closed her eyes. She wasn't going to flinch an inch. She realized Veronica was right.

It'd been four injections, and she already craved the heroin just as much as she did home.

Giants

Iris tries to remember more, but nothing solid comes to her. Does she need to remember more? Iris wonders if she should even care. The time between her becoming a prostitute and ending up with the Adlers doesn't really matter. She knows the end of the story. She found herself in Joseph's hands and then Augusta's.

She takes her attention back to the more pressing problem—the giant.

But the man outside doesn't fill Iris with fear the way it should. She's battling depression. Alone and without her sickness or drugs to distract her, her thoughts begin to turn dark.

Iris doesn't know how to spend the time in her room. No phone. No TV. There is nothing in the room for entertainment unless she wants to hunt cockroaches with her shoe.

Even the Gideon bible has been picked clean. Half the pages are torn out. Probably used to roll or snort drugs. The parts that are left have been scribbled over satanically in black marker by someone on a bad acid trip from the looks of it.

Later in the afternoon, the rain lets up, and Iris considers going to the bar. It feels like she's trapped in this room with Michael.

She can't stop picturing his parents. Her brain has even created a younger sister who's sobbing at this very moment. They all think his death is their fault. They're reading the last texts they exchanged with him, and this time they read too much into his stoic responses. They think they see signs of suicide that were there all along.

But it was Iris. It was the psycho girl who shot herself in the head who's the reason their son is dead.

She finds herself pacing the room in tight circles, biting her cuticles.

Panic builds.

Her existence has felt like it's become a net-negative to the world. Everyone would've been better off if she'd wandered off to die when the fentanyl was shot into her bloodstream on that riverboat. If she'd let her organs fail and faded off into oblivion.

She had gotten what she was after. She had gotten her answers. Now she lives for...what? She's driven by the animal fear of being caught by the cops, but in the back of her mind is an emotion she keeps in a cage.

She's embarrassed by it. It feels twisted.

Wrong.

Augusta's face appears in her mind, and Iris's breathing gets quick. She doesn't love that woman, does she? That doesn't matter. Iris feels like she owes her a debt. Up until a few days ago, she had believed Augusta had died to save her life.

Maybe she really did change from a cut-throat matriarch to someone who wanted to right their wrongs.

Iris believes every word she said on the riverboat about burning it down. About handing over documents to the FBI that incriminated the Adler Corp.

Seeing Augusta again might just be all that drives her now, and it makes Iris feel ridiculous, like loving that woman is falling for manipulation.

Iris is thirty years her junior. She was Augusta's brain-damaged dependent. Even now, she can't help but think her affection for Augusta is some form of Stockholm syndrome.

Iris can't take her thoughts anymore. She snatches the gun off the nightstand and sticks it in the front of her pants. It sits snug and hidden in her jeans.

She pockets her room key and opens her door without even looking out the peephole. She doesn't glance over her shoulder, either, as she makes her way to the bar.

It's still early, but there are a half dozen men sitting around tables drinking in silence.

A few look at Iris as she enters but not all. Those who do look don't stare for long. The bruises on her face and neck make eye contact with the abused girl awkward, and their eyes quickly glance elsewhere. The bartender looks at her for a little longer, and Iris wonders if Tilda has told him about her.

He's rail-thin and tall. But not 6'8". His goatee is graying, and he wears a black biker's bandana over his head.

He speaks as Iris sits at the bar. "What're ya drinkin'?"

"Gin and tonic."

He nods and makes her drink in all of ten seconds.

He serves it to her in a clear plastic cup. The same kind her Brompton cocktails were served in. This is the kind of bar with enough fights and people wandering outside that they don't have glassware. She looks into the fridges behind the bar and sees that all the beer is canned as well.

It makes Iris feel safe. This is a rough place. Nobody here is calling the cops on her. Nobody here is looking twice when she downs her gin and tonic in two minutes. She orders another and looks around this den of thieves.

It looks like the men are all attempting to drink away their hangovers. Def Leppard plays on an old set of scratchy speakers with torn felt. The walls are orange pine, and the only interesting part about the place is a giant stuffed alligator that is roped off and takes up the entire back corner of the room. A placard in front of it reads: *Big Bart, 18 feet, 2 inches.* Coins lie in the diorama of the bayou it rests on like Big Bart must be some sort of swamp deity. A lucky alligator.

His tail is coiled so it takes up perhaps only twelve feet of space. Iris looks at him as she drinks her second gin and tonic just as quickly as the first. By the time it's gone, she's starting to feel buzzed, but her mind hasn't stopped turning.

She makes eye contact with the bartender and nods down to her empty cup. He quickly makes her another, and the cup rests dripping in front of her.

She considers getting dangerously drunk tonight. Drunk enough to say something stupid or fall asleep with her door unlocked. Or perhaps, Iris ponders, wander into the dark water of the bayou and never surface.

The gun in her waistband would be an easier out. This time she'd hold the gun with both hands. This time the barrel would be pressed against her forehead. She reaches out quickly and takes a deep drink of her gin and tonic. The burn of the liquor takes the thoughts away for a moment.

There is a TV here, but it plays SportsCenter. Asking to change the channel to the local news would only get her a side-eye. She drinks her third gin and tonic slower, and by the time she's finished, it's closer to five and the bar is beginning to get busy. She doesn't want to be too nonchalant hanging around this place. She orders a fourth and heads out to the picnic tables. It's stopped raining, but the sun is still nowhere to be seen. It's darker than the hour suggests it should be.

She's relieved to see she's not the only one out here. The tall man is nowhere in sight, but one of the tables is occupied by a younger trio of men in flannel shirts with cut-off sleeves who look at Iris a little longer than the hungover bikers inside the bar did.

She takes the table farthest from them. Tin buckets filled with sand act as ashtrays on the table, and she almost wishes she smoked so she didn't look so awkward. She leans back and watches the water as she drinks. She's at the same table the tall man was leaning against, and she can see that he would've had a good view of her room's window from here.

She has already made up her mind that she's not going to run away scared from Tilda's. If she sees him again, she's going to confront him, as long as there are other people around.

She thinks it should scare her more than it does, but she's too drunk to be truly afraid. She knows this fourth gin and tonic will probably push her across the line. At five drinks, she'd be good and drunk. Six and she'd probably puke. Seven and she'd black out. She plans to keep it to five but makes no commitments.

She doesn't feel any differently about Michael. She's no less numb, and she hopes it's this next drink that will erase her thoughts, but she knows the feelings won't stop bobbing to the surface. The alcohol makes things feel a little less real, but it doesn't delete anything entirely.

Her fourth drink is gone quickly, and she looks down into its ice and jiggles the cup, as if there might be more gin hiding there.

She turns around and quickly freezes. Someone has sat at the picnic table behind her. A man with a can of beer peeking out from the top of an enormous hand. He writes in a notebook.

Iris notices his legs. They make towers of his pant legs. His knees are pressing into the bottom of the table. His shoulders, too, are broad and say that he's in possession of great height.

It's him, the giant, but she's surprised by his age. He couldn't be a year older than her. Twenty-eight, maybe. He notices her gaze and looks up at her for a moment, and then he darts his head back down to his notebook. She watches his massive hand move. The pen wedged in his giant fingers looks like a cocktail straw.

He writes quickly. Almost furiously.

He wears a long-sleeved collared shirt with a pocket on either breast and strap sandals that show long, pale feet.

He looks busy, but Iris thinks it's just a ploy. He's here to watch her. He certainly doesn't look like any of the other customers. He's too clean, and he's dressed like a tourist. All he's missing is a safari hat.

Iris lets the liquor do the thinking, and she stands. She walks right over to his table and sits on the bench opposite. He leans back, and his gaze travels the length of her bruises.

"Were you watching me earlier?" Iris watches his face as it wrinkles with confusion.

He's handsome. Clean shaven with a defined jawline and bright-blue eyes contrast well with his black hair. The skin of his face is spotless. As smooth as a child's. He doesn't have the oblong features of a giant—his nose and ears are normal-sized.

His face turns to a look of understanding, and he points across the water to her room's window. "When it was raining earlier?"

"Yeah."

He smiles and looks back down to his notebook. "I thought you were watching me."

Iris widens her eyes at the sound of his voice. *It* matches his size. It's Deep. Cavernous. The sound you'd picture if a canyon could speak.

"Two nights ago, in the woods." Iris nods her head towards the porta-potty where the trail starts. "I saw you in the middle of the night."

His big eyebrows furrow and then relax in recollection. "Oh, that was you. I heard someone talking in the middle of the night. You went by my cabin." He holds up two long fingers. "Twice."

"I asked Tilda. She said no one else was staying in the cabins."

"When did you ask her?"

"Yesterday morning."

"She would've been right. I checked out yesterday morning and moved into the motel. There weren't any rooms available when I showed up, so they stuck me out there."

Iris is quiet for a moment as she considers his story. She believes him. Maybe because she wants to. Despite his size, he doesn't come off as threatening. Quite the opposite. There is a charm to the way he grins.

"Sorry. I don't mean to sound so paranoid."

"That's alright. I'm not most people's favorite sight when they're in the woods in the middle of night. But can I ask? Are you staying with someone here? I heard someone arguing that night."

Iris smiles. "I was talking to an alligator."

"What?"

"I had to use the bathroom in the middle of the night, and there was an alligator at the foot of my stairs. I was trying to get him to move."

"Did he?"

"With some encouragement."

He grins but goes back to his writing. Iris realizes he probably thinks she's trying to flirt. With her bruises and boozy breath, she must seem like a desperate barfly. She's embarrassed and considers standing again, but he sets his pen down and talks.

"Where'd you get those bruises?" He looks left and right as if Iris might still have a boyfriend lingering nearby.

"Fell off my motorcycle."

He stares at her again and considers this. She knows it doesn't look like she was beaten. The bruises are too large to have come from a fist.

"You don't look like the biker type."

"Why do you say that?"

"Not enough tattoos."

Iris notices he has an accent, but it's slight. Southern but not Louisianian. "You're definitely not a Harley owner yourself," she fires back.

"So?"

"So what brings you here?"

"To be honest, I was looking for an interesting place to write."

"Write what?" She looks at the pages of his notebook, and her brows knit together. It's not written in English. It's not even written in the Latin alphabet. There are not letters as she recognizes them. It looks like Russian.

"A book."

"A book not written in English?"

"I'm from Russia, originally. Adopted. I learned the language in my teens when I was looking for a connection to something."

Iris is genuinely curious about him. She didn't expect to find this blue-eyed giant writing in Russian in the middle of the bayou. Still, she can't help but think his presence is somehow connected to her own here.

"What drew you to this place, specifically?" Iris asks and watches him closely as he answers.

"The people. The language. The fact that this place feels like a country within a country."

"So, what's the book about?"

"The same thing every attempted masterpiece is about. In one way or another."

"And what's that?"

"America."

"Are you actually any good?"

"At writing? I don't know. I hope so. I think I'm self-aware."

"Is that what makes good writing?"

He leans back, and his giant hands close the notebook, indicating she's earned his full attention. "That's what makes *insightful* writing. Storytelling is another skill."

"And which are you best at?"

"Insightfulness." His bright-blue gaze lingers on Iris. She's nervous but stops herself from looking away. "A good writer acts as an interpreter. They take things and events and put them into words others can easily understand. Ideas people easily agree with. A bad writer makes you frown. You disagree with their description— it's too wordy. You disagree with their ideas—they're just plain wrong."

Iris grins. "What if I think you're wrong about that?"

"Fine..." He pauses, considering. "Let me change my description for you. A good writer should make you feel a little *seen* when you meet them."

He squints at her, and Iris has to break eye contact again. She looks towards the water as he continues.

"You know that they see the world at least as cleverly as you do. But there's something slightly uncomfortable about that, because for a moment, when they look at you, you fear that they might know exactly who you really are."

Iris gulps. She can't tell if these are his honest thoughts or if he's just using what he says to deliver a subtext: *I see you, Iris Adler.*

"But who am I kidding." He takes a sip of his beer. "It's really the writer who reveals themselves. Isn't it?" He pats his notebook.

"And what do they reveal?"

"Some guys that they have mother issues. Most that they're sexually deviant. But nearly all reveal that sharpest stab of all... That they're not nearly as smart as they think they are."

"So, which are you? The adoption thing makes me lean towards mommy issues."

"Sexually deviant, actually. You can't tell because it's in Russian, but all the words on those pages you saw were introducing my female protagonist's breasts."

"Oh really." Iris lightens up. "What's your favorite adjective to describe boobs?"

"Pendulous. Voluptuous is overused."

Iris laughs. She's drunk, and it's easy to let her guard down again. She decides she's not going to question who this man is. The two start talking about Tilda. They share their thoughts on her and her rough establishment, and Iris starts to sober up a little.

She's feeling loose enough as it is, and with her mind off Michael, she no longer feels the urge to get sloppy drunk. They talk about bikers. The American South and the town of Dustin. They don't ask each other questions about their backgrounds. There are no questions about work or hometowns, and Iris finds it a relief, but again, she can't help but wonder if his lack of interest in her life is intentional.

After about two hours, he goes to get another beer and promises Iris one, too. He comes back with two sweating cans of Modelo.

Iris's isn't opened yet, and she cracks it herself and takes a long drink. They're both silent for a minute watching the bar.

The place has grown rowdy. A dozen more motorcycles have pulled up, and the music is louder. But the roar of laughter and men shouting stories over each other is still far enough away that neither of them have to raise their voices to be heard.

Iris takes another sip of her beer. "How long are you staying here?" she asks.

"A couple more days. Then I'm crossing into Texas to New Mexico."

"What's in New Mexico?"

"More Americans, but they wear cowboy hats."

"Ha-ha."

He smiles and evades the question. "Anyway, Iris, I haven't asked you what *you're* doing here?"

Iris is about to answer when her mouth closes.

Despite all the drinks, Iris feels her pulse start to pound. She's suddenly sober. She's almost certain she didn't tell this man her name.

"Um. I'm just staying away from home while some family matters blow over." Iris is talking but she's hardly thinking about what's coming out of her mouth. She's going back over their conversation like she's thumbing through a book. There was never a moment when she mentioned her name. If she had, she would've asked his.

There are two answers to what happened, and both make her equally anxious. Either he knows who she is and why she's here, or her memory has proved again to not be something she can trust.

"But to be honest, I should um…" Iris stands from the picnic table. She looks at the tall man. His expression hasn't changed at all. He doesn't seem surprised she's leaving or frustrated at himself for saying her name.

"I should get some sleep."

"Sure, sure," he says. "I probably should, too, soon."

"It was nice chatting with you."

"Yeah. I'll be here tomorrow. I'm sure I'll see you around."

Iris starts to walk away.

"I'm Alexi, by the way."

She stops and turns. "It was nice meeting you, Alexi."

He raises his beer in a gesture that says *likewise,* and Iris turns to go back to her room.

Stalked

When Iris is behind her locked door, she realizes it can't be much later than eight. She's not drunk enough to pass out. She's starting to have the unpleasant sensation of sobering up with nothing else to occupy her mind.

She considers leaving on foot, but she'd have to hitchhike to get anywhere. She could have Tilda call a cab to take her to an electronics store, but they'd all be closed now. She needs to hurry up and get a charger for the phone now that she's feeling better.

She turns her lights off and goes over the blinds. She should be able to see if Alexi is still at the picnic table. She lifts the corner of the blinds and looks out with one eye. At the table they sat at is a group of four bikers smoking.

He must've called it a night. Or gone to another location to try to watch her.

Iris lets the blind drop and walks back right back out the door. She makes her way to reception, hoping to get some news from Tilda, but when she rings the bell, there's no answer from the back room. She heads back to the bar.

She doesn't understand why there's a smoking section. Apparently, there's no enforcement stopping customers from smoking inside. She walks through a haze and leans against the bar with a twenty in her hand. She doesn't feel great about abusing a substance to get to sleep. Then again, she could do worse. She's sure she could buy heroin from any number of these bikers. But she won't. She can't go back to that.

The trapped Iris. The addicted version of herself she has begun to remember is her nightmare.

She does notice she's getting a lot more stares now that it's later. A lot of the men in here are drunk and don't seem to care if Iris catches them looking at her bruises. Coming back here was a mistake.

It was one thing to show her face briefly to four or five people, but a crowded bar is a different story. Someone is bound to recognize her.

She taps her foot anxiously, but the bartender is busy, apparently engaged in an argument about someone's tab. All Iris wants is to buy a few beers and go back to her room. She looks around the bar. Most people who had been staring at her have turned back to their conversations, but there's one table of three men who are still staring. They lean over and speak in one another's ear. Iris doesn't think it's a stretch of her imagination to think that it looks like they're conspiring.

This feels like a mistake. It doesn't matter if it looks like she fits in. This is not a safe place. There's more than two dozen people in this bar but only one woman that Iris can see, and she looks tougher than Iris. Her lip is pierced twice, and she's covered in tattoos from head to toe. She chews gum with her mouth open. As Iris watches her, the woman squeals and then laughs as a man gives her a spank as he walks by.

The table of three men who had been staring at Iris haven't stopped, except now they're not talking to each other. Iris looks them over to try to remember their faces. They all look like they could be brothers. Forties. Graying. They have the same uniform as nearly every other man in here—leather jackets and blue jeans. One of the men is much fatter than the others, yet meth scabs blister on his forearms and neck. This one winks at her, and Iris spins back to the bar.

She leans forward and yells at the bartender. "Hey!"

He gets a last word in over his tab argument and walks over to Iris.

"Three Lone Stars. Tall boys," she says.

He plucks them from the fridge and sets the three cans on the bar. Iris leaves him the twenty and doesn't wait for change.

She makes a triangle with the three tall cans and carries them with both hands. Not being able to touch the pistol in her waistband makes her extra anxious, but she doesn't plan to stick around. She walks to the door in the bar that leads to reception. She pauses here. The TV in the backroom is now off.

Tilda is still nowhere to be found.

Iris goes through the next door that leads to the row of motel rooms, and just as she steps onto the dock, the door to the bar opens again. Whoever comes into reception is out of sight, and from the sound of the booted footsteps, she knows it's not Tilda. It's not just one person either.

Iris is in trouble. She pitches the beers over the dock's railing and into the water. She goes for her room key instead of the gun. She doesn't want the attention of a shooting, but it takes her only a second to realize her mistake.

The three men who had been watching her from their table are only a few steps behind.

"Help!" Iris shouts. She knows she won't have time to stop in front of her door to unlock it. "Help!"

She drops the room key, puts her hand on the revolver grip, and pulls it from her pants. But just as she's about to level it, one of the men tackles her to the dock. The gun goes clacking on the wood boards, and she hears it fall into the water with a plop.

The man is straddling her waist, trying to hold her hands together, but she moves her arms free quickly.

Before the other two can help him, Iris finds the key to her room on the dock and jabs it up into his eye.

Iris feels it sink deep, and the man screams. Blood runs warm over Iris's wrist and all the way down her arm.

She's so occupied with pushing the key harder that she doesn't see the black boot that's swung towards her head. The world spins and goes starry as she's kicked in the face.

Her grip goes limp, and her arms slap down on the dock. The man is still screaming, and Iris grimaces. She's furious. She had this smelly fucker.

If it was just her and the one that tackled her, she would've *won*. Maybe it's the booze, but she's not afraid for her life as she feels herself being lifted. She's angry. All she can focus on is the unfairness of being attacked three-on-one.

The man has finally stopped screaming, and Iris feels herself being carried around the motel, avoiding the bar. She can barely see the picnic tables. Her vision wheels, and it's dark on this side of the motel. She can tell from the smell that they're by the dumpsters. There are a couple other parking spots here.

She hears keys jingle as they're passed off. One of these bikers has a truck. They're taking her to a second location.

To hold for ransom or kill, Iris isn't sure.

Her head lolls and she looks at the trees. She realizes she couldn't scream if she wanted to. A warm clammy hand is pressed over her mouth. She's looking at the branches when she suddenly frowns.

One of the trees is shorter than the others, and Iris notices it's moving.

It's drinking a beer.

Alexi.

She feels her heart sink. So, he was the mastermind behind this. He walks forward casually from the shadows, but to Iris's surprise, he stops, widens his legs in a pitcher's stance, and brings his arm back. The bikers seem to notice him at the same time the beer can leaves his hand. It flies so fast the can is a blur. It meets one of the men's faces with a crack, and Iris suddenly falls.

"Fuck! Son of a bitch!" one of the bikers yells.

Iris is quickly on her feet, but the world is still spinning. She watches the fat biker with meth scabs pull an eight-inch knife from a sheath on his belt.

Alexi's movements are best described as casual. He doesn't look panicked, nor is he lowered into a karate stance.

The fat man swings the knife. Alexi reaches out with his branch-like arm and grabs the man by the wrist, and then he yanks him forward violently. The biker loses his footing, and there's a dull thump as his head slams into the door of the truck.

Iris realizes it was the same biker she wounded who Alexi had hit with the beer can. He was curled in the fetal position, apparently waiting for this all to be over.

The third biker was younger, fitter. Even in the shadowy light, Iris could see veins bulging in his forearms. He's also pulled out a knife, but the blade is short.

He holds the handle in his fist and levels his arm sideways like he holds a shield. It looks like he's been in a knife fight before.

Alexi steps forward, and Iris can see from the way the man moves his arm back that he's about to try to stab Alexi. But just as he starts to bring the knife forward, Iris watches one of Alexi's long arms swing out from the dark.

It doesn't move particularly fast and the biker moves his head back to try to dodge the blow, but Alexi's arm is much longer than he anticipated and he doesn't move out of the way of the blow.

Alexi's fist clips his chin, and the man drops like a rock. Suddenly, the music from the bar is the only thing that can be heard.

"Are you okay?" Alexi asks in his baritone, but his interest isn't on Iris. He bends to the fatter biker that he threw into the side of the truck.

He rolls him over and puts a couple of fingers on his neck. "Oh..." Alexi sighs for several seconds. "Shit."

"What?" Iris steps forward.

"He's not breathing. Can you pick up those knives for me?"

The other bikers are both starting to roll around, and Iris scours the ground. She finds the shorter knife quickly, but the longer one has a black blade, and it's a minute before she finds it. She sets them next to Alexi, who's begun chest compressions. But when Iris is standing next to him, he stops and sighs again.

"His neck's broken."

"He's dead?"

"Definitely."

"What are we doing with these two?" Iris glances towards the injured bikers. They look like they're getting ready to stand, but Iris doubts they'll try anything while Alexi has the knives.

"Let 'em run. They've got cameras in the bar."

The bikers both stand and find each other for support. They walk doubled-over into the dark.

"What if they have friends at the bar?"

Alexi picks up a set of keys and opens the driver's door to the truck. "We're getting you out of here. I'll call an ambulance."

Iris hesitates. She looks back towards the motel. "I can't leave without my things."

"Be quick." Alexi is already dialing, and Iris takes off. Her head hurts as she runs, but she doesn't let it slow her down. The key is right where she'd dropped it on the dock. It glistens wet with blood and surrounded by bright-red drops. She picks it up and sticks it in the door, but the key won't turn.

She backs up and curses. The door she's stuck it in is blue. She's not even outside her room. She goes to the end of the dock and unlocks her door. She leaves it hanging open as she stuffs the PI report, cash, and stray clothes back in her backpack.

She flings it over her shoulder and trots out. When she gets back to the truck, it's already started, and Alexi is behind the wheel. She hesitates again for a moment before she opens the passenger door but doesn't get in.

She's been quick to think of Alexi as her savior, but he just might want the spoils for himself. Those men wanted her for a reason. Iris is valuable.

To the cartel. To the police.

If Paulo caught wind that the FBI raided Sweet Blood looking for Iris, he might have decided she's too much of a liability to keep around.

Is that why Alexi is here? Is he a hitman? He's no stranger to violence, but it doesn't look like he has much formal training in martial arts. He just used his size to his advantage. It was three-on-one, but one of them was injured and the bikers were wasted. The one's death seemed more like a freak accident than intentional.

Iris realizes he's staring at her with expectant eyes, wondering why she's waiting with her hand on the door handle.

She relents and climbs in. She doesn't know what she was expecting, but the biker's truck smells like mold and cigarettes. Fast food bags and beer cans crinkle at her feet.

"Where are we going?" she asks, but Alexi doesn't answer.

She buckles in, and then they're roaring down the road.

Alone

They take a winding series of turns until the road they're on dead ends at the bank of the bayou. The water ahead shines under the moonlight, and Alexi turns the headlights off so they can't be seen from nearby roads.

Iris looks at him. His forehead is wrinkled in thought. He has to know more than he let on. She blurts out the question that's been burning in her since they began driving. "Were you sent here?"

Alexi takes a moment to come out of his own thoughts. "What's that?"

"Were you sent to this motel? Were you watching me?"

"No."

"Then how did you know my name?"

Alexi seems unconcerned by this. It seems like he's thinking of the man who's neck he just broke and all the people who will want retribution for it. Alexi isn't easy to hide. "You told me your name."

Iris moves in the passenger seat so she's facing him. "I know for a fact that I didn't."

"But you did. About twenty minutes after you approached *me*. And sat at *my* picnic table."

Iris suddenly doubts herself again. It is possible she did. Her memory of their first couple hours talking has all but slipped away now. The alcohol. The lack of sleep. The kick to the head.

She decides to leave it. "Forget it."

"So, these guys didn't just randomly go after you, did they?" He moves his hands off the wheel. "You do something to piss them off?"

Iris watches his face in the green glow that comes from the truck cab's buttons. His expression isn't readable. It doesn't look like he's lying. He doesn't know her.

"Something like that."

"I just saved your ass. The least you could do is be honest with me. Are more of those bikers going to be coming for you?"

"I don't think so. Those three had been watching me."

"And why were they watching you?"

"I honestly don't know."

"Give me a break."

"I meant... I don't know what was going through their heads."

Alexi sighs. This feels like a subtle interrogation. "A few days ago, I was watching TV in a bar. There was this girl the news couldn't stop going on about. CNN. FOX. The local station, you name it. She was posted everywhere. Probably still is. You share a resemblance to her, only you're a lot more blonde and bruised."

Iris chews the inside of her cheek. "You've known who I am?"

"Not until we'd been talking for about five minutes."

Iris remembers him shutting the notebook. Growing interested in her. She feels relieved. *It's why he knew her name.*

Her interest is piqued, and she leans forward in her seat. "What did they say I'm wanted for?"

"They say they want to question you in connection with the murder of your husband and the poisoning of your sister-in-law. They say you're mentally challenged. That you're more of a threat to yourself than the public."

That biker missing an eye should sue, Iris thinks. "What else are they saying? Anything about Annabelle Adler's baby? Did it make it?"

"I didn't go on this writing road trip to be caught up on the news. I don't know."

"Do you know if there's a warrant out for my arrest?"

"Not really. The report made it seem like you were a vulnerable missing person. At least that's the story they're putting out."

A cyclops eye of light appears across the water and blinks, stuttering as it passes behind the trunks of trees. In another few seconds, they can hear the motorcycle. It gurgles and roars, and Iris gulps. The bayou feels like a kind of badlands and there are bandits out looking for her.

"We should get moving," Alexi says, and he points across the water to where the motorcycle passed. "I can tell you what those bikers were doing. They know you have no recourse with the law. They were probably going to hold you for ransom. The news is fond of talking about how much money you have."

"They weren't smart enough to realize that all my accounts would be frozen."

"Criminals aren't famous for their brains. But what's the plan for you? Wait around in this cesspool until the police pull you out?"

"I have a plan, and it doesn't involve staying here. I need to talk to Tilda."

"I'm not big on the idea of going back there."

"I'll sneak in."

"I'm not big on that idea, either."

"You saved me, okay. Thank you. I mean that. But I don't need a guardian."

Alexi holds his hands up. "Fair enough."

Iris can tell from his tone that he thinks she's being unreasonable, and he's right. She can't go back to Tilda's. Iris remembers Alexi has a working phone. "We could call reception."

"She's probably not there when there's an ambulance outside. And there's probably gonna be a cop there, too."

"You can drop me off at the edge of Dustin."

"We're in a stolen vehicle, Iris. We shouldn't go back in the direction of the city."

Iris suddenly feels sick. "You should get out."

"Why? And walk?"

"You should get out so you don't get arrested for aiding a fugitive and grand theft auto."

Alexi chuckles. "You think you're corrupting me?"

The words make her think of Michael, and suddenly she feels like she could cry.

Alexi must see her expression crumble. His tone softens. "Iris, you're not the only criminal in this truck."

She looks at him, hoping he'll elaborate, but he only turns the headlights back on and puts the truck in reverse.

Confessions

Alexi hasn't elaborated on what he meant by being a criminal, but Iris isn't going to let him get away with it. She waits for them to get a half hour away from Tilda's.

No bikers appear in the rearview. No cops pull out from behind billboards. They're safe for the time being.

Their destination is the southern suburbs of New Orleans. Iris plans to go to a Best Buy or a Walmart to find a charger for the Nokia.

She wants to hear about his past. She still doesn't trust him, but before she can ask what he meant by being a criminal himself another question begins to bother her, and she doesn't hesitate to ask.

"You drove to Tilda's, right?"

"Yeah. I'm heading to New Mexico, remember?"

The fact that he's going to New Mexico suddenly seems like a bigger detail. Was he just parroting facts that he already knew about her? She was going to Mexico. He was going to New Mexico.

"Where's your car?"

"It's in Dustin at the mechanics. Part of my pitstop in the bayou was getting new brakes. They got too squishy for comfort."

This feels like the first time he has obviously lied. The words come out so matter of fact, it feels like the sentence was prepped.

"You're fine leaving it there?"

"It'll be fine. Whenever I drop you off and we part ways, I'll make my way back there."

Iris has nothing to add but doesn't want her silence to come off as her being suspicious. "So are you actually a criminal, or were you just trying to make me feel better?"

Alexi doesn't laugh. He doesn't react at all. If anything, Iris notices, he's stopped blinking. He stares at the road ahead in deep thought. "I wasn't convicted, but I uh... I shot someone. A long time ago."

Iris waits for him to continue. He takes her silence as a cue and starts from the beginning.

"I grew up in Casper, Wyoming, in a dumpy little duplex. You ever been there?"

"No."

"Well. It's less of a city and more of an island of buildings in an ocean of grass. It's not the kind of place dreams are made of. Lots of drug trafficking. *Human* trafficking, even."

Iris's guts knot. *Is he hinting that he knows about her past?*

"The other unit in the duplex was a mother and her young son. I was ten when he was three, and over the years, I spent a lot of time watching the kid. When he got older, he'd come over to play video games or watch movies when his mom worked. He was a sweet kid. Shy but just naturally kind. Big brown eyes..." Alexi smiles. "A sweetheart. He wasn't raised the best, but he always said please and thank you. Like it pained him not to. Anyway, his dad didn't live there, but every now and then the guy would come by and beat the shit out of the kid and his mom."

Alexi sighs. "Me and my dad would go over and break things up and call the police, but it was always after the damage was done. By the time the yelling came through

114

the walls, it was too late. The kid and his mom were huddled in the corner, bleeding and scared. The dad kept getting out of jail. He wasn't a drunk or a druggie. He had some kind of mental disorder that seemed to help him never see the inside of a cell for long."

Iris isn't sure she wants to hear the end of the story. Her hands are balled in fists. She doesn't want to hear about this little boy dying.

"One day, the dad's really having a breakdown. The mom screams like I haven't heard before, but I don't move right away. My parents are gone and I'm afraid to face the guy alone, so I take my dad's rifle out of the closet. When I get to the unit, I see things are different. The mom's hunched over holding her gut. Blood is dripping through her hands. The boy is fine, crying at her side. Dad's pacing the room with a kitchen knife, looking like he's truly lost it. Eyes wide. Fists clenched. He sees me enter with the rifle and pulls the kid over to him."

Alexi suddenly stops telling his story and puts both hands on the wheel as they pass a cop stopped near the ditch. Its lights don't turn on. The car doesn't follow them. Iris thinks the truck hasn't been reported stolen. She doubts any of those bikers would talk to the cops.

Alexi is quiet for a minute, but when they don't follow, he keeps telling his story.

"It all happens in a fraction of a second. He puts the knife to the boy's neck and spews some curses at me. I don't remember what. I just remember the spit flying from his mouth. The mother is already stabbed. I think he's really going to do it, right? He's really going to kill this kid. He sits on the couch and brings the boy into the lap like this is going to be some long hostage situation, and I don't even think. I level the rifle so it's aiming right at his head as discreetly as I can and boom. I pull the trigger."

Iris's heart thumps. From the horror in his eyes, she thinks he's going to say he missed and hit the kid.

"Have you ever seen the exit wound from a rifle? The bullet takes everything that it passes through with it. A guy can have a dot in his cheek from where the bullet went in while the entire back of his head is gone. The boy was positioned a little bit behind the dad, so he got... messy. That's what I remember. The little boy's face frozen from shock. The whites of his eyes shining bright in all that blood."

"I'm sorry," says Iris.

"I tried to clean him up with some paper towels and talk to him, saying it was okay, but I never heard him speak again. The paramedics took him and his mom to the hospital. She survived and moved out. But I never saw the kid after that day. I said goodbye and I'm sorry buddy, but he never said anything back. I know I'm not a criminal, I guess. I wasn't charged with anything. The city actually gave me a fucking medal. A little civic citizen award. The cops called it a good shooting. They all patted me on the back. There was envy in their eyes, like all those men had wished they could've been the one to pull the trigger. To traumatize that kid."

Alexi shakes his head. "Anyway. I guess I'm not a criminal, but I know what it's like to do something that changes lives forever. That feels wrong, even though everyone tells you it was right."

"I'm sorry you went through that."

"Thanks. I didn't mean to lay that on you."

"It's okay."

"I still think about it in some way or another every day."

"Do you know what happened to the boy?"

"Last I heard he was in prison. Drug possession. He was a nice kid, but being nice doesn't always keep you from picking up the habit."

Iris nods. Again, his words seem to hint at her past, or maybe she's paranoid, connecting dots that don't exist.

In another fifteen minutes, they pull into the parking lot of a Walmart.

"You said you need a charger. Can I see the phone?" Alexi unfastens his seatbelt. "I'll just go in."

"No." Iris holds her hand out over his chest. She's not about to let him out of her sight. He's had the opportunity to call the police on her twice now. Once when she left the picnic table, and again when she ran to her motel room after the assault to get her things, but she still doesn't trust him.

"I'm coming, too."

"Yeah... Iris, even if you weren't on every television in the country, you and I would stick out like a sore thumb together."

"Even in a Walmart?"

"Even in a Walmart."

Iris thinks of Alexi's height and remembers her bruises. He's right. "Okay. I'll come in after you."

"Fine," he says through a sigh and gets out of the truck. Iris waits until he's most of the way to the entrance before she gets out, too.

She walks with her head tilted to her feet. She needs a baseball cap and some aviators, but the bruises help, Iris realizes. It's not suspicious for a woman who looks beaten to want to hide her face from others.

There are only a few customers inside, and everybody is too busy minding their own business to so much as glance at Iris. It's late, and everyone coming in seems to be shuffling from their night shifts or their insomnia like zombies.

There's no greeter, and Iris walks quickly towards the electronics section at the back of the store. She expects to see Alexi when she gets there and grows nervous when he's not towering in any of the aisles.

She starts to search frantically. She thinks he's in the back telling the manager to lock all the doors and call the police. She's about to head towards the exit when she hears a familiar voice. But it's no baritone.

A woman's voice is coming from electronics. Iris walks backwards slowly. Her face is scrunched in a frown. Why can't she place that voice? It's weak, scratchy, but undoubtedly, it's someone she knows.

She freezes in front of the wall of displayed TVs. They all play the same channel. The same program.

It's the NBC nightly news. It's an interview.

"Let's talk about bravery," says the interviewer. It's a brunette woman in her forties. "Because you are so, so, brave for what you went through and remaining so positive."

"Let's talk about forgiveness." The synchronization of all the TVs playing the same program at once creates an eerie echo of the audio.

The camera pans to a woman in a hospital bed. Her face is a smorgasbord of makeup. Bright-red lips. Blush.

Enough foundation to frost a cake. It all juxtaposes poorly with her pale-green hospital gown.

Iris could get shot in the head again, she thinks, and she'd still recognize that sharp chin and crescent-shaped face anywhere.

Annabelle.

"Because I *forgive* Iris Adler for what she did to me."

"Oh," Iris says aloud. "You've got to fucking kidding me."

Spite

Annabelle sounds like a talking cigarette. The acid must've damaged her larynx. How it didn't kill her entirely, she has no idea.

Iris suddenly feels too weak to stand. She looks left and right to see there's no one watching and sits on the stained tile floor.

The interviewer gestures with her pen. "You think your sister-in-law was behind your poisoning?"

Annabelle nods solemnly. "I know for a fact she was."

"Can you tell us why?"

"Iris...didn't like to see other women succeed. She thought she should be the next CEO of the Adler Corp."

"But Iris had no background in business, correct? She had been recovering from a brain injury. A gunshot wound. We're all familiar with that story by now."

"Yes. And I think it caused a lot of *delusion* in her." Annabelle says the word delusion like it has a question mark at the end. "She was deluded. Angry at me and my mother-in-law for being successful women. She had planned to be a housewife with her husband, Joseph. When that fell apart with his death, I think she became untethered."

"But..." The interviewer reaches out and touches Annabelle's leg. "Can we talk about the elephant in the room?" The question was rhetorical, and she continues. "There are more than just rumors... Apparently, an entire police *report* leaked to the press suggests that Iris might've actually been behind her husband's murder."

"And her own shooting," Annabelle adds.

"And her attempted suicide, yes."

"Well..." Annabelle says. "It's shocking to hear that someone so close to you could be a monster."

"But do you think she did it, Annabelle?" The interviewer is shamelessly fishing for a sound bite now. "Do you think she shot her husband and then herself?"

"I can say that Iris was a very bitter person. When you're surrounded by wealth and talent, it's easy to get insecure with yourself. Iris was the kind of person it just ate away at."

"So it's possible?"

"Of course. Iris played the victim well, but it's important to note that she's a pathological liar. When she was living with us, she said so many things that hurt our family. She tried to tear us apart, but we were stronger than her."

"What do you have to say about the night surrounding the death of Augusta Adler? Your mother-in-law died in what was reported as an accident just a few months ago. At the same time, Iris was *overdosing* on Fentanyl. Do you think Iris had something to do with her death as well?"

"I really can't say. I think accidents do happen, especially on a riverboat cruise where there's lots of alcohol flowing. And drugs. They never found Augusta's body. They don't know what was in her system."

"Are you saying Augusta Adler used drugs?"

"I'm saying she and Iris got close. Drug use would explain a lot is what I'm saying. I mean, people underestimate that river. There are currents where if you go under for a second, you never come up. Her nephew went overboard, too. He might've been trying to keep her from falling when he lost his footing. They fell together."

"The police are still investigating that, right?"

"Yes."

"Now I want to talk to you about your recovery, Annabelle. First off, again, I'm so thrilled that your baby boy is okay."

"Thank you."

"What have the doctors said about your health? About what exactly happened to your body after you swallowed that acid?"

"That I'm a miracle, basically. They tried so hard to get me to not do this interview. For me to rest. But I have to get my story out there."

"Wow, we thank you for that. But what about your body?" The interviewer won't let her dodge the gruesome details. "The acid you ingested was industrial grade. What's your recovery look like, Annabelle?"

"I drank it quickly enough that my throat didn't suffer the worst of the damage. I received residual burns there. But my stomach is destroyed. My esophagus is directly attached to my...um..." Annabelle stutters like she knows the word but it's indelicate.

"Intestine?" the interviewer adds for her.

"Yes."

"Wow."

"It's called a gastrectomy. That was my last surgery. The other concern was the acid hitting my spinal column, but it missed by millimeters."

The interviewer juts her chin forward. "By millimeters?"

"Yes."

"Wow."

"I'm alive, but I'll never eat whole food again. I won't ever sound much better than this, either." Annabelle points at her throat. "But from the way I laid on the floor, the acid never had a chance to damage my vital organs."

"Gravity saved you?"

"God saved me."

"And you went into cardiac arrest, right? You stopped breathing for six minutes?"

"Seven and a half."

"Wow. Do you remember anything from that time?"

"From being medically dead?" Annabelle asks.

"Yes."

"I do. I remember seeing this light." Annabelle spreads her hands out before her. She looks towards the ceiling like she's seeing visions. "A light just like I've always heard, but it was bright blue, and there was a voice. A woman's voice actually, and she said to me, *Annabelle you're not done yet.*"

"That's incredible."

Annabelle nods.

"What are you looking forward to most after your recovery?"

"Being a mother."

"I can only imagine. He's a beautiful boy. Can we see a picture?" The TV picture flashes to a red, wrinkled sleeping baby. He's wrapped in wires.

"So adorable," says the interviewer. "He's currently being monitored in the NICU, but they're expecting him to be perfectly healthy, correct?"

"He's actually just been released. He's home with Daddy."

"Oh." She puts her hand over her heart. "That is amazing. Just amazing, Annabelle. *You* are amazing."

"Thank you."

"I wish we had all night, so I've got to cut to the chase. A lot of your fans are wondering... Any business plans still?"

"I'm not used to having fans." Annabelle closes her eyes and smiles like she was immensely pleased by the word. "But to all those wondering, I'm going to be the CEO of the Adler Corporation as soon as I walk out of this hospital."

The anchor shakes her head. "You can't be stopped."

"Nope."

"And if you could say anything to Iris, what would that be?"

Annabelle pauses. "I'd say... that I forgive you, Iris. That I hope you find peace."

Iris balls her fists. The crocodile tears. The pageantry. Apparently, her near-death experience has had little change on Annabelle's bearing. *This bitch is unbelievable.* In some ways, Iris thinks she *is* incredible.

"And I hope she's brought home safe."

"You said you *know for a fact* that she poisoned you. Have the police shared any information with you?"

"I can't comment on that. I really can't."

"Okay." The interviewer looks off camera for a moment, as if her producers are communicating with her. "Thank you so much for your time, Annabelle. This has been an interview to remember for me."

"Thank you, Kathy."

The shot goes back to the studio, and Iris stares into space. The last several days, she'd been questioning what she was living for. That stagnant puddle of feelings has evaporated in a scorching sun of rage.

She has to live as long as possible. She feels as determined as she's ever felt to stay alive, if for no reason but to spite this bitch.

Recharged

Iris is still sitting cross-legged when Alexi finds her. He comes up to her and stuffs a handful of dill pickle chips in his mouth.

"Hey," he says with his mouth somewhat full. The sound of his crunching echoes through Electronics.

Iris looks up at him to see he holds a white box in his free hand. He wiggles it. "Universal pin charger. Works for pretty much all old burner phones. You said it was a Nokia?"

"Yeah." Alexi looks ridiculously tall from where Iris sits on the floor. So much so that it makes her uncomfortable and she stands. "You couldn't wait to pay?" She nods at the chips.

He shrugs. "I've been looking for you for ten minutes. Thought you bailed."

"I thought the same of you."

"I was distracted by chips. I get hungry easy." Alexi crinkles the regular-sized bag and licks his fingers. It's already gone. "You ready to go?"

They both pause and stare at the TV screens as Iris's face appears. It's an old picture of her. Tilda was right. There was something about how she smiled in it that didn't bear the biggest resemblance to Iris. There's a number beneath it telling viewers to call it if they know anything about her whereabouts.

"She's pretty," Alexi says.

"Yeah. Pretty gay."

"Oh." Alexi shrugs. "It was more of an observation."

"Let's go, Gigantor," Iris says and gives Alexi cash.

He pays for his empty bag of chips and the charger at the self-checkout. He was smart enough to grab a car charger adapter so they didn't have to go somewhere to find an outlet.

"So what's with the phone?" Alexi asks as he turns the truck on so it idles, and Iris plugs it in.

"I'm supposed to receive instructions."

"Someone's helping you run?"

"Something like that."

Alexi doesn't pry.

The phone doesn't take long to charge. In a minute, it turns on and vibrates with a text.

It takes Iris a moment to navigate to messages. Her fingers are slow on the small buttons.

There is a single message from a restricted number. It's an address. A lengthy one.

11985 Lafourche Parish Road 16.

Afterwards there's a single command.

Come alone.

The text was probably sent days ago, but there is no mention of a date or time when she should arrive at the address. She texts it back, not knowing if there is anyone still waiting there to help her.

On my way.

Then she shows the phone to Alexi. "Can you drive me here? It can't be far."

"It says come alone."

"Drop me close?"

He nods and opens his maps app on his phone. When he's entered the address, he turns the screen to her. "Fifty-eight minutes." The red line to her destination snakes into the bayou. The address is at the very edge of land. It's practically on the Gulf Coast.

Neither of them says anything as Alexi puts the truck in drive and pulls onto the highway. Meanwhile, Iris is considering if she's driving into a trap.

The letter asking her to come to Mexico was sent *before* the FBI was after her. She can't stop thinking that Paulo might simply see her as a liability he should dispose of as quickly as possible. Iris weighs her options, but only for all of a few seconds because really, she has none.

Float

Iris and Alexi drive into a maze. It's a right and a left and another right. They both lose track of how many turns they've taken. The roads are in greater states of disrepair the farther into the bayou they drive.

They stopped passing towns and houses fifteen minutes ago. All they see is the cracked blacktop ahead of them.

"Destination in one mile." Alexi starts to slow the truck. "I hate the idea of you walking the rest of the way there in the dark."

I hate the idea of you being shot and killed, thinks Iris. "The instructions were clear. These people—"

He interrupts her. "I know. I know. I'm only saying. Here." He picks the Nokia up from the cupholder and starts typing.

"What're you doing?"

"Putting my number in your contacts."

"I don't think you should do that."

"Just text me when you're safe." He holds the phone out to her, and she puts it in her pocket.

"Okay."

"I'll be here for a bit in case there's no one waiting for you there."

"I appreciate that."

He holds out a giant hand, and Iris shakes it.

"It was nice to meet you, Iris."

She can't help but think how much different she'd feel if this was how she and Michael had parted.

"It was nice to meet you, too."

"Stay safe."

"Thanks." She leans forward, puts on her backpack, and then opens the passenger door. She closes it wearing a tight smile. Alexi doesn't drive off yet, and she figures he won't until she's out of sight.

She walks in the road that's lit up by the truck's headlights, but soon she's swallowed by the dark.

The headlights are pinpricks of light in the black behind her. She passes a rusted sign on a green fence post that reads, 11983.

There is no house. It's a lot overgrown with weeds. These are parish emergency numbers, not home addresses.

She's one away. 11985 will be on her right. The address post doesn't appear for another ten minutes, but when it does, Iris stops.

There's a dirt road here that continues into the dark. There's water on either side of it. Suddenly, something splashes into the water, and Iris just about has a heart attack. She watches the ripples settle. She must've startled an alligator.

Down the dirt road, there's a structure ahead directly on the water. A boathouse, maybe. She doesn't want to scare anyone. "Hello?" she says aloud. She hates how far she can hear her voice travel. It reverberates across the water, echoing in the bayou. No one appears, and Iris keeps walking towards the boathouse.

"Hello?"

Iris flinches as a shadow appears in the doorway. They wear a plaid shirt and blue jeans. It's a man about 5'9" or so. He turns on a light in the boathouse, and Iris sees that he's Hispanic. He has a round, hairless face with thick black eyebrows and a potbelly. He's probably forty-five years old.

"I'm Iris."

He still doesn't talk. He looks bored. Tired. She thinks she might've woken him up. He could've been waiting for her here for days, she realizes.

"*Teléfono,*" he suddenly says.

"Hmm?"

He holds his hand up to his ear mimicking a phone.

"Oh." Iris takes her phone out of her pocket and starts scrolling to show him the text. But he takes the phone from her fingers and casually flings it over his shoulder into the water.

So much for texting Alexi.

"*Mochila,*" he commands.

"I'm sorry... I don't speak Spanish."

He gestures like he has straps on his chest, and Iris realizes he wants the backpack. She takes it off and hands it over.

"There's a few thousand dollars in there," she says, but he doesn't look up. He unzips the bag and puts in a jagged hunk of cement.

"*Mucho dinero.*" She points at the bag.

The man doesn't seem to care. He gives the backpack a hardier swing into the water, where it sinks with a splash. Then he goes into the boathouse. Iris isn't sure whether to follow. She hesitates outside for several seconds before stepping in.

Inside, there's a sleeping bag on the floor but no pillow. There are some oil drums lining a concrete floor and snack wrappers.

In the water where a boat would be is a small float plane. The man walks to the end of the boathouse and begins opening the doors. When he finishes, he unties the plane from where it's tied up to dock cleats.

Iris realizes they're already leaving. No introductions. No questions.

He opens the door to the plane and gestures for Iris to get in. He could've easily shot her in the head by now and dumped her body in the water. Iris doesn't see any reason to hesitate, and she obliges. She gets into the plane.

"*Gracias*," she says but doesn't get a *de nada*.

He slams the door and stays on the concrete walk of the boathouse, guiding the plane out of the stall.

He disappears for a moment as he goes through a door at the end of the boathouse that leads out to a dock. He walks alongside the float plane, guiding it with a rope. When it's near the end of the dock, he unties this last rope and hops aboard. When he's at the controls, they're almost knee to knee.

There is no back seat. There's room for a bag or two behind the cockpit, but that's all.

He puts on a headset, gestures for Iris to do the same, and then he starts cranking dials on the dashboard. The motor spurs to life. He hits a few more buttons and stares at gauges as he turns the wheel. As soon as they're pointed in a straight line, he pushes the throttle forward and the plane begins to buzz like a giant bug. They start to bump along the water, and after nearly a full minute, the plane begins to lift.

He yawns and then wiggles his shoulders into his seat.

That's all there is to it, Iris realizes. Not the Coast Guard nor Border Patrol is going to care about a plane flying *out* of the United States.

Iris gazes out the window and sees the dark road she walked on to get to the plane.

She sees the headlights of the truck, but then she frowns as she sees another set next to them. There's another car down there now. Pulled up right next to Alexi.

Iris cranes her head to try and see better, but the plane banks towards the Gulf.

All she could tell was that Alexi had company.

Lukewarm Welcome

The dark shore of Louisiana is soon out of sight and they are flying over the black expanse of the Gulf of Mexico. Ships and oil rigs shine below. She thinks better of asking where they're going. She thinks she knows.

Sinaloa. Western Mexico.

She doubts a plane this small has the fuel to get them all the way there, but she isn't sure. They're not moving very fast. She guesses they're going less than half the speed of a commercial airliner, and when they get back over land, the sun is just beginning to rise in the east.

Below them is farmland, and Iris jumps as her pilot speaks into the microphone attached to his headset. She realizes after a moment he must be talking to ground control. He begins to yell and speak at twice the speed. He mutters a curse and says something calmer into his microphone. Then the plane banks south. And suddenly he's laughing with whoever he was just yelling at. He slaps the control panel a few times in satisfaction.

He points out the window, and Iris realizes he's doing so for her. Past his fingertip, a city shines in the distance. "Monterrey," he says.

"Is that where we're going? Monterrey?"

"*Sí. Sí*, Monterrey." He gives her a thumbs-up, and Iris is twice as awake from his sudden burst of energy.

Whatever he heard on the radio must've lifted his spirits. They begin to lose altitude once they pass the city. In another ten minutes, they're gliding over the heads of cows. Iris is confused. She thinks seaplanes have to land on water, but her limited knowledge of aviation proves wrong when the plane bumps down gently and comes to a smooth halt on a gravel runway.

They taxi to a hangar, and the pilot kills the engine. He gets out of the plane and quickly trots to Iris's side. He offers her his hand. She doesn't need the help getting down, but she takes it out of politeness.

It's hot on the tarmac. She looks up as a small propeller engine plane passes overhead. She's about to try to ask her pilot a question when he suddenly walks off towards another man wearing camouflage fatigues who's walked out of the hangar. Camo man doesn't look like a soldier or a cop. His shirt is wrinkled and untucked. It seems more like a personal style choice. He carries a plastic bag stuffed with white takeout containers, and her pilot takes it with a big smile. He finds shade under the wing of another parked plane and starts to scarf down his breakfast.

Iris realizes he might not have eaten in days. If Aurelia contacted Paulo or Augusta the same night Iris took the backpack with the phone, they might have sent the plane to that address that night, not knowing Iris would be stranded sick for days.

An official-looking white pickup pulls up. It says *Policiá* on the side in green letters. Her pilot doesn't seem to care, but then again, he's too preoccupied with his food.

An officer in an olive shirt and pants gets out of the truck. His boots shine black, freshly shined. *His* uniform looks genuine, and Iris eyes the handgun on his utility belt.

He strolls over to her pilot, and they have a brief conversation that her pilot doesn't bother to stop eating for. He gestures with his tortilla and speaks with his mouthful. He seems to have won. The officer walks off but watches Iris the entire way back to his pickup.

He doesn't drive off, and Iris worries this exchange isn't over. She's staring so intently at the pickup that she doesn't realize the camo man who'd given her pilot his food is now standing at her side.

"*Señora*?"

She turns to see he's holding another white takeout container. He bows his head at it, and she takes it.

"*Gracias*."

"*De nada*."

Iris isn't hungry, but she changes her mind when she opens it. It's eggs and peppers with chorizo on charred tortillas. The tortillas drip with oil as she lifts them.

She wasn't offered a fork, so she does as her pilot is doing and finds some shade under a plane wing to eat her breakfast with her fingers.

She finishes the entire container, and when she's done, she wipes her hands off on the box.

She looks up to see her pilot has already laid down in the shade and pulled his baseball cap over his eyes. He looks settled in for a while, and Iris realizes they must have some kind of layover.

When in Rome, do as the Romans. Iris lies down and gets as comfortable as she can. The cement in the shade is still cool from night, and it doesn't take long for her to doze off.

She's never fully asleep. Her brain is aware of the sounds around her—the sputter of airplanes and truck engines and shouting in Spanish. It's maybe an hour before she wakes up. She's blinded and hot. The sun has risen to an angle, so her airplane wing no longer gives her shade. She's thirsty and decides to head into the hangar to look for something to drink.

She doesn't seem to be chaperoned. Nobody is watching her as she walks inside. There are two mechanics bent over the engine of a small airplane. One of them must sense Iris is behind him, because he stops his work and turns to her.

Water, Iris is thinking. *Come on... What's water in Spanish?* Suddenly it hits her. "*Aqua?*" she says and mimics drinking. He points with his wrench towards a room with long glass windows that bumps out of the back of the hangar.

"*Gracias.*"

Both mechanics are staring at Iris now. She doesn't think they know who she is. Do they know she's being transported by the cartel? Their wary expressions seem to say that they know something is amiss.

There's no one in the back room, thankfully. There's an ancient coffee maker with the fake wood paneling, a rectangular table with a dozen chairs, and an old cream-colored refrigerator.

Iris bee lines to the fridge. It's full of workers' lunches and half-drunken containers of juice, but the crisper drawer is full of plastic water bottles. She takes two and drinks one on the spot. She tenses as she hears shouting from the hangar. She's not sure if it's just a work argument or something more serious, when suddenly her pilot appears in the break room.

He tilts his head back and rolls his eyes in relief as he sees Iris. Then he quickly says something in Spanish.

"Fly. *Ahora.*" He tilts a flat hand out like an airplane.

"We're leaving?"

"*Sí.*"

"Okay." Iris starts to leave the break room, but her pilot ducks his head suspiciously and walks in farther. He chuckles to himself and picks up a box of chocolate cookies that was on the break table. Then he holds his finger to his lips and gives Iris a big grin as he hightails it back across the hangar.

He takes short, shuffling steps and keeps looking back and forth at the mechanics as he passes. Obviously, he wants them to see that he's making off with their cookies.

The mechanics jeer at him, and her pilot laughs and shouts something. One of the mechanics waves him off and blows a raspberry.

They still regard Iris wearily as she walks by.

Outside, a new plane is idling. It's not any bigger than the last one, only it's a coral pink color and has big tires instead of floats. Her pilot opens the door on the passenger side and gives Iris a hand up. Then he goes around to the driver's side and gets in himself.

He's still eating cookies as he punches the dials and throws on a headset. This time he doesn't have to gesture for Iris to put hers on.

He offers the cookie box to her, and Iris takes one. It's a chocolate cracker cookie with a hole in the middle.

"*Más. Más.*" He shakes the box for her to take more, and when she pinches a handful, he laughs and nods in approval. "*Bueno!*"

He has a contagious, annunciated laugh. It's like he's actually saying ha-ha, only it's genuine.

"*Sí,*" Iris says, pinching her cookies.

"Ha-ha-ha-ha," her pilot says and throws the throttle forward.

Iris's stomach stays where they'd been parked, and they bounce off the concrete pad and onto the gravel runway.

Monterrey International Airport must be a ways off. That's probably where she'd find customs officers and more cops. But she's not going to encounter any of that. She realizes she's in the clear.

If Paulo wanted her dead, she would be.

If the police wanted to arrest her, they had their chance.

She feels like she's made it. Her pilot extends his hand to her, and Iris shakes it.

"Luis!" he says.

"Iris."

Soon they're airborne. Iris lets herself daydream more about Augusta. She thinks of what their relationship will be like. What Iris will say to her when she first lays eyes on her again.

But the thought turns her daydreaming into something more like a memory.

Iris remembers.

She remembers the first time that she ever laid eyes on Augusta.

Weeks blurred to Iris. She remembered sweat.

Sweat from sex. Sweat from withdrawals. Sweat from waking up high under too many covers.

She had spent time in many hotels and whorehouses now. She wasn't just tied to Veronica's bed anymore. She was free. Technically.

There was no one monitoring her every movement. No one stopping her from wandering off or wandering home. But she was chained to her addiction. She was sure she could find another heroin dealer who could support her habit, but the drugs wouldn't be half off. And if she left this life, she'd need to lock down a job to afford it.

With prostitution, she could be high all day. In fact, being high helped. She couldn't do it any other way.

Tonight, she had to stay somewhat sober. Sex wasn't her only job. She'd been hired to be arm candy. She was dressed to the nines in a gold sequined dress, gold heels, and sapphire eye shadow. She didn't pick any of it out herself.

She just wore what Veronica left for her.

She was in the ballroom of a five-star hotel. Marble floor. Grand piano. Car-sized chandeliers. A hundred mingling millionaires getting wasted in their tuxedos and gaudy ball gowns. Iris had taken to wearing a watch. Only because it let her know when she could expect the next hit.

She was pretending to be some tool's girlfriend. He was high on coke and wouldn't stop sniffing and wiping an anxious index finger under his nose. But he wasn't interested in Iris. He hardly talked to her.

She'd shaken hands with a hundred people. Introduced herself with the same fake name—Lily—a hundred times. It had been more exhausting than sex, far more, because Iris was beginning to sober up more than she had in weeks.

She got panic attacks whenever she became too lucid. It wasn't just because she was fiending for another dose. She panicked because she could reflect on her life. In a month, she'd gone from good student to prostitute. What was she doing? Who had she become?

A monster. A whore. A drug addict.

She was easily addicted. Therefore weak-willed, she thought.

Iris began to binge drink. She plucked glass after glass of champagne from the trays the waiters paraded around.

Her date disappeared, thankfully. The last she saw him, he'd run into some old acquaintances and was downing bourbon shots. She thought about vanishing herself and getting a ride back to the house where she bunked with a few other girls.

They'd have some H. But she could get in trouble for that. Trouble meant having to do even *worse* jobs. Working with *worse* clients. Men who thought they were Casanova but pulled her hair with the care of a toddler. Problem customers. She'd bear her boredom and cravings and stay.

Iris sat down in an armchair in the corner of the ballroom next to a fire exit. She was remembering too much about herself. There was a desperate pleading voice in the back of her head. It told her to run away. Get clean. Go back to school before she was too far down to pull herself out of this life. It had only been a few months. But Veronica had told Iris she was probably a strong responder. Heroin, any opioid, was an even better experience for Iris than it typically was for most people.

She was staring off into the crowd when she heard the fire door open. She looked in time to see an older woman flick a cigarette away into the parking lot.

Iris met her eye when she walked in. She had a mane of white hair done up elaborately with black chopsticks. It seemed a little quirky and uncaring for the seriousness of the ball, but she looked fantastic. Her tan, full breasts pressed against the fabric of her red dress. She looked at Iris, and Iris spun her gaze away too quickly.

Guilty.

The woman walked like she was going to rejoin her friends, but then she froze. She turned toward Iris and pointed at the armchair across from her.

"Anyone sitting here?"

Iris shook her head but didn't speak.

The woman sat and crossed one leg over the other. She sank lazily into her chair and blew a bored raspberry. "Some party."

"Yeah," Iris said. She noticed the woman's eyes examining her closely. *Can she tell I'm a call girl?* Iris crosses her arms. "You come to a lot of these?"

"Too many. Did I see you here with Justin Peters?"

"Yeah."

"Oh. Are you with him for the evening or the long haul?"

Iris didn't give a shit about her date's reputation. She was fine outing herself as a lady of the night and letting this stranger know Justin had hired her. "Just the night."

"Oh, thank God. I was going to say...you poor thing."

"Is he that bad?"

"Not if you consider a man basing his entire personality around bourbon and golf a good thing."

"He's not really my type, anyway."

The woman narrowed her eyes. "And what is your type?" Her expression seems to suggest she might have a hunch.

Iris's cheeks flash red. "Not him."

The woman leaned back and seemed to mull this over for a moment. "Do you smoke?" she asked suddenly and flashed a pack of cigarettes from her small purse.

Iris was about to shake her head but stopped herself. Maybe she should smoke. It would give her an excuse to get out of places like this for a moment. Plus, there was something arresting about this woman. She had Iris's interest.

"No, but I'd join you. I'm scorching."

They both stood and went out the fire door.

"I'm Augusta, by the way. Augusta Adler," said the woman as the fire door shut.

Iris skipped the fake name. "Iris." They didn't shake hands.

Augusta raised her brow, expecting a last name.

"Iris, Iris," Iris said, not revealing anything more.

"Mysterious."

"Just business."

"Would you tell me your last name if I were a client?"

Iris perked up. She had not had a woman client yet, but she'd heard of it happening from other girls. Usually, it was a bored housewife who wanted to try something new. Something gentler and better-smelling than hubby. She stared at Augusta. "I'd tell you whatever you wanted to hear if you were a client. It would just cost you."

Augusta grinned and lit her cigarette. The two were silent for a moment. It was a warmer winter evening but still not temperate enough to be comfortable in just a dress. Iris cooled off quickly and was soon holding her arms across her chest.

"Do you like what you do, Iris?"

"It's a means to an end."

"And what's that?" Augusta's eyes jumped to the needle marks in the crook of her arm that Iris had done her best job of concealing. To a close eye, however, they were obvious.

Iris didn't respond.

"I apologize. I don't mean to pry. You're just... gorgeous is all. Stunning."

Iris had to look away from Augusta's gaze.

"I don't think you have to do what you do to make a living."

Iris had heard this line from several men already. It was her least favorite. Too pretty for this. Too pretty for that. Too pretty to so much as look sad. "You don't know my life."

"I'm not making a generalization. I'm making an offer."

"And what's that?"

"A chance for you to enjoy what you do a little more genuinely. I've been meaning to talk to you tonight. I saw you looking at that brunette with the hips."

Iris almost choked on her spit. She cleared her throat and tried to center herself.

"Yeah," Augusta said with a smirk. "That one. I was having trouble keeping my eyes to myself, too."

"So what? You want to hire me for a night?"

Augusta tossed her cigarette away and stepped directly in front of Iris. "Not a night. No."

Iris looked at the ground sheepishly. This woman's confidence made Iris too aware of the lack of her own.

"I want to hire you for good. No more men. I couldn't keep my eyes off of you. You're pretty, Iris. But you look tortured."

"I don't need a savior." But she did. This life was going to eat her alive. It had only been weeks, and she'd lost more than ten pounds. She needed to get out, but she didn't want to give up the drugs. She wasn't ready for that.

"Oh, it doesn't come free." Augusta pressed her lips against Iris's.

Her mouth was slow to respond, but eventually, Iris untensed and kissed her back.

When the kiss broke, they were silent. There was nothing but the sound of traffic and dull clatter of the boring party on the other side of the door.

"I have a room. Upstairs." Augusta nodded up at the hotel above them. "Let me whisk you away."

Iris smiled. She had been about to try to negotiate a price, but as Augusta moved in to kiss her again, Iris's breath became shallow with excitement.

That was fast. Forward. And Iris got the understanding that Augusta was the kind of woman who got exactly *what* she wanted, *when* she wanted.

The butterflies Iris felt were just a bonus, because she just got promoted from prostitute to mistress, if it would fly with Veronica. Her only question was where the heroin would come in, but for now, she let her thoughts fade and her tongue wrestle with Augusta's.

Ambush

Iris is confused by the memory. One thing doesn't sit right. Augusta had told Iris she saw her for the first time the night Joseph had beaten her. After she'd come to her son's rescue at the Nile Hotel.

So that wasn't true. There was history before that. She and Iris were even closer than Augusta let her believe. Probably closer than Augusta let *herself* believe.

But Iris can't think for much longer. Her pilot is no longer the silent grump she met in the bayou. He must've been starving, waiting for her to show up to the boathouse.

With food in him, he can't stop talking, singing, and pointing at things out the window as they fly. Iris can't understand a word he says, and he must know this, but his friendly tone and laughs make her feel comfortable regardless.

She begins to think she might have a nice life in store for her. After all, that's what this is—a new life. She hasn't had time to let the fact sink in that she's probably never going back to America.

Maybe Paulo's cartel isn't as violent and sadistic as the news would lead her to believe. She pictures an actual villa. Rolling hills. Tennis courts. Something like Sweet Blood. But who is she kidding? It takes violence and deception to build an empire in America. In Mexico, it takes more.

But what Iris really hopes is that she doesn't even step foot on Paulo's property. What she daydreams now that the memory is gone is Augusta waiting for her with a duffel bag at the next stop.

She tells Iris that she's got accounts in the Cayman Islands and they board another plane. Only this time it's to a secluded cabin.

A beach house in a country with no extradition treaty with the United States. No cartel. No Paulo.

She's only able to daydream for an hour before she realizes her mistake of not finding a bathroom before they took off again. The next hour is spent trying to redirect her thoughts away from the pressure building in her bladder.

Luis points into the distance. "Culicán."

Iris can see a city and, miles beyond it, the sea.

"We landing there?"

He gives her a thumbs-up. His conversation with air traffic control seems more serious than the last time. These must not be friends. Luis seems a little nervous as they begin to descend, and to Iris's surprise, she can see jetliners in the distance parked at a terminal. They're landing at a legitimate airport.

The concrete of the runway is rubber-stained cement, and they add their mark as they skid to a stop and sputter off towards another hangar. Luis talks quietly to air traffic control and seems to sign off. He parks the plane and turns off the engine. Again, he gets out first and goes around to help Iris down.

He doesn't pause. He motions for Iris to follow and walks quickly with his head down. What looks to be the main terminal of the airport is a half a mile away, and Iris realizes this is where they're walking.

It's late afternoon, about as hot as the day gets, and Iris watches the patch of sweat grow on Luis's back until it engulfs his whole shirt.

She doesn't feel much dryer. Her own clothes are sticking to her, and she wishes she had a second top to change into. She doesn't want to meet anybody in the clothes she's wearing now. But she's being absurd. Augusta is not here. She's not a half mile ahead.

But her heart is already beating hopefully.

Thirst is the only thing that distracts her. She left the second water bottle in the plane, and now she wishes she hadn't. She's thirsty, *and* the urge to pee has gotten to the point where the impact of each step physically hurts.

It takes ten minutes of walking along the runway to get into the airport. They go through a tiled hallway and back outside into a throng of at least hundred people.

They're at arrivals. There are cars honking and a couple buses loading people. There's a road above them that shades them from the sun. It's a small comfort, but Iris can tell from how Luis is surveying the street that they're going to get in a car.

Iris looks at the wall behind the sidewalk. "Um. Bathroom?"

"*Sí.*" Luis seems to understand. He points to his feet, indicating he'll wait for her where he stands.

Iris can see a bathroom sign in the distance, and it takes her a while to weave through the crowd.

She notices she's being watched. A pair of police officers, a man and a woman, stare at her intently. The man says something into a radio on his chest while making eye contact with Iris. *If they were going to arrest her, they wouldn't be so obvious, right?*

Her worry is going to have to wait. Right now, if she was put in handcuffs, she'd have to piss her pants.

The women's bathroom is doorless, and she heads inside and finds a stall. She relieves herself for nearly a minute, and when she's done, she goes to wash her hands. But she doesn't turn on the faucet. She hears some kind of argument coming from just outside the bathroom. A woman is yelling.

Then one of the cops who had been watching her comes in and leans against the wall. Iris knows it's over.

A Hispanic woman in a blazer comes in. She's older— 5'6" and fifty or so. She has a small nose and a small set of brown eyes, and her black hair is pulled into a ponytail. She walks right up to Iris.

"Hello, Iris."

To Iris's surprise, she speaks perfect English without a trace of an accent. She's American.

She parts her blazer on her hip, exposing a firearm, set of handcuffs, and a badge.

Iris just stares at her dumbly while she pulls the handcuffs out.

"Would you turn around for me?"

Iris is too shocked to turn around, and the woman doesn't ask again. Instead, she goes behind Iris and pulls her hands together over the small of her back. She does so gently. Then she cuffs them.

The woman doesn't read her any rights, and Iris doesn't feel the need to ask any questions. Iris is not even particularly angry or afraid. She's simply defeated.

But what confuses Iris is that they stay put. The woman stays standing still with her hand on Iris's handcuffs. She's waiting for something, and in another few seconds, Iris sees what.

Someone comes into the bathroom with a briefcase.

A giant.

Iris glares at him, but Alexi doesn't make eye contact.

The woman in the blazer gives the introductions. "Iris, this is Special Agent Alexi Akers, and I'm Special Agent Grace Beltran. We're with the FBI."

Cooked

Iris is confused why they're all still in the woman's bathroom. They don't escort her out. Maybe they're waiting on a plane to fly her back. Or neutralizing the cartel threat before leaving.

Before she can think too much about it, Alexi talks.

"I'm sorry, Iris." His deep voice sounds genuine. He still doesn't look at her. "I'm glad you had a safe flight, however."

He seems to be saying that he's glad she wasn't shot in the head when he let her out of the truck in the bayou.

His deceit only makes her feel stupid for falling for it. She doesn't hold an angry grudge.

Agent Beltran cuts in. "I know your situation is very bleak at the moment, but you have options."

A woman janitor in a gray jumpsuit suddenly appears next to the cop who has posted up by the entrance. Agent Beltran talks to her in Spanish, and she nods.

The cop comes into the bathroom, and the janitor wheels a trash bin to where he was.

Iris realizes they're using the janitor to block off the bathroom. They're going to make it look like it's closed for cleaning.

Alexi sets his briefcase across one of the sinks and opens it, and then he turns back to them.

Beltran speaks. "Iris, how much do you know about Paulo Delgado and the Colinas Cartel?"

"Hardly anything. How'd you know I was coming here? Did you find the letter?"

The agents look at each other with a hint of confusion they can't hide. Apparently they didn't find it.

Iris continues. "He was a family friend—Paulo. He sent a letter addressed to me to Sweet Blood. It's destroyed now, I remember," Iris says, wanting to protect Aurelia. "But he invited me to his estate. This was all just before the raid."

"He left you instructions on how to get to the float plane?"

Iris doesn't mention the phone that was left. "Yes."

"Why would he send that in a letter? How would he know the FBI was about to come after you?"

If Iris is getting arrested, she still can't help but lie to protect Augusta if she is still alive. "I think he figured it was only a matter of time. The letter getting there when it did was coincidence."

"Do you know he's a member of one of the largest drug trafficking organizations in the world?" asks Beltran.

"I know nothing about it. Or him. But he liked me and invited me to Mexico to visit back in August."

"We know this wasn't just a vacation for you. You were evading law enforcement and fled the country. We know he, or his people rather, were helping you."

"Look, do I need a lawyer?"

Beltran crosses her arms. "No, not if you're smart."

Iris realizes why they're still in the bathroom. They're not arresting her. She has leverage. Some kind of advantage, but they haven't told her what it is.

Alexi begins to talk. "We've been working with intelligence to try to pinpoint who is in charge of the organization for years now. But the Colinas Cartel is smart about leadership. They don't have a big boss driving around in a Rolls Royce. They don't show the head of the snake. They keep it ambiguous."

"We don't know who's calling the shots," adds Beltran.

Iris understands what they want already: they want her to be their mole.

Alexi keeps talking. "We know Carlos Delgado, Paulo's father, ran the shell company for some time, but we don't have proof that his influence goes beyond that. Intelligence suggests he retired to Panama, and the latest cartel paperwork we've gotten our hands on shows a variety of signatures. We want to find out who the big boss is."

Iris wonders how much they know about the Adlers' empire. She pretends to play dumb. "Do you know why this cartel had a business connection with the Adlers in the first place?"

"Delgado is a legitimate business, in that it does import agricultural products to the United States. The Adler Corp is a purchaser of these. Was, I should say. They severed all ties in September," says Alexi.

Holy shit. They don't know, Iris thinks. *They don't know the Adlers were helping traffic drugs and the girls. Should I tell them?* She decides to keep it to herself until she can think how best to use it.

Alexi asks another question. "Iris, do you know why Paulo invited you to his estate?"

"I think he's... enamored."

Alexi and Beltran share an expression like this is what they thought.

"And obviously," Iris continues, "he thinks I might not have qualms with his lifestyle. Being that I'm under investigation myself."

"But he's put in an awful lot of work getting you here. Did the two of you have a relationship previously?"

"No." Iris shakes her head vehemently. Then she realizes maybe she should change her tune. They want a motive for why Paulo's interested in bringing Iris to Mexico. They'd never guess it's because Augusta is likely alive and hiding there, but she doesn't want them sniffing that out. "No. I swear. Nothing like that." Iris exaggerates her expression of distaste and crosses her arms defensively. She hopes it looks like she's lying.

She did hint that she was gay to Alexi, but he's probably chalked that up to her wanting to keep a strange, giant man who was driving her around from attempting to make a move.

Beltran gives Iris a venomous look. "Quite the choice in partners. You do realize the snake's den you chose to run to? When he's bored with you, he'll cut you up into little pieces or feed you alive to a tiger. You know what this cartel is famous for? They tie their victims' intestines around their throats after they're dead so it looks like they're wearing a pink noose."

Her tone pisses Iris off. "But you want me to go into this snake's den, don't you?"

Alexi and Beltran are silent.

"So why do you think I'd do that after all the shit you just said?" Iris wants to see their hand.

It's Alexi who talks. He almost sounds sorry as he says it. "Because if you don't, we'll arrest you right now and charge you with the murder of your husband."

155

Iris figured that was coming. "And what if I do agree to help you? Does that just delay that?"

"No." Alexi pulls out a set of papers from the briefcase. "If you agree to help us, you get immunity."

Iris's eyes go wide, but she's not going to jump to agree. One, that makes her look guilty. She knows the police were having trouble proving she was the one who shot Joseph anyway. She knows they were afraid to take it to trial. Marshall told her as much. Plus, there's more than one case they can screw her with. "And what about my sister in-law's poisoning? Am I being charged with that?"

Alexi looks confused. "You're not even a suspect."

"I saw Annabelle's interview on TV. That's not what she's saying."

"And she didn't know what the hell she was talking about. Dominic Hurtz is currently in police custody. He's not elaborating on his motive, however."

Iris nods. "I want a guarantee I won't be charged. Annabelle's not some nobody anymore. She runs the company."

"Sure. You have a guarantee." Alexi holds out his hand.

"Is this a joke? You want me to shake on it? With the US government? That's who you represent, right?"

"Yeah."

"You don't have a great track record."

"And you don't have much choice. Do you expect us to find an Office Depot to print out a new contract?" He pauses to make Iris feel foolish. "Your husband wasn't a nobody either. The DA has their charges drawn up, and they want you locked up. It took a lot of convincing to get you into our hands. You got lucky that a drug lord caught a crush."

Iris doesn't have the bargaining power she thought she did. She'll have to take the deal as is. "So you want me to infiltrate the place?"

"You could say that."

Iris sighs. "Okay."

"Okay what?" asks Beltran. She wants Iris to commit.

Iris has a feeling in her stomach. It's not quite fear, nor anxiety. It's a mixture of both.

Anticipation.

It's like she's on a roller coaster as it clicks higher and higher. She's going to be back in the thick of it.

Empire. Drugs. Murder. They don't even know about Augusta's presence there. They just want the source of the drugs.

The head of the snake.

"Okay..." Iris says, trying to keep the smile from her lips. "Okay, I'll help you."

In Ink

Alexi takes Iris's handcuffs off, and she sits cross-legged on the floor as they go over what they want her to do once she's staying on the property.

The big problem, of course, is that Iris doesn't speak Spanish, and her enthusiasm wanes when they tell her they want her to plant listening devices throughout the house.

"They'll kill me if they catch me doing that. They'll do exactly as you said they would and wrap my insides around my neck."

Alexi looks guilty, but Beltran looks annoyed. She's the bad cop, and it doesn't seem like an act. "You do this to our instructions, or we put the handcuffs back on and march you into a Louisiana courthouse. You got it?"

Iris doesn't respond.

"Even if you don't speak the language, the hierarchy should be visible. Does Paulo call the shots, or do decisions happen after he makes a phone call? Do all the men call him *Patrón*, or does he bow and show deference to someone else?"

Suddenly, they all go silent as the janitor starts speaking in Spanish. Iris can hear Luis's voice. He's looking for her.

The janitor leans into the bathroom like she's looking for someone and then turns back. Iris can see her shake her head.

She hears Luis say, "*Gracias*," and just like that, he's gone.

Iris sighs. "What am I going to tell him?" She points.

"That you had the runs and used the bathroom in baggage claim."

Iris nods. "Okay. They're probably going to search me when I get to the property."

"Of course they are. And we're not going to send you in there with any hardware. The estate is walled in. We're going to have a team in place to toss over a bag."

"What?"

"Don't panic. We've surveilled the place enough to know the guard schedules. Between 11:30 and midnight, sometime in the first three nights, we need you to make it to the wall on the southeast corner."

Beltran holds out a hand, and Alexi goes to the briefcase and pulls out an aerial view of the compound. He gives it to her. "That's here." Beltran points. "Past the koi pond. You'll need an excuse to wander out that late. You don't smoke, right?"

"No."

"Does Paulo know that?"

"I doubt it."

Beltran pulls out a pack of cigarettes and hands it to her. "Now you do. Go out for a smoke around that time, and when you're close to the wall say aloud to yourself, *What a beautiful night*, and the bag will be tossed over. It's small. Black. Don't worry about it making noise or being seen. Even if you're being watched, I doubt they'd see the bag come over. It's not a well-lit part of the property."

"Will the bag fit in my pocket?"

"Alexi?" Beltran motions towards the briefcase, and he takes out a small black bag and hands it to her. "It has a strap on it. Like a garter." Beltran extends the elastic. "Wear something with room and pull it up your leg."

Beltran unzips the bag and starts showing Iris the listening devices and explains the kind of places she should put them. Then she shows her a cell phone that will be in the bag that Iris can use to communicate with them. Text only.

Their plan seems more thought out than Iris expected. But how long could they have possibly known she was going to flee to Mexico?

There's more they're not telling her. She feels stupid for believing them initially when they made it seem like they knew nothing about the Adlers' drug connection to the cartel. And if they've been surveilling the place, wouldn't they know who was there? Wouldn't they know about Augusta?

When Beltran puts the bag away, Iris asks a question. "Do you know everyone who's on the property?"

"Only how many people there are and if they're male or female. We can't risk being seen during surveillance, so we're too distant to pick up faces. At any given time, there's a dozen guards and nine permanent residents. Guests seem to come and go weekly. Plant these bugs. Text us updates. Keep your eyes and your ears open. We've been trying to get someone on the inside of the Colinas Cartel for seven years. If it weren't for that fact, you would've been pulled out of that shack on the bayou still vomiting. Don't fuck this up for us, and you get your freedom."

She wants to weigh how thorough their plan is. There is something about Iris's involvement that feels hasty. "And after I'm done reporting back to you, how do I get out?"

"We'll text you instructions when the time comes," says Agent Beltran.

"Are you going to raid the place?"

"Again, Iris, we'll share the necessary information with you when the time comes."

Vague. She can tell from the guilt on Alexi's face that something doesn't sit well with him about this. Do they expect her to get caught? Is there no exit plan? "I want to see the agreement," Iris says. "The one that says I won't be charged."

Alexi hands her the paperwork offering immunity in exchange for her cooperation. It's several pages long, and most of it is in a legalese she can't understand.

"Can I have my lawyer go over this?"

Beltran just smiles, amused, as if this was a juvenile question.

This is an intelligence operation, Iris realizes. A handshake under the table. There is not even a guarantee she lives.

"One more thing." Alexi pulls a photo of a man out of the briefcase. "We've had eyes on one fella in particular running this cartel. Emmanuel Barrera. He's Paulo's uncle on his mother's side. He vanished four years ago. He's wanted for the deaths of two DEA informants, so if he's alive he'd be lying low. If you see a man like this"—Alexi taps the photo— "let us know."

Iris studies it. Emmanuel has wide cheeks and a mean little mustache. His eyes are so brown and beady, they look black. He's a killer if she's ever seen one.

Alexi hands her the contract and pen, and Iris writes her signature on the bottom line. Maybe she sighed her life away, but she's not in much of a position to barter, not when she shot her husband in the head and the world seems to know it now.

Beltran looks at her signature, satisfied. "You did the right thing, Iris. Go about your visit as you would. Be calm. Be gracious. But most of all, be smart. We don't have time to go over everything twice. We've got to get you back to your escort now, or they might be too suspicious of where you were to let you into the compound."

"But if they don't let me in, what would they do with me?"

Silence.

Iris realizes why Alexi can't hide the guilt from his face. This very meeting is risky enough that Iris might end up dead an hour from now. She doesn't feel anticipation anymore. She's just afraid.

Iris looks at Alexi. She wants to hear some encouragement from him, but he just chews his lip. He won't even look at her. She can tell that the fear in her eyes is not something he wants to remember if she dies.

"Eyes and ears," Beltran repeats. "That's all you have to be."

Iris nods, feeling like she'll be lucky by the end of this if those body parts of hers don't end up on a platter.

Colinas Azules

Iris is in a cold sweat as she walks out of the bathroom. She looks and feels tortured, but she plans for her pained expression to be part of the reason she was gone.

Luis is not where he'd been standing. It's been nearly twenty minutes since she left him. *Shit. Shit. Shit.* He left already. She's sure of it, and she feels a kind of relief.

Maybe the cartel has just left her here. Her disappearance has proved too suspicious. Without the option to spy, she'll be arrested for her husband's murder.

It doesn't sound so bad anymore. What pushes her onward just as much as her fear of prison is that she doesn't want to look like a coward. She has an out. She should take it.

Maybe she'll rip up the contract anyway. She doesn't want to do this anymore, but just then she catches Luis's eye. He's standing next to an older black sedan stopped in the street. He waves and runs over to her.

"*Señora! Señora!*"

"I'm sorry." Iris puts a hand on her stomach and rubs. She grimaces as he approaches her. "I'm not feeling so well."

"Ahhh. Okay. Okay. *Bueno?*" He holds his hand sideways and shakes it.

"I can go. *Sí.*" Iris points at the car, and Luis helps her step off the curb. He helps her into the back seat and then sits shotgun.

Their driver is already seated. He looks at Iris in the rearview. He's younger than them both. Little more than a teen. His face is deathly serious. His hair is cut short, and his eyes are hidden by aviators.

He looks dangerous: a boy working for the cartel who is probably itching to prove himself as a man. These are the people who are so eager to slice open people's stomachs and wrap their insides around their necks.

Luis doesn't bother to talk to him. Maybe he knows this kid's an asshole.

Iris hadn't been that worried on either of her two flights, but now it feels like there's a hot coal burning through her guts. She's being driven into the dark by two strangers. She doesn't know what they saw at the airport.

She's not in intelligence, but she thinks Alexi is too damn recognizable to even be in the field. If they saw him follow her into the woman's bathroom… Iris assures herself the FBI was smart about making contact. They waited until they knew they wouldn't be seen.

After twenty minutes, they've left the buildings of the city behind. They drive through farmland towards mountains in the distance. The sun casts shadows as long as skyscrapers over the flat land.

Soon, they stop passing homes. The road begins to wind up into the foothills. The darkness comes on quickly. The road they're on turns into gravel, and they drive through a tunnel of trees. The gravel road ends at a gate.

There's a man in loafers and a blue dress shirt standing in front of it. His business-casual outfit contrasts poorly with the assault rifle strung across his chest.

He nods at the driver, and the gate opens. There's another guard on the other side. This one is in camouflage fatigues and a black face mask. He gestures for the driver to roll down the window. They have a quick conversation, and he makes him pop the trunk. After the guard investigates, he shuts it and slaps the roof twice.

They drive on.

The road they're on rises, and Iris realizes the scale of this place is enormous. It's not just an acre or two that's walled in but ten. *Past the koi pond. Southeast wall.* Beltran's directions no longer seem so straight forward.

The road crests and a fountain appears. It's a story tall and tiered like a wedding cake. It's illuminated with lights stuck in the grass, and Iris can see water pour from the mouths of snakes.

The estate house is behind it. It's made of cream-colored stone and has a red-tile roof. It's not that different from what Iris envisioned. There are four balconies that extend from what Iris assumes are the bedrooms on the second floor.

They don't stop in front of the main entrance. They drive down a side road toward a garage with six stall doors. The garage is the size of a large house itself. They stop, and the teen driver says something Iris doesn't understand.

Luis mumbles something and gets out of the car. He opens Iris's door, and she gets out quickly, thankful to get away from the driver.

Luis motions for Iris to follow him. They walk down a path lined with paving stones. A tall hedge runs along each side, making another tunnel, and they come into a clearing—the backyard of the house. There's a lit swimming pool shining turquoise in the night, and in front of it is a dinner table.

There are a few people seated and one man standing. Paulo. He wears a white suit with no tie. He's barefoot, and his wavy black hair is cut a little shorter than it was in August. His sharp facial features look even more handsome shadowed in the dim light of the backyard.

"Iris Adler." He looks at her, but Iris is already scanning the table looking for Augusta.

There are two women in dresses in their early thirties. One is white, blonde, with a floral tattoo on her shoulder. The other is a Hispanic woman with small wrists, a tiny nose, and intense eyes like Paulo.

At the head of the table is an older Hispanic man with a bushy, gunslinger's mustache. None of these three meet Iris's eyes. One of the women, the white one, pulls on her own earlobe self-consciously.

Iris can see broken glass on the lawn. There's a cracked plate on the table. She's come during the middle of an argument. A fight.

A man crawls into view from the other side of the table. She can tell from his matching black pants and shirt that he must be a servant. He shuffles, picking up bits of glass and placing them in his palm.

"Won't you join us? We still haven't had dessert." Paulo gestures to a chair.

"Can't you see she wants a bed and a shower?" the Hispanic woman snaps. "She doesn't want to eat cake with you, Paulo."

She's in a satin, sapphire dress, and she makes eye contact with Iris as she picks up her wineglass and has a sip. She's beautiful. She has the same handsome, dark features as Paulo. Maybe a little sharper. The longer Iris

166

looks, the less beautiful she becomes, but Iris realizes that this must be Paulo's sister.

Paulo says something in Spanish but then shakes his head as if he's trying to get out of a trance. "Of course. Of course. How ungracious of me. You've had a big week of traveling. I suppose you'd like to put your feet up."

"That would be nice. Thank you." Iris looks towards the house. She can see the kitchen through the windows, but there's no one there. There isn't an empty place set at the table either. *Where is Augusta?* She's too embarrassed to ask so soon.

Paulo's sister tosses her napkin on the table and stands. "Let me show you to where you're staying, Iris."

Paulo just smiles awkwardly. The older man with the mustache clears his throat. He has some food on his chin, a fleck of what looks like salad, but obviously, no one has called it to his attention.

He drums his fingers on the tablecloth. Iris sees his nail beds are cracked and dirty. He seems anxious to resume whatever it was they were talking about before Iris interrupted. He's fatter than the photo of the man Alexi showed her and the mustache is different, but this could be the same man.

"We look forward to seeing you in the morning," says Paulo. "And welcome."

The woman takes Iris's elbow gently and starts to lead her to the back doors. As Iris starts to walk, she turns to Luis. He's standing with his chin tucked towards his chest. "*Gracias*," Iris says. She wants to thank him for everything.

He only smiles and nods at her. Sweat builds on his brow. He looks terrified.

They keep walking towards the house. "My brother is a fool," the woman says loud enough that Iris is sure Paulo can hear her. "I'm his younger sister, Esperanza. Let's get you comfortable, okay?"

They step into the kitchen. It's as beautiful as any Iris has ever been in. The cabinets and sinks all have copper fixtures. The countertops are white granite with gold flakes. There's a variety of half-picked-at dishes sitting on the kitchen island, and Iris can hear what she presumes are servants talking to one another in a butler's pantry.

"Don't worry. We won't make you stay in the main house. We have a lovely guest cottage all made up for you. I just need to arrange some things." Esperanza peeks into the butler's pantry and speaks in Spanish.

A girl no more than fourteen wearing black pants and a black shirt comes out. When Esperanza is done talking, the girl walks down the hall quickly.

Esperanza turns to Iris. She has a model's bony face, and her arms are freakishly thin. She is beautiful, Iris decides, but in a bulimic kind of way. Her diet looks like it consists of white wine and Tic Tacs. Her black hair is thick, lush, and healthy, however. Iris looks at it bouncing glossily over her shoulders.

"She's going to get you some of my clothes." Esperanza holds a long finger out at Iris and curls it. "I might not fit."

Iris isn't sure if this is some kind of insult. She's as light as she's ever been. She can't weigh more than 130 pounds. "Okay... thanks."

"I hear you're staying for some time?"

"Um... the foreseeable future, I guess."

"The *foreseeable* future," Esperanza repeats with understanding but with the undertone that she's never heard the phrase before. Iris supposes she probably hasn't. "We've been following your story on the news. You're quite the sensation in your country. A Black Widow, they say. Did he deserve it? This husband of yours?"

Iris is quiet.

"I'm just kidding. That was in poor taste. Let me show you to your cottage."

They walk across the kitchen and go out a separate set of back doors than the ones they came in from.

The pool is now on their left, and the dinner table is on the other side of it. The older man with the cracked nail beds is talking now. Paulo still doesn't sit, and the servant who was on all fours picking up glass is still doing so, but now he's at Paulo's feet.

Iris and Esperanza are clearly visible as they walk along the grass, but no one bothers to give them a wave or a glance. The older man's voice builds to a yell. He finishes his sentence by slamming a fist on the table. His mustache twitches and the glassware jumps.

The last thing Iris wants to seem is nosy, so she looks at Esperanza's back as they pass through the backyard. In fifty yards, they come to a bungalow of the same style and color as the main house.

Esperanza opens the front door. It's an open floor plan, apart from the bathroom. It's all of eight hundred square feet, but there's a kitchenette, sitting area, and a queen-sized mattress. The floor is tan tile, and a pile of fresh towels sits on the bed. There aren't any windows on the far side of the room. Instead, there's a set of French doors that are open to a garden.

It's lovely.

"Step into the shower, and by the time you're out, there will be some fresh clothes for you to change into," says Esperanza. "I'll make sure you have a pen and paper, and you can write a list of your sizes. Tomorrow, I can have someone go shopping for you."

"Thank you."

"*De nada*, Iris. We are privileged to have you."

Esperanza turns to leave and closes the door behind her, and Iris is left alone. Just like that. But Iris stays where she stands and looks around the room suspiciously. There have to be cameras.

At least a microphone hidden somewhere. They didn't even pat her down. She wonders what the argument at dinner was about and can't help but fear it's about her. What if they think she's too high risk to keep here?

Her greater anxiety comes from the fact that Augusta is nowhere to be found. But the letter sent to Sweet Blood was in *Augusta's* handwriting. There was no doubt about it.

She tries to block it from her mind. She's not having any epiphanies now. She has to sleep. She hasn't had a full night's worth since she was in America.

She showers, and sure enough, when she comes out of the bathroom, a pile of clothes has appeared on the bed next to the towels. There's a toothbrush, toothpaste, and an entire bag of makeup and toiletries. Next to it all is a paper pad and pen as well.

Iris dries off and moves the stacks of towels, clothes, and toiletries to the countertop in the kitchenette. She freezes as there's a slow, hesitant set of knocks on the door. "One minute!"

Iris fishes through the clothes and throws on an uncomfortable pair of silver silk pajama pants and a plain white T-shirt.

She opens the door to see Paulo standing several feet back with his hands crossed in front of his crotch. Luis stands off to his side. Luis is making an *O* of his mouth and exhales nervously.

"Sorry to bother you, Iris," Paulo says. "But I'm afraid there were some business items we forgot this evening. Would you mind?" Paulo holds out his palm like he'd like to come in.

"Of course." Iris opens the door wider, and he and Luis enter.

"You didn't have a bag, did you?"

"No. Just the clothes on my back."

"Great. Do you mind if we give you a quick search? This should've been done at the gate, I'm afraid." He gives an accusing look to Luis, who doesn't react at all. They're speaking in English, and Luis must not know what Paulo is saying.

"Sure!" Iris says, widening her eyes. She's trying to be as agreeable as she can.

"I'm sorry. It's just protocol." Paulo waves his hand, as if these silly rules are not his.

He steps back and gestures for Luis to step forward. He pats Iris's pajama pants and quickly goes over her waistband. He steps back and nods at Paulo.

"And the clothes you wore here?"

"They're in the bathroom."

Paulo clicks his teeth at Luis and tilts his head at the bathroom. Luis goes in and comes out with her dirty jeans and top.

"I have cigarettes in my jeans pocket."

Paulo takes the clothes from Luis and pulls out the cigarettes. He opens the top, obviously looking to see if she smuggled anything inside. "Do you mind?"

Iris shakes her head, and Paulo takes a cigarette. "Thank you." Paulo is looking at the room as if he's wondering where she could've hidden something. He takes the cigarette from his mouth and holds it between two fingers. "I heard Luis lost you at the airport?"

"My breakfast didn't want to stay in me very long." Iris looks at Luis. His stare is far off and fearful. It looks like he believes his life is being debated.

"Sorry to hear that," says Paulo. "I promise you, you'll find the cuisine here a lot more palatable. But Luis should've stuck closer. Something could've happened to you." Paulo nudges Luis's ribs with an elbow, and he begins to tremble.

A pit opens in Iris's stomach. A warm breeze blows through the open door. It's a quiet, lovely evening. It's hard to contemplate, but the fact is clear; she's arguing against a man's execution.

"No." Iris shakes her head vigorously. "He did great. I kinda ran off on him. The urge came quick."

Paulo squints. "Did you?"

"Yes. It wasn't his fault. He was a great pilot. Very professional."

Paulo tilts his chin up. "Was he? Well, I suppose we all make mistakes." He slaps Luis on the shoulder, and the man flinches. "I think we'll let him keep his job!" Paulo says loudly and laughs as he shakes Luis by the shoulder. Then he winks at Iris, and she gulps.

She's not able to hide her fear. It's clear Paulo brought Luis to her door to suggest to Iris that he was going to kill him. To say to her, *This is how thin the ice is around here.*

"Sorry to have bothered you." Paulo heads towards the door. "We shall let you get some sleep. *Buenas noches, señora.*"

"Yeah." Iris's voice quivers too much for her to attempt to speak Spanish. "Good night."

Paulo and Luis step out, and she shuts the door gently behind them. She keeps her hand pressed against it as she collects her breath. A question has begun to form in her mind.

She thought Augusta invited her here. It was her handwriting in the letter, and Iris was under the impression that Paulo's signature was just a ploy in case anyone intercepted the mail. But if Paulo sent the letter and Augusta isn't here, why is Iris?

He could be attracted to her, but she doubts that's it.

She had thought this would be a reunion with Augusta, but now she fears that her presence has a purpose.

She's not just a guest. Paulo plans to use her for something, and whatever it is, Iris doubts she's supposed to be alive by the end of it.

Night Walk

Iris isn't going to be able to go to sleep anytime soon after Paulo's visit. She takes the cigarettes and heads out the back sliding doors of the bungalow that lead to a rectangular yard enclosed in prickly bushes. She wants to establish a pattern so it's not strange when she's seen walking to the southeast wall, cigarette in hand. She needs them to think she smokes.

The grass here is as short as that of a putting green, and on it is a patio table with four chairs. Iris walks barefoot to the end of the yard and peers out through the bushes that act as a barrier.

There's a road, and about fifty yards from where she stands are two metal structures with large garage doors.

Iris ducks lower when she hears footsteps crunching the gravel. The sound of an argument soon follows. One voice shouts, and another tries to quietly reason. At the same time, Iris recognizes the louder voice and the men come into view.

It's Paulo and the man with the mustache. Is this his father? Iris remembers her job the FBI sent her here to do. It would've been helpful to have been shown a picture of him, too. From the inside, it doesn't look complicated— this older man is still calling the shots. They stop when they're in front of Iris's bushes, and the man presses his finger into Paulo's chest.

"*Mátalo*," he says the word slowly, with deliberation.

Paulo nods and starts trotting back the road the way the two had come. Iris takes the opportunity to duck even lower. She hunches down and lies flat on her stomach so she's watching the man from under the bush.

He whistles and sings. He seems to be waiting for Paulo to return. He has a lovely tenor voice. It's light and dreamy. She can't understand the lyrics, but she has a feeling they're about love and a woman.

Iris starts to tense her entire body as the man walks towards the bushes and pinches some of the needles between his fingers. He tsks as if there's something wrong with the plant but then walks back to the center of the road quickly, as if he was out of position in a play that was about to begin.

Iris can hear why. A man's pleading voice wails in the night.

There are more footsteps on the gravel, and several men come into view. Paulo and two guards. Between the guards, with his feet dragging limp under him, is Luis.

No, Iris thinks. No, no, no. The men start going towards one of the metal garages. They're going to kill him in there. Iris isn't even thinking when she stands. She's pricked and stabbed as she climbs over the bush.

"Shit. Shit. Ow. Ow." The stiff branches and sharp needles feel like they draw blood. She stumbles onto the gravel road and wipes her hands off on her pajamas. When she looks up, she realizes all the men have stopped and are staring at her in silence.

"Excuse me." She walks closer. "Excuse me."

They all look at her with expressions between total confusion and amusement.

"Don't do that. Kill him, I mean. I'm not kidding. Luis took good care of me. He was cautious, and he was smart."

Luis is looking at Iris from one open eye. The other is swollen shut from being hit.

All the men look at Paulo, and Iris thinks for a moment that maybe he is the boss before she realizes they want him to translate.

A big grin appears on his face, and his eyes don't leave Iris as he begins speaking Spanish.

Iris talks again as soon as Paulo finishes. "And it's not very good hospitality to do this right behind the guesthouse."

Paulo adds this last part, and they all begin to laugh. He turns to the man who may be his father or uncle, and they whisper to each other. Paulo looks back at her. "Okay, Iris. You have my word. Luis lives."

He whistles at the guards who hold Luis, and they drop him to his feet. He almost falls before he's able to find his footing.

"You mean that?" Iris asks. "Or are you just going to take him into the hills when I'm not looking?"

"I mean that," Paulo says, and his face wrinkles, offended. "Just because I'm Mexican doesn't mean I don't honor my word."

"Oh, I didn't mean…"

Paulo suddenly erupts into laughter. He puts his hands on his knees and wheezes. "Oh, I tease, Iris. I tease. It looks like Luis may need to stick around to heal." He points at Luis's left foot, and Iris realizes that he's avoiding putting any weight on it. "We'll get him back to health." He pinches Luis's chin. "You can keep your baby bird, Iris."

Suddenly, a flashlight bobs in the distance as someone runs towards them. They all watch the light approach in silence. A younger guard drenched in sweat

176

stops, panting. He gestures at Iris with the flashlight. "*La mujer habla español?*"

"No," says Paulo.

But Iris knows enough Spanish to understand there's something they don't want her to know. He and Paulo begin talking quickly. Paulo seems exasperated. He turns back to her. "Go inside, Iris. I'm afraid one of my tigers has gotten loose on the property."

Iris chuckles awkwardly, but Paulo's serious expression doesn't morph into a laugh this time.

"Her name is Lola, but you know cats. They don't come much when they're called."

Paulo issues commands to the guards and to Luis. The guards trot off in different directions while Luis limps.

Paulo turns to see Iris still standing there. "Go! Now!" He points at the back of the guesthouse, and Iris looks at her feet, reddening at being chastised like a child. She goes around the hedge to enter through the front door.

Iris is thinking about what Agent Beltran said about being cut into pieces and fed to a tiger. Apparently, that wasn't hyperbole but a totally possible scenario.

When she gets to the bungalow, she pauses before she goes in. She can see flashlights searching in several different places. There's no doubt they're looking for something, but Iris doesn't believe it's a tiger.

She can't help but think they're looking for a woman. That someone they're keeping here has escaped.

Bathed

Iris wakes to a knock on the bungalow door. She isn't able to respond before Esperanza comes in, trailed by a servant holding a breakfast platter.

Coffee and eggs steam. A glass of orange juice refracts some sunlight around the room. It looks like late morning. Nine or ten.

"Good morning, Iris. How'd you sleep?"

Iris is still in the process of waking up. "Oh. Fine." She sits up and rubs her crusty eyes.

Esperanza looks like she got up at six a.m. to do her hair and makeup. She's wearing a peach-colored dress with matching strap sandals and gold earrings. *Who puts this much effort in just to walk around the house?* She makes the way Augusta and Annabelle would dress at Sweet Blood look frumpy.

"Would you like your breakfast in bed? Or left on the table?"

"The table is fine."

Esperanza gestures at the table, and the maid girl sets it down and leaves.

"Have you made a list of things you need?"

"No, not yet. Sorry."

"That's okay. You eat breakfast and freshen up. I want to give you a tour of the house. Would you meet me where you saw us dining last night, by the pool? I'll be reading there."

"Sure. That sounds good."

"Great." Esperanza gives her a big smile and turns to leave.

"Esperanza, one thing."

She turns and cocks a brow at Iris.

"I don't know if he was teasing me, but last night, Paulo said his tiger escaped. Is that still…"

"Oh, Lola is safe and sound. Don't worry about her anyway. She is a…what's the word in your language? *Feminista*. Lola only eats men."

"Ah," Iris says. "My kind of tiger."

Esperanza smiles. "Not much reason for her to eat women. They are typically well behaved here."

Iris senses the threat and nods. "I'll see you in a few."

"Yes, see you in a few."

Iris eats her breakfast but doesn't want to keep Esperanza waiting. She showers again, keeping her hair dry, and puts on a navy dress with a tennis skirt. There's a pair of sandals left for her by the door. Iris slips them on and starts towards the pool.

Morning transforms the estate. There are blooming flower bushes everywhere. Bright-green parrots sing in the trees. Iris wants to take the sandals off. All the grass is the same soft manicured kind that's on putting greens. There are orange and lemon trees polka-dotted with the bright colors of their fruits.

Esperanza paces the side of the pool slowly. It looks like she's watching her reflection in the water as she walks.

"Okay," Iris says, and Esperanza startles.

She puts her hand on her heart and smiles, but Iris can see the malice in her expression. "You sneaked up on me."

179

"Sorry."

"Come. I want to show you our home."

They go into the kitchen, and Iris speaks first. "So, who's house is this exactly?"

"Our father left it to Paulo, but he lets many family members stay here. There are two kitchens. Eleven bedrooms. It's easy to stay here yet not see others."

"I heard Paulo talk about your father when we first met. Is he retired?"

"Yes. He spends most of his time in Panama."

"So... Paulo took the company's reins?"

Esperanza just smiles, and Iris realizes she should've used a clearer word than *reins* because Esperanza changes the subject. Perhaps out of embarrassment of her ignorance. "This is the primary kitchen. The second one is for house staff. But if you want a drink or a snack or something, feel free to come here."

They go towards the front entrance of the house. There's a wide spiral staircase and a large living room off to the side.

In the living room is a black sectional that is twice as long as any couch. There's a large tan stone fireplace, and the skull of a bull hangs above the mantel. It's one of the few signs that this place used to be a ranch.

It's clear this is not Paulo's bachelor pad. There is that orderly woman's touch that single men can't quite replicate without giving themselves away. Usually they do it by hanging a sword on the wall or making the focal point of the room their whiskey bottles.

"This is usually where we entertain if the weather isn't good. Otherwise, you will always find us in the garden."

"It's lovely there," Iris says genuinely.

"Yes. It's been decades in the making, and today it truly is something, isn't it?"

Iris can see an office and a formal dining room behind the living room, but they don't enter either, and Esperanza starts up the stairs to the second floor.

"Who is the other man I saw here?"

"The older hombre... That's our uncle, Manny."

Manny. Short for Emmanuel, no doubt. Iris feels a little jolt of victory. The FBI will be very happy to hear this. She almost wants to ask straight out if he runs the business, but that can all wait.

Esperanza shows her into a poker room on the second floor. There's a round table with black felt in the middle of it. One of the walls is a full bar, and across from it is a plush leather sofa. The room smells like cigar smoke.

"The boys like to do their serious business here. Makes them feel like their fathers, but it gets smoky quick." Esperanza wafts invisible smoke away from her nose. She walks through the room down a short hall and into a vast bedroom.

"This is the master."

A four-poster king is in the center of the room. Its curtains are bloodred. The furniture has fancy swirling wood grains and gold handles. The rest of the house has been tasteful, but this king's chamber feels tacky.

Esperanza doesn't seem very enthusiastic about this tour, and Iris curses herself that it's taken her this long to realize it's an excuse to get her away and out of sight of the bungalow.

They're searching it, no doubt.

Iris is in her own head, hardly listening as Esperanza speaks. They stand in a cavernous bathroom with a copper bathtub in its center. Iris wants to get this tour over with, but suddenly the hair on the back of her neck stands up. She stares at the copper tub. Her mouth creeps open. She remembers this tub. She's seen it before.

Here.

One of her very few memories she has of Augusta before she was shot was in a bathtub. She was in the bubbles while Augusta knelt at her side. Iris suddenly shuts her mouth and stares at Esperanza.

"I've been here."

Esperanza pauses. She brings her hands together calmly. "What?"

"This estate. I've been here before."

Esperanza smiles. "I think you are mistaken."

Iris looks back at the bathtub, willing the memory to reveal more of itself.

"I was bruised then, too, wasn't I?"

Esperanza doesn't respond this time.

"She took me here... She kept me here to recover."

"Paulo said you were a little loco. It's no big deal. I was on antipsychotics when I was a young girl. I have a few ex-boyfriends missing eyes. Another also has only one of something else when he should have a pair. Come." Esperanza gestures. "Do you like wine? I shall show you to the cellars."

Iris walks, but she has to watch her feet. She remembers the bathtub, and it's not just a snippet. She's shocked how clear it all comes back to her.

Past Tense

Iris lay back in the bathtub while Augusta ran her hands up and down her arm gently. She was bathing her, and the slight sensation of touch and hot water made it difficult for Iris to keep her eyes open.

There had been an argument. One that had left Iris exhausted.

"You should quit. At least cut back. My God, Iris. You're going to kill yourself if you're not careful."

"You don't know what it's like to want something this badly."

Augusta seemed like she had something to say to that. She pursed her lips and brought up an orange pill bottle and rattled it. "OxyContin. Forty milligrams. Delayed release. If you're mine, then no more heroin. No more needles. Understand?"

Iris's eyes were locked on the bottle like a dog's on a treat. "Yes."

Augusta unscrewed the cap, and Iris moved her hand out of the water, but before Iris could offer her palm, Augusta was holding the pill in front of her mouth. She slipped it between Iris's lips, and she swallowed.

"I'll hold on to these. We'll wean you down to twenty milligrams and talk then. Okay?"

Iris smiled contentedly. "Deal."

"I can keep you away from everything. Every bill. Every enemy. Everything bad." Augusta lifted Iris's hand from the tub and ran her fingers over the back of it gently. "You won't ever have to see any men."

Iris relaxed more and wiggled her shoulders into the slant of the tub.

"When you're feeling up for it, we can discuss it more."

Iris turned her head. She looked into Augusta's shining green eyes. "Just tell me now and get it over with. What? You want me as more than a mistress?"

Augusta smiles. Her white hair was held back in a ponytail, but with her tan face completely exposed, she looked almost youthful. Her teeth flashed white as she smiled. "Is it awful if I do?"

Iris suddenly felt as naked as she was. She took her hand away from Augusta. But Augusta didn't respect her body language. She moved her hand to Iris's head and stroked her hair instead. "You don't have to pretend anymore. I know I'm not a job to you, Iris." She caressed Iris's arm again.

Iris's pulse didn't relax. Her heart raced.

"You like me, don't you?"

"Yes." Iris said with quivering breath.

"Then I don't believe you were in the right line of work." She lets a rope of Iris's wet hair slap on her shoulder.

"You're married," Iris eked out.

"I'm many things, sugar."

Iris was quiet.

"What do you say?" Iris watched as Augusta's hand sank below the bubbles into the water. She felt her fingertips on her thigh, and Iris's breath caught in her throat.

She couldn't speak.

"I can keep you here as long as you like. Keep you here. A penthouse. Wherever you like. You won't have to work. You won't have to lift"—Augusta started to walk her fingers up Iris's thigh in tandem to her words—"A. Single. Little. Finger."

Augusta slipped her hand between Iris's legs, and Iris tilted her head to the ceiling.

"What do you think? Do you want to be *mine*?"

Iris brought her head down to look into Augusta's eyes. "Yes." Her voice was so breathy, she practically panted.

"That's what I thought," Augusta whispered and pushed her fingers in up to the knuckle.

Iris felt like she was beginning to dissolve into the hot water, and then the memory too, fades, as the Oxycontin and Augusta's hand got to work.

It dissipated into something wordless. A recollection of only pleasure.

Tiger

Iris stares at the bathtub. *What came after that evening?* Iris doesn't understand the timeline. Was she here before or after Joseph got his hands on her and beat her at the Nile?

But regardless of the order of events, why was she here at all back then? What did Paulo have to do with her?

Perhaps Augusta was worried about keeping her around Louisiana. A gay lover is bad press. This estate could've been a safehouse. But Iris can't help but wonder if she was here then for the same mysterious reason she is now.

Esperanza is explaining where the marble was sourced for the vanity top when Iris interrupts her.

"I'm sorry, but why are you letting me stay with you?"

She pauses and speaks like the line was scripted. "Because you are important to close business associates of the family."

"Important to Augusta Adler, you mean?"

"Yes." Esperanza stands up straighter.

"And where is she?"

"Last I heard, she was in the river."

Iris should be confronting Paulo. Esperanza is harder to read. She's not as fluent in English, and her tone is not something Iris can scrutinize, listening for a lie.

Iris walks around the bathtub and looks at it as she talks. "It was her handwriting on the invitation that brought me here. Why would Paulo stick his neck out to host a fugitive?"

"I cannot answer why my brother is as foolish as he is. Life to him, people's lives, they're all part of a game. Paulo's game. Maybe he wanted you to think your mother-in-law was alive so you'd trust him enough to come visit."

Iris feels the floor wobble beneath her. For some reason, she hadn't let herself really consider that possibility. Augusta might *really* be dead. Iris might've been baited here.

"Now come." Esperanza waves. "Let me show you the main office."

They walk back out to the hallway and pass closed doors that most likely lead to more bedrooms. There's another office at the end of the hall. There aren't many books. Nor do any diplomas hang on the wall.

There is a large black desk centered in front of a window. "This was a recent expansion. Paulo drives me crazy with how much he always wants to change something. We can't have a year when there isn't a construction crew here hammering from morning until night."

Iris looks out the window. From the second floor, she can see the white stone wall that surrounds the property. The top is lined with barbed wire. The wall is perhaps two-hundred yards away, and in front of it is a row of single-story townhouses.

Iris points out the window. "Who lives there?"

Esperanza makes her way over to see what Iris is talking about. "Employees."

Iris isn't so sure. A guard with a rifle paces the path in front of the townhouses.

"See that black fence?" Esperanza says quickly. "That's the enclosure."

Iris sees a black fence that's extremely high. Maybe fifteen feet. It's to her left, closer to the estate's garden. "Lola's enclosure?"

"Yes. Would you like to see her?"

Iris is here on business. She should be scouting out a location to hide the listening devices she's going to get from the FBI. She might be *fed* to the goddamn thing, but she can't say no to seeing a tiger.

"Yeah." Iris shrugs. "Sure."

"Who can resist? She's beautiful. You'll see."

They leave the house out the same back door they came in from and walk through the garden, hanging a right instead of going to the guesthouse. They cross a gravel road, and at the end of another stone path lined with mature trees is the black fence. Esperanza goes right up to it and starts to tick her tongue against her teeth. "Lola? *Dónde estás*, Lola?" she says in a chipper, questioning tone.

The ground of the enclosure is all wood chips. There is a large, plastic structure in the center that looks like playground equipment.

"Lola?"

The tiger suddenly jumps out of the structure so fast that Iris stumbles back. It's no miniature tiger.

It's huge. If it stood next to Iris, she thinks its head would be next to her ribs. It trots the rest of the way to Esperanza with the same cool, casual air of a house cat and then rubs its side against the fence. Lola reaches through the fence and pats Lola's back.

"Give her a touch. She's friendly."

Iris watches the tiger's muscles twitch under its fur. She reaches forward slowly with her arm flexed, ready to yank it back. She touches Lola as far from her giant mouth as she can, right on the hip. The orange and black fur is soft, but when she takes her hand away, her fingers and palm are gritty with a film of dirt.

"Paulo rescued her. She used to work for a circus that went out of business. If they couldn't find a buyer, they were just going to shoot her. Animals."

To Iris's shock, Esperanza moves her hand all the way up and starts scratching Lola right behind the ears. The big cat tilts her head towards the fence. Her eyes are partially closed in pleasure.

Iris watches, amused. "Do tigers purr?"

"No, but they can roar. Only it doesn't sound like it does in cinema. If you ever hear a sound in the night that sounds like a scream out of your worst nightmares, do not worry. It's just Lola."

Iris senses movement behind her and turns to see Paulo walking towards them. He's as casually dressed as she's ever seen him. He's in a khaki polo and black pants. He holds a half-empty bottle of Gatorade. "Good morning, ladies."

"Good morning," says Iris.

"So you've met the troublemaker?" Paulo gestures at Lola with his Gatorade.

"Yes." Iris looks back to the tiger. "She seems like a sweetheart."

"Don't let her fool you. If I were to reach in to scratch her ears, she'd tear my arm off. She was in the circus, and her trainers were men. I don't think they were as kind as I am to my sweetheart."

The tiger has wandered away from the fence and rolls onto her back. Her tail flicks, and she wiggles against the ground. The tiger's behavior is hardly any different than a domesticated cat. Iris finds herself smiling.

"But Esperanza…" Paulo clears his throat. "You should show Iris the hills."

Esperanza pauses like there's a hidden meaning in this. She's slow to respond. "I can do that."

"Great. Do you like to hike, Iris? I promise it's nothing too difficult, and the views… They are beautiful. Best to go this time of morning." Paulo rotates his hand to read his watch. He taps the dial with a finger. "Before the heat of the day becomes unbearable."

"I'm not sure I'm outfitted." Iris looks down at her sandals.

Paulo follows her gaze. "We can get you some sneakers."

"I have some in my room."

"Okay, okay. You go to your room, and Esperanza will wait for you outside. Then have a hike, and we shall all have lunch together. Sound like a plan?"

Iris looks at Esperanza. She wants to see what her reaction is to these commands that are being played off as plans.

She starts speaking in Spanish, and Paulo interrupts her by holding up his hand.

"From now on, we only speak English around Miss Iris. It's not very polite to have conversation she can't partake in. Enjoy your hike, ladies."

Paulo turns around and walks off with his hands clasped behind his back. A guard with a rifle is waiting for him on the road, and the two then walk together.

"So… we will take a *hike*." Esperanza says, like it's an activity that's not worth her time. "I'll change and meet you at your cottage."

They start back towards the gardens, but Esperanza doesn't take the same path as Iris towards the house. She takes a sharp left without a goodbye and follows Paulo down the road.

Iris looks back at Lola's enclosure. It feels obvious that Paulo was lying yesterday. The tiger never escaped. Last night, they were looking for a person.

And from the looks of it, Iris thinks they still haven't found them. She feels hopeful Augusta is still somewhere around here, but when she looks at the hills, the hope sours.

She's not confident that taking a hike isn't a metaphor for getting a bullet to the back of the head.

Blood Trails

When Iris gets back to her guesthouse, it's obvious the place has been searched. The maids have made the bed and taken away her breakfast platter, but her clothes aren't where she left them. Even her sneakers are crooked, and one of the pads is half hanging out like they'd checked the soles.

The TV she couldn't work was now on to an American news channel, but they were covering the economy.

She wonders if the media has gotten bored of the Adlers' drama with no new leads to follow. What Iris wants is an internet connection so she can see everything they're saying. Then she realizes that even if she asked, Paulo probably wouldn't give her a phone or a computer or anything she could contact the outside world with. She thought she was escaping when she first decided to come to Mexico, but now she's worried she walked into her own jail cell.

And here, there is no trail before she's on death row. For all she knows, her execution already has a date.

Iris watches the news on the end of her bed and ruminates for a half hour before Esperanza comes knocking. "Are you ready to walk, Iris?" she says, opening the front door before Iris can answer.

Iris stands and looks at Esperanza. She's wearing big black sunglasses, a black sunhat, and black jumpsuit. Her sneakers are canvas and have about two inches of lift and look like something from the 90s that is attempting to come off as futuristic. She's a *Real Housewife* going for a hike.

"*Vamos*," Iris says with a smile that quickly fades.

The two of them head towards the back of the compound. The ground slopes up, and they ascend a set of stone steps until they reach a small black pedestrian gate in the wall.

Iris hasn't been this close to the wall yet. With its crowning of barbed wire included, it's probably twelve feet tall. She feels like she's at the border of an empire.

Esperanza pulls out a plastic card and holds it against a black box near the gate lock. There's no buzz or light that flashes green. The gate unlocks with a clank, and she pushes it open. She holds the gate while Iris steps out, and then she closes it behind them.

On the other side of the wall, there is a man immediately to Iris's right. He wears full camouflage fatigues and a black ski mask. Another guard. His gun has a scope, like it's his job to look for long-distance threats. He nods at the ground in respect and avoids eye contact as they pass.

"Ah, *puta madre*," Esperanza says.

Iris turns from the guard to see her staring at the stone steps that continue up. "Paulo says this is not *dificil*. Paulo plays tennis every morning. Paulo ran track at boarding school. Paulo. Paulo. Paulo. Paulo calls the shots. If I were born a man, I would be in charge of this cartel already."

"Is Paulo already in charge?"

"Ha! He wishes. He doesn't have the respect of the men. They fear him the way you'd fear a kid who enjoys shooting dogs. Fear without respect is a problem waiting to happen."

Iris wonders if Esperanza's tone changed so suddenly because they were out of the compound. No cameras. No listening devices. Is this just the conversation of a sibling rivalry, or is Esperanza saying something more?

Soon they're both too winded to speak. The trail they're on is somewhat shaded but still hot. The trees they pass have white bark and twisted, gnarled branches.

Esperanza catches Iris looking at them. "Ficus." She points at the trees. "It's about the only flora here that won't cut you open if you brush against it."

The earth is hot and white and every other plant around looks spiky.

Iris lets Esperanza talk while she takes deep, panting breaths through her mouth.

"This place is a… Oh, how do you say it? *Thorn* forest, and that's not a nickname. It's a climate just like a rainforest. Nice, huh?"

"Yeah." Iris pauses and puts her hands on her hips. They're already several hundred feet above the compound. Iris can see it all. The guest house, the main house. She spies the tennis courts near the entrance she first came in from, and not far from them is standing water that doesn't shine the same turquoise blue of a chlorinated pool.

It's the koi pond. The wall just past it is where she'll need to get to in order to receive the listening devices.

The FBI didn't think this through whatsoever. The koi pond is not a place Iris can be without being asked what she's doing there. Exploring, she'll have to say. A suspicious enough answer.

"Come, Iris." Esperanza keeps walking. "I'll show you the view on the other side of this hill."

They crest the hill and descend so the compound is out of sight. Another hill perhaps a hundred feet high is in front of them.

"Paulo calls this the tit. It's as far as we go."

Iris sees its likeness—the tall hill bulges higher than the others like a single breast. "Sounds good."

They march silently to the top. There are no Ficus trees anymore, just spiky shrubs that shade only their ankles. Iris realizes neither of them has remembered to bring a water bottle. Genius.

They couldn't hike any further if they wanted to. The hill isn't that high, but the climb feels like a ninety-degree angle. They're both panting with their hands on their knees when they're at the top. There's a breeze here, as cool and refreshing as a glass of water. There's a gorgeous view of the thorn forest. It stretches for miles, all the way to the shining sea. To the east is a town at the top of one of the mountains. There's a spattering of brightly colored buildings and what looks like a cell tower.

Iris looks back to the ocean but is too exhausted and stressed to see any beauty in it. She just holds her arms up so the breeze hits her pits. "Shit."

"*Sí*," Esperanza says and spits. "Shit."

They both find boulders to sit on and catch their breath. By the time they're cooled down, Esperanza extends an arm. She's pointing towards the sea. "Can you see those boats?"

Iris squints. She can see some structures on the shore and large ships beyond them. "Yeah. I see them."

"That's our port. There's farmland north and south of here. What product we send to America that doesn't go by train is shipped from there."

"And what product is that?"

Esperanza smiles. "Fairy dust."

Iris watches Esperanza. Her grin is boasting. Cruel.

"Do you have a job in your family's business?"

Her smile fades as her lips tighten. "What do you mean?"

"Do you work?"

She scrunches her face in disgust. "No," Esperanza laughs. "It is not a woman's place to work when she is wealthy. I manage social business."

"Oh."

"When I say I could do a better job than Paulo, that's just me saying he's doing a *shit* job. We have a half-brother, Santiago. He's who should lead this business when it leaves our uncle's hands. But never mind that."

Iris is surprised the FBI has been so stumped as to who leads this cartel. But then again, she's on the inside. And they may be willing to let Iris hear and see a lot if they don't intend to let her ever leave alive. The compound with its high wall and many trees and dozens of guards must make it impossible to surveil.

"Your work." Esperanza looks over at Iris. "You were a whore, yes?"

Iris has to blink away her shock before she can respond. Luckily, she's too hot already to blush more than she already is. "Who told you that?"

"As you say... a little birdie." She plucks a bit of branch off a bush and begins to tear it up with her fingers. "My brother."

"You don't know that because I was here at your ranch before?"

"No, Iris. It's not because you were here before."

She nods. Anger builds in her stomach. Esperanza is another rich bully, and Iris isn't going to take it—even if they could have her killed at the drop of a hat. "I was actually an assassin. That was my last job."

"You mean when you killed your husband?"

"Yeah." Iris makes a finger gun and points it at Esperanza. "I shot him right between the eyes." She shoots and flicks her wrist back with imaginary recoil.

Esperanza laughs, but it sounds faker than the last time. Iris made her uncomfortable. "When Paulo told me you were going to stay, I didn't know what to think. *Mankiller*. I thought we already had one tiger. I said, why do you need two, Paulo?"

"And what did he say to that?"

"I'm only joking. I never asked what he wanted with you."

"Really?"

Iris watches Esperanza's gaze move over the landscape. She's smiling. Loose. Suddenly her features all tighten in concern.

"We should get back," Esperanza says and stands abruptly. "It's only getting hotter."

Iris looks to where Esperanza had been staring. She sees it immediately—about a hundred feet from the base of the hill they're on is a pale splotch of color among the dark greenery of the shrubs.

Iris stands like the rock she's sitting on turned into a hot iron. She's looking at a corpse. "Holy shit."

Esperanza doesn't react, and Iris doesn't say another word as she starts to descend the other side of the "tit."

It's steep, and she quickly loses her footing. She's sliding down with her feet in front of her as Esperanza shouts after her.

"Iris!"

Iris still doesn't respond. She feels her dress tear and thorns slide her legs. When the ground levels out, she stands and tramples off trail to reach the body. She slows as she gets closer. The air buzzes with black flies.

The woman is naked. She doesn't appear Hispanic. Her hair is blonde and her skin milk white where it isn't red and scratched by thorns.

Iris feels her throat tighten as she sees a large floral tattoo across her shoulder. It's the woman from dinner last night. The one pulling on her earlobe who looked the most nervous. The woman's face is hidden, pressed into the ground.

Iris can hear her heart drum in her ears. It's quiet down here where she's protected from the breeze. There's just the sound of flies and Iris's feet crunching in the dirt.

A pool of blood expands out from the woman's head. It's been baked black by the sun. There isn't much of a smell, Iris realizes. Nor is the corpse bloated. Iris bends and moves the body gently by the shoulder so the face isn't pressed into the dirt.

By moving her head, Iris reveals the stone that punctured the woman's skull. From the looks of how her body is sprawled, it seems likely that she tripped.

Iris doesn't pretend to be a detective, but what happened to this woman seems clear enough. She was afraid enough to be running through this thorn forest naked and likely at night when she lost her footing.

Running from what? Iris hardly needs to ask the question before the answer appears obvious in her mind.

Paulo.

This woman is who those flashlights were looking for last night. She'd escaped. Not a tiger. Which points to an obvious fact: Paulo has captives, of which Iris might now be one.

"Oh my God." Iris turns over her shoulder to see Esperanza coming over to her. She takes long cautious steps and pinches the fabric of her dress up over her nose. "Iris, get away from there."

"Was this your friend?" Iris asks, still holding the woman's shoulder when she suddenly jumps back. The corpse takes a gasping breath, and her eyes roll back into her head.

"Shit!" Iris says, and her heart starts to pound harder. She's still alive.

It takes several seconds for Iris to recover her composure. She bends down again and shakes her shoulder ever so slightly. "Hey. Hey. Can you hear me?" She looks over to Esperanza. "What's her name?"

Esperanza has backed up. She stares down at Iris and this bleeding woman with shared disdain and juts her chin out. "She doesn't have a name." Then she begins walking back up the hill.

"Esperanza!" Iris lets the woman's shoulder down gently and follows her. "We've got to get her help."

"What the fuck do you think I'm doing? Going for my siesta?"

Iris wants to fire back, but she keeps her mouth shut for this woman's sake. "Do you have your phone on you?"

"There's no service out here."

Iris looks up at the cell tower on the mountain. She's not sure she believes that. "Fine, but one of us should stay here."

Esperanza pauses. "Then that should be me." She stares at Iris. The implication is clear: Iris isn't allowed on her own outside of the compound.

"That's fine. I can run and get help."

Esperanza glances at her smart watch. "It's fifteen minutes there and back. I imagine you'll be running. Call it ten. Be back in twenty minutes. Don't take any longer."

"I won't."

"And bring me something to drink."

"Of course."

Esperanza sighs and walks farther from the woman to sit on a stone that's partially in the shade of a lone Ficus.

Iris can see that the woman is moving now. She's gasping for air like a fish out of water. "You should really stay by her side."

Esperanza points at her own feet. "What does it look like I'm doing? Go!"

Iris hesitates a moment longer before turning on her heel and breaking into a run. As the thorns cut little razor scrapes into her legs, she pictures the woman's last moments before she fell. This slicing pain is what she felt.

The scuff of footsteps and her own ragged breathing is what she heard. Iris doesn't feel lucky to be alive. She's hit with an odd feeling that this is not the last time she will run through these thorns.

And it's her turn next to be forced naked, running into the night.

Mercy

The guard's expression is wary when Iris appears alone out of breath at the little pedestrian gate.

"*Doctora!*" Iris shouts, and he adjusts the rifle in his hand. He points the gun at her feet and asks a question in Spanish she can't understand a word of.

"Um... Paulo! I need Paulo."

He moves a finger to the trigger and takes a radio off his belt with his free hand. He speaks into it quietly and steps so his back is against the gate. Another guard responds on the radio.

"Wait," the guard says in English.

Iris paces impatiently, and the guard's eyes never leave her. Thankfully, Paulo is fast. He's running up the stone steps, and the guards following him are several steps behind and sweating. They evidently don't play tennis every morning.

Paulo speaks as the guard lets him through the gate. "My sister... Is she okay?" he says with a lack of concern. It's like he's half expecting, and maybe even hoping, Iris is going to say she fell off a cliff.

"Esperanza is fine."

"Hmm." He tilts his head up.

"We found a woman. She's badly hurt."

"White woman?"

"Yeah."

"Oh, Iris." He steps forward and squeezes her shoulder. "You are a godsend. *Donde?* Where is she?"

"Esperanza stayed by her side. She's just at the bottom of the...tit."

"Ahh. Life, it writes itself. You'll understand. Come! Show us." Paulo starts walking and appears to translate everything Iris said to his men.

Paulo, Iris, and two guards start back in a trot. When they get back and get down to the other side of the tit, Esperanza no longer sits.

"What took you so long, Iris?"

Iris doesn't bother to respond. Paulo doesn't let her anyway. He's already breaking his rule and talking to Esperanza in Spanish. Then he starts toward the injured woman.

"You don't have any water?" asks Esperanza.

Iris hasn't had any either, and she was the one doing the running. She brushes past Esperanza towards the woman but suddenly freezes. She can't comprehend what she sees.

Something is wrong.

Esperanza comes up behind Iris's shoulder and speaks into her ear. "She didn't make it."

Iris can see why. Fresh blood stains the dirt. A new hole has appeared in this woman's head. She's been finished off with the same stone she fell on.

"She would've made it, I think," Esperanza hisses, "if you were *quicker*."

Whore

Iris sits under the stream of her shower. Paulo said the girl's name was Nadia. He said she got paranoid when high and must've got lost last night. He said she was here for entertainment, and Iris takes the hint.

She was a prostitute from eastern Europe, probably. But she didn't just wander off high. She looked frightened at the dinner table last night. Alert. And as they walked back through the gate, Iris marveled at the wall and wondered how Nadia got over it. It's too smooth to scale, and the tangle of barbed wire at the top poses another problem even if you somehow did.

Iris can see why Paulo was looking for her inside of the compound all last night. It would've taken a plan to get over it, but why was she naked? Her clothes might've been torn from her body. Depending on what she wore, it was possible the thorns stripped her as she ran.

Iris spends the better part of an hour under the hot water. It never gets cool, and she sits next to the drain with her arms wrapped around her knees. Hearing about violence and seeing it are two completely different experiences.

She's not a stranger to it. She remembers pointing the handgun at Joseph and pulling the trigger. But she can't imagine picking up a stone and taking it to a wounded woman's head.

Iris pictures Esperanza as a black-haired little girl. She can see Paulo leading her around a barn and sneaking under a window to watch their father cut men's throats. They grew up with this.

Iris should never have come here, but she can't help but remember she thought Augusta would be waiting for her. Now she pictures her white hair sticking up from the dirt. Her corpse half-buried somewhere in the thorn forest.

She's trying to decide what to do, when suddenly the answer becomes clear—she'll do what she promised the FBI she would. Before this dead girl, she wasn't dead set on helping them. She didn't want to collect the hardware and risk her life to plant listening devices.

She figured she'd run off with Augusta as soon as she got here. That this would be a little pit stop to freedom.

It was selfish, but she didn't want to risk being hanged with her own intestines so the federal government could notch a win in their belt. So what if they catch Manny? This cartel will continue to exist. It will be run by Paulo or Santiago, and the killing will go on.

Iris has made up her mind. Once she plants the bugs the FBI leaves her, she's gone. She'll find a way over the wall herself. She knows the leader is Manny. It's obvious here from the inside, and Iris will tell them so. She'll tell them about the girl as well. Nadia.

Iris has a feeling that drugs aren't the only thing Paulo traffics. Augusta said it was Joseph and Paulo who started the prostitution rings throughout the South. He probably already had operations in Latin and South America before that began. Veronica comes into this somewhere. Iris suddenly remembers the Spanish-speaking woman who came into the apartment to inspect her when she was cuffed to the bed.

There's a connection to this cartel and her capture.

Iris hears a knock on the door to her guesthouse. She lifts her head but doesn't move. The knock doesn't come again. She stands and turns off the shower and then dries off in the bathroom.

"Hello?" she says once she's wrapped in a towel. She leaves the bathroom and opens the front door. There's no one there, but a note has been left on the step. Iris stoops over and picks it up. *Dinner at 6.*

She has a couple hours before then to plan how she's going to do it, but she's going to confront Paulo. It is time to ask questions. What will he say when she brings up Augusta's handwriting? Will he laugh at her?

The realization is creeping up on Iris that maybe she was just wrong. That it wasn't Augusta's handwriting. After all, she did compare the two in a hurry while her brain was still reeling from what she saw happen to Annabelle.

Iris debates getting dressed and going to find Paulo so the two can talk one-on-one, but she can't bring herself to leave the guesthouse again.

She gets changed and sits in bed. She puts the American news back on and turns the volume down until it's background noise, and then she pulls the sheet over her.

She knows she won't be able to sleep, but she doesn't want to face reality, either. She can't stop seeing Nadia's cracked skull. She pictures Esperanza kneeling over Nadia as the woman gasped for breath. Picking up that stone... lifting it over her head.

Birds squawk outside. The groundskeepers are shouting at one another in Spanish and laughing. Iris goes to the thermostat on the wall and cranks up the A/C so the fan whirls. Then she closes the blinds over the glass doors.

She manages to doze off, but before she's able to get into a deep sleep, a familiar voice begins to wake her.

"And I just want her to know women like me can't be stopped. There are stoppers and then there are movers."

Iris lifts her head from her pillow. One of her eyes is still shut. She sees Annabelle on the TV. She's in a hospital bed, but it isn't a rerun of the last interview she saw. Annabelle appears on a webcam. Her interviewer talks to her from a news studio.

"Iris is a stopper. It's about *self* for people like her. What do *I* get out of this outcome? What can *I* do to better my situation?" Annabelle talks with drawn-out syllables like an idiot trying to sound wise. Her voice is still scratchy. In fact, it sounds much worse. Iris bets she's bucking the doctor's advice by giving interviews. They are probably advising her to try not to talk at all.

"I'm of the doer class. We don't let selfish people get in our way. We pity them and put them to the side. Then we get back to work."

"Oh, you fucking go, girl boss," Iris says aloud and springs out of bed. She's already fuming. *Why is Annabelle even still talking about her?* Then she reads the banner at the bottom of the screen. It reads, *Iris Adler Prostitute Past?*

Her cheeks burn red. Her shoulders sink.

"So. So—" The interviewer is trying to interrupt her. He's a thin, graying man that Iris doesn't recognize. At least Annabelle isn't getting prime time anymore. "So Annabelle?"

"Yes?"

"What can you say specifically to reports coming from the Memphis police that Iris was involved in prostitution? Did anybody in your family *know* about that?"

There's a delay before Annabelle responds to the question. "No. Absolutely not. She played the part of perfect partner to our Joseph until he wanted a divorce. Probably because he found out about this past of hers on his own. She just wasn't going to let him get away from her without getting the money she was after."

"So you think this past now constitutes a motive to why she shot her husband? If she did?"

"Absolutely. What's puzzled the police is *why* Iris murdered Joseph. It's why they're not directly saying they're going to charge her. And I do think that's what this is. A motive. It's not something Iris wanted others to know about, obviously. She hid it from all of us in the family."

"And what do you have to say about the suspect the police currently have in custody for your poisoning. Dominic—"

"She paid him," Annabelle interrupts. "She has millions of dollars. She paid him to poison me. The police saying he likely did this independently is a *farce*. It's a joke, really. The fact that it's been revealed that Iris was a *prostitute* says everything you need to know." Annabelle looks off camera with a grimace of distaste.

"Right." The interviewer picks up a folder and clacks its bottom on his desk. He's clearly uncomfortable from the hate Annabelle doesn't bother to hide. "You've just been so strong through this. Thank you again for joining us. I think I speak for the country when I say we continue to wish you a speedy recovery."

"Thank you," Annabelle says, entitled.

Her feed is cut and the reporter signs off before it cuts to commercial break. Iris turns off the television and stares at her shadowy reflection on the black screen. Annabelle just said a lot of words to effectively say to the world that Iris was a gold-digging whore.

They believe her. Iris is the black widow. The criminal.

She wants to be angry. She wants to feel injured, but Iris suddenly feels seen. She sits back on the bed and then wraps herself in the sheets again. She's not tired anymore or angry.

She's just trapped.

Replaced

Iris waits until five to get out of bed. She's contemplating skipping dinner entirely. She can't see herself making small talk or taking any more of Esperanza's barbs without causing a scene.

She realizes she hasn't been this depressed since she moved to Sweet Blood after her brain damage. Maybe even longer.

She stands to go pee, and when she's done, she stares at her reflection. Her bruising is mostly gone. It's a shadow now. It almost looks like it could be a trick of the light. Nothing some concealer and foundation couldn't fix.

The thought gives Iris an idea. She goes to the clothes she's been brought and pulls out a plain black dress. It's like Esperanza gave her the ugliest clothes she could find, and then Iris realizes she probably did.

Esperanza is insecure. That's clear enough. She's not confident. She's just bitter. Maybe tonight Iris doesn't give Esperanza the choice to feel superior. She's looked like hell ever since fleeing Sweet Blood. She's yet to style this new blonde bob. She looks through the makeup she's been left.

Hair spray. Check. Hairdryer. Check. She'll be a half hour late to dinner, but it'll be worth it.

Besides, Iris thinks, it's best not to wallow in misery.

By the time she's done, her fingers are sore, and she's only just not lost her mind getting her hair to behave, but she hasn't looked this good in months.

The little black dress is a size too small, but instead of looking like she's in her mother's clothing, it tightens well across her butt. Iris smiles. Her lips are painted dark red. Her pale skin and bright hair contrast well but not too sharply with the dress. She's taken on the identity. Played along. They want a black widow, then she'll show them one.

It's past six thirty as she makes her way through the garden towards the dinner table that's set up at the pool. There's talking in Spanish, but as she gets closer the table goes quiet.

There's Paulo and Esperanza, but Uncle Manny is not at the table. There are two new faces Iris doesn't recognize.

One is a white girl, several years younger than Iris. She looks like a college kid. Twenty-one. Twenty-two. The other is a Hispanic man with darker skin and spiky black hair. He has a chubbier face that looks like he never grew out of his baby fat.

"Iris. We weren't sure you'd be joining us." Paulo stands and pulls out a chair to his right that has been reserved for her. "*Dios mio,*" he says and freezes as he really *sees* her.

Iris steps forward, and he extends his hand. Iris gives him hers, and he kisses the back of it. "You look incredible."

"Thank you."

Iris sits, a little wary. Paulo looks at her like she's something to eat. Maybe she'd made a miscalculation in dressing up. She was better flying under the radar as the frumpy fugitive girl.

"You like fish?" Paulo asks.

"Yeah."

"We are having red snapper tonight. It's being prepared the ancient way. Cooked in earth ovens with herbs and spices. And butter of course. This you will love. It melts in your mouth."

"Hmm." Iris scoots her chair in and looks at the younger girl. She's sitting in the exact same spot to Esperanza's left as Nadia was the night before. She looks like a replacement. Her eyes are just as alert. There is no sign she's drugged. This time Iris has the chance to talk to her.

"What's your name?"

Esperanza answers for her. "Sorry, Iris. Not everyone speaks English, you know."

"Oh."

The girl smiles awkwardly. It seems like she has an idea of what is being said.

"But I think Ana was just going in for the night, yes? She's had a long day traveling." Esperanza looks at the girl and then whispers in her ear. Iris thinks she hears English.

The girl nods and stands from the table. Then she gives a little bow and takes one of the garden paths that snakes behind the house. From what Iris can see, a guard doesn't follow her. She's headed towards the townhouses, not the main estate.

"She's a little young for dinnertime conversation," Esperanza says.

But she's not too young to be used for sex, Iris thinks, and despite skipping lunch, her appetite leaves her.

"She's quite the bitch, isn't she?" Paulo suddenly says.

Iris isn't sure she heard him right. "What's that?"

He picks up a bottle of beer and takes a sip. He sighs in satisfaction and then speaks again. "Your sister-in-law. The shit she said about you on the news... Disgusting. I always hated her, for the record. I'm sorry she's still with us."

Iris can't respond right away. She's too caught up on the fact that Paulo is speaking as if he was in the room with her when she watched Annabelle's interview. She shakes her head. "It's not surprising behavior. Don't worry about it."

"But she wasn't wrong, isn't that so?" Esperanza says. "You were just a whore, right?"

The table goes silent. The baby-faced man with spiky hair must speak English. He coughs awkwardly into a fist.

"In English, there are many more words that are more polite to describe the profession with, sister." Paulo takes another sip of his beer.

"Profession?" Esperanza says with a laugh.

Iris watches Esperanza's eyes travel from her forehead and down her black dress. Her nose wrinkles a little in envy. She seems to be even more bitter seeing Iris dressed up.

Iris almost wants to keep her mouth shut. Then she pictures Esperanza holding a bloody stone over her head.

"So, what's got you acting so childish? Is it because even with a nose job, you're still not even as hot as a whore?"

Paulo chokes on his beer. Esperanza wasn't ready to have it dished back. Her jaw drops for a moment before she pretends to have not heard.

The man to her right with the spiked hair is staring at Iris, unblinking, like she is something dangerous no one else at the table is taking seriously enough.

"Who's your friend?" Iris points at him, and Paulo speaks immediately. He's happy to fill the air.

"This is our stepbrother, Santiago. Santiago, Iris."

Santiago nods at Iris but doesn't say anything. He still doesn't blink.

"Santiago didn't go to boarding schools," says Paulo. "Our father married his mom when she was a single mother after she'd been widowed. He doesn't know much English."

"Esperanza said he was a half-brother."

Esperanza cuts in. "Stepbrother. Half-brother. Whatever the fuck it is in your language. I don't care."

The table is quiet again, when suddenly their eyes lift as there are footsteps coming from the direction Ana had left. It's their Uncle Manny. He wears a white suit with big gold rings bulging at his knuckles.

He walks along the length of the table until he gets to Paulo and then puts a hand on his shoulder. Paulo whispers something to him and stands. An argument begins in Spanish, but Paulo doesn't raise his voice.

It's Manny who is yelling while Paulo seems to quietly try to calm him. Iris is trying to catch a word in Spanish that she knows, something to give her a hint of what's going on, but before the argument continues, Manny lands a sharp slap on Paulo's cheek and walks off the way he'd came.

Paulo rubs his cheek with an amused expression. Even Esperanza, who had been silently stewing over Iris's barb, was now grinning.

Paulo sits back down. "Manny doesn't like it when I use the house for parties. He is going out of town for business tonight. I thought he was already gone. He must've seen the servants setting up."

Iris doesn't buy the excuse. That fight had something to do with the girls that are around here.

"This is the first I've heard of a party," says Iris.

"I was just trying not to be rude. It's a bachelor affair. I'd invite you, but...the clubhouse is boys only tonight."

Iris looks at the path Ana walked down. No doubt that girl is here to be prostituted. Nadia's replacement for the night.

Paulo points to get Iris's attention. "Anyway, you are no stranger to family feuds. Although, my uncle is more of a bull and your sister-in-law a tick."

"But you worked with her, didn't you?"

"What can I say? Business is business. But believe me, even when she was making me money, it was hard to stomach her."

Iris leans forward with her elbows on the table. "And did she help you traffic girls or drugs?"

There are more silent stares. Another awkward silence. Iris doubts they speak this openly about their operation when there's company, but these people don't deserve to not confront the ugly reality of what they do.

Paulo grins. "She worked in imports, generally."

"So both?"

He shrugs.

"And these European girls you have here... Are you shipping them off after you're done with them, or this a final destination?"

"I wouldn't be a good businessman if I didn't sample the product."

Iris has to make an effort to keep the hate from showing on her face. That's what these girls were to Paulo—product.

When one falls and splits her head open running for her life, that's just a cost of business. Iris can't cool down. She opens her mouth to say something she'll surely regret, when suddenly a train of waiters appears down the path.

The table watches as they each carry a large plate of steaming fish. They set one in front of each guest, and Iris stares down at hers.

It's a whole snapper. Its eye has turned white and gelatinous like a boiled egg. Its scales are a pinkish red. The steam smells like lemon and rosemary, but she pushes her plate back.

"Not hungry anymore?" Paulo asks, lifting his fork.

"No."

"Maybe we can get you some mac and cheese," Esperanza says mockingly and takes a tiny bite of fish.

Iris sighs. She's losing patience. Beating around the bush seems ridiculous. These people are all murderers, even if they like to pretend they're not at dinnertime. "Are these girls being shipped to the States?"

Paulo's mouth is full and it's Esperanza who answers. "Of course not. It's too risky there, thanks to you. The police are asking questions. They can't all be bought off in your country," she says this like it's a flaw in the American system. Perhaps it is when you want to be an oligarch.

"I want to get rid of her." Paulo wipes his mouth with his napkin. "Just so you know, Iris. Annabelle is not good for business. She's nothing like your mother-in-law."

This is the first mention of Augusta, and Iris's gulps. She's almost afraid of the answer, but she has to ask. "And Augusta... Is she here?"

Paulo frowns as he spears another bite of fish. "Pardon?"

"The letter you sent me... The handwriting was Augusta's."

"Ah. I see you do pay attention to details." Paulo narrows his eyes and nods. Apparently pleased with himself. "Some people told me I would have to be more obvious. That you wouldn't pick up on that. But I think you're far cleverer than a lot of people think."

"You didn't answer my question."

"Augusta? Alive? Come on... I was on the boat. We both saw how dark that water was."

Iris watches Paulo's face closely, but she can't read him. Esperanza's words come back to her. *It's all a game. Paulo's game.* "Then why was I invited here if Augusta didn't send the invitation?"

"I'm sorry..." Paulo points back and forth at himself and Iris with his fork. "Are we not friends?"

Iris goes quiet. The crickets have begun to chirp. A few night birds are calling to each other. It's all amplified by the silence at the table that Iris lets linger.

"No, Paulo."

"That's too bad. You're an interesting one. I think if you were a man, Iris, we'd be great friends."

"Uh-huh."

"But if we are not friends... Then yes, good question. What purpose do I have for keeping you around?"

The rest of the table has stopped eating. They watch Iris and Paulo. The waiters who stand nearby sense tension and watch them as well.

"I was hoping you'd answer that. Because I haven't the slightest clue."

"Hmm." Paulo touches his chin. "Have you never heard the expression in your language, keep your friends close, your enemies closer? You could hurt me, Iris. You know things others don't."

"Then why not kill me?"

Paulo takes a bite but suddenly stops chewing and tilts his head like he's had an epiphany. "I guess I never thought of that."

"Why are you being cute?"

"You shall see, Iris. Just be patient." And then he winks at her and starts to cut harder into the fish with his knife and fork.

Everyone else at the table goes back to their food, but Iris stays still. She's been used enough in her life to know when it's happening again. But for the life of her, Iris can't guess for what.

Rendezvous

Iris is going to get the listening hardware tonight. The FBI said they would give her three chances to be at the southeast wall around midnight. She'd have one more opportunity after this, but she needs it over with. A clear part of the contract she signed was planting those devices.

She doesn't think she can get away with just telling the FBI that the leader is a man with a potbelly and a mustache named Manny. They probably want recordings. Documents. She wonders what the FBI will think of Nadia's murder. Is that something they even care about? Nadia wasn't an American. She wasn't a shipment of fentanyl. They care about drugs, not foreign prostitutes.

She knows girls and whores are thought of as two separate things. Human and not. They are not equal.

Not to the law. Not to men, and definitely not to the sum of those two things—the United States government.

After dinner, Iris goes back to the guesthouse and plays with a cigarette as she thinks. She doesn't turn the television on again. She's done listening to Annabelle.

Her own anger isn't helping her sense of self-preservation. She's saying what she wants to say but, Iris thinks... but perhaps Paulo respects her for that.

He clearly doesn't care for prostitutes. Maybe the only reason she's being kept around *is* because he finds her interesting. He wants to keep the pseudo celebrity around for a bit before he's bored with her.

Iris keeps looking at the clock, and when it's 11:30, she puts the cigarette in her mouth and goes and lights it on the kitchenette's stove.

She walks out the front door in a nightgown and the same pink sneakers she got from Marshall's wife. She takes a light drag of the cigarette every minute or so. It's dark enough that anybody watching her wouldn't be able to see that she's not inhaling.

She can hear music coming from the main house. Bass thumps loudly. Behind the sound is the muted laughter of men. When Iris walks to where she can see the front of the house, there are half a dozen cars parked in the driveway.

There are Ferraris and Mercedes. A classic Mustang convertible. A lime green Porsche SUV that looks like one big, congealed ball of cartoon vomit.

Paulo's friends for the bachelor party apparently weren't invited to dinner. She hears them sing the lyrics together to the song that plays. There is only one guard in sight, and he stands smoking a cigarette by the front door.

Perfect—the smell of her own cigarette is masked.

She sticks to the shadows and tries her best to act like she's walking aimlessly. She ends up at the koi pond when her cigarette is halfway gone. She can see the dark-orange shadows of the fish under the water. A little waterfall gurgles into its center. She stays here for a full minute, pretending to be entranced, making sure no one followed her, and then makes her way over to the wall.

Iris opens her mouth to say the code phrase for them to toss over the bag, when she freezes. *She doesn't remember.* "Shit," Iris hisses aloud. "Um..." She looks around to make sure no one is watching, but it's too dark to be sure.

The FBI did pick an unlit corner of the property, but it also makes it impossible for Iris to see if she's being watched or not.

"What a lovely evening," Iris says. It was something like that. For all she can remember, that might've been the signal phrase verbatim.

No bag comes out of the darkness over the wall. It's quiet enough outside that Iris would hear it, she hopes, but the waterfall of the koi pond does act as white noise. If a soft bag landed in the bushes, she might not hear it.

She's about to repeat the phrase when someone steps out of the dark.

"That it is." It's Paulo, and right as he speaks, Iris sees something fly through the air out of the corner of her eye.

"Oh!" Paulo says and ducks. "Did you see that?"

Iris is still so terrified she can't move. She slowly blinks and lifts the cigarette up to her mouth. She takes a trembling puff. "See what?"

"I think it was a bat." Paulo has walked towards her now, and she can smell the beer on him. He's wearing a navy suit. Again, he is barefoot. He kicks at the bushes. "I've never seen a bat do that." He kneels and starts to paw through the leaves with his hands.

If he finds the bag, I'm dead.

"Paulo," Iris says with intention. Like she has something serious to say. He looks at her from a crouch and then stands. He's standing inches away from her. Iris brings the cigarette up and puts it in his mouth. He smiles and sucks. Then he blows the smoke up over his own face so it doesn't hit Iris. Her pulse rocks her chest.

He goes in for a kiss and puts her bottom lip between his and then pulls back with a bite and laughs.

"I didn't mean to stalk you. I just saw you wandering." He looks over her shoulder at the wall and then leans close to her ear. "I had to make sure where." He bites her earlobe, and Iris feels like she's going to explode. She can't do this with him. Not now. Not here in the grass.

Not anywhere.

He flicks her throat with his tongue, and Iris clenches a fist. He's drunk. There's a round rock about the size of an apple just a few feet away in some of the landscaping by the koi pond. She eyes it as he runs his tongue down her neck. She can feel the sour reek of beer being left like a snail trail.

He backs up and smacks his lips. "I should get back to the boys. I'm afraid I'm a little…" He looks down at his crotch. "Spent already this evening."

"That's okay."

Paulo takes a stumbling step backwards. "I'll see you."

"Yes."

He chuckles and sticks his hands in his pockets, and then he walks into the dark towards the house. Iris has no way of knowing if he's still there or not. His footsteps are silent on the grass. The foliage is too thick to see through. She waits for a minute and smokes. When the cigarette is burned down, she bends over to stub it out, and with her free hand she frantically pats the ground beneath the bush, looking for the bag.

She finds nothing but wood chips. If she's down here any longer, Paulo will know she's looking for something if he's watching. She moves her hand out, when she suddenly feels something on the grass.

It's the little bag. She flips it over so the elastic strap is facing her, and then she lifts her foot and pulls it up her leg at the same time as she stands.

She has no way to know for sure, but her action felt smooth. She thinks it probably doesn't matter, anyway. No one saw her. But just as she thinks it, a shadow moves on the other side of the pond.

It's Paulo. She sees his face illuminated in orange as he lights a cigarette. He exhales a plume of blue smoke and waves to her, but he doesn't wait for her to wave back.

He walks into the dark, and Iris can feel the wet spot his tongue left on her neck as the night breeze blows.

Bachelors

Iris follows Paulo to make sure he's going back to his party. She stays behind a tree while Paulo passes the guard at the entrance and goes back into the house. Did he know? Iris is afraid that as soon as he sobers up, he's going to put together what he'd seen.

Her time here is running out already. She can feel it.

She needs to plant the bugs tonight. She kneels and pulls back her nightgown so her thigh and the bag strapped to it are exposed. She rotates the bag and unzips it. There's all the hardware the FBI showed her during their meeting in the bathroom. But there's also a note and a touchscreen phone. There's a phone number on the note. Below that, it reads, *Text everything you have so far. Delete after sending.*

Iris reads it over again. *Text everything you have so far.* Iris doesn't have to wonder why they're impatient. They don't want to wait to hear a full report because they don't want to risk losing what she knows already.

They don't know if she's making it out of here alive.

She zips the bag closed and stands. She stays in the shadows as she walks into the back gardens by the pool. She can tell the party is in the living room, but she wouldn't be able to spy from the front without being seen by a guard.

She takes one of the stone paths around the house. Near the end of it, with the path to the tiger enclosure just across the road, Iris can see inside. There's a hedge in front of the window, and she climbs over it so she's pressed against the side of the house. Then she crouches and leans her head towards the glass so she can see in. Her eyes widen in shock. What Iris registers first is skin.

The living room is filled with naked women. She counts quickly. There are six. There's one black girl and another who looks Hispanic, while the other four are pale and white. Ana is among them, but the others she doesn't recognize. All of them have a sheen of sweat over their skin or have been covered in oil. They glisten under the light like goddesses.

The men are all Hispanic. They wear suits with no ties, and each has a woman by their side. Some of the women sit straight up, while others lie back on the giant sectional couch lazily. None of them speak.

The men are being too loud. They smoke, laugh, and push each other's shoulders playfully like boys. Paulo sits in the center. His stepbrother is seated closest to him.

Iris stares at the tattoo on the thigh of one of the white escorts. She has short black hair—shorter than Iris's bob. But that isn't what makes her hold her breath.

The tattoo on her thigh is of an eagle. *Adler*. It's like the one used to mark Iris. She squints to get a better look, when suddenly the girl crosses one leg over the other and the tattoo disappears from sight.

Surely these girls aren't part of the Adlers' sex trafficking network? Paulo could still be working with Annabelle. Iris realizes his talk at dinner was probably all for show. Why wouldn't he still be working with Annabelle? He even said earlier that business is business.

Girls are still being trafficked. Iris thinks of the private investigator's report and the trouble they're having finding girls who worked with Iris. Then there's the two who vanished with blood found in their bathroom. Katie and Jasmine, wasn't it? They're getting rid of the ones who know about Iris. Who know too much.

These girls are their replacements soon to be shipped to America to take their place.

Iris scans the other women for tattoos. She can see that some are inked, but she's too far away to tell what the tattoos are.

The black girl suddenly turns her head towards the window, and Iris ducks.

She sinks all the way to the ground below the window and takes a deep breath. She's struggling to keep it together. She hears a glass break inside, and then there's a roar of laughter from the men.

Iris is going into the house tonight. She's not just going to plant these bugs. She's going to try to talk to one of these girls.

One of them must speak some English.

She stays under the window for what she figures is a half hour. No guards seem to be patrolling the garden paths, and the party inside doesn't sound like it's dying down. For all she knows, it might be four in the morning before she gets the opportunity to sneak inside.

The one thing she has going for her is that Paulo and any of his friends who stay the night will be passed out drunk. Her hurdle will be avoiding the housekeepers, and that might not prove to be difficult either. They'll all be on the first floor cleaning up after the party, while she'll plant the devices on the second floor. All she has to do is get up and down one flight of stairs unseen.

Iris is sick of hearing the men yell and laugh. If she's going to have to wait for hours, she doesn't plan to spend the entire time lying under the window. She ducks and walks in a crouch back to the garden path, and once she's out of sight, she stands and begins to walk normally.

She crosses the road towards Lola's enclosure, and once there, she walks along its black fence. Tigers are mostly nocturnal, if she remembers right. Iris scans the grounds, looking for a set of glowing eyes, but she doesn't see anything.

The area is better lit than most of the grounds. There are no trees or bushes in the enclosure. It's mostly a wide-open space apart from the plastic structure in the center. When Iris reaches the far side of the enclosure, she stops walking. Lola is lapping water from a pond about the size of a kiddie pool. The big cat suddenly stops and brings its giant head up to stare at Iris. Its tail begins to flick up and down. But Iris is no longer looking at Lola.

It takes her a moment to be sure of what she sees. It's dark, after all. But her eyes have adjusted by now. There's no doubt that on the ground of the enclosure is a set of human legs.

There is no torso or head. Just the two pale legs still connected by a pelvis.

Nadia.

Lola seems to know where Iris is looking. The tiger walks over to the set of legs and picks an ankle up in her teeth. She looks over her shoulder at Iris and seems to gloat in her dinner. Then she walks slowly, dragging the legs behind her, into the total darkness of her structure.

Tiptoes

Iris is too bothered to go back and spy on the naked women and drunk men. She doesn't think she'd be able to keep her composure. She stays near the enclosure and at one point she jumps when there's a crack from the other side of the cage that sounds almost like a gunshot.

She can hear Lola munching and chewing and realizes the big cat must've broken one of Nadia's femurs with her massive jaws. She's a *feminista* in life, maybe, but food is food.

Iris sits on the grass, contemplating how long she has before she's cat food herself. It depends on whether Paulo truly has a plan for her or if she's a plaything he could get bored with at any moment.

Or, Iris thinks, if she gets caught planting these devices. At one point she realizes something is wrong. It's become dead silent outside. The music from inside has turned off.

She stays put for another ten minutes, and the silence is still uninterrupted. She gets to her feet and crosses the road to the house. There's the distant hum of something inside. A vacuum cleaner. She heads to the bush she hid behind to peer into the living room.

One housemaid is vacuuming, and another picks up trash. She doubts the men are asleep yet. Some are probably having one last run with the girls. It's still somewhat early—not yet two.

Iris crouches under the wall until the vacuuming stops and the living room lights turn off.

Somewhere in the house is the sound of exaggerated sex. A woman screams, but they're not cries of pain or pleasure. It's an act. Ego stroking.

It doesn't last long. After a couple minutes, the sound stops as suddenly as the vacuuming did. The house is silent. Iris watches a batch of the garden darken as more lights inside are turned off.

Iris doesn't wait any longer. She moves. She walks quickly towards the pool where the back door to the kitchen is. She's relieved to see the lights are out. She kicks her sneakers off and hides them behind a planter.

The door handle doesn't make any noise as she turns it. It's unlocked. She steps inside. Lucky for her the house is newer. It's all tile and marble. Even the stairs. In nothing but her socks, she moves as silently as a ghost.

She walks quickly towards the living room and front hall and takes the stairs two at a time. The upstairs hallway is lit, but she doesn't hear anyone. She goes to the poker room and grows nervous when she sees it hasn't been cleaned yet.

There are beer bottles littering the table and a giant ceramic ashtray stuffed full of cigars. She starts to walk quickly out the opposite door towards the upstairs office, when she stops.

There's a black pistol resting on the armrest of the leather sofa. Iris looks over her shoulder and walks closer to the gun. She picks it up.

She knows a little about guns now. The basics. There's a safety on the slide, but below that, near the trigger guard, is another button. She holds it down and the magazine ejects into her hand.

It's heavy and filled with bullets. She slaps it back in and puts the gun down. She doesn't want to take it. If a gun went missing, they were liable to search her and her room all over again.

She's about to leave when she pauses. There's something else on the cushion of the sofa. It glints like gold in the light, but it's not blonde.

It's a woman's strand of hair, about twenty inches long. Iris picks it up with a pinch and looks at it under the light.

Her heart races. She moves her head left and right like an idiot to make sure it's not a trick of the light, but it's not.

The hair is white.

"Augusta?" Iris says aloud, and then there's the clap of a door shutting down the hall the way she'd come. She scrambles out the poker room and walks the rest of the way down the marble hall to the office at the end. She opens the door and shuts it gently behind her.

It's dark in here—pitch black apart from the square of the window. She pauses and lets her eyes adjust to the dark. There is no more noise from down the hall, and she begins to calm down. She forgets about the white hair. She can think about that when she's out of this house.

She takes the bag off her leg and unzips it, and then she walks to where it's brightest by the window. She empties the listening bugs into her palm. There are three. Each is the size of a dime.

They're simple enough to set up—there's a bit of plastic on the back that peels back to reveal an adhesive strip that will stick to almost anything. The FBI said there's no switch to flip or anything.

She feels under the office chair and manages to put one into the plastic covering that the height adjuster lever sticks out from. It's the perfect place, completely hidden. She almost doesn't want to risk hiding the others but climbs onto the desk and sticks one more inside a fogged light fixture in the ceiling.

She steps down, wipes the desk off in case she left footprints, and then goes over to the wall and feels until she finds a light switch. When they come on, the bug doesn't cast a shadow in the fixture. That's it. She's done.

She turns the lights off and leaves the office.

When Iris passes back through the poker room, she stops again. There's no one here, but the light is still on. Her eyes narrow on the sofa. The only thing that changed is that the black pistol is gone.

Contact

Iris gets back to her guesthouse, and from the clock on the microwave, she sees it's only 2:15. She pulls out the phone the FBI gave her and plugs in the number they left for her into texts.

She sums up the events as best she can. She focuses on Uncle Manny, his description, altercation with Paulo, and the fact that from inside the compound, there is no question as to who the boss is.

She mentions the girls, likelihood of sex trafficking, and the death of Nadia. She decides to leave out the part that her body was fed to a tiger.

She hits send and then deletes the text message a minute later.

She sends another that reads, *I am not safe. When am I getting out here?*

The response she gets mere seconds later isn't reassuring. *Soon. Sit tight.*

Iris deletes both messages and puts the phone down. Her ears begin to ring. She asks herself a single question: Does she trust the FBI to get her out of here?

The answer is absolutely not. Alexi didn't seem incompetent, but it was his guilt in the bathroom that alerted Iris that something was wrong. He couldn't hide it—they were sending her on a suicide mission.

Iris's thoughts deteriorate as she hears a rumbling in the distance. Something groans, hisses as it quiets, and then groans again. It's a truck. A big one. And it's already in the compound.

It's the raid.

Iris springs up and goes to put on her shoes. She's realizing how delusional she's being as she opens the door. There are no gunshots. Nobody yells. If this were a raid, the cartel would not just go quietly. She keeps walking through the garden and towards the front of the house.

There is a semitruck idling in the front of the driveway. It hauls a full-size orange shipping container. The guard who was by the front door during the party is opening the metal latches on the back and swings open the container doors.

The girls she'd seen in the living room walk around from the other side of the house. They must have been staying at the townhouses.

They're clothed this time. All six girls who were at the party walk across the driveway. They're not dressed like women of the night. They're in lounge clothes. Sweatpants and pajamas.

A few of them carry plastic bags that presumably carry their things. They're given a hand into the back of the container, and then the guard latches it shut and pulls out a can of spray paint.

He paints a big number six on the door in a smooth arch like he's done this dozens of times before and then yells something towards the driver. The truck rumbles forward. A black pillar of diesel exhaust shoots from the tail pipe that sticks up over the cab.

Paulo wasn't lying. He was just sampling the goods before they went to market. The truck drives down the road, and Iris stays in the shadows, watching it long after it disappears.

Was she transported like this? Iris tries to picture the darkness. To imagine the engine roaring just on the other side of the metal container. But there's nothing. No, Iris thinks, she was never trafficked like this.

Demands

It's three a.m. when she finally gets to sleep, but it's not long before she's up again. There was a sound like the door to her guesthouse closing. It's enough to make Iris sit up in bed.

She jolts as she sees a shadow sitting by in the dark next to her feet.

"Turn on your light."

She hears Paulo's voice and takes a moment to realize he's talking about the lamp on her nightstand. She reaches over and twists its plastic switch.

Paulo appears. He looks haggard. He's still wearing his suit, and it's wrinkled to hell. His thick hair is a wavy mess. He puts on his signature grin. "Sorry to bother you so late, *señora*."

He pats her legs, and she recoils. In his other hand is the black pistol she'd seen in the poker room.

She waits for him to speak again, but he seems content letting the silence grow. "What do you want?"

"Your phone."

Iris freezes.

"Come on. Where is it?"

Iris looks around, thinking about what to do, when Paulo thunders, "Show me the fucking phone!"

Iris pulls the bag the FBI gave her out from under her pillow and holds it out.

"Open it yourself." He points the pistol at her.

She unzips it and takes the phone out slowly.

Paulo snatches it from her and starts to scroll through it. "You got this tonight?"

"Yes."

"What have you told them?"

"Nothing yet."

He tilts his head at her and widens his eyes crazily. His expression says enough. *Lie to me, you die.*

"I told them that there was a girl who died trying to escape. The names of who was here. The number of people."

"And this is who? DEA? FBI?"

"FBI."

Paulo nods. "You're going to call them right now." Paulo sniffles hard, like he's been snorting drugs. "You're going to call them and say I'm on my way to Mexico City. That I said I was going to stop at a town called San Marcos before going to the airport. That there's some kind of deal happening there." He sniffles again.

"Okay, but I can only text."

"Then fucking text it!" He tosses the phone at her face, and it clocks her in the corner of the eye.

"Fuck!" Iris presses her palm against where it hit. She uses her other hand to pick up the phone and starts to text.

"And say I have light security. That I went there in only one car."

"Okay." Iris starts to text with both hands and keeps her injured eye closed. Before she hits send, she shows him the message.

Paulo nods. "Okay." He takes the phone, presses send, and pockets it. "I'm disappointed in you, Iris."

"They were going to arrest me if I didn't agree."

"And you didn't think to tell me? We could've double-crossed them the whole time. Let me guess... They said you'd be free if you did this? No charges?"

"Yeah."

"I invited you into my home, only for you to rat on my family."

Iris looks at the bed sheets.

Paulo grabs her by the chin. "*Look* at me, Iris."

She glances up at his dark-brown eyes. "This can be salvaged. Lucky for you." He shoves her by the jaw and stands from the bed.

Iris watches him walk to the counter and pick up a glass with clear liquid. He takes something out of his suit coat. A pill. He twists it in two and taps the contents into the glass. Then he takes out another and does the same thing again. He mixes the drink with his finger, takes it out, sucks it clean, and then spits on the floor.

He walks back to Iris and holds out the glass. "Drink."

She takes the glass but only stares at it.

"We've got to move you, and I don't want you remembering where. You lost that privilege."

Iris still hesitates, and he raises the pistol. She can see the bullet down the barrel—a faint flash of bronze. This time there won't be a ricochet. She considers the possibility that the liquid in the glass is poisoned but doesn't think it's likely.

Paulo can make as big of a mess of her murder as he wants. If he wanted her dead, she thinks he'd just shoot her right now.

Iris tilts the glass back and tries to let it fall down her throat without tasting it. She brings the glass down and sucks air into her mouth. It's a chemically, chalky concoction. It makes whatever Tilda put into her cold medicine cocktails taste pleasant.

Iris coughs and gags.

"Keep it down," Paulo orders.

Iris holds her breath and flexes every muscle in her body to keep from vomiting.

"Good girl." Paulo steps back and looks at his watch.

Iris already feels the room begin to move around her. The glass falls from her hand onto the bed sheets.

"Go to sleep, Iris," Paulo says, his voice more distant.

She thinks it's just the drugs making him sound farther away until she hears the front door shut. He's already left. She stands. She's going to the sink to make herself throw up, but as soon as she's upright, her feet can't find the ground.

Iris falls hard.

Something should hurt, but she can't feel a thing. The ceiling fan spins above her, and it's the last thing she sees before the black begins to creep in from every corner of her vision, and then she's gone.

Thunderstorms

Iris wakes to the sound of rain and a pain in her back. The floor is hard beneath her. Tile. Ceiling fan.

She looks around. She's still in the guesthouse.

She hasn't moved an inch.

She gets to her knees and then stands. Her body buzzes. Her head is foggy. The feeling is somewhere between getting wrecked by a long midday nap and a wicked hangover. It looks like early morning from the weak gray light, but with the rain and overcast sky, it could be much later.

Iris goes to the bathroom and pees like this is any old morning and then asks herself if last night was a nightmare.

But the empty glass of whatever she drank is still in the sheets where she dropped it. The bag the FBI gave her sits empty next to it. Paulo never found the third bug she didn't plant. He didn't make her empty the rest of the bag. Iris walks over to it and grabs the Post-it Note that has the FBI's number on it. She holds it in her fist as she thinks.

Paulo was sloppy. Then again, he was far from sober last night. Is that why she's here this morning? Did he just forget about her? She has a feeling he's far from the estate by now. But he had said she was going to be taken somewhere else.

Iris puts on the pair of jeans she came here in and her heather gray sweater that had been washed. What she doesn't have in her room is a raincoat.

She opens the front door. It's not a downpour. Right now, it's only a drizzle, but from the size of the puddles spread throughout the gardens, she knows it must've been raining harder at some point while she was asleep.

Iris puts on her shoes and starts towards the house. There is no birdsong. No sound at all apart from the water dripping from branches and leaves. She pauses when she sees the back door to the kitchen is wide open. There's water that's been blown in from the storm shining on the tiles.

She doesn't need to look further to know that the entire estate has likely been abandoned. No servants. No groundskeepers. No guards.

She goes inside. The lights are off, and with the clouds, it's dark inside. She tries the lights, but when she flips them, nothing turns on. She looks around the kitchen to see that the LED screens on all the electronics are black.

The power is out. Was it that way in her guest house? Iris can't remember if the ceiling fan was spinning above her or not when she woke up.

She walks into the house and through the short hall to the living room. The rugs still have marks on it from where the vacuum was run.

Nobody has been here since last night. She makes her way upstairs to see that the poker room has been cleaned. The white strand of hair she left on the table is gone. The room smells of lemon cleaner. Iris doesn't want to open any of the bedroom doors without announcing herself. "Hello?" she says loudly.

There's no response. Iris opens the door to the master. The curtains of the four-post frame are flung back, revealing an unmade bed. There's a pair of pink women's underwear on the floor.

"Hello?" Iris says again and steps into the bathroom with the copper tub. It looks the same as when she was last in here. Untouched. Immaculate.

She leaves the master and opens the bedroom doors one by one. Some of the beds are made, others not, but each room has a similar layout—there's a queen-sized bed in its center, windows to the garden behind it, and a private bathroom off to the side. The rugs and wall art are different, but for the most part, the rooms have the similar look of a hotel.

She comes to the upstairs office, and the first thing she does is check if the bugs are still there. She reaches under the chair and finds the first one in place and then stands on the desk. The second hasn't been moved either.

Iris gets down and stands still in the middle of the office. There must be a hidden camera in her room. Paulo must've seen her use the phone. What was she thinking? There's no obvious place for there to be one in the guesthouse, but for all she knows, there could be one hidden in the screen on the microwave.

Iris curses and looks around the office. There are some documents in Spanish on the desk. There's a Post-it Note on top which reads, *Urgente!*

Iris flips through the papers. There are some tables with dollar amounts in them. On the last page is a signature line. The name is printed—*Emmanuel Barrera.*

Manny. That's the name the FBI mentioned. It's him, alive. Iris isn't going to flee from here empty-handed. She grabs the documents and turns to leave, but just as she does, she pauses in front of the window.

She sees something. It's not movement that catches her eye—all the trees and bushes are swaying in the breeze.

It's Lola's enclosure. There's an open gap in the black fence where the gate is supposed to be. It blows open, back and forth in the wind, and from where Iris stands, the tiger is nowhere in sight.

Bait

Iris feels like the one who's in a cage now. She remembers what Esperanza had said about Paulo playing games. This feels like some kind of rich man's hunting sport.

Leave Iris alone in the compound, and cue the hidden cameras.

But Paulo fled from the FBI. They had real reason to go. Maybe she's not being watched. Maybe Paulo's plan was to forget about Iris and let the tiger take care of her.

Iris doesn't plan to believe their comments that Lola's only interested in eating men. She's already seen that when it comes to a meal, she's indifferent.

She goes downstairs and heads past the kitchen into a part of the house she hasn't been to. There's a large mudroom with a tiled floor.

There are doorless wooden lockers, piles of shoes, and two sets of washers and dryers. She finds a navy raincoat in a men's size and puts it on. Then Iris takes a small black Adidas duffel bag off a coat hook. She unzips it to find it empty, and she stuffs in the papers she's taken from upstairs and then goes into the kitchen.

Her gaze is drawn to the window, where she can see the garden. She expects to see a blur of orange and black. That long tail flicking maliciously. She's still numb from whatever cocktail of drugs she was fed, but there is a feeling in her spine that skitters up the back of her neck with a tingle.

It's an anxiety she hasn't felt before, an ancient fear: She is being hunted by something that wants to eat her.

But this is the time when she should move. Tigers are far more active at night. She'll head into the dry forest towards the town she'd seen in the distance. The one on the mountain with the cell tower. It's not much of a plan, but it's better than waiting around to get eaten by a big cat.

She goes to the fridge and opens it. She chugs what's left of a glass container of fresh-squeezed orange juice and sets it back. Then she takes out a liter container of milk out of the fridge, goes over to the sink, dumps it out, and fills it with water.

Outside, it's cool and wet, but for all she knows, it may be blistering hot in an hour. She drinks more water from the liter bottle and then holds it back under the faucet. She twists the cap on, tilts it upside down to make sure it's not leaking, and stuffs it into the duffel.

She steps into the food pantry. It's the size of some of the kitchens Iris has been in, but the room is windowless, and with the power out, it's almost too dark for her to see anything.

She grabs a box of full-size Snickers bars from a shelf and dumps it into the bag. She tosses the empty cardboard onto the ground. There isn't much for healthy snacks that she can see. It's mostly canned goods and ingredients in glass jars.

Paulo's family is so rich they mostly only eat prepared meals. Iris adds some apples to the duffel and zips it up. She doesn't plan to be in the forest for long, but she doesn't want to worry about hunger when her head is fuzzy enough as it is.

Iris lifts the duffel's strap so it's over her shoulder and goes to the front door. She opens it and stares out at the driveway. The rain has stopped and been replaced with a violent wind.

The trees rock and the breeze booms through their leaves when it gusts.

Iris thinks about what she should do. She might be able to find a gun if she searches the other structures on the property. There's no way they took everything with them during a hasty departure into the night. The problem is that searching the buildings would mean more time wandering the property with Lola around.

Iris sets one goal—when she's outside, get to the other side of the wall as fast as she possibly can.

She shuts the front door, steps forward, and looks right and left. There's nothing there. The wind blows towards the house from the direction of the gate. Lola would only be able to sniff Iris out if she is behind her, which she likely is since most of the compound stretches behind the house. Great.

Iris sighs and breaks into a trot with the duffel bouncing on her shoulder. She keeps her head on a swivel, but seeing Lola likely wouldn't change the outcome of an encounter with her.

She's out of breath and already sweating and humid beneath her raincoat when she reaches the front gate.

Iris looks up at it. There is a bar on the bottom that runs horizontally that she can set her feet on, but the metal bars that make up the fence run vertically. It can't be easily scaled.

There is no pedestrian gate or guard house. There are no trees that she can climb and then jump out of to fall on the other side of the wall. All the trees have been well pruned, and their branches don't begin until about twelve feet up their trunks.

"Shit, shit, shit," Iris says and spins around, looking at the road she walked on. The breeze blows directly against her back. Her scent is being carried over the entire compound. She tries to think, but the fear and brain fog don't let her focus on the problem at hand.

She leans against the bars of the gate and breathes. Lola doesn't appear stalking down the road. With a full belly from last night's meal and the bad weather, Iris tries to assure herself that the tiger's probably fast asleep.

Three options appear in her head. She could walk around the entire perimeter of the compound looking for a tree to climb to hop over. She could go back to the house and look for a keycard like Esperanza used to open the gate yesterday, or she could start looking for a ladder.

She likes the keycard idea best. She likes the safety she feels when she's inside. Walking the entire perimeter feels foolish, and a ladder would likely be found in one of the buildings behind her guesthouse, which is smack dab in the middle of the property. Then she'd have to carry the thing half a mile.

She starts back up the road and is almost to the house when she ducks in panic. A growl sounds behind the wind. It takes a full second for her drugged brain to realize the sound is mechanical.

It's an engine. Iris stands up straight and turns around. There's a truck coming down the road. She can hear the rise and fall of its engine as it shifts gears, climbing up the windy road just as she did last night.

She starts back towards the gate and positions herself behind the wall so she's only watching the road ahead with one eye.

Sure enough, it's the same truck pulling a shipping container behind it. Iris scrambles away from the gate and gets behind a tree. She hears the engine rattle as the truck idles. They're stopped in front of the gate.

She hears the cab door shut, and suddenly the black gate begins to swing open. The long nose of the semi comes into view as the truck crawls forward. When the container clears the gate, it immediately begins to close behind the truck. But the gate doesn't crawl. It glides closed, and Iris can't hesitate.

She sprints out from behind the tree and throws herself through the sliver of opening before the gate latches. She falls flat on the wet road and spins, leaning on her elbows to look up and see if the truck has stopped, but there's no indication they saw her. The truck creeps on up the road, and she can see the same number spray painted on the door of the orange container. Six.

She wonders if they are coming back to make her a seventh. Perhaps Paulo underestimated how long the drugs would keep her out.

She stands and brushes the dirt and rocks that have stuck to her palms off on her jeans. She doesn't plan to walk down the main road she came in from. This is cartel country.

The police can't be trusted. Neither can most of the farmers. No one is going to shelter Iris when they know that their entire family could be strung up by their organs for doing so.

Iris has already done everything she needed to do for the FBI. She can get out of here. All she needs to do is find a phone. There could have been one in the house, Iris realizes. Maybe in the townhouses. But that would mean maybe meeting Lola.

She's too distracted by her own thoughts to realize something is wrong. The sound of the engine is back to an idle, but the truck isn't at the house yet. It's stopped on the road.

The passenger door to the cab hangs open.

In the middle of the road, a man is pointing a rifle at her. It's her drugged brain that keeps her frozen in place, even as the muzzle flashes.

Then comes the crack of the bullet. There's a whizz and a chunk of road is flung into the air. She starts to run but trips. She takes wide, wobbling steps and keeps herself from falling over. Then she finds her footing, and her feet soon pound evenly under her and Iris is running for her life.

Run

Iris goes right and follows the compound wall north. She's going in the same direction Nadia was running, only Iris is going to go east, inland.

If she's getting anywhere, it's not going to be by going through the thorn forest. She needs to stick to the Ficus trees.

She runs for what she thinks may be fifteen minutes before she stops and catches her breath. She's been going at a slight incline up into the hills, and she has a good vantage point from where she is. The compound is below her now, but the truck is nowhere in sight.

Iris frowns. She didn't hear them drive away, but with the wind gusting in the trees around her and her heavy breathing, it's entirely possible she didn't hear it.

It has to be possible, she realizes. Her gaze sweeps the compound, and as big and tree covered as it is, there aren't many places to hide a seventy-foot truck and trailer.

She sits on the ground and opens her duffel bag. She unscrews the cap to her water and takes some gulps. She tosses it back in and zips it up with a quick flick of her wrist. Then she surveys the country below her.

Iris doesn't have a plan that goes further than making it to the small village with the cell tower she saw and saying *teléfono.*

She doesn't have money to barter with, but if she approaches someone clean and calm, maybe they will think she's just an extremely foolish tourist and not a fugitive from the cartel. That or she could try to steal a phone. She gets to her feet and starts walking instead of running. She looks at the ground, and while wet, thankfully it's not muddy enough for her to leave an obvious trail of footprints.

She keeps walking up and over the next ridge. She thought the little village would be visible from here, but the landscape bowls immediately into a little valley. It's the hill on the other side of it that she'll have to get to the top of in order to see the buildings.

The valley floor is full of Ficus trees and is perfectly halved by the brown scar of a creek. It's running high and quick from the rain, and Iris figures if she follows the water, she'll find farms along the banks once she's out of the valley. But that's likely the same direction the cartel is anticipating she'll end up. She decides she'll head straight across the valley and keep climbing.

The clouds begin to part as she starts down into the valley. The sun comes out, and the wind begins to lighten. At first, it makes for a pleasant walk, but in another half hour, the wind and clouds are gone entirely.

From the height and heat of the sun, Iris can guess it's roughly midafternoon, maybe three o'clock. The sunshine starts cooking the water in the air, on the leaves, and what's puddled on the ground, and soon it feels like Iris is walking through soup.

She takes off her raincoat and her sweater and puts both in the duffel. Her T-shirt is soaked in sweat in just several minutes, but at least she's cooler.

Her body odor is sour and unfamiliar. It's the drugs she was given making their way out of her system. She pauses again and looks at the forest in front of her.

It's not sparse and scrubby woodland like the terrain around the compound. The forest foliage on the valley floor is thicker than that on the hills, and it has come alive since the storm. As Iris begins to walk, birds come out and scream at one another. Little squirrels skitter up and down the trees and join the chorus as they shout at Iris as she passes.

Everything seems angry. Violent. Or, Iris thinks, she's just seeing the world through the lens of just being shot at and hunted by a tiger.

"Just breathe. Just walk," she says while ducking a branch. She keeps talking to herself quietly. The sound is an anchor in this noisy forest. The heat gives an unreal feeling to everything. She can feel the heavy air part around her as she walks.

It takes her longer than she had hoped it would to reach the creek, which means she doubts she walked in a straight line. Now that she doesn't have the height of the hills, she can't tell if she veered right or left. To get lost means dying for sure.

She looks up and down the creek. Its stream is only about ten feet at its widest, and there are places where it narrows to just six. But she doesn't want to have to attempt a long jump. She follows the bank back to where it's narrowest and tosses her duffel bag over. Then she takes a few running steps and casually leaps across.

She picks up her duffel in stride and slings it over her shoulder. She thinks she likely veered right while she walked. *Towards* where she expects there to be road access. Towards where the cartel will be coming in to find her.

Now, she purposely veers left. She didn't think the valley was much more than a mile across, but after a half hour of walking, she begins to grow nervous. The forest floor stays flat, and Iris expects that any minute she's going to realize she's walked in a circle and come across the creek again, but finally she sees the trees in front of her begin to rise on sloped earth.

She's so excited to see the hill that she climbs quickly, and at times where it's steep, on all fours. She climbs up and up, and when she reaches a rock ledge clear of trees, she looks back down into the valley. She watches the forest darken beneath her. It's sudden. The dark is spreading at a speed not unlike a cloud eclipsing the sun. Iris turns east. The sun is dipping under the rim of the valley. The light leaves here early, but she should find it again as she climbs.

She positions herself with her back to a tree so she's not in the open, and despite being more nauseated than hungry, she makes herself eat a Snickers bar. She crumbles the wrapper in her fist as she chews the last bite and leans out from behind the tree to scour the valley.

Birds dart over the treetops. A black vulture loops in tight circles, but from what Iris can tell, he's not circling the dead. She's about to stand, when she pauses. There's movement by the creek.

It's far from her, but she can see clearly enough. Two men walk slowly. She thinks they're by the narrowing where she hopped the creek. They inspect the ground and then walk onward in her direction.

She would've left prints from the impact of when she jumped and landed on the other side. Iris realizes with a cold fear that her hunters are smart. They probably followed the length of the entire creek looking for where the ground would show her leap.

But what bothers her the most is how slow they are walking. There is no rush.

Slow, deliberate steps. It's as if they know they're going to get her eventually, no matter how far she runs.

Dark

Iris is driven by panic. She doesn't try to stay out of sight as she climbs the hill. She doesn't conserve her energy. By the time she passes the trees at the top, she's gasping for breath and her legs burn so badly she has to cling to a tree branch to stand.

She looks up, expecting to see the little village and cell tower in the distance clinging to the mountainside, but her bearings are all wrong.

The village on the hill she'd seen with Esperanza is nowhere in sight. She steps out of the trees into an open field. The forest is gone. The landscape ahead of her is a type of shrubby plain with massive boulders sticking up out of it. Dead ahead, little mountains rise miles away in the distance.

To her right, east, the forest hugs the edge of this plain, and to her left, west, is a rocky ridge that is several hundred feet high, but not as tall as the mountains ahead of her. There are places where the ridge is vertical, and she wouldn't be able to simply hike up it. She'd have to work her way up sideways.

It doesn't make sense, she thinks. Iris realizes that when she went on her hike with Esperanza, they must've ended up more due west than she realized. The walk there had been uphill and hard, and she was looking at her feet most of the time. When she ran back, she was too panicked after finding Nadia's body to orient herself. She was wrong about where the village was.

Iris has no idea where the hell she is. The terrain in front of her is flat enough that if she doesn't walk low, she'll be easily spotted.

Iris stops trying to orientate herself and remembers she's being hunted. She starts moving forward.

The sun is visible again and the breeze is once again strong, but at least out of the forest, it's much less humid. Iris walks so she'll be blocked by boulders when the two men enter the plain where she did. She can see why there's no more Ficus trees. The ground here is all rock.

The bushes that grow have shallow, sprawling roots that run over the stone and into pockets of earth.

She's only been walking ten minutes when she jumps as something rattles a few feet to her left. A fat rattlesnake lies coiled. Its sharp, scaly head follows her as she keeps walking.

Great. Iris won't be so confident about her footing if she has to run again.

She hasn't given up on making it to this village. She has an idea of where it is and grows confident that it's just over the next hill, a little more west now. But she knows how that went last time.

She walks for an hour and sees another three rattlesnakes getting the last of the evening sun. The last one she sees slithers down between a split in a rock.

It's already getting to be evening, and when the sun dips below the tree line to the east, the plain goes from warm golden light to being cast in shadow in only a few minutes.

It's immediately cooler, and in another half hour, Iris realizes she's going to have to put her sweatshirt on and find a place to settle in for the night. She decides to abandon going west. The ridge she'd have to climb is too open and too steep to climb at night.

She makes her way for another mile west towards the distant tree line where the plain dips into forest again. She's still most of a mile away when she finds herself in a natural courtyard of tan boulders. There's an area about half the size of a tennis court that's blocked off from the rest of the plain. There are four boulders, or maybe, Iris thinks, rock formations. They're long—about the size of school buses, and two are sort of shaped like Tennessee.

It's cozy blocked in by these boulders. There are many wide entrances between the stones, so it's not like she'd be easily trapped. Iris opens her duffel bag and takes out the water and the apples she took. She leans against a smaller boulder in the center of this courtyard and has her meager dinner. There's still a little water left when she's done, but not much more than a couple mouthfuls.

She puts her gray sweatshirt back on and surveys the ground around her. There's a dip of earth under one of the rock formations. She walks over and stares at it with her hands on her hips. It's a kind of hole leading under the rock that's about as long as a person. It wasn't dug. It looks like the soil has washed out. It's still big enough to be a coyote den, but Iris doesn't see any sign that it's occupied—bones, paw prints, or scat—around the entrance.

It's not a cave. It must not go very deep. She just doesn't have a flashlight to see. Her alternative for the night is to sleep under the prickly bushes in the wide open.

She could fit in this crevice and would be completely hidden by any passersby while she slept. She'd stay dry if it rained.

Iris bends to get a better look when she suddenly realizes this hole is probably a palace for rattlesnakes.

She kicks a loose rock into it, and while she only hears it clack against other stones, she still can't shake the creepy crawlies. She's not going in there. At least the snakes have their own place to sleep and won't bother her in the bushes, she hopes.

There doesn't look to be any difference in comfort between the places under the shrubs, and Iris chooses the spot by the widest opening in the stones.

She watches the plain she'd walked over until it gets darker.

No figures appear. Iris bites her lip. She doesn't know if they're going to keep looking for her at night. Her heart drums at the idea of those two men, walking slowly, looking for while she sleeps. It's soon too dark for her to bother staring into the distance.

She's not tired in the slightest, but that might change quickly. Her brain still feels like an open wound from whatever Paulo forced her to drink. She lies down so she's partly covered by a shrub and uses her duffel as a pillow.

She had expected the white noise of night insects or birds, but the plain is silent. There's a whoosh of wind in her ear, and that's all. She turns on her side and brings her arms together against her chest.

Soon she feels her heart rate begin to decrease. She pictures herself deflating. It's like she's letting out one never ending exhale. Strange images flash in her mind's eye. Her thoughts are running, but they're not the concentrated kind that keep one awake. They're fleeting, momentary, and soon, Iris is fading into sleep.

She comes to with a gasp. A sensation of falling throws her up so she's sitting upright on the dirt like she'd been hit by defibrillators. She hears some small mammal screeching in the distance.

That's all it was, she tells herself. That's what woke her. She isn't even sure she was ever asleep. Her sense of time is gone. It could be four hours from when she first lay down or thirty minutes. She moves to lie back down when she pauses. There's another sound in the air. A low hum. Not near, but not too far either.

She stands and wanders out, stumbling towards the gap in the rocks.

Her eyes adjust quickly to the dark. There's starlight and quite a lot of it. There is nothing in sight, but she hears the engine clearer now. The sound is not the same bass depth of the diesel that came into the compound. It's a smaller vehicle. She steps out so she can see farther in the direction she spent the afternoon walking.

There's a shadow moving in the night. It's a half mile away, closer to the ridgeline in the west. There under the starlight, a shadow is creeping forward. A spotlight swivels to and fro, creating a yellow patch of the plain in the distance. It's a truck, and it's looking for her. It's lifted twice as high to be able to go offroad, and she can see its giant wheels turn even from this distance.

They're going in the wrong direction. They've passed her horizontally. They're headed towards the little mountains in the north.

She should be relieved, but something else bothers her about this truck. She's standing with her mouth slightly agape trying to figure out what it is, when suddenly, it clicks.

The sound of the engine she hears doesn't match the shadow in the distance. It doesn't seem to be coming from the same place. It could be a trick of the terrain or...

Iris spins to her left and sees it immediately.

There's another truck. Close. Three hundred yards, maybe.

This is the engine she heard, and she's facing its hood—they're coming right towards her.

Two more shadows appear on either side of the truck—the men she'd seen by the river. Still, there doesn't seem to be any urgency to their movement or the truck's speed. Iris is trying to think when she's suddenly blinded.

She's centered in the ugly yellow beam of the spotlight. She doesn't hesitate this time. She bolts into a sprint. She goes back between the rocks and hears the truck's engine accelerate behind her. She sprints past her duffel and out a gap in the stones on the opposite end of the natural courtyard.

She can see the tree line of the dry forest to the east, but it's too far away. She'll never make it.

She stops. In less than a minute, the truck will be around the rocks. This is her last chance to hide. Thick as it is, they'll find her in the scrub grass, she's sure of it.

She sprints back to the rock formations, all the way to the hole that leads under one of the boulders. She hesitates at its entrance. There's a high chance they'll check this spot, too, and this snake-filled crevice is just a coffin.

The truck hiccups as it shifts gears, and Iris drops to her stomach and moves sideways, inside. She shimmies in until she doesn't fit anymore. She doesn't feel any snake bites. She doesn't hear a rattle. She puts her cheek against the dusty ground and prays.

A minute passes. She hears the truck grow more distant, but she knows she didn't get that lucky. In another minute, she hears slow footsteps scrape in the dirt. There are two sets, but that's the only way she can tell there are two of them. These men do not speak to each other.

They're listening.

One of the pairs is coming closer. There's less hesitation. They're walking deliberately. They see the crevice, Iris is certain. She's crying silently when suddenly, something brushes against the back of her leg.

She flinches and tosses a hand over her mouth. She fights the urge to fling herself out to the mercy of a quick bullet. The feeling begins to brush against her butt at the same time.

It's long. Silent. Slithery. It's a rattlesnake, and a big one at that.

She's lying on her side, and to Iris's horror, there's a gap at the bottom of her T-shirt and she feels the snake begin to slither in.

Her mouth is open now, her hot breath warms the rocks. She's almost in a state of shock. She can feel its cold scales and the muscles of it contract against her back as it curls up between her shirt and skin.

A beam of light hastily illuminates the top of the crevice but doesn't reach Iris. She half considers calling out, ending this nightmare, but the light is gone as suddenly as it appeared. The footsteps get farther away.

She almost doesn't want them to, but she couldn't even whisper if she wanted.

She feels the snake begin to coil itself into a ball, and then it's still. It's been attracted by her warmth. It's not exploring, Iris realizes.

It's sleeping.

Crawling

Iris is afraid of crushing it. There's no chance she'll sleep. She's terrified of falling asleep, because if she rolls, it will sink its fangs into her back.

A snake this big has more venom than smaller ones. A bite to the back close to her vital organs, and she'd probably be dead in a couple hours.

She tries to take noticeably deep breaths. She even risks a sniffle here or there. She wants this snake to not be surprised by a little bit of movement. It *has* to know she's a living, breathing thing, right?

The last thing she wants is this snake thinking she's a soft warm rock and biting her the second it realizes that is not the case. The snake doesn't seem bothered when she breathes, and after an hour of unmatched terror, Iris begins to calm down.

She even realizes she's going to get bored. She'll have to wait for the snake to move, which might mean midmorning. And if it's an overcast day, it might decide to sleep in longer.

She can't hear the truck in the distance anymore. The footsteps don't return. She thinks it's just as likely that the cartel men are waiting as well. Waiting for morning and for Iris to show herself, thinking she's lying low in the shrubs.

An hour passes, maybe. Then perhaps she thinks it's been three. Snakes re-adjust themselves while sleeping, too, she learns. At one point she thinks it's leaving, just for the snake to switch sides.

She keeps her eye fixed on the sliver of sky she can see. Stars filter in and out of it as the planet spins. Her thoughts can't fix on any one thing. She doesn't want to start crying, and she's afraid that's what will start to happen if she thinks too hard about where she is and what likely awaits her in the morning.

It doesn't take as long as she feared for the sliver of sky to lighten, and in the same minute that she realizes it must be dawn, the snake begins to move. It crawls out of her sweatshirt and then up over her hip. She can see it clearly as it moves towards the opening.

"You're welcome," Iris says aloud. The snake doesn't seem very thankful for its warm night as it slithers out quickly. It's too early to sun itself, Iris thinks. It must've gotten hungry.

Once it's likely the snake has moved on, she climbs out, too. She isn't immediately met with a bullet. There's a morning breeze rustling the shrubs. She stays in a crouch and then decides to lie flat. Her duffel lies ransacked. The water container is empty on the ground, and the bag itself is upside down in the dirt. She didn't even hear them going through it.

With her arms in front of her, she starts to army crawl. They're watching the plain. There's no way they believe that she ran all the way unseen into the dry forest. If she stands, she'll be chased down and shot. She hasn't even thought of her plan fully before she started doing it—she's going to crawl the entire mile or two to the forest.

While it's still somewhat dark, Iris moves the fastest. She keeps her sleeves down and holds them in place with her fingers so they don't get pulled back. Even with the jeans and sweater, the sharp stones are enough to keep her cringing in pain. It's more tiring than she thought it would be, and she can't be moving faster than a half mile per hour, and that's not counting all the breaks she's taking.

She stops to breathe. To listen. To find the path that follows the shrubs most closely so she's never in the open. It's hard but manageable, until the sun comes out. As soon as it's out, it begins to bake her.

The humidity is back, and the wind feels like it's shifted and is coming from inland. It can't be nine a.m. when it already must be close to eighty degrees. Iris is quickly soaked in sweat, but the alternative is taking her sweatshirt off and getting cut to bits by the little sharp stones in the dirt.

She hasn't risked rising to her knees in order to get her bearings. It's possible she veered in a circle like a hiker lost in the woods. She has deviated a lot from a straight path to avoid open patches of rock and boulders. She might be smack dab in the middle of the plain for all she knows. She stops for a minute and then rises partially so she's on all fours. Her back doesn't arch above the bushes. A fraction of her head does.

She's able to see treetops only a couple hundred yards away. Her course stayed straight, and she has to resist the urge to get up and sprint the rest of the way. Her thirst is going to quickly become a problem, and another twenty minutes of crawling is only going to delay a drink that much longer, but she doesn't risk running.

She keeps crawling until she's under the canopy, and then she stands and looks back at the plain. Nothing moves out there. An eerie feeling sits heavy in her stomach. Out there are men with rifles still waiting for her to show herself. She spins around and descends a slight hill into the dry forest.

Those same men will be in these woods, too. Only here they will be harder to spot.

Graveyards

The first thing Iris does is take off her sweatshirt and stuff it under a bush. She doesn't care if there's another chilly night or if she'll need to crawl again. It's a sweaty, stained mess of dirt. Taking it off feels so liberating that she reasons it would be better for her morale to leave the stinking thing behind.

After twenty minutes in the woods, her arms glisten with sweat. Her T-shirt sticks to her skin. She can feel the film of dirt on her face from crawling. The dry forest doesn't offer total shade, and soon she has a headache from dehydration. She keeps daydreaming about encountering that creek again or even a puddle from yesterday's rain, but the dry forest is back to living up to its name.

Her view doesn't change for what must be miles. It's all short trees and prickly bushes. She takes note of landmarks—boulders, a burned-out trunk, in case she sees them again. But Iris never retraces her steps.

It must be near noon when she comes to a rusty chain link fence. On the other side are mounds of scrap metal and stacks of cars. A junkyard.

The tan dirt on the other side of the fence is unshaded and sizzles in the sun.

She could go around it, but Iris is driven by an animal want for water. There's a chance this place isn't a business. That it's just a place people can freely dump their trash, but she bets there's an office. She needs there to be.

Her head pounds. She can't think straight. She'd risk her life to quench this thirst.

Tree branches have grown through the chain links, and some are rusted away entirely, leaving head-sized holes. She knows she won't have to go far to find an opening in the fence, and after about thirty yards she finds a place where it's been crushed by a fallen tree. She climbs onto the trunk and walks over it then jumps down onto the dusty lot.

She doesn't hear any engines running or the shouts of people working. No dog comes charging out from behind a scrap pile. The world is silent except from the slight whoosh of a jetliner leaving a wide contrail across the sky.

Iris makes her way into the yard slowly. It's not a mess—the place is organized. It's arranged in aisles. There is one of junked sedans and another of pickup trucks. One aisle is just a heap of engines and car parts fifty yards long on either side. Iris instinctively starts down the row of old buses.

There are classic yellow school buses and flat-roofed city buses. Their wheels have been removed, and they've been stacked two high. This row is higher than the others. It gives more shade and cover.

At the end where the stacks end is a pile of tires two stories high. Iris starts down the row and moves slowly. She lets herself cool off in the shade. Before she even reaches the tires, she stops. Out of the corner of her eye, something reflects.

She looks over so fast that her hair blinds her for a moment, but then it appears. Water. It's a puddle in a gap between two stacks of school buses.

The water is the same color of the sandy soil around it, but Iris gets to her knees in front of it. She cups a handful and smells it first. Minerally. Cool. There's no hint of oil or filth. She takes a sip and lets it sit on her tongue. It tastes a little of rust and the dirt that clouds it, but good enough. She gulps it down and closes her eyes in relief.

For the first several seconds, she scoops handful after handful to her mouth but loses more between her fingers than she gets. She gets frustrated and drops her lips to the surface. She sucks until she feels her stomach get heavy.

She leans back with a sigh and wipes her mouth with her wrist. The feeling of being tired hits her instantaneously. It's like now that she has achieved her quest to quench her thirst, her body has put forth a new priority.

Her eyelids bob closed. She totters on her knees in the cool shade. Her mind is elsewhere fighting sleep, but she fixates on a sound in the distance—a deep metal thump.

She can't always hear it. One second, it's there, and then the wind shifts and it's not. The thumping comes again but more frantic, and Iris feels her heartbeat spark as something else accompanies the noise. A scream. A woman's scream.

Again, the wind blows, and the sound is gone. Iris tries to calm herself. To say she's exhausted is an understatement. She's *dead* tired.

To trust what she heard would be ridiculous. It could've been a bird. A screech of crumping metal. Her hunted brain is only jumping to the worst conclusions.

She needs to find a place to lie down and wait out this heat. The buses are the easiest answer to that, but most don't look like they can be easily accessed. Their doors are shut, crumbled and broken in their frames. But a school bus on the ground level across the row is missing some of its back windows. Iris staggers to her feet and walks over to it.

Without wheels, the bus sits lower to the ground, but the windows are still high enough that it would take someone six feet or taller to see in if they were just passing by. Iris grabs ahold of one of the empty frames and scampers up and into the bus.

It's hotter in here than it is outside. She doesn't even inspect her surroundings. She doesn't try to find something to use as a pillow. Iris crawls under the benches so she won't be visible even if someone does look through the windows. With her cheek pressed against the shaded metal floor and no rattlesnake curled against her back, she's asleep in only a few seconds.

Iris wakes sweating. Her head throbs. Blinking hurts her brain, and the air she breathes in feels hot in her lungs. She hasn't forgotten where she is for a moment. The first thing she's thankful for is that the water she drank isn't coming back up. She's not nauseated. If anything, she's thirsty for more.

She crawls back out from beneath the benches and looks out the window. The sun is even higher. She only got a couple hours of sleep, but it's plenty, she thinks, sighing. She doesn't need her brain for much. She's running for her life, not doing arithmetic.

There's no one visible out the windows but there are voices in the distance now. She's tense as she listens to them until she hears one laugh.

Still, it's not an indication the conversation wasn't about looking for her. Life is cheap to these men. A joke could be cracked about who gets to wrap her intestines around her neck when they're done with her.

The voices vanish and ten minutes pass without anyone walking down the row of buses. Iris makes her way back to the water and drinks until she's full again. By the time she's done her headache has already lessened. She pauses and tries to think.

The junkyard might have a phone. A landline. If it was a business, it was plenty possible. She could scout the place out and wait until nightfall. That's option one.

An option two doesn't come to her. She doesn't want to try to find a house. The less open ground she travels, the better.

She steps out of the row of buses and to the pile of tires. There's a white cinderblock building near a gate. Two cars, an old white Toyota truck, and a newer black Volkswagen sedan are parked outside. Both are coated in dust.

There's one visible window in the building, but it's stuffed with a large and yellowing air-conditioning unit. The door to the building is metal. It doesn't look like the kind of thing she could kick in.

She makes her way across the yard to see if the building has any more windows. It's the only structure around and if she's going to find a phone somewhere, it's there. When she gets to the back of the building, her shoulders sink. There are windows, but they are barred with rusting iron. On the other side, the blinds are drawn to keep out the sunlight, but she still doesn't step where she'd be visible if someone peeked out.

The little building is a fortress. She's sure there's crime in this area, and if this place buys and sells scrap, they probably keep cash. Which means they have a safe to protect. She's not going to be able to get inside to use a phone if there is one.

She spits in frustration. There's grit on her teeth from the dirty water and she runs her tongue over them as she thinks. Unbrushed and unbathed, she's beginning to feel like a wild animal. Her brow furrows as she looks at the area behind the building.

It's not organized like the rest of the junkyard. There are two old couches and a pallet that's been placed on top of old tires acts as a table.

Beer bottles and cans litter the ground. But that's not what Iris's eyes end up glued to. Near the wall of the building is a heaping pile of clothing.

There are camouflage pants and collared shirts stained with blood, but there is also women's clothing. Bras and panties glow against the dark blue jeans and camo shirts in a feminine rainbow of purples, pinks, and reds. The bottom of the pile is rimmed with the shoes of both sexes. There are black combat boots, sneakers, sandals, and high heels.

Iris is frozen. There are flies in the pile feeding on what congealed blood there is on the clothes.

The air conditioner hums. She looks at the closed blinds behind the glass and bars and walks closer. The pile of clothes is sizable but not massive. It's about four feet high. She turns over her shoulder. There is something familiar about what she sees. There is a line of shipping containers just in front of the chain link fence.

She's surprised that it took her so long to notice. One of the containers sits apart from the rest. There are fresh tire tracks in the dirt in front of it. It's a rusty orange and spray painted on the doors is a big number six.

She stares at it for a full twenty seconds. There is no shade near the shipping containers. The sun beats down unabated. A part of her already knows what she sees, understands what she'll find if she opens that door. She turns from the clothes and starts walking slowly to the container.

The flies get thicker the closer she gets. The air is suddenly alive and pulsing with dozens of them. Hundreds. And the doors... Iris stops and stares at the doors of the container.

She can easily be seen out the window of the little building if someone opens the blinds, but she doesn't care. She's too afraid. Her mouth is open—the door is black in parts from the number of flies that have landed on it. They're trying to get inside. They crawl over the paint, and some find success and disappear between the cracks.

Iris grabs the metal handle in her fist and drops it immediately. She grimaces and inhales a curse. It is so hot from the sun that it is hot to the touch. She sticks her hand in her shirt and tries again. There is no padlock keeping it in place. This time she can get a grip, and the handle straightens and the door creaks as she opens it. She's hit by a blast of stale hot air. The temperature inside of the shipping container is easily in the hundreds.

The flies pour in past her, prepared, like they've done this many times before. They don't have to go far. They settle on the corpses by her feet. Six naked girls are heaped on top of one another. Their eyes are wide. Their mouths are caked with white crust, but some of their lips and chins are still wet with fresh foam.

Iris is trying to see through the tears that have suddenly blurred her vision. It's not their lifeless eyes that shock her—it's their cracked, bloody nails that they used to try to claw themselves out of this cooking coffin.

She looks over her shoulder at the building. The blinds are still closed. The monsters who helped do this are still inside.

She crouches down and tries to shoo the flies away, but they land as soon as her hand is back at her side.

She tries to listen past the buzzing and looks at their chests for signs of breathing, but they're still. These women are all dead. She puts the back of her hand against one girl's forehead and recoils her hand. Her forehead is not just warm. It *burns*.

Iris puts her hand over her mouth and stares at them. She thinks of the muffled screams. The banging she heard before she fell asleep in the bus. She could've found them. She could've gotten here in time if she'd cared enough to investigate. The container has no way to open it from the inside, but the outside is unlocked. Iris could've simply let them out.

And then what? she asks herself. Try to all run out of here together? Overtake the guards in the building? No. They'd all just be shot. Iris can't feel guilty for long. She frowns at the girl's tattoos.

She can read them all. Two of the girls have cursive names on them. *Liberty. Justine.* Another girl's tattoo that runs the length of her forearm reads, *trust your vibes.*

They're all in English. She thinks for a moment that maybe these Eastern European girls were being hip with western tattoos before she sees one tattoo on one of the girl's biceps.

It's a bridge. She'd recognize it anywhere. Two slight humps represent the M bridge that connections Tennessee to Arkansas. Below it is the number, the area code, *901*.

These girls were from Memphis. Paulo wasn't testing the goods before they went to market. He was fucking them before he killed them.

Iris stands up. Her mind is trying to understand what she so clearly sees. She might've known these women. They might have been shipped back here because the police were sniffing around her past and these girls knew things.

It's still quiet in the yard, but she'd rather hear voices. The silence is disturbing now. Iris turns towards the building, and the hairs on the back of her neck stick straight up because the blinds are now open.

Disposal

Iris doesn't run. She waits ten seconds. Twenty. If this is it, so be it.

But no one comes out of the building. No bullet comes bursting from the other side of the glass. She supposes it's possible that the blinds were opened for light and whoever opened them didn't even glance outside after. They just pulled the string. Twisted the little plastic dowel.

She shuts the door to the shipping container, but it won't latch. There's something in the way. Iris opens the door again to see that one of the girl's pale arms has fallen forward into the dirt. It blocks the door from shutting all the way. Iris thinks of moving it with her foot for a second before showing more respect and bending over quickly and tossing the arm back in.

But it wasn't enough. The arm flops back out into the dirt. Iris is about to pick it up again when she hears a door whine. From the direction of the sound, she doesn't have to guess—it's the metal door to the building.

She runs in a low crouch around the other side of the building and presses herself against the wall. Footsteps crunch quickly in the dirt. A man is muttering annoyed in Spanish. They don't sound like they're looking for something. If anything, they sound annoyed.

Iris risks a peek and sees a fat man in black cowboy boots and a black silk shirt walk to the container. He shouts something back over his shoulder towards the building and starts dragging the women out by their ankles. He doesn't seem to find it strange that the door was ajar.

Iris hears a truck start—the white Toyota, she guesses. It quickly comes into view driving in reverse with its bed facing the container. The fat man now has all six girls lying in a row.

The driver puts the car in park and gets out. Iris recognizes this one. It's the dangerous-looking teen who drove her from the airport. He tosses a cigarette into the dirt and puts his hands around one of the woman's ankles. The fat man takes the wrists, and they hoist the girl so she's level with the truck bed and drop her in with a thump. They do this with the other five and don't even bother to put the tailgate back up.

They drive forward, slowly, and Iris walks to the other side of the building to watch them. They don't take a left towards Iris and the exit of the junkyard. They drive to the other side of the giant tire pile, where there's a gray metal contraption the size of a large dumpster. From the twisted pile of scrap behind it and the black oil that stains the lip of the inside that she can see, Iris can tell it's a car shredder. She knows what's going to happen. This is a good time to run. To sneak inside and try to use a phone or find a gun. But Iris can't move.

The truck stops in front of the metal shredder, and the men get out. The younger one drags the bodies out of the bed while the other strolls to the cab of a crane.

The kid has put the bodies into a pile. The shredder is turned on and coughs a black cloud of diesel into the air.

The crane adds to the steady roar of engines, and the claw hook that's attached to its boom spreads its talons as it descends towards the girls.

Iris looks closer at the shredder. She can see flies from here. A black swarm hovers near the mouth of the thing, and she can see why. It's not oil stains that she sees—it's blood that's been thickened and darkened by the sun.

These girls aren't the first to be fed into the mouth of this thing. The pile of clothes. They all belong to victims of the cartel. Men and women. Old and young.

The crane starts to lift all the girls at once like a hand of God. It takes clumps of earth with it that rain down in clouds as it gets higher and higher. Iris turns her head away and starts walking back the way she'd come. She sticks her fingers in her ears and closes her eyes as she trots towards the fence.

She doesn't want to hear the women fall. She doesn't want to hear the shredder protest as it starts to churn them through its grinder. But it doesn't matter how far away she gets. The image is all she can picture.

Caught

Iris leaves the junkyard through another opening where the chain link has curled away from the fence posts. She's back in the dry forest.

Her frantic state of self-preservation has been replaced by a dull shock. She walks in a stupor. Cracking twigs and at times tripping over roots. There are men looking for her still, but a part of her is beginning to want this to be over. Pull the Band-Aid off.

Die like the six women before her.

If Iris hadn't dug into her past, if she hadn't kicked the hornet's nest that is the Adler Corporation, the police wouldn't be turning over stones in Memphis and Paulo wouldn't be paranoid. He wouldn't have felt the urge to clean house. Those women would be alive.

She trips over another root, but this time she's walking too fast to catch herself. She hits the ground, and the air is knocked out of her lungs. Iris puts her palms against the earth to push herself up, but she just keeps them there. She stays with her cheek pressed against the dirt.

The FBI have left her for dead.

Even if she lives, the agents might decide she didn't do enough to fulfill the contract she signed. Maybe they'll pretend the piece of paper she signed doesn't even exist. She had no lawyer look it over. No assurance that it wouldn't find the shredder and that they'd use her to get their cartel boss and then send her home for prosecution.

Iris pushes herself up and starts walking. She hasn't looked where she was going for an hour. Trees and bushes begin to look familiar. The fence of the junkyard doesn't appear again, but that doesn't mean she hasn't ended up walking in a circle.

The air gets cooler. The forest gets darker and louder with insects. The sky has grown indigo in the dusk, and a few stars shine when Iris spills out of the dry forest and suddenly finds herself in a field. Whatever was planted has been harvested. The field is empty.

Iris stays on the edge of the woods and reassesses her situation. Her defeatism has passed. With the cooler night air comes a new vigor. It takes a while, but her confidence comes back some.

She should live, if for no other reason than to kill as many of these sons of bitches as she can. She crouches in the shadows and waits for the darkness to become absolute. She breathes in deeply and ignores the rumbling in her stomach. Her thoughts feel sharp for the first time since before she was drugged.

A dog barks in the distance. It comes from where the field ends. A mile away, dead ahead, there are greenhouses and what look like short stucco structures on the other side of them. They aren't visible for much longer. When it's finally dark, all that can be seen are a few weak orange lights where the buildings were.

It's not a village. More of a lone farm from what Iris can tell. It's the only kind of settlement around. The field is only a mile long ahead of her toward the buildings, but to her left and right, the open earth stretches for four times that before being obscured by the trees of windbreaks.

She's done running without a destination. She's getting to a phone or she's finding a gun.

When it's too dark to even see her feet, she starts to cross the field confidently. Away from the birds and the bugs of the forest, her footsteps become the only sound. She reckons she's halfway to the greenhouses when a pair of lights to her left make her stop.

They're far away. Close to the windbreak, she reckons. But the lights don't belong to a new farmhouse. They're a twin set, and they're bobbing up and down. The slight groan of an engine follows. They're headlights. She's looking at a vehicle.

There are no roads that intersect this field. She wants to believe that she simply didn't see one. That she was too tired and missed the scar of a dirt road. But the headlights are pointed directly towards her, and then Iris hears the engine rev angrily.

They're accelerating.

She pushes off her feet into a sprint. They must be able to see her run, because the sound of the engine gets louder.

She runs for a minute, maybe, before the vehicle catches her. It's a black SUV. American made. A newer Suburban, she thinks. It cuts her off twenty feet ahead and comes to a jerking stop. A cloud of dust is illuminated red in its taillights.

Iris doesn't move. She turns like she's going to run the opposite way, but it's hopeless. She looks back.

"Just fucking shoot me, then!" she screams.

No response comes from the SUV. The windows don't roll down. A rifle barrel doesn't appear. It idles quietly for several seconds, and then Iris hears the driver's door open.

Someone steps out slowly and then starts to walk around the vehicle.

The man is clearly cartel. He wears a bandana face covering. Both hands grip an older AK-style rifle.

Iris can't stop staring at the gun. "Do it."

He doesn't move.

"Fucking do it!" Iris charges forward, but instead of raising his gun, the man reaches out and grabs the door handle to the SUV's back seat. He opens it, and Iris goes still.

A black sneaker and then a woman's leg appears. Staring at her from behind a bruised and swollen face is Augusta.

"You been looking for me, I hear."

Iris is too shocked to talk.

"Come on." She holds the door open and waves. "Let's go, sugar."

Beaten

It takes Iris a moment to start walking forward. If it weren't for her voice and flowing white hair, Iris would have to question if the woman who stands in front of her is really Augusta.

This doesn't feel like real life.

Her face is puffy and purple. Her bottom lip is so fat it looks like it has been stung by a bee.

She'd been beaten by Paulo's men, no doubt. But why is she alive? Why is Iris?

"Are you okay?" Iris manages to speak as she gets closer.

"Am *I* okay? My, aren't you something. Come on, we need to go." Augusta doesn't say anything else as Iris gets in and she pulls the door shut.

They wait for the driver to get into the SUV. Iris doesn't feel like she should have to ask questions. She looks at Augusta expectantly, waiting for her to explain this, but she doesn't speak.

"Are they... going to kill us?"

Augusta shakes her head. "No."

Iris looks at the driver as he starts to crank the wheel and give the SUV some gas. His rifle rests on his lap. He turns on the radio and starts to hum along quietly to the song that plays.

Iris blinks as if she expects to wake up. She'll open her eyes to find a rattlesnake curled against her back again. But the cool leather against her skin is real. Augusta is real. "No one's trying to kill me?"

Augusta won't make eye contact. She pulls on her fingers. Touches the bruises on her cheeks. "No, and they sent me out here to convince you of that."

Iris can't bear the silence any longer. "How long have you been here?"

"In Mexico?"

Iris nods.

"As long as I've been gone."

"Why didn't you—"

"Iris?" Augusta interrupts. Her eyes are closed, and she's cringing like Iris's questions are giving her a headache.

"Yeah?"

"The questions can wait. They'll be answered. All of them." Augusta leans her head back like she's going to sleep. Like this is the end of an extremely long day for her, too.

Iris looks at the driver. One of his hands still rests near the trigger of his rifle. Her pulse begins to pick up again.

Ever since she got the letter at Sweet Blood, Iris has been expecting some kind of grand reunion with Augusta. That she would be thrilled to see her. That they'd rekindle whatever it was that they had.

But this is all wrong. It feels like a bad dream.

Augusta is quiet. Afraid. Beaten.

Soon, they're on a paved road, and the SUV is roaring ahead and into the night.

No one talks. For an hour, they ascend into the hills. They take what must be little more than an off-road vehicle trail into the woods. The SUV bounces up and down and side-to-side for ten minutes before the trail ends.

Iris watches a small cottage made of orange clay appear at the end of it. It's one story, and smoke pours steadily from its chimney.

The driver puts the car in park and makes a phone call. He says something quickly and then hangs up and tosses the phone in the cupholder. He doesn't move to get out of the SUV. He sniffs and pinches his nose.

Iris leans forward to catch Augusta's eye. "What do they want with us?"

"One more thing," Augusta says and squeezes Iris's thigh.

"One more thing?" Iris repeats, confused. "What do you mean? What was I doing?"

But before she can answer, Iris's attention is taken outside as a man opens the door of the cottage.

She can see him out the front windshield. He's backlit. Iris can't see his face, but he wears a navy suit and no tie. Her heart sinks when she studies his build longer and notices the thick black hair.

Iris has no such luck that the FBI got Paulo. He's standing right here. A pistol in his hand.

"Bait," Augusta says, finally responding. "You've been bait."

Hook

Alexi Akers sits in a windowless conference room. He's pushed out from the table because his knees don't fit comfortably under it, and he taps his foot anxiously.

He's deaf to the conversation happening right in front of him. This is it—the moment he's been after since he was a high school freshman obsessed with spies, dark suits, and America's national security. He's a hundred feet from the pinnacle of his career and he's having a crisis.

Iris Adler is dead. That or about to be killed. And it's all because of his ideas and his lies. He pulled his trigger in the field before. The story he told Iris about the dad he shot was not entirely a fabrication. But this murder by word of mouth... the conscious lies he told her to use her life as chum in the water for these sharks...

A hole burns in his back pocket. There, ten pages are folded in a square. It's the end of a report from a PI firm that Iris had paid for. Private no longer—their findings in Memphis were so serious that the firm reported them to the FBI. Iris has no idea. He needs to get these papers to her. She deserves to know.

Deserved, Alexi thinks glumly. It is too late now.

"Alexi?"

It takes him a moment to look over at Agent Beltran. Her brow is raised incredulously. Her look is accusing—*were you seriously not listening?*

"Would you like to continue, Alexi?"

"No," he says quickly and crosses his arms. "You know this part best." He doesn't even know what part she's talking about. Alexi scratches his ear and looks at the video monitors set up on a desk at the far wall. Ernie is watching the screens—a skinny junior agent with wire-frame glasses and a shaved head.

The space they're in has been converted into a kind of situation room, and the screens show live footage. Some is aerial. Some is from cameras on the ground. They're surveilling three different structures.

Agent Beltran sits to his right, and an older man sits across the table from them both.

He's bald, wears a black suit, and his white mustache seems to twitch in anticipation as he listens. He looks like an old colonel because he was one before starting a career in intelligence. His name is John Riley, and it's his decision whether this operation goes forward or not. He's flown all the way from D.C. to their makeshift headquarters outside of the city of Durango to make it.

For the last hour, they've been filling him in on the basics. The time for the final pitch is near.

Beltran is getting there. "We've been tracking two sets of vehicles that left the compound yesterday in the early morning. Neither has gone anywhere near the small town of San Marcos. Meaning, the last message Iris Adler sent was likely a fake. She got caught after sending the first batch and was then fed false information."

"And how do you know the first message wasn't false information?"

"We can't for sure. But it conveyed a lack of panic. It was organized. Thought out. The last message she sent felt... random."

"If she even sent that last message herself," Riley adds.

"Yes. They could've taken the phone from her and texted that to us. Regardless, all persons of interest fled the compound. One set of vehicles went to a small house about eighty miles from the Colinas estate. We believe this is Paulo Delgado, using a safe house for the time being."

"And the other vehicles?"

Beltran looks at Alexi and licks her lips nervously. This is it, the ask. But Alexi just lifts his brow. He doesn't give a shit about any of this anymore.

Beltran looks back to Riley and continues. "At nine p.m. on October 25th, two trucks left the Colinas estate traveling west. We've kept an eye on them with a drone, and they're currently at a house in a residential neighborhood in the city of Durango. Another safe house, we believe. We've looked up the address, and it's owned by a subsidiary of Delgado International—the cover company in the States."

Beltran glances at Alexi again. They're partners on this. He's expected to talk. He's being petty if he doesn't help her out, but Alexi still can't help but sigh in disinterest before he begins. "We believe that the man they're transporting is Emmanuel Barrera."

John Riley widens his eyes and leans back in surprise.

Alexi keeps speaking. "The messages Iris Adler sent to us refer to an uncle of Paulo's that goes by Manny. She said it was evident that he was the authority inside of the compound. Of course, Emmanuel Barrera hasn't been seen in four years. He was the number-two man in the Colinas cartel before he vanished. Iris was briefed on what he looked like, and this Uncle Manny fits it. We also saw this man she described in the second convoy that went to Durango when they stopped for gas before reaching the

287

city. He was assumed dead, but now it seems he's been calling the shots from inside the compound."

John Riley taps the table with his pointer finger. "This is the same guy who was known as the butcher, right?"

"*El Tallador*," Beltran cuts in. "It translates more to sculptor, but yes. He was known for cutting up rival gang members or..."

"DEA informants," Riley interrupts. "This guy killed two American citizens in 2019. We were after him before he disappeared." He taps his fat finger on the table again. "We went after him *hard.* Now you're telling me he didn't just resurface but has done so as the head of the Colinas cartel?"

Beltran has to stifle a satisfied smile. Riley is informed and doesn't need the full sale. This operation is going better than either of them ever expected, but she's the only one still enjoying herself.

Beltran opens a folder and pulls out a few old pictures of "*El Tallador.*" One is a mugshot from the 80s of him as a thin-faced teenager with wanting, dangerous eyes. Another is of him nearer to middle-aged. He's in a club, chubby, wearing a white polo and gold chains and a gold watch. The people around him are smiling, but his face is serious. He is busy giving a death stare to whoever is taking the photograph.

Beltran rotates the pictures and slides them over to Riley. "It sounds like it. Iris Adler sent a description of him. He's gained more weight and grew out a different mustache. It's no surprise. After the DEA informant's deaths, he's done a great job staying hidden. If we lose him again, I don't know if he'll surface."

They're all silent now after the last line of the pitch. It had been easy for Beltran. She was lucky that Riley knew who Emmanuel Barrera was. The last thing they needed was for this operation to be dead on arrival because the greenlight had to pass through a bureaucrat who didn't understand the significance of the name "*El Tallador.*"

Alexi can hear the analog clock ticking on the wall.

Riley's chair creaks as he leans back and intertwines his fingers in front of his face. His brow furrows in thought. He takes the pose of a powerful man about to make an important decision. "So, you want an arrest?"

"We want our team to move ASAP on the location in Durango, yes," says Beltran.

Riley doesn't respond right away. "And tell me the downsides to moving this quickly? Why trust this information from the Adler girl?"

"She's a unique informant," Beltran begins, and Alexi almost wants to excuse himself. This is the part he can't bear to hear.

"We've had moles in the cartel before, *but* they were always there for business. They had a purpose. Chemical company reps selling drugs to be used in P2P meth manufacturing. A ship captain negotiating his bribe. Iris is different. To put it simply, the cartel wouldn't be afraid of hiding things from her because we don't believe they intended to let her leave alive. That's what this operation has hinged on and why I think we're going to be immensely successful here."

Live bait. Beltran just admitted it. They've used Iris's life. But instead of disgust, Riley nods like he's pleased with this answer. "And what about this girl?" he asks. "Have you had any more contact?"

"After the phone was discovered, cartel security around the property increased and our surveillance team had to retreat. But no, we don't think Iris would be kept alive long. The bugs she planted are still active, meaning we believe she hasn't been... interrogated about their location yet."

Alexi cringes. The cartel is merciless. They don't interrogate—they torture. They'll cut off Iris's fingers and toes, and when they've got what they've wanted, they'll take a blow torch to her breasts just to make a point.

"You don't expect Iris Adler to resurface?" Riley asks.

"No." Beltran shakes her head. "The news will just have to speculate what ended up happening to her."

"It sounds like everything came together on this one."

"It really did, sir," says Beltran proudly.

Riley still hasn't given the thumbs-up. He just nods. He won't stop nodding. His head bobs up and down and up and down like he's loving everything he's hearing. "What does the Mexican government think of moving in now?"

"The new president wants to send a message. The call is ours. The agreement has already been struck that we would get extradition privileges for Emmanuel's murder of the DEA informants."

The room goes silent again as Riley thinks. Alexi can't care less what they do. They all know that the cartel is not a snake—it's a hydra. Cut off one head, and another will take its place.

Capturing or killing Emmanuel Barrera will do nothing to stop the flow of drugs into America. His absence won't start a civil war among the cartels. All intelligence agencies thought he was dead until a day ago.

What his capture *does* do is make the current administration look strong against drugs and tough on the mayhem that's happening beyond the southern border.

This operation is all about posturing. All about optics. Lives won't actually be saved. The spoils are internal promotions and back patting. And all of it comes at the expense of using the life of a young woman. There's not even any remorse from Beltran about what they did to Iris.

Riley sighs, and there's a finality to it. Like he's thought everything through as much as he needs to. "If the Mexicans are satisfied and we can release a joint statement on the arrest, I say go ahead. Move in."

Beltran beams. She doesn't hide it anymore. Alexi figures he should feel the same. They've struck career gold by coming upon Iris. Lifers in the FBI and DEA have tried to make an arrest like this but failed. Their informants were killed or got bad info. Beltran was right. It was Alexi's idea in the first place—Iris was perfect. The catch was that they had to send her in there knowing she was going to die.

"Okay. I'll make the call," says Beltran.

They all stand and shake hands. Alexi catches Ernie looking at them for a second before he glances back to the monitors.

Alexi turns back to John Riley and musters his best fake smile. If this goes well, he'll be twice the rising star that he already was. This arrest will be international news. He'll probably field a call from the president.

As Riley and Beltran chat as they leave the room, Alexi is in his own head, pondering the morality of this murder.

He didn't kill Iris, technically, but he could just as easily say the same after pushing her into a pit of snakes.

Line

Alexi and Beltran strap on their bulletproof vests and utility belts. Then they get in an SUV to rendezvous with the Special Forces team they have waiting three blocks down from the residence where Emmanuel Barrera is staying.

It's two a.m., and the street is tree-lined and cast in hundreds of shadows. It's not a wealthy neighborhood, but still, there are just as many security lights and cameras as trees. Three blocks seems like a safe enough distance to not have to worry about being picked up by the cartel's security, but then again, you can never be sure.

Alexi calms down. They're using the best undercover vehicles they could find—utility trucks that bear the city's name. And so far, there's no additional activity around the address to suggest they've been spotted.

The door is opened to one of the trucks, and Alexi and Beltran get inside. It smells like wintergreen chewing tobacco and Red Bull. They shake hands with Coleman—the raiding party's squad leader.

He has a crew cut and stubbly beard. His eyes are wide in anticipation. "We're itchin' to go. I take it you two are here to join the party?"

Alexi is indifferent, but they're here because Beltran wants to be here for the bust.

"I want to put the cuffs on him," says Beltran.

"Cute, but we're putting you two in the rear."

"I'd rather be point, but—"

"Look, you don't got the hardware to be point." Coleman pats his rifle. "Rodriguez. Jefferson." Two young men in camouflage vests sitting farther back in the van wave. "These boys will be next to you in the rear. Stick with 'em. Got it?"

Beltran doesn't try to argue any further. "Okay."

"Okay. Gather around now."

Alexi starts biting his nail as the Special Forces team goes over the entry plan. To be honest, by the time they break huddle and the truck starts to move, he doesn't even know what they're doing. He decides he'll follow Beltran's lead. It should be easy enough to be rear guard.

Things move quickly. The trucks accelerate all the way to sixty miles per hour before coming to a screeching halt in front of a large, wrought iron gate. They accelerate again and smash through the gate. They drive into a large dirt yard. The sliding doors open, and the team moves out in silence.

Alexi and Beltran follow with their sidearms drawn. There's an old maroon sedan parked in the middle of the yard, and Jefferson and Rodriguez signal to stay put behind it.

One of the soldiers sets his rifle over the hood to keep watch, and the other does the same over the trunk. Alexi and Beltran are crouched behind the middle of the car.

There's a bang as the door to the house is breached, and then they hear a woman yelling. Alexi peeks over the car. He can see the raiding party's flashlights sweeping around inside. They yell commands in Spanish.

"Hey. Hey." Alexi spins around as Beltran hisses. Her pistol is aimed towards a shed on the other side of the yard. His breath stops as he sees movement in the shadows.

"Guys," Beltran says. "We got contact six o'clock."

"Hey!" she shouts, and the figure moves. It's a person. Two people. "*Policía! Levanto las manos!*"

Alexi watches something raise, but it's not their hands. "Gun," he says at normal volume. He puts one of the shadows in his sights, and then they both start shooting. The figures vanish behind his muzzle flash. He takes six quick, controlled shots.

Either Rodriguez or Jefferson fires as well, and there's the deafening crack of a rifle for several seconds. When the shooting stops, the figures are gone. They're now heaped on the dirt.

The smoke clears, and Alexi's adrenaline morphs into something else. A deep anxiety spreads further and further through his body with every beat of his heart. He stands casually and starts walking towards the bodies.

"Alexi! Alexi, stay down!" Beltran yells.

"Anybody hit!" another soldier shouts from the house.

"No!" Beltran says. "Two bogies down."

Alexi can't speak. He stops in front of the bodies and bends. They're still moving, just barely. There's no breath, but their limbs are sliding mindlessly, slowly in the dirt. One of them opens his hand and closes it as if he's grasping for life.

Alexi's eyes are stuck on the rifles they held. They are not guns. He reaches down and picks up a stick.

They are two boys in soccer jerseys. Thin and maybe thirteen.

They are little more than children.

A woman is wailing now. She screams just outside the door that was broken in. Alexi doesn't need to listen to what she's saying to understand.

This woman knows what they've just done.

Sinker

Alexi finds his way out of the compound. He goes back through the gate that lies sideways on its hinges and sits on the curb. He's too shocked to cry, although he tries. He wants to feel something, but his body is still in fight or flight.

Gun. He was the one who said it. He could've had one of the soldiers look first. They have night vision. They could've seen that they were kids with sticks.

Alexi stops himself from spiraling. In the heat of the moment, the soldiers, too, would've mistaken them for guns and opened fire. There is no world where those boys are alive.

Paramedics and the Mexican authorities that had been waiting for the all-clear move in. A stream of two dozen people pass Alexi before Beltran comes wandering out from the lot.

"They're not gonna make it."

"Really?" Alexi says sarcastically.

Beltran extends her hand. "Come on. You need to answer some questions with me."

He takes it, and his giant hand hides hers completely as he gets to his feet. They walk to the dirt yard that smells of sulfur and blood.

Three men and two women have been taken out of the house. They're handcuffed against a wall.

Alexi watches as Coleman comes over to them. His face is tight in a frown. "No weapons were found so far or any drugs. We're still looking for hidden compartments."

They don't respond. Alexi has more than a bad feeling about this.

"None of these three men admits to being Emmanuel Barrera, but that's our mark, don't you think?" Coleman points at one of the handcuffed men, and Alexi knows it's Barrera. He's chubby, sixty, and has a wide mustache.

"Yeah. That's the guy," Alexi says.

"You two gotta stand back for a bit. There's going to be an investigation into the shooting, and until then, no business. I'll keep you updated though." Coleman walks back to the suspects.

Alexi grows quiet. He's watching the paramedics load the boys onto stretchers and cover them with blankets. It's Beltran who starts asking the questions he feels like they both already know the answer to.

"Why were they out playing at two in the morning? I mean... it doesn't make any fucking sense."

Alexi doesn't bother to give a response. Soon, Alexi, Beltran, and Jefferson, the soldier who fired his weapon, are corralled away from the rest of the raiding party because of the shooting.

They start to hear things regardless. The boys were brothers and lived in the house. Why they were out late playing, the mother can't say. In fact, the mother can't say much of anything.

"It's hot," Jefferson reasons with a shrug. He's got a southern accent and a bigger gut than Alexi thought was allowed for soldiers who operate in the field. "The kids probably couldn't sleep and went out to play war. It don't look like these hombres can afford an Xbox."

That's the other thing that bothers Alexi. These people *are* poor. The stucco walls of the house are runny with dirt. The car in this lot doesn't look like it runs. The SUVs they tracked from the Colinas Estate are parked out front, and they have the right address, but Alexi knows something is wrong.

He watches as the Mexican authorities question Emmanuel. Manny sits against the house. His belly stretches a dirty white T-shirt. His hands are cuffed behind his back, and he speaks quickly, emphatically. Moving his head and yelling at times. He does not look like a cartel kingpin waiting to see his lawyer.

"How'd they get here so fast?" Beltran says, and Alexi looks to see what she's talking about.

Near the gate is a throng of reporters. More news vans are pulling up, and there's shouting and honking from out front as they clash with the Special Forces and first responders.

"Hey!" Alexi shouts at the Mexican police. He knows Spanish but doesn't command the language with the confidence of a native speaker. He nudges Beltran. "Tell them this entire block is supposed to have a perimeter."

Beltran shouts in Spanish, and the police shout right back and shrug like there's little they can do.

Alexi gulps nervously and looks at his watch. "Someone tipped off the press."

"Wasn't me," says Beltran.

"I'm not saying it was."

The reporters have all been stopped on the sidewalk just in front of the broken gate. One of them yells in English.

"Is it true? Has Emmanuel Barrera been captured by US authorities?"

"Shit," Beltran whispers. "How the hell do they know who we were after?"

The back of an ambulance is slammed shut. It's been loaded with the dead boys. Even as it cranks its siren and starts driving out onto the street, the reporters are slow to move out of the way.

"Because it wasn't some no-name cop who leaked this."

"You got any bets on who did?"

Alexi turns and watches a Mexican cop exit the house wearing a pair of purple latex gloves. He holds a file in both hands. Whatever its contents are, he starts sharing them with the other men who are interrogating Emmanuel Barrera. He hands them each a few sheets of paper.

Even though they're only twenty feet away, there's far too much commotion for Alexi to hear what they're saying. But he has a feeling.

Alexi starts walking over to Manny.

"Alexi! They told us to stay here." Beltran yells.

He doesn't respond.

"Alexi!"

The cops all look up at him as he gets close. They seem to marvel at his size. He points to the folder that was brought out of the house. "*Que es?*" Alexi asks in Spanish, but he's answered in English.

"The man's papers."

"Identification papers?"

"Everything. Yeah. Conveniently in one place. Birth certificate. Driver's licenses. Marriage certificate. You believe this shit. He's trying to say his name is Juan Carlos Ramos."

Alexi looks Manny. He's shaking his head with a grin. The Mexican cops think the paperwork is phony, but Alexi has put it together.

The kids. The lack of security. A cartel compound without a single weapon.

"Can you believe this?" asks a cop. They're all laughing with each other. "He's trying to tell us he's a gardener."

Alexi looks at the paperwork. It's not counterfeit. The cartel has been ahead of them from the start. This man isn't Emmanuel Barrera.

"That's because he is."

The cops stop laughing.

Alexi speaks barely louder than a whisper. "We just shot two kids dead and arrested a gardener."

Party

Iris stands stiff as a board as Paulo wraps her in a hug at the doorway of the little cottage, the gun still in his hand. "Oh, so good to see you, Iris! So good to see you!" He gives Augusta a big hug and then steps out of the way and waves them inside. "Come in! Come in. Please. Both of you."

She and Augusta enter the house and Paulo continues.

"I'm so sorry, Iris. We had to leave you behind for it all to look believable. Like we were really afraid the FBI was after us. I heard one of my guards shot at you. They were supposed to pick you up, bring you here easy. He panicked when he saw you off the property but he's been punished, okay?"

Paulo is talking a mile a minute. Iris is nervous to see that his big brown eyes are now black. His pupils are so big they've eclipsed his irises and a small ring of chocolate brown is all the color that's left.

He walks past them into a small dining room, and they follow. There's a table with four men. All of them are smoking. Two have cigars. The other two have cigarettes. They all wear suits, and the youngest is still at least several years older than Paulo.

"My money was that you fell and hit your head like the other whore," a woman says, and Iris and Augusta turn to see Esperanza sitting in a leather lounge chair. She wears a silk romper, like she's just been roused from bed. A bottle of white wine sits on an end table next to her. The glass in her hand is empty, and what little wine is left in the bottle doesn't rise above the punt.

"Ah, forgive my sister. She is bitter at my victory," Paulo says, tucking his pistol into the back of his pants. "She didn't so much as think you could keep your feet steady beneath you. I believed you were capable of much more than that, Iris. Now." Paulo gestures at the table. "These are my business associates. Tonight is a very special night that could not have happened without you. Do you like the US government? Uh, uh, uh..." He waves a finger. "Don't answer that. You shouldn't! They used you like a fucking goat, Iris." He snaps his fingers. "Like in...in *Jurassic Park*! Have you seen *Jurassic Park*? Where they put the little goat on the leash for the T. rex?"

He doesn't give Iris time to respond before speaking again. There's no cocaine on the table, but it's obvious Paulo has had a lot. She can see a little white residue under his nostrils. "No? That's okay. That's okay. Please, sit."

He pulls out two chairs. Iris doesn't sit. She looks at Augusta, but she won't make eye contact back. It's like she knows something about this situation that Iris doesn't.

They're not out of danger.

Iris keeps looking at her, and eventually Augusta gives her a little nod of assurance. They sit down in the blue haze of smoke. It's Augusta's fear that has Iris so on edge. She was the authority in every room she entered, and now, it looks like she's ready to beg for her life.

"I thought I would introduce you. You have done more for the cartel than any living American. There should be a statue of you, Iris. Scar and all."

"You don't even know if your plan worked, Paulo," Esperanza says and pours the last splash of wine into her glass.

"You wouldn't be such a sad drunk right now if you thought I failed."

The two begin to bicker, and the four men at the table are having their own conversation, also in Spanish.

The man seated next to Iris's right is the oldest in the room. He's got a patchy gray beard and a large cigar wedged between his fingers. He looks her over and then says something loudly towards Paulo, which stops him from speaking to his sister.

Paulo responds in Spanish, walks to Iris, and bends to her hair. Then to her disgust, he sniffs her.

The rest of the table chuckles, and Paulo says something witty that makes them all laugh louder. Then he slaps both shoulders of the older man who's seated next to Iris and goes back to his chair.

Iris is growing more angry than she is afraid. Her tongue can't be held. "Is he saying I smell?"

Paulo holds out a pacifying hand. "Forgive my friends' manners, Iris. They are not as civilized as I am." He smirks.

The man next to Iris isn't free of a scent himself. He has the sour reek of someone sweating alcohol. His neck and cheeks have a sheen of sweat. Iris sits up in her chair. "Ask him why he stinks, too." She points directly in his face. "I've run twenty miles and slept in a den of rattlesnakes. So how come he smells half as bad as I do from just sitting on his ass?"

Paulo translates this, and the table bursts out laughing. The sweaty man next to her does not join in.

Paulo says something else, and the man's eyes widen. He looks at Iris with a mixture of fear and respect.

"I just told him you were the *mujer* who shot her husband and then herself. He thought it was the old one." He points at Augusta. "Silent and Loco. But no, it's this beauty. Go on. Show him the scar."

Iris says nothing.

"Really, please. Show him, show him. Show all of us."

Iris pauses and brings her palm to her forehead. She parts her matted, grimy blonde hair away.

One man whistles in exclamation. The others just stare.

She lets her hair fall back and crosses her arms. "Why are we here?"

Paulo is busy lighting a cigarette. When he's done, he snaps his metal lighter shut and yells something in Spanish. A teenager comes into the room and picks up a remote. He turns on a TV hanging on the wall.

The table takes their attention to the TV. There's a woman reporter speaking into a camera. A light show of emergency vehicles flickers on the street in the background.

They listen for a minute, until the reporter says something that makes the men erupt in applause. Paulo spreads his arms and holds them in a boastful shrug. His friend closest to him pats his leg.

"Ah! I fucking told you!" Paulo says and rockets to his feet. He points at Esperanza. "The Americans thought they were too smart to be double crossed by a Mexican. I know. I know. Paulo is the greatest!"

He spins and gestures at Iris with his cigarette. "You got me in a lot of trouble. The FBI, DEA. They started poking around where they shouldn't. A lot of people thought I ruined our imports into America. A lot of people wanted me gone. Including..." He points at Esperanza. "Some of my own blood. But then I had an idea. Can you guess what, Iris?"

Paulo starts walking around the room. The other men are having a different conversation now. Iris doesn't think they speak any English.

"Come on." He nods at Iris. "Guess."

Iris grits her teeth, and Augusta must be able to tell she's trying not to erupt. She sets her hand firmly on Iris's thigh to try to calm her. "I'm done playing, Paulo," Iris says.

"Ah, that's too bad. But it is the end now, so okay, okay. All your country's feds, they've wanted to show their guns against us for some time. Make your president look like a macho man. Mexico's people, its drugs, you can't stop either from coming into your country. They can only look strong. Problem was they didn't know who to arrest. They know I'm a big player, but not that I'm the leader. My uncle Manny on the other hand, may he rest in peace, was another story."

"Uncle Manny hated you," Esperanza says.

Paulo grinds his teeth and shakes his head like a mad man about to explode. "Oh, would you shut up! Imagine wanting to be right so bad that you don't care about good news for the business. Just keep your trap shut."

Esperanza purses her lips. "Whatever."

"Uncle Manny... I was more like him than I was my papa. He was a psycho man. Liked to kill and ask questions later but to the point that it was bad for business. So, I find a man that looks like him. Hire him to be my gardener. Pay him to pretend to be the boss. Make sure the FBI can get to you, Iris, before you reach the compound. You see where this is going? The FBI thought you were perfect. A one-time lover of a drug lord soon to be thrown out with the rest of the garbage anyway."

Iris is clenching her fists. She's so angry, she's not even afraid of getting herself killed.

"They were desperate. I thought they'd at least investigate the bait before they bit. It's like catching a fish on a bright-pink lure. What are you doing? That doesn't even look like food. You know? They saw a shiny object, and then didn't even think. They just opened their mouths..." Paulo opens his mouth. "And chomp," he says and then bites down, baring his teeth. His mouth twists into a smile, and he smokes his cigarette.

Iris has enough guilt in her life. Now she just helped the cartel gain the upper hand over the US government. "And what do you get from making them look like idiots?" she asks.

Paulo's face turns serious. "Time, *señora*. Their operations will be much harder to fund next time. With this embarrassment, we have proved to simply be more trouble than we are worth." He walks over to Iris and gives her a long, smooching kiss on the forehead before she squirms away.

"And I could not have done it without you."

Iris looks at Augusta and realizes she had been glancing in the direction of Esperanza. Esperanza's mouth finishes moving. She was talking silently. Mouthing words to Augusta. Iris feels her butt clench. She's in the dark about something.

Paulo throws himself back into his chair and pulls out a small glass vial. He sprinkles a dime-sized pile of what must be cocaine on the back of his hand and snorts it right off. He tilts his head to the ceiling and blinks rapidly. Then he shouts something in Spanish so loud that Iris and Augusta jump.

He pounds his fist on the table and stands straight up. His business associates have quieted. They watch him warily, like they know he's dangerous in this state.

Iris is trying to hold the fury from her tongue, but she can't hold back any longer. "And what did the girls you murdered have to do with it?"

She feels Augusta's fingers dig into her thigh. She's pleading with her. *Stop.*

Paulo narrows his eyes. His devilish smirk returns as he spreads his lips in a smile. "Ah... The whores, you mean? That was cleaning up your mess. The FBI was asking around in Nashville or Memphis or whatever fucking town it was you crawled out of." He tilts his head back again and sniffs violently. "Some of those girls knew people." He speaks with his head towards the ceiling. "They were loose ends, that's all. Ones who are easier to dispose of without a trace here than in the States." He brings his head down and shakes it vigorously. "Don't think too much of it."

"And the two girls who went missing in Memphis... Jasmine and Katie, the two who shared a house together... Did you have them killed because they didn't want to be trafficked to Mexico?"

"Two what? Who?" Paulo suddenly looks furious. "Why the fuck do you think I'd know their names? I don't know these things. Your brother-in-law, the pudgy one,

308

Jamie, could tell you. He's the one helping us clean up this mess. So there." Paulo looks at Augusta. "And that's my last favor to you, too, Augusta. That's all. No more questions. We're done."

Iris isn't sure what he means. *Done.* But something isn't right. Why keep her alive? Why is Augusta beaten but not dead?"

Another question comes to Iris's mind, and it feels less dangerous to ask. "Why was I drugged?"

Paulo's eyes brighten. "I had almost forgotten! Come." Augusta and Iris both flinch back in their seats as he pulls the large silver pistol back out of his pants. "Come, come." He points the gun at them and waves them forward.

Iris's eyes start to water in fear. Her anger is finally overridden. At least it's not torture she's facing. At least it'll just be a bullet.

Augusta is the first one to stand and follow Paulo. Iris is a few steps behind. He takes them through a small kitchen and out the back door. Paulo leans back inside before closing it.

"Sister, I think it's best if you join us in our final parting with these lovely Adlers."

"With pleasure," Esperanza shouts and joins them outside.

The backyard is all dirt and stone pavers. There is no grass.

Iris is looking for the words to beg for her life. What could she possibly say to have him change his mind?

Augusta is the one to speak. "Paulo, we had a deal."

"And you fulfilled your end, yes. I appreciate that, Augusta. Truly, I do. Esperanza." He points at the far end of the yard where there's a few rusty lawn tools lying on a tarp next to a mound of dirt. A mound of dirt where a fresh hole has been dug, Iris realizes. "Grab a shovel."

Esperanza walks over to get one.

"I'm not one to go back on my deals. I'm telling the truth. I'm seeing you off." Paulo raises the pistol, but he points it in the opposite direction. He points it at Esperanza's leg.

Muzzle flash illuminates the backyard like a lightning bolt, and Iris jumps back towards the door.

Esperanza screams so loud that Iris puts her hands over her ears. Her leg has buckled under her, and she holds the area around her knee with both hands.

"Paulo! Paulo! Please!" She starts to crawl, as if she somehow has a chance to get away.

"You see what happens when you lead a charge to replace me?" He shoots her in the other leg, and she screams again. "When you try to have our stepbrother replace me? Go ahead and look in the hole. Whose face do you see? Santiago's."

Esperanza just cries.

"He died like even more of a dog."

"You two." Esperanza looks at Iris and Augusta. Her mouth keeps closing in a grimace as she tries to speak. "Paulo will kill you when he's bored of you. Help. Help me!"

"Sister, these are business associates who have been nothing but good to me. You embarrass yourself. Die like a Delgado, with pride."

"Fuck you, Paulo."

"Go on, keep crawling to the hole." He waves the gun for her to move. "I'll shoot you in the head once you're there. No more pain, I promise."

Esperanza stays where she is and breathes heavily.

"Fine." Paulo raises his pistol again and shoots her right through the head. "You're light enough to carry, I suppose."

The silence lingers for what feels like an eternity as the echo of the shot is carried into the distance.

Paulo breaks it by blowing on the pistol barrel like a gunslinger but there's no smoke. He whistles commandingly. A guard comes into the yard from the other side of the house. He steps to Esperanza and begins to drag her under the armpits.

"I hope I have been a good host to you, Iris. I apologize for all these inconveniences."

Iris is too shocked to talk.

"I understand you hate what we have done to those girls in the States, yes? What we did to girls like you. I feel bad. Truly." He reaches out and puts a hand on her shoulder. She recoils, but not far enough to stay out of the grasp of his long arm. He ducks his head so they're eye to eye. "But Esperanza, she worked there. She probably even crossed paths with you in Memphis. It was she who selected girls. She who decided which ones would make good whores."

Paulo pats Iris's shoulder and moves his hand to her face, where he pinches her chin. "You have earned what you came to Mexico for. Please, enjoy the beach for me. Think of this as my reward for your help. No more prostitutes in America. You have my word." He heads inside and shuts the door gently behind him.

Iris and Augusta stay frozen in the backyard. Neither looks at the other. What feels like a full minute passes in silence until the guard who dragged Esperanza into the hole comes back over to them whistling. He doesn't say anything, but the indication is clear that they're supposed to follow him.

They walk slowly, stiffly, as if they both expect to be shot in the back. But no bullet comes.

They walk around to the front of the cottage, where the back door to the SUV they came here in is opened for them. The cartel could be taking them to another destination to kill them, but Iris doesn't think so. Paulo could've done that here.

She turns back to the cottage, and the SUV begins to roll forward. Augusta is silent. She doesn't offer her hand this time or a kind word. She's just as shocked as Iris, and the two look out their windows as they drive back through the woods. Speechless.

Extraction

Alexi stares at the headrest of the car seat in front of him. He's trying to keep his breathing under control, but Beltran won't shut up.

"Bad is an understatement. I mean... this is our careers. They're done if this is true. Do you understand that at all?"

Alexi grunts. He's picturing the two dead kids in soccer jerseys. He's envisioning Iris Adler's stomach being cut open while she's still alive. Beltran is imagining being sent to the mail room.

"It was your idea, Alexi. You know that? It's in email. You were the first one to suggest using Iris as a mole."

"Uh-huh. You can try the blame game, but we're both cooked."

Another field agent is in the passenger seat of the car. He hangs up the phone. "That was Alinsky. The Deputy Directors want a call ASAP. Peterman wants to know if he should wake up Erikson."

Erikson—the Director of the FBI. Luckily, Alexi couldn't feel any more anxious than he already does. "We probably should. Yeah," he says.

Beltran puts her face in her hands. "How'd we fuck up like this?"

"Because we thought we hit the jackpot," Alexi says, but he knows there's more to why they lost. Using Iris Adler's life wasn't enough of a sacrifice. The cartel made them kill teenage boys just to make them look like idiots.

"Because you can't beat an enemy with no morals without becoming just as debased."

Beltran shakes her head and punches the inside of the car door. "Fuck!"

They don't speak for the rest of the drive back to the field office. They don't take off their tactical gear as they enter the makeshift war room. Ernie comes in shortly after and sets two coffees on the table.

"There was a development while you two were gone."

Beltran raises her head with the enthusiasm of a child. Alexi's expression doesn't change any. They wait for Ernie to continue.

He points at the video monitors at the end of the room and walks over. "About an hour after you left, the drone we have circling the safe house Paulo Delgado fled to picked this up on its infrared."

He moves the mouse to a video player bar, rewinds the footage, and then hits play. Their three faces crowd the screen. "You see this? A vehicle arrived at the safe house at 2:34 a.m. It was carrying two women."

To Alexi, the bright shapes on the screen don't have a sex, but Ernie has been taught to read infrared imaging with the skill of an X-ray tech.

"They were there for all of fifteen minutes before leaving in the same vehicle. And just before they left…" He clicks the mouse and zooms in. He plays the video. Four people stand behind the house, and one who walked farther from the others suddenly falls over. They're on the ground for a few seconds, and Alexi can see a flash come from the hand of another person.

They're being executed. A fifth joins them all and starts to drag this shot person. A body.

"This guy's dragging her." Ernie points. "But I don't think it's one of the women who arrived in the SUV."

"So who is it?" Beltran blurts out impatiently.

"I don't know. Maybe a nobody. But watch this." Ernie turns back to the screen and clicks until it shows what looks like a man filling a hole with dirt. The heat signature of the dragged body gradually vanishes. "You could find a body here. She was buried in the backyard."

"This is Sina-fucking-loa, Ernie. We could find a body in every goddamn acre of the place."

"Okay." He puts his hands up. "Just thought you might want to know about a fresh corpse."

"Do you have any idea what just happened in Durango?"

"Come on. Cool it," Alexi says.

Beltran glares at him.

Alexi taps Ernie's shoulder. "Tell me about the women. What are you thinking?"

Ernie is quiet. He opens his mouth, but it's a few seconds before the words come out. "I'm thinking what I'm sure you're thinking—one of these women is Iris Adler."

Beltran scoffs. "Iris Adler is worm food already. That was probably her grave."

"Look, the heat signature of this third woman, the one who ended up in the ground, it's thin. This woman is thirty pounds smaller than either of the other two who arrived in the SUV. Maybe not to your eye, but I'm telling you, there's a noticeable difference."

This shuts Beltran up. She crosses her arms and twitches her eyebrows. "So what?"

Ernie shrugs. "After all that just transpired in Durango… What if Iris isn't dead? What if she's around to tell her story?"

Beltran and Alexi go quiet. Alexi understands exactly what Ernie's saying. He's ahead of them on this one. Right now, they might be able to keep this story under wraps. The American press is already talking about the accidental shooting. It'll be leaked soon that they arrested a gardener. But what happens if the media finds out this was all instigated because the FBI used a brain-damaged fugitive to try to infiltrate the most powerful cartel in the world? If Iris is dead, they can refute it. But if she turns up again…

Beltran's eyes go wide. "Ernie, please tell me you started following that SUV after it left again."

Ernie exits out of the video, and the screen shows an SUV traveling down a highway. "I already told the operators to leave the safe house behind, but we're going to need to refuel in two hours, and unless the SUV stops before then, we'll lose contact. They headed south. They're not far from here now."

"Can we get a tail on them?"

"Mexican police can, sure."

Beltran shakes her head. "We can't trust them on this. Someone leaked this operation to the press."

"I'll do it," Alexi says. "Get me a car."

"You might not even have a job in twenty minutes," says Beltran.

"Then this will help me keep it a little longer."

Ernie stands and makes for the door. "I can get you a car. Sit tight."

He leaves, and Alexi adjusts his utility belt. He takes the magazine out of his pistol and replaces it with one that's fully loaded.

"I can go with you," Beltran offers.

"One of us needs to be on this call."

"This is more your fault than mine."

"Great. Then it should be you. Throw me under the bus when I'm not there to defend myself."

Beltran doesn't respond.

"They'll probably want to send in a Special Forces team to extract Iris, but I need to keep eyes on her."

Beltran smirks. Her eyes are squinted in amusement. "Sometimes I wonder how you got this far in the Bureau, Alexi."

He pauses and waits for her to explain what she's talking about.

"You think they're going to want to *extract* Iris after all this?" She walks close to him and reaches up to pat him contemptuously on the chest. "But you know what? I think you might make a good assassin. A little easy to spot, maybe."

"Agents?" Ernie leans in the doorway. "The deputy director is on the line now."

Beltran sits at the table and reaches a finger towards the conference speaker in the middle of it. She hovers it above the answer button. "Give that bitch my best," she says to Alexi and accepts the call.

Alexi is glued in place. She's exaggerating, surely. The FBI isn't going to kill a US citizen, he thinks, but he's not certain.

After all, he's never been in the middle of a mess this bad.

The Surf

Iris and Augusta have both been dozing in and out of sleep for the past few hours. Their driver doesn't speak any English, or if he does, he doesn't feel any need to inform them where they might be going.

Iris was alert at first—marking road signs, north and south, and trying to recognize the names of cities. They passed through the metropolis of Guadalajara and into a state called Jalisco. Sinaloa is behind them. The junkyard. The metal shredder used for corpses. The beating heart of the cartel.

Iris doesn't want to trick herself, but she's hopeful. Paulo had his chances, but then again, there is no such thing as being out of the woods with a man who treats life like a game.

Iris comes to attention as they stop at a gas station in the middle of nowhere. From the shadows of hills on either side of the road, she can tell they're in elevation, but that's the only thing she can say of the terrain. No doubt their driver made sure to pick a place where they were the only vehicle at the pumps.

The urge to run causes her heart to thump. Their doors are unlocked. She can see the little red tag of plastic next to the handle indicating so. They're not on rural back roads anymore. This was a highway. All she'd have to do was wait until morning. And then what? Hitchhike?

Iris wraps her fingers around the door handle. Their driver whistles at the pump. She looks over at Augusta. She doesn't look like she's in any condition to run.

She didn't even seem to stir when the driver slammed his door shut. She seems resigned to their fate, whatever it may be. There's a deeper, deathlike exhaustion to her.

Iris wonders if Augusta's bruised face is just the tip of the iceberg. She looks at her shirt and envisions what burns and cuts might be hidden beneath.

Iris takes her hand off the car door and leans into Augusta. Augusta wakes suddenly then relaxes. She wraps her arms around Iris's shoulders, and the two hold each other in silence—not as lovers, but as two people in the same situation. Both trying not to be consumed by the feeling that they're being ferried to their deaths. They start to drive again, and with her head against Augusta's collarbone, Iris is finally able to sleep.

Iris is shaken lightly awake. The world is darker than it was when she fell asleep, and she realizes it's because her face had ended up pressed into Augusta's lap. She lifts her head and blinks at the brightness. Augusta isn't looking at her. She's staring out the window. She's staring at the sea.

They're on an oceanside highway, and the water is ablaze in the light of morning. It's textured with tens of thousands of little whitecaps. The view of the Pacific is suddenly obscured by palm trees, and then the SUV turns inland and the ocean disappears entirely.

Iris leans back so she's in the middle seat next to Augusta. "Do you know where we're going?" she asks.

Augusta nods. "A beach house. It's near Puerto Vallarta. It's private, don't worry."

"Did he tell you?" Iris looks at the back of the driver's head.

"Yes. I knew where we were going. But I just wasn't sure…"

"We wouldn't end up in a hole somewhere?"

"Yeah."

The SUV pulls off of the highway and onto a sandy road with palm trees on either side. The dark-blue water comes into view dead ahead, and then the SUV turns onto the beach. The shore horseshoes here. It's a cove. The beach at the center is sandy but fringed with coral rocks farther out.

There's a small house set back about fifty yards from the water. It's painted baby blue—the same color as the early morning sky. There are wooden trellises running up the sides, crawling with vines. Iris can't really believe it. This house, this cove—it looks like heaven. A flock of birds flies from a palm as they get close and settle in another on the other side of the cove.

The driver gets out, opens the doors for them, and hands them a key. Then he starts walking into the sandy palm forest. Iris and Augusta watch him nervously until they see him plant his feet and reach for his crotch.

They go closer to the house as he finishes peeing, and before they even put the key in the door, he's back in the SUV, and it whips around in a circle and disappears down the road they came here on in a roar.

Iris and Augusta stay still until the sound is gone completely and is replaced by the soft beating surf. Seagulls glide and call. The wind that comes off the ocean is so fresh that each breath Iris takes makes her head feel clearer.

Augusta starts walking to the house's front door.

There's a wooden deck surrounding the entire structure. It's on ground level, and all the planks are covered in thousands of grains of sand. Their steps crunch as they walk to the door.

Augusta puts the key in and unlocks it. She pushes the door open but doesn't step in right away, as if the place might be booby trapped. The breeze butts in first, rippling window curtains and dish towels that hang over brass handles in the kitchen. The inside of the house has the brackish smell of beach. Salt and seaweed decay. It's not entirely unpleasant, just strong. Augusta steps inside and takes off her sandals.

"You'll track sand in."

Iris takes her sneakers off, too. She isn't expecting the wave of relief that follows. She's had these shoes hugging her feet for days. She peels off her socks, and it feels like they're taking a layer of skin off with them. She tosses them outside. She spreads her toes on the cool hardwood of the beach house. Augusta is already going room to room investigating, but Iris is still.

The place is tiny and fully furnished. There's a tiny den with windows that look out to the ocean, a kitchen, and one bedroom and bathroom. Iris walks into the kitchen and opens the fridge. It's fully stocked with meats, cheeses, juices, and something pre-cooked in Tupperware containers. There's silverware in the drawers. Coffee and chips in the cabinets. A bowl of oranges and bananas sits on the blonde wood kitchen table. Next to it is a yellow legal pad with a note written in English.

"Augusta, Iris, make yourselves at home again. For any requests..."

There's a ten-digit phone number listed below. Iris doesn't have a phone, but maybe Augusta does. Augusta walks into the den and starts tossing the cushions off the couch. "I'll take the pullout. You can have the bed, Iris."

"Are you sure?"

Augusta grunts as she finishes pulling the bed out and unfolding it. She opens the linen closet and pulls out a stack of sheets and blankets like she's been here before. "I'm positive."

Iris watches as Augusta concentrates her energy on making the pull-out bed.

"How bad did they hurt you?"

Augusta ignores her for a moment as she yanks the fitted sheet over the mattress corner. "Just what you see, sugar. I'm fine."

"Why did they do it?"

Augusta stops and stands up straight. "How about we both get a nap in before we get into the details? You could use a shower, too, Iris."

Iris nods, and Augusta starts to fluff her already plump pillows. It's clear she wants Iris to go away.

Iris nods nervously and goes into the bathroom and takes off all her clothes. She has random bruising, scratches, and patches of dirt all over her body. Her hair is a frizzy blonde ball of grease. She steps into the shower and waits for the water to get warm. It never does get hot, and she steps into the tepid dribble and starts to scrub herself with a bar of rough soap.

She rubs harder and harder, and it seems like no matter how much she cleans herself, the water that circles the drain stays just as dirty. She shampoos and rinses her hair twice for good measure and dries herself off in front of the mirror that never saw the steam it takes to fog over.

She looks rough. The bags under her eyes are as dark as bruises. Her skin is discolored and splotchy all over. Some bug bit her a few times just above her butt, and the welts are the size of silver dollars and just starting to itch. Now that she's clean, she can smell her rancid clothes. She wishes she had a broom handle to pick them up with and take them to the trash, but instead she wraps a towel around herself and wraps her hand in toilet paper and lifts the clothes.

She stuffs them into the kitchen trash and sees that Augusta is already fast asleep on the pull-out. She's opened the windows in the den, and the house is alive with the sound of the wave's crashing and the breeze as it funnels in through the windows with a soft whistle.

Iris goes back to the bedroom and opens the dresser drawers. There are women's clothes in two different sizes—Iris's and Augusta's.

This place wasn't thrown together for their arrival. The beach house has been part of the plan all along. Iris puts on a pair of generic white underwear and a white T-shirt and crawls under the covers. She thinks she should be able to sleep. The hour or two she got on the ride here had done little to make her feel rested. But Iris stares up at the still blades of the ceiling fan. She's stuck in her head. An hour passes like this, then maybe another.

She's just starting to feel tired when she hears the door to her bedroom creak as it's opened. She sits up with a jolt, expecting a gunman or Paulo's wide, wicked smile.

But it's Augusta. She's barely dressed, like Iris. She's in her underwear and a T-shirt that's a size too small for her and shows the bottom of her tan belly. Her white hair has been combed. Her face has been touched up with foundation and concealer. She doesn't say anything as she walks to the end of the bed.

It looks like she's here to talk, but Iris doesn't prompt her. She doesn't say a word as Augusta sits near her feet. She reaches under the sheets and starts rubbing Iris's leg. It's not a comforting touch. It's wanting. Her hand moves higher towards Iris's groin, and Iris pulls her legs up. Augusta glides up the bed so they're face to face, and then she closes her eyes, ducks her head, and puts Iris's earlobe in her mouth.

Iris's eyes are not closed in pleasure. They stare wide at the ceiling. This is not the time for sex. Nothing about this feels right or normal or attractive.

Her heart beats nervously, but it's all bees, not butterflies.

She feels exposed.

"Augusta," Iris says, but Augusta just moves her mouth down Iris's neck towards her breast. She feels a sharp sensation as Augusta bites her nipple through the thin cotton of her T-shirt.

"Augusta!" Iris shouts and scooches back so she's sitting up against the headboard, and Augusta looks up at her with guilty eyes.

"I don't want this."

Augusta's face scrunches up like she's been struck, and Iris adds gently, "Not now."

Augusta slinks back so she's kneeling on the bed. "I'm sorry." She blinks rapidly like she'd been under a spell and is just coming to grips. "I'm sorry," she repeats and stands.

She walks quickly out of the bedroom and slams the door behind her.

Iris is left in silence. There is no sound of the breeze or the sea in here. Her nipple still stings. Her heart still pounds. She frowns and squeezes her fists until they're white, trying to will the past to come to her.

A memory hangs just out of reach like a dream she's trying to remember. Augusta in her bed. Her breath on her neck. This has happened before. Plenty of times. She knows this.

Augusta saved her from these monsters once, but Iris isn't sure she can succeed a second time. It's Paulo who makes her skin crawl. She can pretend otherwise, but she feels it in her heart like a fact: he'll be back.

Followed

Alexi isn't fired. Not yet, at least. They want him on the next plane to Quantico, Virginia, where he awaits a full inquiry into the failure of the operation. Beltran has already been taken out of the field. As soon as he's relieved from his surveillance duties, he's gone too.

They say twelve hours—that's how long it will take to get a team down to Puerto Vallarta. For now, he's on his own, with nothing but his phone, service pistol, and a musky Volkswagen Amarok the Mexican authorities were able to procure for him.

It's a midsize pickup, black with tinted windows the same color as the paint. It's not as inconspicuous as he would have liked, but he doesn't think the SUV that was carrying the two women from Paulo's safe house noticed him tailing them.

He kept a half mile back until the drone was able to refuel, and then he stayed out of sight. When Alexi got word that they turned onto a sandy road that went towards the beach, he had a feeling they'd reached their destination.

He drove past the sandy road about a mile ahead until the shoulder was wide enough for him to pull onto.

He sits in his truck now, looking at the satellite maps on his phone. It shows that the sandy road has no exit. It runs to a little cove with a small house in the center set back from the beach. There is no address posted. No neighboring structures either. It's probably another safe house. He holds his phone in his hand, waiting for the surveillance team to call him with an update. It's only five minutes before they do.

The phone vibrates, and Alexi accepts the call. "Yes?"

A male voice he doesn't recognize begins to speak. "Two females have exited the SUV, but we're too far out to get an ID."

"Okay, I've got my satellite pulled up. I see there's a structure."

"The women entered that house. We're not seeing any other cars or a garage, but the forest is thick. They could have wheels and are transferring vehicles."

"You want me to sit tight?"

"We want you to try to get a visual on these women. If neither is Iris Adler, get back in your truck and make for Guadalajara international airport. Terminal one."

"And if one of these women is her?"

"Then you are to surveille her movements until you're relieved."

"And what's the plan? Are we extracting her?"

There's a pause on the other line. "You don't have clearance on this operation. Your duties are observation only, do you understand?"

Alexi exhales. He feels light with relief that he hasn't been instructed to kill her, but it doesn't last. He probably will be. This is his problem to fix.

"Call if the women leave," says the voice on the phone. "Call once you get an identification."

"Understood."

The line goes dead.

Alexi brings the phone down and stares at it in his palm. A part of him doesn't believe what Beltran said—the FBI can't just murder Iris Adler. That can't just be an acceptable play in their book. But this isn't about national security—it's about the Bureau's pride. The director's pride.

The countless other federal employees who would see their careers suffer for this. He's seen the FBI ignore threats to national security before, but never their pride.

They're not going to let themselves be embarrassed more than they are. A botched operation is one thing. Alexi already knows what the FBI's media strategy will be.

They'll say the Mexican government is too corrupt to work with. That it wasn't the cartel who set them up but legitimate Mexican officials who must've taken bribes. Iris changes that. Iris is smart and capable, but the media will rip her apart. She'll be labeled a brain-damaged prostitute. If it comes out that the FBI recruited her to infiltrate one the most dangerous organizations in the world, America's incompetence will be impossible to refute.

The FBI isn't going to let her live. Not when it would be so easy to just snuff her out here, when the world still thinks she's missing.

But really, this is Alexi's fault. Chess master, Mensa member, 6'8" giant. The Russian orphan and the Bureau's next prodigy. Everybody took his ideas as gospel. When he came up with the plan to use Iris as a mole, the higher-ups all thought it was genius.

There was no second-guessing. They were hungry for an opportunity to look strong against the drugs and human trafficking of Mexico, and the golden child had a solution.

This is Alexi's failure, and it isn't going to be pawned off to some assassin. No, Iris is his problem to fix, and at the back of Alexi's mind, an idea is already forming.

He checks his sidearm to make sure there's a round in the chamber, and then he gets out of the truck. He looks both ways down the cracked highway strewn with sand and browning palm fords. There is no one else around here. No one for miles.

He locks his truck and starts trudging through the thick foliage towards the beach house.

He uses the satellite on his phone to make sure he's headed in the right direction. The ground here is all soft sand, and while his steps are silent, the grains constantly fill his shoes.

He moves slowly, hunched, looking for guards. Alexi comes to the tree line on the far side of the cove. There is no one on the beach. No cartel sentry strolling back and forth with a rifle half the size of him. It's not a good omen if Paulo doesn't believe these two women are worth protecting.

Alexi stays under the palms and starts to walk the crescent cove to its center where the house lies. There is no TV or talking happening inside. The surf and the breeze both boom in his ears. Suddenly, he freezes. A window opens on the side of the house.

He sees a white curtain of hair blown by the wind, and then it's tucked back by a tanned hand. The face he sees is bruised but unmistakable. Alexi feels his brows stitch together. A shiver skates down his spine. *Augusta Adler?*

She disappears away from the window, and Alexi bolts forward. He gets onto the wood deck that surrounds the house and stays close to the wall. He peeks through another window.

Hair dripping wet, body splotched with bruises. Iris Adler is bent over a dresser pulling out clothes.

Alexi leans back against the wall and licks his lips. Augusta and Iris Adler. *Alive.* Alive and staying in the same safe house. He walks away from the house and back under the palms. He goes deep—a quarter mile away from the house—before he pulls out his phone and crouches on his heels.

He dials the FBI, and they pick up on the first ring.

"Yes?"

"This is Agent Akers."

"Report. Have you achieved a visual?" the man demands.

"Yes." The words then freeze in Alexi's throat. It takes them a moment to thaw, and when they do, they are something different entirely. "It looks like they're just a couple of Hispanic call girls. Probably here to service the next cartel hotshot staying by the beach."

"Copy. You are to make your way to Guadalajara immediately. This operation has been terminated."

"Okay." Alexi begins to lie. "One problem—I think I've been spotted. No one has approached me but back on the road, and there's a motorcyclist waiting about a half mile back. They're just watching me."

"You're about twelve miles from Puerto Vallarta. We could notify the Mexican authorities there, and you could rendezvous with them."

"I'll do that. You want me to head to the police station?"

"Yes."

"Okay. Tell them I'm en route."

"Stay safe, Akers."

Alexi hangs up and stares at his phone for a moment before he drops it in the sand, grips his long fingers around a heavy coconut, and cracks the screen.

Together

Iris doesn't fall back asleep after Augusta's visit. She stays in bed and listens to her making something in the kitchen. Augusta's not trying to be quiet. She hears cabinets shut and dishware clink, and the burner ticks noisily as it's turned on.

Iris hears something frying in a pan, and in another minute, she smells eggs and a spicy sausage that almost makes her sneeze. Chorizo.

Hungry as she is, she's nervous Augusta is going to try to apologize by bringing her breakfast in bed.

The thought makes her cringe. Iris had wanted nothing but Augusta since she first ran from Sweet Blood, but not anymore. She feels too vulnerable. Augusta has been hiding out with this cartel for two months. Then Iris remembers her bruises. This has been no vacation for Augusta, either. They were in this together.

As much as Iris wants Augusta to know she's upset with her behavior, she can't hold a grudge. She gets out of bed, finds a clean pair of black athletic pants in the dresser, and goes out into the kitchen.

Augusta doesn't look up from cooking. There's a visible layer of smoke in the air, and out here the odors are burnt. "I tried to make omelets." Augusta curses under her breath as she wrestles eggs with a spatula. "But we're having scrambles."

Iris goes to the coffeemaker and pours herself a mug and then takes a seat at the little kitchen table. Augusta sets a plate of dry scrambled eggs in front of her with little blackened bits of burnt sausage.

"It's been a long time since I've cooked." Augusta is staring at Iris's plate with disappointment. "I'm sorry."

Iris doesn't want to make small talk. She's either going to eat so she can face the day with a full stomach or question Augusta as to what the hell they're doing at a beach house and if they're actually safe. Iris takes the plate from her. "I'm so hungry I could eat the raw ingredients. It's fine. Thanks for cooking." Iris digs in, and Augusta sits across from her in front of her own plate.

It's not a lot of food, and Iris finishes in a few minutes. When she comes out of her trance, she realizes Augusta hasn't even picked up her fork. Her expression is sorrowful. Far away. Iris suddenly feels guilty for being short with her. "Do you want something else?"

Augusta grimaces. She points at her bruised cheek. "Hurts to chew."

Iris looks around the kitchen and then stands. "Here." She takes both plates to the sink and takes the pitcher of mango juice out of the fridge. She places it on the table and then grabs two glasses from the cabinets.

She gives Augusta a glass and then starts pouring her own. They drink in silence. Augusta sits straight and just nurses hers with small, delicate sips, as if anything else would be improper.

How Augusta can prioritize manners after all the violence they've seen, Iris doesn't know. Putting on a seat belt feels foolish now—like a strange act of self-preservation. Caring enough to eat like a proper lady when Iris is starving seems even stupider.

Iris wolfs down the juice in gulps. She slows only so it doesn't pour out and down the corners of her mouth. In her starved state, the syrupy, sugary drink is as good as any hit of a drug that Iris can remember. She finishes her glass with a satisfied sigh. "Wow."

Augusta licks her lips and sets her juice down. She's had maybe a quarter of the glass. "I'm sorry, but I can't just sit here and eat breakfast. My mouth doesn't actually hurt."

Iris is quiet, waiting for Augusta to continue, but when she doesn't, she asks, "Should we be running?"

Augusta shakes her head. "No. I was..." She sighs and pinches the bridge of her nose. "I had been staying here the last couple months. Before you got to Mexico, and before Paulo came up with his plan. I've been safe here. We're safe. This was the deal."

"So you're sure? He's not going to change his mind?"

Augusta tilts her head in a little shrug, as if to say Paulo changing his mind is always a possibility.

It's not reassuring. If Paulo is bored, he might just decide to make a game of this. Iris wouldn't be surprised if he let a hungry Lola into the house or locked all the doors and lit the place on fire when they were sleeping. They need to get out of here.

"Do you have access to any money?" Iris asks.

"Yes. I have offshore accounts."

"Then let's go."

"Go where, Iris?"

"Anywhere. Somewhere Paulo doesn't know where we are."

"All we'd be doing is ending up in the same place only somewhere else. A secluded beach house. This is what we need."

"Can't we go to South America? Where he doesn't know where we are?"

"I don't know any Realtors down there, do you? I have money but no fake identification papers. And you, Iris... Your face has been all over the news in America. One tourist sees you, and then what?"

"I don't see how you think he's going to let us live."

"He let me live for two months. You understand that? He was planning to do so indefinitely if I kept paying him, which I could."

"Then why'd he beat you?"

"Because I made a bit of a scene when they lost you."

"After I was shot at?"

Augusta nods. "I was... difficult. But at the time...I thought you were dead. Lost in the Sierra Madre."

"What did they do to you?"

"It was just a punch. Which to the cartel might as well be a literal flick on the wrist. It's fine, Iris. Please." She reaches across the table and tries to take Iris's hands in hers, but Iris yanks hers back down to her lap quickly.

Her pulse hiccups in her chest. Has Augusta not seen the same violence she has? Does she just not care? Iris has more questions. Her memories of Memphis and what Augusta had told Iris about her own past don't add up. She was protecting her from something.

Augusta stares at the floor and then slaps her hand flat on the table twice.

"Would you judge me if I had something stronger than juice?" she says and stands.

"Go ahead."

"I could go for a little relaxant." She reaches into an upper cabinet and pulls down a brown bottle of rum. "There's club soda and lime juice. Mojito? Breakfast of champions."

"Sure." Iris still can't smile, but the offer of a drink isn't something she can turn down. Her anxiety is still telling her to run. That there is no such thing as being safe as long as Paulo knows where she is. Augusta brings all the ingredients to the table. She twists a couple ice cubes out of a plastic freezer tray, adds them to the glasses, and starts to pour the rum.

"Strong or weak?" Augusta asks.

"Strong."

The ice cracks as she pours the rum in. She fills half the glass with it, pours the club soda and squeezes lime over the top. It's a hasty mojito but Iris agrees with the preparation. Perhaps more than any drink she's ever had, it's a means to an end.

Iris takes a big first gulp and then sets her glass down. Her stomach still feels empty, despite the eggs and juice. The liquor burns making its way into her bloodstream. She closes her eyes. Pictures her heart beating. They both drink and listen to the waves crashing out the open windows.

There's nothing awkward about the silence. It's not the sound of there being a lack of things to talk about. That panic between two people realizing they don't have enough in common to easily continue a conversation. It's a silence of exhaustion.

Augusta finishes her drink first and pours more rum. She hovers the bottle horizontally over Iris's glass and gestures down with her green eyes.

"Go ahead," Iris says, and Augusta refills her cocktail like it's a cup of coffee.

It's quiet for another couple minutes before Iris talks. "I want to kill Paulo."

Augusta huffs humorously. "I think the best thing you can do, at least for today, sugar, is *forget* Paulo."

A ticking sound on the roof startles Iris. It's raining. She glances over her shoulder out the window to see clouds have come in from the ocean, and it goes from no rain at all to a downpour in all of a few seconds.

Forget Paulo? It seems all but impossible, but she reckons Augusta may be right. Iris brings the glass to her lips and hesitates before tilting her head back and letting the rum pour down her throat. Maybe she can at least try.

Cozy

The rain doesn't stop, and neither does their drinking. Iris and Augusta are on their fourth cocktails when they finally begin to become lively. They're talking about the posh culture of rich southern society.

It's intricacies. It's hypocrisy.

Augusta has had an easier time loosening up, probably because she actually believes they're safe.

She's smoking a cigarette as she talks. "I'm telling you, sugar. The rule of thumb down south is the angrier something makes someone, the likelier it is they indulge in it. Almost every Bible-thumping homophobe I've met has a gay lover. Every woman who hates Mexicans hires a dozen of them to maintain her house. If I had a dollar for every time one of them rich women went off about trans fats or drug use and I found they had a pantry full of Hostess cakes they vomit up or a bottle of Vicodin in their bathroom, I never would've gotten into this mess. I'd be richer than King Tut." Augusta takes a drag of her cigarette. "People hate that which they hate about themselves. *That's* God's truth."

"What about you? Were you ever a homophobe?"

"Oh no. No, I admitted I was gay. To myself, I mean. The closeted men down there can be taking it in the ass at breakfast and still go to bed that night swearing they're straight. Pardon my French."

Iris shakes her head with a smirk. She's never heard such words come out of Augusta's mouth, and they sound ludicrous in her lush southern accent. "Did you have anyone else? Before me?"

"You mean a lover?"

"A woman one, yeah."

"Of course there was. The only pro of all that projection was that it made it easy to spot which women were hiding a little bit of a lesbian side."

"What about Joseph, your husband... Did he know?"

"Oh, he knew." Augusta blows out a long plume of smoke. "He said to knock myself out. Our marriage became one of convenience. Power. He wanted me to run the business and in exchange send him pictures of our pastor's wife's chest."

"Wait, is that a figure of speech, or did you..."

"Pastor's wife. Judge's wife. A lot of those bored southern belles were looking to explore. That was another thing about the culture there. You grow up your whole life being told something is so very wrong that it's hard to resist at least trying it."

"I had you pegged as a love-starved lesbian," says Iris.

"No, I was having a grand ol' time. They weren't beauties like you. They were *never* beauties like you, don't get me wrong. And it was a one-and-done kinda thing with most."

"Is that why you liked me? I was a pretty young thing?"

"I liked you because you were strong."

Iris leans back, slighted. Something about the way Augusta said it felt cheap. Manipulative. She remembers their first meeting. Augusta's attraction had nothing to do with strength. Iris decides not to share that fact. "Come on. Enough with sappy bullshit."

"I mean it. I was around people who pretended to be someone else all their waking life. Myself included. You were just you."

"I'm not special. I just wasn't raised in a culture of shame. My mom worked at a gas station. No one cared if her daughter was queer. The biggest source of pride in my neighborhood was if your kid was sober or not in jail. Graduating college was seen like climbing Everest. The bar was different."

"Maybe. But don't discount yourself. The things you've done..."

Iris feels her heart jump. She doesn't like to be reminded of the things she's done. There was nothing strong about shooting her husband. Nothing strong about shooting herself. It makes her feel like some psycho bitch. Like the person Annabelle has painted her out to be. Annabelle. Iris suddenly grows quiet.

Augusta can tell. She leans forward. "What is it?"

"Your daughter-in-law."

"Oh." It seems like Augusta doesn't want to discuss her either.

Iris tilts her head up. She's got an idea. "Hey, now that the world thinks you're dead, what's stopping you from releasing information that incriminate her? Anonymously, of course."

Augusta suddenly looks pained. "It would put my son in jail, too."

"Jamie was never your favorite," Iris jokes, but Augusta's face doesn't lighten.

"I know I said I'd take the fall. But I can't do that anymore. Not if you want to be..."

"Be what?"

Augusta looks up into Iris's eyes. "Together."

Iris looks away and ignores her question. She's still not done trying to pin Annabelle. "What about Marshall? Does he have information? Could he be selective and only release things that incriminates her?"

"Iris, let it go. You won. Annabelle is shitting in a bag for the rest of her life."

Maybe it's the rum, but Iris is angry again. She knows Augusta is hiding the answer. Of course Marshall could do that. He's a fixer. It's what he does. "Someone has to pay."

"And what about Esperanza? Paulo wasn't lying. She worked to set up the sex rings. Stop looking for vengeance. It's over, Iris."

Iris is quiet. She takes a sip of her drink.

Augusta sighs. "Did you know I first found out I was gay at a horse race? I was eight years old." She's smiling, trying to lighten the mood.

Iris decides not to sulk. "How so?"

"Those horses' penises." Augusta swings her head in disgust. "I mean, have you ever seen one?"

Iris smiles. She can tell Augusta is trying to humor her, but she accepts it. "Yeah, Augusta. I've seen a horse's penis."

"I didn't know about the birds and the pees. I'd never seen a penis. Not my father's. Not my brother's. Hand to God. My parents must've kept me from cherub statues my whole life till then. I remember seeing this thing *dangling*." Augusta waves her arm up and down like an elephant's trunk. "And I ask my older cousin, what is that thing? And she just smiles, and then at eight years old... I hear it all. She tells me everything. How babies are made. I had nightmares for weeks about it."

"You thought men were hung like horses?"

"Yes! Which I suppose for some women would've turned out to be a giant disappointment later in life, but for little Augusta, it was too much. I decided to like girls."

"You're saying you decided to be gay?"

"No. No, I was probably always gay. I admit it. So maybe it was just happy coincidence. But maybe, Iris, just maybe..." She holds her cigarette in a pinch and emphasizes her words with the burning tip. "It was that horse's penis."

The room goes silent, and Iris's smile turns into a cackling laugh. They both start laughing till they wheeze.

"You're ridiculous," Iris says and shakes her head.

"I can be anything I want to be."

"So that's it. You want to think you chose to be gay. I see the psychology now. You want to have power over every last thing in your life."

"Oh, don't be so serious. It was just a story."

Iris laughs again, and Augusta can't keep a straight face either. An hour passes of them bantering and talking like this. Iris doesn't forget the violence, or Paulo, but it does all feel farther away.

The thing is, Iris trusts Augusta. She's the woman who calls the shots. Someone so tough it's hard to imagine harm coming to her. If she feels safe here, Iris should, too.

They can leave at some point. Slowly plan to get a house somewhere Paulo doesn't know about.

Iris begins to feel elation. It's the perfect amount of alcohol she's had and the cozy rainy day. She can see for the first time the rest of her life playing out in front of her. She and Augusta could get a place just like this. Iris could tan in the afternoon. Read every single book she's ever wanted to. Swim in the ocean in the evening and sleep till whenever she wants in the morning.

She's *giddy.* It might just be a brief high after all the lows of the last weeks, but she doesn't dwell on that. She accepts the moment.

Augusta finishes her drink and goes to the fridge. "I'm actually hungry now. I'm not going to lie to you... I've been surviving off candy bars and tortilla chips most of the time I've been here. I get the place restocked once a week, but the cooked food doesn't last the whole seven days. Can you cook?"

Iris shrugs. "Maybe. Can't remember."

"You want to find out? They restocked without a list, and there's a bunch of ingredients. I think it's a prank. The housekeeper who comes by knows I can't cook."

Iris investigates the Tupperware. It looks like beef seasoned in chilies and a red sauce.

"You got tortillas?"

Augusta produces a clear white bag of them from a cupboard.

Iris takes them. "Lucky for you I've been able to make a cheese quesadilla since I was ten."

"You sure you're any good at it when you're drunk?"

Iris grabs the rum bottle and takes a little sip. "I'm even better at it drunk."

Iris burns both quesadillas so bad that they have to open every window to air the place out. They both have two Mexican candy bars and more mango juice for a late lunch instead and wash it all down with more rum.

Iris is solidly drunk by the time they stumble outside to get some fresh air. The rain has stopped. The sun is out.

Iris is looking at the sea sparkle when Augusta suddenly grabs her shoulder. It's too rough to be a romantic gesture, and Iris's heart nearly flies out of her throat. "What? What is it?"

Augusta is staring into the palm trees. "I thought I saw someone. But it's a bird." She points to some little songbird fluttering across the cove. "The booze has me seeing things."

Iris keeps looking into the palms but sees nothing but dripping fronds and cracked coconut husks.

Seeing Augusta on edge has erased all of Iris's good feelings. "Can you tell me something honestly?" Iris asks. "Do you *really* think we're safe here?"

"How many times do you want me to say it? Yes. I really do." Augusta takes her hand and squeezes it. "I'm allowed to be startled and not think we're going to be killed, Iris."

The breeze outside is sobering. Iris and Augusta both stare at the ocean together. Their silence is no longer that of exhaustion. It feels more like contentment. Iris contemplates her life that has led her to this moment. She thinks about Augusta.

She's funny. Clever. Self-effacing when she needs to be. And here, when it's just the two of them, the charade of cold-blooded matriarch is gone entirely.

"About earlier... When I went to your bed." Augusta gives Iris's hand a couple pumps. "I didn't mean to come on like a bulldozer. It's just that when I'm afraid or overwhelmed, something like that helps me forget. Booze, I suppose, is the next best thing."

"It's fine."

"How are you feeling?" Augusta turns to face Iris and peers down at her intensely.

"What do you mean?"

"Like... are you better than you were this morning? Do you trust that you're going to be safe here, with me?"

Iris can hardly believe it. There's a wanting in Augusta's green-eyed gaze. Her pulse begins to quicken once more. *She wants to fuck me.*

"Um..." Iris blinks and tries to think, but her nervousness doesn't let her string much of a thought together. The memory of the last few days has an unreal quality to it. A lightness, like it never really happened. But Iris isn't so drunk she can't see the future. Paulo. The girls. The murders. It will all come back as soon as she's sober, and she can't just stay drunk forever.

Augusta is playing with her hand now. She trails her thumb softly up the back of it, tracing the tendons and veins. Iris is still trying to think. Still trying to come up with an answer that isn't bullshit, when Augusta turns so she's facing her.

"Because I promise you there's nowhere safer in the world. You need to relax. You need to just breathe and spread your toes in the sand."

"It's not just—" Iris starts, but Augusta doesn't let her finish. She brings her face to Iris's and lingers so their eyes are just inches apart.

"Augusta..." Iris says, her name trembling on her lips. She's not wired the same. Sex is not something that helps her forget. She feels a hand on her crotch. Two fingers crawling like a spider, prying their way past her underwear. Images flash in Iris's mind. The bloody bathroom in Memphis. The mattresses downstairs on the floor. Naked girls sitting silent in Paulo's living room. Those same women then eternally quiet on the floor of that reeking shipping container.

"Augusta—"

Augusta answers with a kiss and then peels her lips away. "I can stop, but can you trust me? Trust me for just for a minute?"

Thoughts and images become harder to capture as Augusta moves her fingers. A wave of breathlessness overtakes Iris.

She can trust her. She can forget.

Iris manages a nod, and then she closes her eyes tight and focuses on the feeling. No thoughts. No memories. There's the sound of the waves, the feeling of someone else's foreign fingers exploring. Iris gasps. Entering.

Iris rests her mouth against Augusta's collarbone. She opens her watery eyes wide and sees the waves curl and whiten as they crash over Augusta's shoulder. Snarling. Vanishing. Repeating.

Augusta pauses and pulls out her hand. Iris isn't sure how long it's been. Twenty seconds? Two minutes?

"Come on, sugar." She grabs Iris by the hand and pulls her inside.

Augusta shuts the door once they're in, and just then thunder booms over the open water. It rattles the glassware in the cabinets. The rum on the table. Iris's heart.

"Undress," Augusta orders.

Iris doesn't hesitate and slips her pants and underwear off smoothly. She pulls her T-shirt over her head and slings it casually over a lampshade. She stares at Augusta daringly. Her head tilted slightly down, her brow tightening a little more each second like a bowstring being drawn.

Augusta's chest rises and falls in quick, deep breaths. Her gaze darts over Iris's naked body in what looks like utter disbelief. "You're *all* I've ever wanted," she says, staring at Iris's body and not her eyes. There is no trace of love in the words.

They're possessive. Lustful. But before Iris has the chance to question them anymore, Augusta drops to her knees and her mouth is on Iris stomach, and Iris is being pushed backwards onto the pull-out bed.

Fucked

Iris wakes up to evening light. She's lying on top of the sheets, alone. Augusta is at the kitchen table in nothing but a long T-shirt. She's drinking a glass of water with ice and smoking a cigarette.

The wind has died down. The windows are open, but the smoke from Augusta's cigarette hangs in bands of textured blue waves. It drifts slowly.

Iris has sobered up after her nap. She's dry, dehydrated. Her eyes are crusty, and she can feel her pulse at her temples.

"Do you want one?" Augusta holds her cigarette out, and Iris shakes her head.

"Did I ever smoke?"

"No. Although I tried to get you to. I'd say this is a special occasion, but I guess it's going to become ordinary." Augusta smiles.

This? Iris wonders what she means by that. Sex? She brings the sheet over her breasts so she's partially covered. There's a feeling of vulnerability that won't go away. She can't help the feeling that she is not Augusta's equal. There is no feeling of partnership. It's the same as when she was at Sweet Blood. It's the age gap, of course. But there's more to it than that. Augusta knows so much about the time of Iris's life that she remembers the least. There's power in that memory. And Augusta hadn't been honest about the beginning of their relationship. Why had Iris let it slide? Because she'd gotten drunk, she realizes.

"I figure we can try the quesadillas again this evening," Augusta says.

"Sure."

"You can teach me."

"Uh-huh." Iris nods.

Augusta's lips tighten. It looks as if she was afraid Iris might get cold feet.

The sex wasn't bad. It was amazing, actually. It did help Iris forget. Once she got in the mood, it was hard to get out of it. But again, something didn't feel mutual about their lovemaking. Something about it felt servile. Like she was just Augusta's pet.

Iris crosses her arms over her chest and puts her palms over her elbows.

Augusta stamps out her cigarette in her glass. "I think I'm going to get some exercise now that the rain has cleared up. I've got a bit of cabin fever."

"What are you thinking?"

"I was going to walk the beach, maybe go for a swim."

Iris looks out the window towards the horizon. The sun has already vanished. The darkness will be coming on quick. "Be careful if you swim."

"I will, darling." Augusta says, her tone lightening like she's relieved to hear Iris is concerned about her.

Augusta goes to the bathroom to change, and Iris puts on her athletic pants and T-shirt while she's gone.

There's a sour expression on Augusta's face when she comes out in a black one-piece swimsuit. "I was hoping you'd stay naked."

Iris smiles. "It's a little chilly for that." The room is warm and humid with the lack of wind. Iris's bare feet stick a little to the tile floor as she walks. It's not too chilly at all.

Augusta goes to Iris and gives her a hug. "I know the circumstances are shit." Augusta leans back with her hands on her shoulder so she can look at Iris. "But this is the only place I've wanted to be for years. Somewhere like this, with you." Her eyes glisten, and this is what Iris needed—to get a little bit of vulnerability back.

Iris has to stand on her tiptoes to kiss her on the lips.

Augusta smiles, showing the wrinkles that ring the corners of her eyes. "Do you want to come with me?"

"No, I should get dinner ready."

"Okay. I'll be back in a half hour." Augusta grabs a towel off of the back of a chair, her cigarettes, and then smiles back at Iris one more time before she slips out the door.

Iris starts to clean up the table from their afternoon of drinking. She washes the dishes in the sink and contemplates how happy she could really be like this. Life is not supposed to be one long vacation. Iris should have friends. A life. A home.

She worries she'll quickly feel the need to strive for something other than reaching the end of another lazy day. But she needs to weigh the alternative. Would she be safe in the States? She doesn't even know if the contract she signed with the FBI holds any water. She could just as easily face prosecution.

Iris sticks a sponge into a glass and sighs. She doesn't know how she'll ever feel like these dishes get clean when the water doesn't get even hot.

"Iris?" a man's voice booms behind her.

She drops the glass she holds, and it shatters in the stainless-steel sink. She fumbles for a hard of it and holds it out like a knife as she spins around. Her eyes survey Alexi warily.

He's still giant but ragged. His thick black hair is not combed but frizzy, and his eyes have the wild wideness of someone who hasn't slept.

"I'm not here to arrest you."

Iris just gulps and tries to catch her breath.

"I need to talk to you."

"You knew where you were fucking putting me. You knew what those people did." Iris is embarrassed to feel her eyes well with tears so fast.

"Hey. Hey." He gestures at the glass in her fist. "Just put that down. It's actually why I'm here. I swear, Iris. If the FBI wanted to extract you, there'd be an entire team."

She reckons he's right. She sets the shard gently in the sink but keeps her distance and her hand in easy reach.

"Before I say anymore, can we turn off some lights? Sit in the dark so we can keep an eye on Augusta?

"The FBI knows she's alive?"

"Just me."

"And what are your thoughts on that?"

He chuckles, but it's a fake, exasperated sound. "Seriously, she can't see me. It would be a problem."

"Okay." Iris points to the light switch. Alexi reaches out a long arm and flicks them off. Then he turns on a single lamp and sits so he can look out the window. "Is she just taking a walk?"

"No, she was going to swim, too."

"Okay." He sighs and nods like he's trying to calm himself. "Sit." He gestures at a kitchen chair.

"I'm good where I am. So talk. Why are you here?"

"Because I'm sorry. Genuinely, I'm really sorry for what we did to you. God, that just sounds fake."

Iris eyes the pistol on his hip nervously. "You seriously came to say you're sorry?"

"I was tasked with following your vehicle here anyway. And yes, I don't know, Iris. It sounded like a better idea in my head. I thought I could communicate how bad we fucked up better."

"I heard you got played."

Alexi nods.

"Is that why you're here? Because you didn't win?"

"I felt like shit long before the operation fell apart."

Iris tries to keep her anger to a simmer. Alexi has information she needs to know. She needs to play nice. "So, you're only here for an apology?"

"There's something you need to know about the operation..."

Iris waits for him to keep going. He can't stop sighing and running his fingers through his hair.

"The FBI raid at Sweet Blood... We were after the Adlers. Jamie. We know about the drug trafficking."

"Okay."

"What I'm saying is... there is no warrant for your arrest. The police were after you, yes, but the media wasn't lying. You're a missing person of interest, but the district prosecutor doesn't want to bring charges against you for the murder of your husband. No one thinks there's enough evidence to win at trial."

Iris is silent. "Are you saying that I'm not a fugitive?"

"Yeah." Alexi cringes and licks his lips. "You're a free citizen. You have been."

Iris is speechless.

"But the contract we had you signed was legitimate. If the DA changed their mind or new evidence came out, you would've been safe still. What you did, infiltrating the cartel, it wasn't for absolutely nothing."

A tear races down Iris's cheek.

"I'm sorry, Iris."

"Get out."

Alexi spreads his giant hands out apologetically. "I can't just go."

"If you're actually sorry, yes you can. You can do something for me, and that's fucking go!"

Alexi looks out the window, clearly nervous Augusta might've heard the yelling. "We need to talk about Augusta."

"What about her?"

"She *is* wanted. The FBI has a clear case against her for trafficking. We've kept it hidden as we turned our attention to Jamie and Annabelle after Augusta went into the Mississippi."

"So, you're here to turn your misfortunate around? Let me guess, you're in serious shit and think giving the FBI Augusta will save you?"

"I'd like to turn Augusta in, yes. But I'm probably fired either way. She's a criminal, Iris. I don't know your relationship..." His eyes widen like he learned the extent of it this afternoon. "But she's not who you think she is."

"Do you know what Paulo does to the women he traffics?"

Alexi doesn't respond.

"He bakes them alive. He leaves them in a hot container under the sun and lets them claw at the door. Does the FBI give a shit about that, or just the drugs?"

"Just the drugs."

"Yeah. That's what I thought. They're American though, the girls. You know that?"

"We do."

Iris frowns. "And stopping that isn't a priority?"

"Look it's on the list, but we're not losing 100,000 Americans a year to prostitution trafficking the way we are to drugs."

"So why did you really come here?"

Alexi looks out the window for Augusta and then turns back to Iris. "I think I owe you an apology. And I wanted you to know you were safe from prosecution in the States."

Iris doesn't quite buy it. He's after Augusta, obviously. But he doesn't have to manipulate Iris to get her. The FBI could simply raid this place. He really is just here out of guilt. She watches his Adam's apple bob as he swallows nervously. He's her age, a kid really. But she can't give him Augusta.

"If you're really sorry, and not just bullshitting me again, leave. You'll do me one favor—you'll leave Augusta alone." Iris eyes his gun again. Then she looks at the shard of glass in the sink.

Alexi sighs and settles in with his elbows on his knees. "I don't want you to find out in an interrogation room. We've put you through enough already."

"What are you talking about?"

"The PI firm you hired to dig into your past in Memphis reached out to us. The information they found was so serious that it wasn't something they felt they could legally keep private." Alexi reaches into his back pocket and brings out a wad of papers folded in a square. He unravels all four corners and looks at it for a moment before holding it out to Iris.

Iris doesn't move. She doesn't want to walk any closer to him. His tone and reasons for being here seem genuine, but Alexi is not someone she is about to trust again. Then again, violence shouldn't be her worry. He had his chance to kill her when she had her back to the door doing dishes.

Iris takes one step forward, snatches the paper, and walks backwards until she's against the counter again.

"What is this?"

"The conclusion of the report you paid for."

"There's like five thousand words here. What am I looking for?"

"Does the name Veronica mean anything to you?"

Iris looks up from the paper.

"Your investigators kept hearing a rumor of a woman who went by that name. She was a recruiter, so to speak. She'd get girls hooked on drugs. Introduce them to the lifestyle. Your investigators found her."

"And?"

"Veronica worked directly for Augusta Adler."

"My husband and Paulo started trafficking girls. Augusta didn't have anything to do with it."

Alexi's expression darkens. He grows somber and looks like the bearer of bad news, and Iris realizes her own ignorance before he even opens his mouth.

"And who told you that?"

Augusta did. Iris is silent.

"Your husband was a nobody, no offense. He was in charge of nothing. We have texts and witness statements that your mother-in-law has been trafficking girls from both Mexico and the US and running prostitution rings in *nine* different cities in the South. You can read about that in item 10.7." He nods at the paper.

Everything Augusta said on the riverboat. Everything she said about how she was ignorant to what Paulo and Joseph Jr. were... It was a lie. The human trafficking was her.

And Iris just believed her. No proof. No nothing. She just took Augusta at her word that she was honest about wanting to shut it down.

She thinks of the girls in the container. She thinks of the look Augusta exchanged with Esperanza. They used to *work* together. Esperanza's death was partly Paulo's gift to Augusta because she was another loose end.

"I think you can see where this is going?" Alexi says, but Iris is too busy trying to stay upright to talk. She finishes reading item 10.7 and flips the page furiously. There's another interview. It's the private investigator's conversation with Veronica.

"But Augusta..." Iris looks up. "She had a change of heart. At least to me... She saved me from that underworld."

Alexi's silence fills her with dread.

Iris is already putting it together. Augusta running into her for the first time at that ball. Augusta hiring her and keeping her dependent on pills. Then there was the night around Christmas, 2019. The one at the Willard hotel when she first met Veronica. Someone had been watching them. Someone had seen that Iris liked girls...

"She didn't save me?"

Alexi's brows fuse together. He does his best to hide the horror from his expression but fails.

Iris's stomach flips. That night at the Willard becomes clearer. The woman watching her from the far table... The Hispanic woman was Esperanza, but the other one... The one who had been stealing glances at Iris. The one she thought might be blonde.

"Save you?" Alexi says, and the face watching her that night becomes clear and white-haired in her memory. Before Alexi even finishes, Iris knows what he's going to say. "Augusta Adler *enslaved* you."

Broken

The words of the report blur. Iris can't see. Augusta had seen Iris at the bar. She'd seen her on a date with another girl. She'd seen her—young, pretty, and gay—and she'd selected Iris for herself.

She'd called her fixer, Veronica, and she got there just in time. Just as Iris was standing to leave.

Iris was handpicked.

Tricked. Tied up. Injected with heroin.

She was turned from a student to a whore. And when she was at her darkest, Augusta pretended to be the light. But she was the reason. She was the reason for everything.

Iris cries and doesn't bother to wipe the tears as they tickle her cheeks.

Alexi lets her take it in. He gives her what little privacy the little beach house can afford and goes to the window to keep an eye on Augusta.

Iris manages to read the rest of the interview, even though the pages shake in her hand. Veronica's statement confirms it all. She even confesses to getting the call around Christmastime from Augusta about a pretty brown-haired girl at a hotel bar.

"I can come back later," Alexi says, sensing Iris's shock. "We can meet on the south end of the cove in a few hours. Just make the excuse that you need a walk. I'll be there." Alexi moves towards the door.

"Wait," Iris says, managing to wrestle the word out of her throat.

Alexi pauses with a hand on the frame.

"What's your plan?"

"I have a truck parked close to here. You stay here to make sure Augusta doesn't go anywhere, and I drive to Puerto Vallarta. I get ahold of the FBI. I'm going to let them know you're alive, and I'm going to let them know you're willing to sign the strictest NDA possible to keep you from talking to anybody about this operation. Stronger than the documents you already put your name on. Otherwise, I'm not so sure they won't try to stick you with some kind of charge to blackmail your silence. Then we let them know Augusta's location."

Iris turns around. She grabs on to the wedge of counter that sticks out in front of the sink and squeezes until her fingers ache. "And she'll go to prison?"

"Oh yeah. Right now, we've got her dead to rights on tax fraud. She's been cooking the books at the Adler Corp for years to launder the trafficking money."

Iris spins around. "What about the human trafficking itself?"

"It's trickier to prove. She did clean up well. But I think we'll get there. Especially with your testimony."

"Get there? What about Veronica's statement?"

"It will still be difficult to get a human-trafficking conviction without hard evidence. But we'll get there.

"So right now, you've got her for tax fraud? That's it?"

"It sounds light, but these are felonies, Iris. She didn't underreport once or twice. We're talking about the systematic hiding of tens of millions of dollars. She'll get a severe sentence. She's not young, either. She can spend the rest of her life in prison from her white-collar crimes alone."

"But stuff like the container of girls who were baked to death, she won't face anything for that?"

"Probably not. Not unless we get our hands on communications saying she ordered something like that."

Iris weighs what she's been told. There's no reason for Alexi to be lying to her. If the FBI wanted her and Augusta, they'd already be under arrest. But what if he's trying to pin them against each other? Create a prisoner's dilemma. Iris is being gullible again; There's no telling if Alexi still has an angle or not. She's being too trusting.

Alexi must see her doubt. The mistrust. He tries to make eye contact with Iris, but she makes a point to stare past him into oblivion. "No matter how this goes, my career at the FBI is done. I'm done. This is me trying to do right by you. You and Augusta can run. I doubt you want that, but you can. You won't get far, and if you do with the help of the cartel, I'm not sure Paulo would be interested in you as such high-profile guests."

"So now you're threatening me?"

"I'm saving you the trouble of thinking that this is anything other than the end of the road."

Iris lets the silence grow. "How long do you think you'll be before you're back?"

"Two hours."

"Then go."

Alexi opens his mouth, but Iris cuts in.

"And don't...say you're sorry again."

He nods, his head down, and then looks out the door to make sure the coast is clear before he slips silently into the night.

Iris practically collapses. She leans against the fridge and slides all the way down until she's sitting on the floor.

She pulls on her fingers and breathes through her mouth in disbelief.

She thinks of the clothes in her size that are stocked here in the dresser. She thinks of Augusta trying to sleep with her this morning. Failing and then loosening her up with booze and conversation before trying again.

Manipulation. Coercion. She pictures Augusta's tongue trailing down her stomach, and she stands in a rage, her skin crawling.

This is not paradise. It's a playhouse for Augusta's plaything.

Iris leans over the sink. Her stomach churns, and she opens her mouth. She coughs and spits. The shards from the shattered glass sparkle against the steel. *Broken*, Iris thinks.

Not like anything was ever fixed, but little did she think her reality could shatter again so quickly. Just when she felt like her feet were maybe planted under her again...

Broken.

High Tide

Iris goes to the window and sees that Augusta is no longer on the beach. The crescent shape of the cove is illuminated by a rising moon. It's mostly full, and the water is lit up in bone-white light.

She sees a shape cutting across the slight chop of waves. Arms wheel one after the other in a breaststroke. Iris walks outside barefoot to where the waves break. Where Augusta has left her towel.

The shore is closer to the house now. The tide is higher.

Iris sits cross-legged in the sand and keeps her eye on Augusta. How she swims at this hour, Iris doesn't know. Sharks feed at dusk. "But you're in good company then, aren't you?" Iris says aloud.

There is no way Augusta can hear her, even if her head wasn't underwater most of the time. The wind and waves are too loud. She swims for a long time, and Iris can see how Augusta has kept such a figure. Athletic. Tan. She's always been meticulous about her appearance.

The moon is bright enough to read by now. Iris can see the creases that line her palm. She closes her right fist around a handful of cool sand and lets it fall between her fingers. In her left hand are the papers Alexi gave her. She fills her fist with sand and lets it fall again and again until Augusta comes to the shallows.

She doesn't see Iris right away. She isn't looking towards the beach. She faces the ocean with her hands on her hips, and Iris can see that she's naked. Iris looks at the towel and sees part of the one piece sticking out from under it.

Iris's heart begins to shake her chest as Augusta turns and starts towards shore.

"Well, hello," Augusta says, panting, and keeps walking right up to her towel.

Iris hides the papers in the sand while Augusta takes a lighter and cigarette from inside the towel and sparks it. She goes back to the water and stands ankle deep while she catches her breath, yet smokes at the same time.

"Feels like a dream, doesn't it?" Augusta says with her back to Iris.

"I thought I put it together. I thought Veronica worked for Esperanza."

Augusta turns a little too quickly to pretend not to be startled. She pauses. "What do you mean by that?"

"I mean when you decided to make me your personal whore. You did a good job keeping it from me."

Augusta's hands hang at her sides. Her mouth slackens before she frowns and licks her lips. "Who told you that?"

Iris throws the papers at her. They have weight from the way they're folded, but Augusta doesn't reach out to catch them. She watches as the papers pass right by her and fall into the water. They bob gently on the waves.

"Paulo gave me that. Stuck it in my pocket before I left that little cottage," Iris lies, not wanting Augusta to make a run from the FBI.

"Can you answer a question? If I was in your care before it happened, why'd I end up getting beaten by Joseph?"

Augusta flinches. Her face is pained, like she still can't believe this dream is already crumbling. Iris can see her contemplate lying before she sighs and takes a quick puff of her cigarette. "Because you were a prostitute, after all. You were in our books as one. He had access to you. But believe me, I had no idea that was going to happen." Augusta steps closer, and Iris stands up from the sand.

"If I had known what he'd do... Iris, I know how it looks. How this started all wrong. It was manipulative. It was wrong. But my feelings are real. I love you. I really do. That is not a lie," she says while shaking her head slowly, earnestly. "I understand how crazy I sound, but it's the truth."

Iris could tell her what the truth is, but she doesn't waste her energy talking to a mad woman.

"I have a memory at Paulo's ranch. You were washing me in a bathtub. That was before Joseph beat me, wasn't it?"

Augusta nods.

"You pretended like you saved me from being a prostitute? And kept me as a mistress?

"I kept you in Mexico. Sometimes in Memphis where you had friends and were happier."

"How long?"

"It was eight months before Joseph got his hands on you. I realized after that... you were strong enough to do bigger things."

Iris is quiet.

"Everything I did, I did for you. I pulled Nick overboard on that riverboat, fulling expecting to never see the surface. You remember that, Iris? That was my redemption. I died for you."

"Yet here you are."

Augusta purses her lips and flicks her still lit cigarette onto the shore. "Everything I said on the riverboat was true. I would burn the company." She points at her own face with both hands. "Myself. *Everything* to the ground if it meant making it up to you."

Insane. Wicked. These things are true of Augusta, but Iris believes her. Iris is all Augusta wants. It's a strange feeling. Manipulated as she is, Iris feels that control come back—the same kind of power that she first felt when Augusta confessed her feelings for her on the riverboat.

Iris walks to Augusta so they're chest to chest. She reaches her hand up and traces it softly up Augusta's hip and ribs. "I believe you," she whispers.

Augusta hiccups a sigh of relief.

Iris tilts her mouth up. "I can be yours."

"Still?" Augusta asks, her eyes glistening with hope.

Iris softens her gaze to look up at Augusta all doe-eyed. "Still," Iris says, and she closes her eyes.

Augusta does the same, and they lean together to kiss.

Iris's heart palpitates so hard it nauseates her. She lets Augusta lose herself, kissing her lips. Iris glides her hands down Augusta's naked body until her hand reaches her pocket. She thinks of all the violence she's seen while her fingers find it.

Sharp. Jagged. It's the long shard of broken glass she'd picked from the sink.

Iris breaks the kiss and whispers in Augusta's ear. "And what about the girls in Memphis you had killed? Did you do that for me, too?"

Iris doesn't hesitate. She swings the glass in a fist into Augusta's side.

Her hand grows hot and slippery in an instant as blood pours out. Augusta gasps and grabs Iris's arms with both hands.

Iris twists the glass, but Augusta jerks back and the shard falls with a plop into the water. The wound is far from fatal, but it's more than enough to give Iris a chance. She throws herself against Augusta's chest with all her might, and they go toppling into the water.

Augusta writhes and wiggles, but Iris is on top of her. She punches at Iris's side weakly while Iris adjusts her weight so she straddles Augusta's shoulders. She puts her hands into the water and presses them against Augusta's face to keep her from coming up for air.

Augusta stops trying to hit Iris. She sticks her arms out at her sides, and just as Iris realizes she's looking for the glass that fell, she feels a burning sting as Augusta plunges it into her leg.

Iris screams and presses her hands against her face harder. Augusta swings again and again, making contact each time. White-hot flashes of pain erupt from Iris's leg, and she screams even louder.

She feels for Augusta's eyes with her thumbs, and then she pries them into the sockets. She presses with every ounce of strength.

She can't hear the sound of splashing. She can't hear the ocean at all. There's only the roar of her own scream as she pushes harder. Harder.

Augusta's swings become weaker. The glass doesn't cut as deep. Her arm falls limply into the water with a light splash.

Iris keeps pressing for several seconds even after Augusta goes completely still. When she releases her grip, she rolls off into the water. The saltwater stings in Iris's cut. She takes heaving breaths and crawls towards the shore.

She breathes for a minute. Two, maybe, trying to stay conscious through the pain. Then she turns and watches Augusta's lifeless body rise and fall as each little wave rolls into the cove.

Her nose twitches, and she looks to her right to see Augusta's cigarette still smoldering in the sand. She picks it up with a pinch, blows off the sand, and then sucks on it until the smoke rolls thick.

Her thoughts are hard to catch. She waits for the self-loathing to come, but it never does. This violence was not part of a game. As her pulse slows and her breath catches and the night breeze dries the salt on her skin, a feeling spreads from the base of her neck. It tingles out to her hands and feet, raising all her peach fuzz along the way. She doesn't feel guilty for doing what she just did.

It wasn't for her. It was for all girls who didn't make it.

She feels something she hasn't since before she woke up after her gunshot wound to the head.

Since before Sweet Blood and Augusta and the entire goddamn Adler family. It overtakes her for the first time since a syringe of heroin was shot into her arm.

Iris feels peace.

She stares at Augusta's white hair. It glides just under the surface in the moonlight. Back and forth, it moves with the tide, like the tentacles of an anemone. Iris watches her body and contemplates dragging it ashore, or just pushing it out for the sharks, as she smokes the cigarette down to the butt.

Policía

Iris lets the ocean decide what to do with Augusta. Eventually, the waves push her face first into the sand so she lies beached. After another twenty minutes, Iris gets up. Her leg burns too much to stay sitting. She takes a few steps and tests putting all her weight on her wounded leg.

The shallow stabs didn't make for a debilitating injury. It doesn't affect her movement at all. It just stings like a bitch.

She walks back to the beach house and turns on the lights. This little place looks so much different than it did just an hour ago. There's nothing quaint about it anymore. Iris takes the rum back down from the cupboard. About a quarter of the brown liquid is left. She and Augusta did a number on it.

She twists the cap off and rotates her head so she can see her wound. It looks even worse than it feels. Flaps of skin hang loose around a four-inch crater of stabbed and sliced flesh. Iris splashes it with rum to disinfect it and screams once before the wave of pain passes over her. The next splash hurts half as bad, and by the third time, she's used to it.

She looks under the sink for a first aid kit but doesn't find one and ends up using a large white T-shirt from the dresser to bandage the wound.

She didn't mark the time when Alexi left. It could've been an hour already. Her sense of time is spotty. She sits at the little kitchen table and drinks rum directly from the bottle. She has two pulls before she pushes it away from herself and waits.

She doesn't know how long it's been, but she doubts it's the full two hours Alexi said it would take before the little room is lit up in red and blue light. There are no sirens but the roar of truck engines and swoosh of sand under their tires as they come to a stop in front of the beach house.

Iris takes one last pull of the rum and is mid sip when a man in a mask and camouflage fatigues comes through the doorway. She's blinded by a flashlight at the end of his rifle.

She cringes simultaneously from the burn of the rum and the blinding police light that's shone in her eyes.

Another man enters, a carbon copy of the first, and then another. They shout in Spanish. And Iris tilts the bottle up in a *cheers* motion.

"*Hola*," she says and has another sip.

Alexi comes in last. He holds his pistol at his side, and when he looks at her eyes, his features all sink in disappointment. She can tell from his expression that he already knows. He holsters his gun. "Where is she?"

"In the water."

Alexi says something in Spanish. Half the officers rush outside, and the others still there move behind Iris. They pull her up under the armpits and put her wrists together over the small of her back. She feels the cold steel and hears the cuffs click.

"What happened?"

"She saw you."

Alexi sighs. "Did she?" he asks doubtfully.

"Your giant ass couldn't hide from the International Space Station."

"And what happened to her?"

"She attacked me." Iris rotates her leg so the bloody bandage shows. "I confronted her with the papers... She lost it."

Alexi chews his cheek. He knows this would be hard to refute.

"I thought you said I wouldn't be in trouble." She shrugs her shoulders to emphasize her cuffed hands. "I'm a victim here, Alexi. Isn't that what those papers say?"

Alexi hesitates before he points. "*Quitarlos.*"

The cops take her cuffs off, and Alexi gestures for her to follow him outside.

"How bad is your leg?"

"It's fine."

They walk to where the rest of the cops have gathered at the shore. They've dragged Augusta farther onto the sand, where her wet body lies coated in sand like a filet rolled in flour.

Alexi and Iris are quiet as they watch the cops roll over her corpse. The police step back and curse in shock. Iris hears what she assumes are prayers muttered under their breath.

These cops have to be used to the violence of the cartel, but Iris can understand there's something different about Augusta's body. Something horrific.

Her eye sockets are black holes—those emerald irises have been pressed back into her brain.

"Okay," Alexi says. "That's enough."

Iris can't look away. As her gaze flickers over Augusta's body, it's like her eyes search inward, traversing every inch of her thoughts. But even as she looks at the damage of what she did, there is no remorse to be found.

"You got a story?" Alexi asks.

"Yeah."

"Well, keep it consistent, because you're going to be asked to tell it about a hundred times."

"I don't think I'll have any trouble with that."

"Come on." Alexi puts his hand on Iris's shoulders to try to turn her away from the body. "Let's go."

They walk back to the police vehicles in silence, and when they get there, Iris sits sideways with her butt on the car seat and the door open so her bare feet are in the sand.

"Stay put. We're going to be here for a while," Alexi says and walks back to the house.

Iris is alone, unwatched for a while, as a crime scene photographer enters the beach house and a couple other officers bring a body bag down to the beach.

She watches them. There's satisfaction in watching them wrap Augusta up. She'd been manipulated by not just her. It was the FBI. The cartel. And Iris had won.

They carry Augusta's corpse on a stretcher. Her tan skin and white hair are hidden inside the black cadaver bag. And as Iris watches them come closer, she does just as Augusta said. There's a lot to do. A lot to face back in the States.

But for now, she breathes and spreads her toes out in the sand.

Epilogue

Iris sits in a dressing room. The vanity mirror is ringed with lightbulbs. She looks at her face and almost doesn't recognize it from the caramel color from the self-tanner they put on her. But the makeup artist kept it mostly light. Iris figures they don't want to put her in bright-red lipstick or anything that might remind the viewership that she was a prostitute.

There's a vegetable and cheese platter four feet long sitting untouched behind her on a folding table, and of all things, this studio room at NBC smells like ranch dressing.

It's been four months since Mexico. The first week after Augusta's death, she spent in FBI custody.

Once she got back to the States, she was able to get home with the help of Marshall—who has had enough of his own problems staying afloat as the Adler ship sank.

Now she's living out of hotels, spending time in LA and New York and DC running a circuit of news interviews. She needs the money. Her legal fees surmount to four years at a private college, and her stock of the Adler Corp is frozen.

The FBI raided the company. Jamie's in a jail cell while Annabelle has been let off with house arrest as the case builds. Sweet Blood is at auction, and the Adler Corp itself is going to be liquidated to Tyson Foods or a Chinese conglomerate for pennies on the dollar.

She sold the townhouse in New Orleans, and adding the money she's gotten from interviews, it should be enough to last the rest of her life if she lives modestly.

She's made good use of her fame. Iris has become the face of human trafficking in America. No news station can get enough of her. There's a bidding war between publishers for the rights to a book that she hasn't even written.

It's been hard to focus at times. The hotel bars call to her, but she stays clear. Just one drink turns into just seven. She wants to be drunk enough not to dream. Paulo, Lola, a dozen cartel soldiers in black masks silently stalk her through the dry forests of Sinaloa every time she falls asleep.

She doesn't know what happened to Paulo. He's probably at the peak of his power after the failed FBI operation. She could advocate in her interviews that the US should get involved. That the real way to stop human trafficking was to arrest or kill men like him. But she's too scared. And besides, if Paulo is killed, another man just as ruthless will take his place.

There's a knock on the door, and a young woman with a headset peeks in. "We're ready for you."

Iris takes a deep breath. She's given a list of the questions before the interviews and has days to ready her answers each time, but this is the first time she's sitting down live.

Her agent, Jason, has mentioned this particular interview might be different from the others. The requests for media appearances aren't coming through as often. Iris's fame is already drying up, and she has a feeling they're going to have to create some fireworks to keep viewers interested.

The world has found out that she was trafficked by the Adler family. But there's a lot Iris hasn't said. She hasn't shared her affair with Augusta, nor does she plan to.

She's already been exonerated in the public's eye for the murder of her husband. They know about Joseph's involvement in the trafficking. Iris could probably make up a story about how his death was self-defense. But she doesn't want the attention from the police and prefers to deflect. She doesn't say she killed him when she's asked in interviews, but she doesn't say she didn't either. She dances around the question with the skill of a politician and lets the insinuation linger.

Iris walks into the studio. There's a plush tan rug, a small coffee table, and two leather armchairs illuminated by light stands. Jason is standing on the perimeter. He nods as Iris makes her way to an armchair.

He's about 5'9" with receding hair and a black soul patch. She's not sure she made the right call hiring him or if all media agents are sleazeballs.

Her interviewer tonight, Melanie Mayes, sits in an armchair across from her. She sips from a glass water bottle. *VOSS*, it says in silver letters.

Her blonde hair is curled and rolls over her shoulders. Her lips look a little too plump to be natural. Iris didn't know who Melanie was before tonight, which is more confirmation that her media tour is losing steam.

It's fine.

She's gotten what she needed from it and done a good thing at the same time. A foundation set up by Marshall is touted in every interview Iris has given and has raised more than five million dollars for the victims of human trafficking.

Melanie looks up from reviewing her script with a tight, fake smile, like this job of talking to an ex-prostitute who's on her fourteenth of fifteen minutes of fame is beneath her. "Are we ready?" The woman looks at her producer, not Iris.

"Fifteen seconds."

Iris clears her throat. She's nervous from Melanie's cold manners, and her anxiety doubles. She's afraid the words will get stuck in her throat. She's already lisped a word or two in interviews in the past, but luckily, they weren't live, and she imagines it was edited out.

She wouldn't know for sure—Iris hates the sound of her own voice too much to watch them afterwards herself.

"Ten. Nine. Eight. Seven. Six..." The producer switches to counting with his fingers for the final five seconds, and then the newswoman begins with the introduction.

It begins with the same questions Iris has answered a dozen times, and she manages to quell her fears and get into the rhythm she's had in the past interviews. The media has been left in the dark as to what happened in Mexico. They usually stay clear of the subject, but halfway through, Iris's stomach drops when she's hit with a question that was not on the prep sheet.

"So, Iris, there's been a lot of speculation that your presence in Mexico had something to do with the failed FBI operation that left two young boys dead."

Iris's eyes dart to Jason. He looks on with one hand on his chin, seeming unsurprised at the question.

"I can't speak to that," says Iris.

"As in you are legally bound to be quiet?"

"As in I know nothing about it."

"So it's just a coincidence?"

"Yes."

"You said you went to Mexico in the first place because you were afraid of retribution by the Adler family."

"Yes. I thought they might think I had something to do with Annabelle's poisoning."

"You were seen talking to the man responsible for that the same evening it happened. Dominic Hurtz."

"He approached me. I didn't even know who he was."

"His sister was a prostitute who was left brain-damaged after an assault. Did you know her?"

Iris picks up her water and takes a sip. This interview begins to feel more like an interrogation. "No, I didn't."

The newswoman crosses her legs, quickly. There's something aggressive about her movement. She tilts her chin up slightly at Iris.

"And what do you have to say about critics of *you* being the face of human trafficking in America? Don't you think it's representationally inaccurate?"

Iris doesn't hide her confusion. "What do you mean?"

"It's estimated that white women make up less than half of the total victims of trafficking." She gestures accusingly at Iris. "Yet you're the mouthpiece."

Iris stutters. She looks struck. "Um...you emailed *me.*"

"Pardon me?

"Your network. You, not me, sent an email offering ninety thousand dollars if I'd sit down here tonight. I was chosen to be the face of this."

"But don't you think you have a responsibility to put the spotlight on others?"

"That's exactly what I'm doing. Our foundation—"

"I'm not talking about your foundation. I'm talking about you, Iris. Do you think you bear a responsibility to collaborate with victims of color and not just take the spotlight yourself?"

Iris burns red. She frowns and pauses. *Is she being accused of being racist?* Is the media in that much need of a soundbite? Iris licks her lips. She leans forward. "Look, I know it's not just white girls who grow up wanting to interview people on the nightly news…"

Melanie raises her brow.

Iris continues. "So why is it always platinum blondes with not-so-subtle boob jobs who get the gig?"

Iris doesn't get an answer. It looks like Melanie has malfunctioned. After several seconds, she blinks like she's rebooting and smiles up at the camera. "We'll be right back."

Iris takes her microphone off and tosses it onto the floor. She stands and storms over to Jason. "What the fuck was that?"

Jason tilts his head to the floor and grimaces.

"Did you know these were the questions?"

"Not exactly, but as I said, they had some things they wanted to ask that you wouldn't be prepped for. It was conditional, Iris. You wouldn't have gotten this money or this offer if it was the same interview we've done two dozen times now."

Iris doesn't even fight him. It was her fault for hiring an agent who got a percentage of the money from every studio appearance she accepted. Of course he was going to stretch this as long as he could.

"Whatever. You're fired." Iris walks away from the interview.

Jason yells after her. "If you don't finish this interview, you don't get the full ninety!"

Iris flips him off over her shoulder. She goes back to her dressing room for her coat and purse. She's halfway out the door when the same girl with the headset who retrieved her for the interview blocks her path.

"Are you not continuing the interview?"

"No."

"You have a phone call. It came through the studio."

"Who is it?"

The girl just holds out the phone to Iris.

Iris's insides knot. She hesitates before taking it like the phone might bite.

The assistant walks off, and Iris thinks of hanging up. It takes her several seconds to speak. "This is Iris."

"You're hard to get ahold of."

She relaxes some at the sound of the deep baritone. Alexi. Not some messenger from the cartel delivering a death threat.

Still, he's not her friend. Iris's tone turns to annoyance. "You should talk to me through my lawyer."

"I've been trying to. His receptionist has been saying she'll pass along my message for two weeks now, and I doubt you've gotten it. Have you?"

"No."

"You heard I quit?"

"I heard you and that other FBI agent who confronted me in the bathroom got fired."

"I was done before they reached their decision."

"Is that why you're calling me? Because—"

"No, no, no, no, no," Alexi says quickly. "I was told to get ahold of you."

"By whom?"

"Henry Reichert. He's a retired businessman. Owns several thousand acres in Northern Vermont. You heard of him?"

"No, and get to your point."

"He was a bit of a figure in the seventies. Went off the rails with religion after he sold his company and created the largest compound in the Northeast. Some call it a cult. Anyway, his daughter went missing in the nineties. It was always assumed she was kidnapped or killed and dumped in the woods by an unsavory member of his new crowd. But he got ahold of me, and he thinks she was trafficked."

"Okay?"

"He wants to hire me—has hired me, actually—to look into her disappearance. He knows I know you."

"Hiring an ex-FBI agent for a missing girl makes sense, but where do I come in, Alexi?"

"He wants you to get on a media circuit in New England. Put some heat on the cold case, so to speak."

"I think I'm okay."

"He's offering a half million dollars."

Iris pauses. Right now, she has to stifle the urge to throw the studio phone into the ranch dressing. She hates how governed by money she is, but she doesn't want to go back to work. Ever.

She's never even had a proper job. Where would she begin? She could go back to school. Get a job at a nonprofit.

But the thought of sitting in a classroom taking notes feels a bit ridiculous after all she's been through.

No, she'd rather have a few million in savings churning out five percent a year and spend the rest of her life in an RV with two dogs, chasing warmer weather.

"What do you think?" Alexi asks. "I've been looking into the case, and I do have to say it's fascinating. If not a little freaky."

"Let me think about it," Iris says.

"Awesome. Can I get your email? I'll share your—"

"I'll call you back later, Alexi." Iris hangs up and sets the phone on her thigh.

She pictures her options, sunning herself in Arizona in December and having campfires in Montana in the summer. But she knows herself well enough by now to understand she can only sit still for so long. Driving around the country is a cheap antidote to that.

She wants the real thing. A reason to be on the move. And more missing girls... Isn't this call exactly that?

She picks up the phone, and before she even knows what she's doing, she dials Alexi back.

Made in United States
Troutdale, OR
10/12/2024

23707117R00235